The Usurper

First published 2010 by Solaris
an imprint of Rebellion Publishing Ltd,
Riverside House, Osney Mead,
Oxford, OX1 0ES, UK

www.solarisbooks.com

ISBN: 978 1 907519 07 9

Designed & typeset by Rebellion Publishing
Printed in the US

ROWENA CORY DANIELLS

The Usurper

BOOK THREE OF THE CHRONICLES
OF KING ROLEN'S KIN

SOLARIS

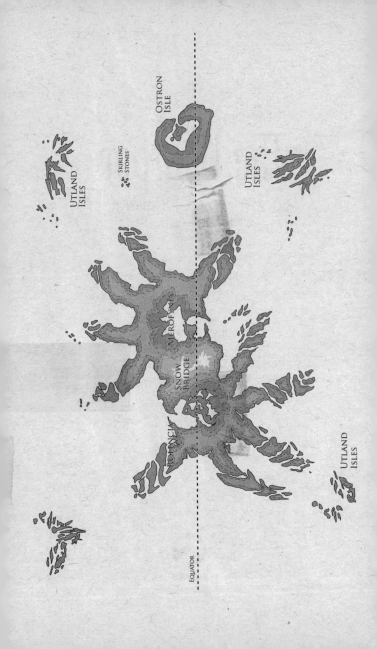

ROLENCIA

NEARLY THREE HUNDRED YEARS AGO, WARLORD ROLENCE MARCHED OVER FOENIX PASS AND CONQUERED THE RICH VALLEY, DEFEATING THE BICKERING CHIEFTAINS. HE NAMED HIS NEW KINGDOM ROLENCIA AND DECLARED HIMSELF KING ROLENCE THE FIRST, CLAIMING THE VALLEY FOR HIS CHILDREN AND HIS CHILDREN'S CHILDREN.

BUT HOLDING A KINGDOM IS HARDER THAN CONQUERING IT. NO SOONER HAD KING ROLENCE MADE HIS CLAIM, THAN KING SEFON THE SECOND OF MEROFYN SET SAIL TO PUT DOWN THIS UPSTART WARLORD, BEFORE THE WARLORDS OF HIS OWN SPARS COULD GET IDEAS ABOVE THEIR STATION.

MEANWHILE THE MERCHANTS OF OSTRON ISLE TRADED WITH BOTH KINGDOMS, GROWING RICHER, WHILE THE UTLAND RAIDERS PREYED ON EVERYONE, INCLUDING EACH OTHER.

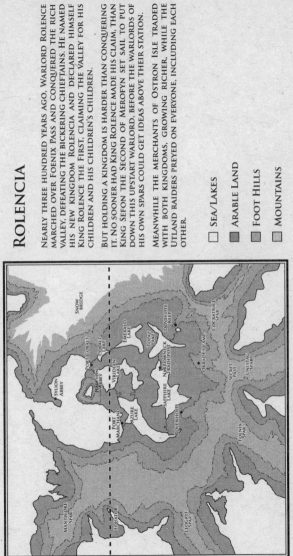

☐ SEA/LAKES

▨ ARABLE LAND

▨ FOOT HILLS

☐ MOUNTAINS

DISTANCE FROM ROLENHOLD TO DOVECOTE APPROX 50 MILES AS THE CROW FLIES

Chapter One

Fyn stood in the crow's nest, squinting into the westering sun to watch the merchant ship's mainmast fall. It groaned like a toppling tree, taking rigging and sails with it, leaving him with a savage surge of satisfaction.

As the two vessels drifted apart, he could just make out the merchant captain shaking a fist at the *Wyvern's Whelp*.

But Fyn felt no qualms. The Merofynians' ship had been laden with Rolencian treasures stolen from his homeland. His vision blurred, hot tears of grief stinging his eyes. His mother, father and eldest brother were all dead. Even little Piro...

He must not think of Piro. Must not dwell on how his thirteen-year-old sister would have felt, seeing their father killed under a flag of truce. Had Overlord Palatyne executed their mother in front of Piro, or had she been killed first? He hoped she hadn't watched. He hoped she hadn't wept and pleaded. Somehow, he couldn't see Piro doing that. She'd be angry and defiant to the end. A sob caught in his throat.

Why was he torturing himself?

Because he should have arrived in time to warn them of the invasion! Fury and shame burned within him. Here he was, press-ganged to serve on the *Wyvern's Whelp*, when he should have been back in Rolencia. All his family were dead except for his brother, Byren, and his cousin Cobalt.

Cobalt lay injured in the castle, forced to serve the invaders as their puppet king, while Byren was in hiding with a price on his head. Before Fyn had been press-ganged, he'd promised Cobalt he'd help find Byren so they could unite Rolencia against the Merofynians.

Frustration ate away at Fyn. If only he could reach Byren to let him know he wasn't alone.

A bird cried. He blinked and looked up, seeing a sea hawk circling above. Far beyond it, a scattering of high, lacy clouds glowed, reflecting the sun's rays from below the horizon. An extravagant display of stars had already claimed the eastern sky.

His hand rose to touch the Fate, which he wore hidden beneath his jerkin. This was the first time he'd been alone since finding himself tied up in the ship's hold.

Pulling on the chain, he brought the stone out. It lay heavy with potential in his hand – Halcyon's

Fate, a mystic's tool. His heart picked up pace, pounding in his chest.

A sense of inevitability swept over Fyn. He'd known he was going to attempt this, whatever the risk, first chance he had.

Slowly, he sank to sit with his back to the mast, and the Fate cradled in his palms between his raised knees.

The opal flickered to life, awakened by his Affinity and need. The same fiery sliver of light that illuminated the high clouds above lurked in the stone's cloudy depths.

Fyn stared into the opal, seeing eager glints. Somehow, he had to bend its power to his will and locate Byren, but Halcyon Abbey had fallen before he could begin his proper training. All he had to go on was basic acolyte training, the whispers he'd heard and the experiments he'd tried on his own. The mystics master would have said Fyn knew enough to get himself into trouble, but not out.

He grimaced. There was no help for it, he had to use the Fate. If it attracted any enemy renegade Power-workers, he'd pull back and hope he could escape. After all, he was stuck here on the *Wyvern's Whelp*, way out on the Stormy Sea. It was not likely they could send Merofynian warriors to capture him.

But it wasn't his physical body that was at risk.

He could feel the power of the Fate, its Affinity-induced heat almost burning his skin. The one – and only – time his friend Feldspar had used the Fate, he'd bled from the nose and passed out.

Ignoring his trepidation, Fyn focused on Byren, trying to recall his brother's essential self. Last midsummer, they'd all gone fishing on Sapphire Lake. He grinned. Byren had hauled him out when Lence had thrown him off the boat. How Piro had laughed...

He mustn't think about Piro.

Gritting his teeth, Fyn narrowed his focus, recalling how Byren had come to wish him luck in the Proving, when his future with the abbey had been decided. Lence hadn't bothered. What a pity Byren wasn't the first-born twin. He would have made a better king than...

Fyn blinked. With Lence dead, Byren was the king's heir. In fact, with their father dead, Byren was the uncrowned king of Rolencia.

How could King Rolen, his louder-than-life father, be dead? Painful loss laid Fyn bare.

His vision blurred and, when it refocused, he recognised the mystics master, although the background was pale and shimmering, as if sunlight danced on mist.

Relief flooded Fyn. Now he wouldn't have to battle the power of the Fate alone. Master Catillum would tell him what to do.

But before they could communicate, Fyn's sight wavered again and, when it cleared, he saw Byren marching across a field, wearing the fabulous manticore chitin breastplate, a faceless host of warriors behind him. A banner flapped in the breeze, depicting a foenix battling a leogryf, which was odd because that wasn't Rolencia's royal banner.

Was the mystics master trying to convey a message with symbols or was Fyn seeing an Affinity vision of the future? Frustration gripped him. Without the proper training, he didn't know what to make of it.

His sight wavered again. This time he saw Master Catillum battling a wyvern, armed only with a hunting knife. The Affinity beast's claws raked the mystics master, but he didn't back off, didn't try to flee. He kept ducking and weaving, trying to slip under the wyvern's guard. A man with a hunting knife could not hope to defeat a full-grown wyvern. Fyn opened his mouth to warn Catillum, but no amount of straining could unlock his voice. He was paralysed, as in a dream. Urgency drummed through him as, with every strike, the mystics master weakened.

Tears of frustration and horror burned Fyn's eyes, streaming down his cheeks. His vision wavered, but not enough to prevent him seeing Catillum fall to his hands and knees.

Wait... Catillum was missing his left arm, but in the vision he was whole-bodied. What did this mean? Why –

Something struck the side of Fyn's face and he fell sideways, thudding into the rails of the crow's nest, his return to the present so abrupt that nausea threatened.

'That'll teach you to doze!' Bantam snapped. 'There's rocks, wyverns and storms, not to mention Utland raiders eager to rob the *Wyvern's Whelp*. So you keep your eyes peeled and if I catch you sleeping again, you'll be down there getting your back lashed, even if you are the captain's golden boy!'

Fyn apologised, and went to tuck the Fate inside his jerkin.

'What's this pretty bauble?' Bantam reached for it, then pulled back with a curse. 'Heathen Affinity!'

'Never.' Fyn bristled, even as one part of him realised the little quarter-master had to have some Affinity of his own to sense the Fate's power. If Bantam had been Rolencian he would have been sent to serve the abbey or face banishment. To abbey-trained Fyn, Bantam was the heathen. Fyn stiffened. 'This is a holy relic, blessed by the Goddess Halcyon herself.'

The little man snorted, clever eyes fixed on Fyn. 'You might have won Cap'n Nefysto's trust with your abbey martial training, but I'm not so easily convinced. What were you up to, boy?'

Fyn licked his lips. Although the captain had attacked a Merofynian ship, Nefysto was no friend of Rolencia. Fyn dared not reveal his true identity, or that his brother, Byren, had survived the invasion.

Bantam's eyes narrowed.

'I was trying to contact the mystics master, to see if he still lived,' Fyn confessed, hoping the half-lie would do. He knew Master Catillum was alive, since the mystic had already contacted him via the Fate, before warning him not to attempt to use it again.

Fyn held his breath, as the quarter-master studied him.

'Utlanders!' the cry went up from the deck below. 'Ship to port.'

Bantam stood and searched the horizon. Fyn sprang to his feet. A dark silhouette rode the star-silvered sea, making towards them.

Bantam cursed and cuffed Fyn over the ear again. 'That's why I sent you up here. Not to practise heathen Affinity!'

Fyn gulped. They'd left the merchant crew alive, with a disabled ship to limp into port. From the stories he'd heard, Utland raiders would not be so generous. The raiders would slit their throats and toss them overboard. 'Can we outrun them?'

The quarter-master grimaced. 'She has three masts, like us. It'll come down to whose hulls are the cleanest.'

'Clean hulls?'

Bantam snorted. 'Oh, you're a landsman for sure. Barnacles, boy. They slow the ship's passage through the sea. The cap'n was going to put her into dry dock and have her hull scraped next time we made port.'

Fyn frowned. He had been hoping for better news. Night had fallen while he endured his visions. Now he stared across the sea at a threatening, dark silhouette. 'They're getting closer.'

'Aye. Looks like you'll have another chance to use your fancy abbey training, then we'll see if last time was a fluke.'

Fyn didn't bother to answer. He hated violence. It made him sick to his stomach. And violence was the one thing these sea-hounds respected.

ROLENCIA

'SOMEONE'S COMING,' BYREN hissed, stopping in the knee-deep, starlit snow to listen.

Nothing.

He glanced over his shoulder. Despite her age, Seela had kept up with them since leaving their hidden camp, high in the foothills of the Dividing Mountains. Her anxious eyes fixed on his face.

Behind her, Orrade brought up the rear. At Byren's warning, his friend froze in his tracks. Seela, after her initial wariness, took the chance to bend double and catch her breath. This was exactly why Byren had not been keen to send her out into the valley to recruit loyalists to the Rolencian cause.

Byren touched her shoulder. When she lifted her grey head, he put his finger to his lips.

She nodded and tried to breathe quietly. Byren felt guilty. He shouldn't have agreed to let her go, not that he could stop her. His old nurse had a mind of her own. And she was right, Merofynian warriors wouldn't suspect an old woman of sedition, probably wouldn't even notice her.

Unsure what had prompted him to call a halt, Byren tilted his head, listening. His gaze was drawn up, past the tall, snow-shrouded pines, up to the froth of sparkling stars. He was glad now that they hadn't paused to make camp, deciding rather to reach the loyalist farmhouse by midnight. If there were enemies travelling the foothills, he didn't want them coming upon him while he was unawares.

The silence lengthened.

Byren met Orrade's gaze with an unspoken question.

His friend shook his head. Orrade's recently developed Affinity visions came upon him in his sleep or as waking dreams, but they were invariably accompanied by headaches.

'Not a twinge,' Orrade mouthed.

Seela glanced from him to Byren, coming to her own conclusions. So much for hiding Orrade's Affinity.

The soft snort of a horse reached them, confirming Byren's fears. He turned to Seela. 'Go hide. Orrie and I will scout on ahead.'

Without waiting for her agreement he set off along the path, cursing the snow, which left clear tracks all the way back to their secret camp.

'Probably someone coming to join us,' Orrade muttered, following in Byren's footsteps.

They crested the rise, crawling on their bellies in the snow. Below, coming around the bend, was a boy of no more than thirteen. He walked as if half-asleep, hugging himself.

Six warriors rode behind him. Over their armour they wore Merofynian surcoats, the azure wyvern on a black background. In the starlight the wyverns appeared pale grey, but the warriors were still recognisable as invaders, loyal to the Merofynian king.

The first rider wore an expensive lincis fur cloak and held a chain, driving the boy before him like a dog on a leash.

Fury ripped through Byren. If there was one thing he hated it was a bully. He might be half-Merofynian but he despised their arrogance.

Byren frowned. It was the Power-worker and his little Affinity-slave all over again. Only, this time, there was no Affinty seep exuding power and the man holding the chain was not a renegade Power-worker but an arrogant man-at-arms.

Last time, Byren had used the Power-worker's own tools against him to free the slave, while avoiding a confrontation with the men-at-arms.

This time he was hindered by Seela, who was used to the comforts of castle life, so it would be just him and Orrade against six men. Lence would have welcomed the odds. Byren flinched, reminded once more of the loss of his twin.

No time to mourn.

Time for strategy. He and Orrade had both brought bows, hoping to snag something for the pot. Between them, they could drop a few of the men-at-arms, but there was the boy. Clearly, the Merofynians weren't above using him as a hostage. Byren cursed softly. How could he ensure the boy's safety?

'I know that lad,' Seela muttered.

Surprised, he turned to see her stretched out on the far side of Orrade. 'Seela, I told you to hide!'

She ignored him. 'That's young Vadik. We're on our way to his ma's farm. He wanted to come with me into the mountains to serve you, Byren. But his ma thought he was too young to get involved in war.'

'Looks like the Merofynians didn't agree.' Byren's voice ground deep in his throat, tight with anger.

'I should have insisted,' Seela whispered. 'But his ma didn't want to leave the farm. Her man was killed when the Merofynians invaded. She thought, with Vadik and his younger brother's help, she could get the spring planting done. Now –'

'The look-outs will spot them by midday

tomorrow,' Orrade muttered. 'They'll lay an ambush, but one or two of those riders might get away, and take word back. We have to kill them, Byren.'

He had come to the same conclusion, but how could he save the boy?

'They're beasts, treating a child like that,' Seela muttered. 'Worse than Utlanders.'

Byren frowned. 'There's something odd about the way the boy's moving.'

Vadik stumbled and put out one arm to prevent his fall. The other, his right arm, ended in a bloody, hastily bandaged stump.

Orrade hissed under his breath.

Seela gasped in horror.

Byren blazed with fury. For a heartbeat he thought of nothing but rending and tearing those men to pieces. The force of his reaction shocked him. Truly feral, it made him wonder if his time with the ulfr pack had affected him on some basic level, bringing out the beast that lurked in all men.

No point worrying.

If he was to save the boy, he needed a diversion to draw the Merofynians' attention away from Vadik. If only the ulfr pack were still following him. Imbued with Affinity, ulfrs were long-haired wolves the size of ponies and, Byren had discovered, they were more intelligent than anyone gave them credit for.

If only they were here now, they'd spook the horses...

Of course!

'Orrie, go across the far side of the ravine, hide and

give the hunting cry of an ulfr pack. Make it sound like a large pack. See if you can startle the horses.'

'What will you do?'

Byren fixed on the Merofynian leader. The beautiful cloak of silver-grey lincis fur patterned with leopard spots rested on his broad shoulders. A trophy of war, no doubt it had been stolen from some rich Rolencian merchant or lord. 'I'm going to kill their leader and set the boy free. Seela, you whisk Vadik into the trees, keep him safe.'

She nodded.

'And then?' Orrie asked.

'See if you can take down a couple of men from a distance, before coming to my aid. None of them can be allowed to live.' Too many lives depended on keeping the whereabouts of their camp a secret.

They slid down from the ridge and Byren chose a spot for the ambush. He strung his bow and selected an arrow, then glanced to Seela. She looked grim, her hand at her waist where she kept her paring knife, ready to act. He hid a smile and prayed she would never have to use it.

First around the bend was the injured boy. Vadik walked like one asleep. Face white, eyes fixed, bleeding stump held to his chest.

Once again, rage boiled in Byren's belly. But it was with cold precision that he notched the arrow and waited for...

The ululating cry of an ulfr on the hunt sounded from the ridge opposite, echoing off the bluff behind Byren. All six horses startled. Two reared, their riders only just retaining control. Another howl came, differently pitched. One man was thrown, another fought his mount as it tried to bolt.

Byren aimed and dropped him from the saddle.

Even as Byren ran towards the invaders, he notched, aimed and loosed another arrow, taking down a second man.

In the confusion, the Merofynians had only just realised the attack came from men, not beasts. Their leader stood in the stirrups to yell an order. Byren rushed up, swung an arm around his waist and pulled him off, stabbing him through his surcoat and the side-lacing of his chest armour. As the man fell, spraying blood on the snow, Byren tore the chain's end from his hands and threw the chain to the boy.

Vadik caught the chain clumsily with his left hand and stared at it, then at Byren.

Seela appeared at his side, snatched his good arm and dragged him off towards the trees.

A warrior tried to cut them off. Byren leaped for him, pulling him off his horse and slitting his throat before the man could draw his sword.

A blow whistled towards Byren's head. He ducked and turned in time to see his attacker clutch his chest, where an arrow bloomed. The Merofynian looked surprised as he toppled from his horse.

And that was it. No more mounted men.

Byren counted horses. Five. He swore.

Orrade came running through the trees, knife drawn. A man tried to rise, an arrow in his thigh. Orrade cut him down and kept coming. Without breaking his stride, he leapt into the saddle of a skittish horse and took off down the track, after the one that got away.

Being half a head shorter and lighter of build than Byren, Orrade was better suited to catch the fleeing warrior. But until he returned safe, Byren could not relax. He went around the churned-up clearing, checking the men for signs of life, dispatching the living without compunction.

Byren collected weapons – his people needed them as well as food and clothing – and tied the bundles to the horses' saddles. The dead men he left for the scavengers to clean up. This close to spring cusp the winter creatures were desperate for food and the ones that had hibernated were waking up, ravenous.

The frightened horses were inclined to scatter, so he led them away from the bloody snow and rapidly cooling bodies, into the trees where Seela had taken the boy.

He found the pair of them perched on rocks. While the old nurse rewrapped Vadik's stump, the boy shivered uncontrollably.

Byren draped the lincis cloak around his shoulders. 'This is yours now.'

'He needs a healer,' Seela said, voice thin with anger. 'They chopped off his hand to show they were serious, then told him to lead them to you.'

Vadik looked up at Byren. He still shivered, but there was some colour in his cheeks. Byren hoped it was not the sign of a fever developing. The boy's eyes looked glassy.

'I failed you. I shouldn't have led them up here,' Vadik said, young voice rising. 'I wanted to be brave, but they threatened to kill Mam and Tikhon. I didn't know what to do. I wasn't brave enough to –'

'You protected your family,' Byren said, throat tight. 'That's the best you could do.' The boy did not look convinced. Byren knelt in front of him. 'It's what I woulda done.'

Vadik blinked, surprised.

'I should have insisted they come with me,' Seela muttered, furious with herself.

'You couldn't have foreseen this,' Byren told her, coming to his feet. 'It's barbaric.'

'Did you kill them all?' Vadik asked.

'All but one. Orrie's gone after him.'

'He must catch him.' The boy came to his feet, an edge of panic to his voice. 'They said they'd go back for Mam and m'brother if I ran away.' Desperate, he searched Byren's face. 'You won't let them get Mam and Tikhon?'

Byren reached out, placing his hands on the boy's shoulders. 'No one is going to hurt your family, I swear. I'll go and bring them back myself.'

Tears brimmed and the boy threw his arms around Byren, who rubbed his back wishing he'd been a day earlier and been lying in wait for those Merofynians. See how brave they were when faced with a grown man. But wishes wouldn't return Vadik's right hand. Everything Byren did was too little, too late. Since Cobalt returned... no, since the old seer told him he would kill his twin and take Lence's place, everything had gone awry despite Byren's best efforts to prove the crazy old woman wrong.

So he rubbed the boy's back and brooded, vowing to do better.

That was how Orrade found them, when he returned riding one horse and leading the other.

Swinging his leg over, Orrade slid to the ground and tied the reins to a branch.

'Any trouble?' Byren asked.

Orrade shook his head once and glanced to the boy, who had subsided in relief.

'Vadik was worried about his family,' Byren said. 'But I'm going to fetch them now. I want you to take him up to camp. He needs a healer. And quickly.' When Seela nodded, Byren knew he was right. The boy's skin was too hot.

Orrade, however, was clearly unhappy about leaving him.

Byren laughed. 'I've managed without you guarding my back before.'

'Aye, and look what happened? I found you wounded in an Affinity seep!'

Which reminded Byren, now that Halcyon Abbey had fallen there were no monks available to capture the untamed Affinity leaking from new seeps across Rolencia. Instead of storing it safely in sorbt stones, it would leach out into the valley, affecting plants, people and animals in ways no one could predict. Although he was glad his wound had been healed while he slept in a seep amidst an ulfr pack, he was not sure if that was as far as it went. Like Orrade's visions, something else might arise, something he couldn't hide.

'What's wrong, Byren?' Orrade asked, perceptive as always and just a shade too intimate for a friend, even a best friend.

Byren shook his head, aware of Seela. He'd had enough trouble evading capture and overcoming his cousin, Cobalt, who had thrown in his lot with the Merofynians, without worrying about the effects of renegade power and Orrade's inconvenient love for him.

'Seela can lead me down to the farm. Orrie, you take Vadik up to the camp. Select a horse, let him ride in front of you. I'll be back by tomorrow evening, the next day at the latest.'

'Will you take the other horses?' Orrade asked.

Byren considered. Mounted, the brother and mother could travel faster, but horses were noisy and might give them away if there were more Merofynians about.

Vadik swayed, deciding Byren. Orrade would have enough to do, getting the boy to the camp, without trying to lead five horses as well, and Byren refused to leave them for Affinity beasts to devour. 'I'll take them with me. C'mon, Seela. Time for you to ride.'

'You know I can't ride,' she protested.

'Thirty years in Rolencia and you still can't ride? Time to learn, I'd say.'

The boy grinned, which was what Byren had intended. Seela played along, grumbling warily as Byren helped her into the saddle of the horse he judged to be the quietest. At least he thought she was playing along.

With her settled, he lifted Vadik to sit across Orrade's lap.

'Now, don't you be worrying, lad. I'll fetch your mam and brother and be back before you know it. You concentrate on getting better. That's an order.'

Vadik nodded, then his mouth twisted. 'But what

good am I without my hand? I can't farm like Da, can't fight for you, can't do anything.'

His bitter words made Byren grit his teeth. 'You've already saved your mam and Tikhon, and led six Merofynians to their deaths. What other boy your age has done so much?'

Vadik looked surprised.

Judging the moment right, Byren sought Orrade's eyes, finding unwanted admiration and affection there. With a nod, Byren sent them off. His friend urged the horse out onto the track.

Byren watched them go, thinking that kiss had been a mistake. But he'd thought he was dying.

Only he hadn't, he'd lived. And now Orrade wasn't the friend who'd protected Byren's back since they were fourteen... well he was, but he was also a potential danger. If Byren's honour guard knew Orrade was a follower of Palos, the legendary warlord and lover of men, they would assume Byren was also one. They'd lose faith in him. He'd never retake Rolencia and avenge the murder of his family.

'War is a cruel thing,' Seela muttered. 'No respecter of age or goodness of heart. I'd hoped my little Myrella's sacrifice would bring an end to all this.'

Hearing his mother described as 'little Myrella' struck Byren as odd, but then Seela had been his mother's nurse, accompanying her from Merofynia, when she was sent as a child bride to ensure the peace after the last war.

The midwinter just gone, his parents had celebrated thirty years of peace, while hoping for another thirty with Lence's betrothal to the new kingsdaughter.

Now his parents and Lence were dead, Fyn was missing and Piro... little Piro had been enslaved and sent to Merofynia. He only hoped she reined in her temper and kept her tongue between her teeth. But when had she ever done that?

Byren gathered the reins of the remaining horses and swung into the saddle of the largest. There wasn't a horse big enough to carry him easily. He would have to rotate mounts.

So much rested on him, the second son, the spare heir. He'd never wanted the crown, never thought he would have to right the wrongs of his generation.

Chapter Two

MEROFYNIA

PIRO HAD NEVER expected to return to her mother's home as a slave. Breath misting, she gripped the ship's rail and stared at Port Mero, painted in dawn shades of grey, gleaming only where early workers had lit lamps.

Her skin prickled with foreboding and she did not need to turn around to know that the little Utland Power-worker approached. His smell was enough to warn her, that and the waves of Affinity, which rolled off him like cold off an icy forge.

Now she wished Lord Dunstany had not gone down to his cabin. There was bad blood between the two Power-workers.

'You're just like him,' the Utlander whispered, hate making his voice thick and tight. His hand came to rest on her shoulder, to outward appearances a friendly gesture.

But Piro felt his fingers dig into her body, while his power burrowed into her Affinity, cold tendrils seeking the source of her power, seeking to steal it, just as he had stolen her mother's essence when she died, sealing it in the stone on the end of the staff that never left his side.

She tensed, shoring up her defences. During this last year, she'd built walls to keep her Affinity a secret from the abbeys' monks and nuns, and she had been safe. But the walls had never had to withstand an assault like this. Her body locked up, refusing to move as she bit down on her bottom lip and strained to keep him out.

'You think you're clever, but I won't be beaten by a pampered Merofynian noble and his pretty little spy. I know Dunstany's given you to Overlord Palatyne as a bride-gift for Isolt Kingsdaughter. I know you're a spy and I've warned Palatyne. You won't –'

'I see you've come on deck to catch a glimpse of Mount Mero, too. Poets have written odes to the dawn sun on these slopes,' Lord Dunstany said, as his hand came down to settle on Piro's other shoulder.

She felt a wave of warmth emanate from the noble scholar and roll through her, driving out the creeping cold of the Utlander. Her knees quivered. Nausea rode up her throat. She swallowed, but failed to keep it down. With a moan, she lurched forwards to retch over the side of the boat.

She shuddered, emptying her stomach in involuntary spasms. At last, she straightened up, wiping her chin on the back of her hand. Since she hadn't had breakfast there hadn't been much to bring up.

'I see your slave still suffers from sea-sickness,' the Utlander observed.

'I see what my slave suffers from,' Dunstany said, voice thin and stretched with fury. His hand rubbed in gentle circles between her shoulder blades. 'Hurt her and you hurt me.'

The Utlander stiffened, the bones woven into his waist-length plait clicking. Piro risked a look.

The Utlander's tilted eyes narrowed. 'What is she to you, Dunstany? By tonight she will be Palatyne's to use as he wishes.'

She felt the noble scholar's hand fall away from her. He'd had no choice but to gift her to the overlord. Palatyne planned to present her to King Merofyn's daughter, as a prize of war, a seven-year slave. Lord Dunstany, try as he might, could not protect her.

A smile parted the Utlander's thin lips, but it did not reach his narrow, sunken eyes. Satisfied, he slipped away.

Piro waited until he was out of hearing. 'He hates you. Why?'

'I wish I knew.' Dunstany sounded tired, as though keeping the Utlander out had cost him more than he liked to admit. 'I fear I haven't done you any favours, Seelon.'

Piro was so used to answering to her assumed name, she didn't even blink. And she knew what Dunstany meant. 'It's even worse. The Utlander told Palatyne I will be spying for you.'

'The overlord's no fool. He could figure that out for himself. But he underestimates women. He thinks Isolt will agree to be his biddable wife but he's very much mistaken.'

'She was betrothed to Lence Kingsheir,' Piro said. Lence was the one brother she was certain was dead, as Seela had heard from Byren and no one knew where Fyn was. A ferocious protective surge warmed Piro as she prayed, yet again, for his safety.

'Oh, Isolt knows her duty,' Dunstany said. 'But there is a world of difference between King Rolen's heir, a youth who was as sturdy and reliable as his father, and a jumped-up spar warlord who seeks to make himself emperor of the known world.'

His description of Lence and her father brought tears to Piro's eyes. As far as Dunstany knew, she was a palace servant with a touch of Affinity. If he discovered who she really was, would he use her as a tool to further his own goals?

She rather suspected he would. Despite herself, she liked him, but she had no illusions.

Going over to the water barrel, she took a mug to rinse her mouth and spat it over the side. She still felt shaky from the confrontation. How was she to survive in the Merofynian palace, if she could not protect herself from one Utlander Power-worker? According to her father's spies, King Merofyn surrounded himself with renegade Power-workers in his quest to prolong his life.

The sun's first rays had reached Mount Mero's snow-tipped peak, making it glisten a rich salmon-pink, but below that everything was still shrouded in shades of grey. Lamps gleamed on Port Mero's docks.

She returned to Dunstany's side as the overlord's ship – first in a convoy of eight, laden with stolen bounty from Rolencia – made its way towards the Port. The sea-hounds, four ships of fierce sea-warriors who had accompanied the convoy to fight off Utland raiders, still patrolled like anxious sheepdogs, only now they were anxious to collect their payment.

Piro could make out the still water stretching far ahead of them. It curved around the base of Mount Mero, reflecting the peak with hardly a ripple. It was a pretty sight but, privately, she thought this mountain did not compare with Mount Halcyon.

The two kingdoms were like mirror images, but there were differences. The fertile valley of Rolencia was dotted with five deep lakes, linked by canals, while in the centre of Merofynia's fertile valley lay a small inland sea which lapped at the far side of Mount Mero. Nearly two hundred years ago, the Landlocked Sea had been linked to Mero Bay by the Grand Canal, a feat of engineering the Merofynians were inordinately proud of.

The king's palace overlooked the Landlocked Sea. Port Mero sprawled around the base of Mount Mero, along the edge of the sea and out around the shore of Mero Bay.

Piro had never seen Port Mero, but she recognised it from her mother's stories. The roofs of the graceful, golden stone buildings were capped with snow now, but in the height of summer they glowed in the sun's fierce light.

Wharves stretched greedy fingers out into the bay, and crowded four-storey warehouses clustered along the shore.

Soon their ship entered the Grand Canal, which was wide enough for two seagoing vessels to pass each other comfortably. Tree-lined streets and buildings three or four storeys high lined the canal. It was a wonderful sight.

As the residents woke and began their day's work, people hung washing off balconies, chimneys smoked and the smell of cooking reached Piro.

'I heard that some of Merofynia's valley farms have been reclaimed from the Landlocked Sea,' Piro said, repeating her mother's tales. 'That in places the canals are walled. That you could step out your front door and see a boat sail by above your head.' She looked to Dunstany for verification.

He smiled. 'One day, if I get the chance, I'll show you.'

Piro thought that was an odd thing to say to a slave. Even odder considering that, later today, she would become Overlord Palatyne's property, and then Isolt's.

Piro held on to the ship's rail as the vessel left the Grand Canal and the Landlocked Sea opened in front of them. The sun had not yet reached it and a fine mist hung over the surface. But the nearest wharves were busy with life. Men waited as the ship's rowers backed their oars, slowing their progress. Ropes sailed across the cold water, drawing them in closer to the wharf.

She glanced thoughtfully at Dunstany. She wanted to ask him about the amber pendant. It still rankled to see her essence trapped there, hanging around his neck. He seemed fond of her. If she asked, would he release her?

Dunstany stiffened imperceptibly. Only Piro, who knew him so well, could sense his wariness. She turned, and sure enough Overlord Palatyne approached them.

Palatyne gestured to the clear, oyster-shell sky. 'Looks like it'll be a fine day to report my success to the king!'

The overlord was dressed in full battle gear, wearing the prized manticore chitin breastplate that had belonged to her father, King Rolen. A Merofynian crested helmet increased his already considerable height and a sword hung fron his waist. Since successfully invading Rolencia, Palatyne had adopted Merofynian royal azure, this time in his cloak. On his chest five of the royal emblems of her family glittered. Her own, Byren's and her mother's silver pendants, her bother Lence's electrum pendant and the king's gold pendant, embossed with the royal foenix. The last time she had seen her father use his seal, he'd stamped the image into an official decree and she'd wished he would hurry up so they could get on with the dancing. Seeing the emblems on Palatyne's chest made her so angry she had to look away.

Dressed in full armour the overlord appeared very grand and noble, but Piro knew that what was inside did not match the fine exterior. He was not quite as tall as her father, but still a fine figure of a man. His nose had been broken long ago and its flattened bridge gave him a belligerent aspect that suited his temperament. Palatyne... now that had to be an adopted name. It harkened back to myths that predated Merofynia's history. She knew he was a barbarian warlord from Amfina Spar. Much more likely his birth name had been something like Strong-arm or Snake-sight.

She turned away to hide a bitter smile.

'Mark this day, Dunstany,' Palatyne said. He never used the noble scholar's title. 'This is the dawn of a new era for Merofynia, for the Twin Isles.'

Her mentor said nothing.

'What? No fawning congratulations, Power-worker?' Palatyne prodded.

'You will only get the truth from me, overlord,' Dunstany answered. 'Look to others for ass-licking, I don't offer false coin.'

As Palatyne stiffened, Piro's heart did a double beat of terror.

At that moment the gangplank rattled into place and sailors started shouting. Palatyne gestured to Piro, looking right through Dunstany. 'Bring her to the feast tonight. I want her decked in the finest Rolencian clothing.'

'No kingsdaughter could look better, I promise,' Lord Dunstany said, with a shallow bow that did him more honour than the overlord. Only Piro could hear the mockery in his words.

Palatyne turned and strode off. Eager to bask in the overlord's reflected glory, the Utlander hurried across the deck just as Palatyne went down the gangplank. The Power-worker scurried after him, having to take two steps to each of the overlord's.

Piro smiled despite herself and caught Dunstany's eye. His lips twitched, one side of his mouth lifting. It reminded her of Byren's lop-sided grin, and fear for him diluted her happiness. It was days since she'd sent Seela into the mountains to find Byren.

And there had been no word of Fyn. Palatyne had been furious when his body hadn't been discovered amidst the corpses in the abbey.

She must take heart and trust to her brothers' quick wits to keep them alive, for it seemed the goddess had abandoned them.

DAWN SAW BYREN packing the family's belongings onto the horses. Pots, pans and bed linen, all of which were needed up at camp. Leaving the horses ready in the barn, he returned to the farmhouse. It was a good size and had been prosperous, but the invasion had robbed it of its workers, leaving just the mother and two boys. How would they cope with the eldest boy now a cripple?

Anger gnawed at Byren.

Even the smell of honey-oat porridge failed to lighten his mood, but somehow he managed a smile. Vadik's mother, Esfira, greeted him warmly, indicating the place she had set in his honour at the table. Day-old bread, spicy sausage, warm beer and a bowl of hot porridge with honey.

As Byren thanked her, he wondered how she could bear to have him at her table, when he was the reason her son had been crippled. If the Merofynians hadn't been searching for his camp, they wouldn't have come here and forced the boy to lead them into the mountains. Yet, she had been nothing but kind to him.

Tikhon climbed up on the chair beside Byren. He was small for his age and his feet swung free, unable to touch the floor as he chattered on about one of the farm dogs which would have puppies soon. Meanwhile, Seela helped the mother rinse the cooking pot and pack the last of the kitchen implements.

When it was all done, Esfira wiped her hands and hung her apron over the back of a chair, just as she must have done every day after breakfast.

She gave an odd laugh. 'Here I am, thinking it's good the kitchen is tidy, and I'm about to leave the farm.' With the back of her hand she brushed tears from her cheeks. She was a small thing, plump with sun-kissed skin and the creases of easy laughter in the corner of her eyes.

The dogs barked.

They all stiffened.

'Strangers?' Seela asked softly.

'Aye. I know that bark,' Esfira whispered.

Byren thrust his bowl aside, catching Seela's eye. 'Go out the back door, over to the barn. Lead the horses out the back way. I'll distract them. If you hear fighting, don't wait for me, head for the hills.'

Byren slipped out the back of the farmhouse with them, but he went right, while the others went left to the barn.

The dogs' barking led him past the farmhouse, down the slope and up over the rise. This was steep ground to farm, mostly suitable for sheep and long-haired goats. But the family had built terraces to plant grains and it was on one of these terraces that the dogs had three men pinned.

Unarmed men, who carried travelling kits across their shoulders. Cold, hungry men, who hugged themselves and stamped their feet to keep warm.

Byren whistled.

The dogs broke off barking and sat, waiting for him. He'd always been good with animals. Had he been better with them since the ulfr pack adopted him?

He put this unnerving thought aside to study the men. They had stiffened when he came into view. He was armed and a head taller than the average man, thanks to his father's blood.

Byren jumped from the upper terrace to the one where they waited.

'We don't want any trouble,' the eldest said. He looked about thirty and had the kind of too-ready smile that Byren distrusted. With him were two much younger men. They looked to be about Fyn's age, maybe sixteen. One was short and skinny, the other a little taller and solid with a thick neck. They were both weary, grey-faced and angry. They hugged themselves as though cold to the bone and did not meet Byren's eyes. No... it was not anger, but fear.

'We're just passing through,' the first said.

'To where? Nothing lies above this farm but steep foothills and, above that, even steeper mountains.' Byren pointed to the west. 'Foenix Pass lies that way.'

As the man glanced over his right shoulder he swayed slightly. They were all exhausted and they had no business here unless they were looking for the loyalist camp. But what was there to stop the Merofynians sending one of their own disguised as a loyalist? He'd only have to speak Rolencian to blend in.

Byren waited.

The first man summoned a weary smile. 'We've come a long way and run out of food. You wouldn't have a bite to eat you could spare us?'

Byren thought of his half-eaten breakfast. This would give him a chance to judge the men's veracity for himself. 'Come this way.'

At his whistle the dogs followed. He put his hands on the thigh-high stonework and swung his weight up to the next terrace, then turned to offer his hand to the closest man.

It was the skinny, short one. As he went to take Byren's hand with his left arm, Byren spotted the bloody stump of his right arm held against his chest.

With a curse, he hauled the youth up. In fact, he pulled so hard, the youth stumbled and Byren had to set him on his feet again.

'What happened to you?' Byren asked, afraid he knew the answer.

'The same thing that happened to all of us,' the smiler said. He wasn't smiling now. He'd managed the climb and had paused to help the solid one, who was struggling. For him the terrace was waist-high.

'Here.' Byren stepped in and hauled the other youth up. Three men, all missing their right hands. 'It was the Merofynians, wasn't it?'

'They're searching the valley for Byren Kingsheir. Every house they come to, they drag out the man of the house and ask for directions. If he can't help them, they chop off his right hand. They figure a man without his right hand is one less swordsman to worry about.' The smiler gestured with his stump. 'I was a player. No more juggling for me.'

'And you?' Byren asked the solid youth.

'A butcher. Just finished my apprenticeship. M'master died so I married his daughter and took over. Now who'll look after the shop?'

Byren looked to the skinny one, the youngest who, on closer inspection, couldn't be more than fifteen.

'I'm a scribe.' He gulped. 'At least I was. What good is a scribe who can't write?'

Anger made Byren's breakfast an indigestible lump in his belly. Unless the Merofynians had crippled one of their own men so he could blend in, Byren could trust these three. 'Come on. You can share my breakfast.'

They followed him up over the rise. From here they could see the farmhouse in the hollow.

'I told you we shoulda kept walking last night,' the butcher complained.

'Eh, just as well you didn't,' Byren told them. 'Last night six mounted Merofynians arrived here. Chopped off the right hand of the man of the house. He was all of thirteen. Then they tied a chain around his neck and told him to lead them to Byren Kingsheir, or they'd do worse to his mam and little brother.'

The butcher swore softly.

'What is Rolencia coming to?' the scribe muttered. 'Where's King Byren when we need him?'

'But, how did you escape? I don't –' The player broke off, staring at Byren with suspicion. 'You're no farmer. You're too well spoken. Where are these Merofynians? Where were you when the boy was taken?'

'He's safe. The Merofynians are all dead. Couldn't have them running off and leading others back to –'

'You're Byren Kingsheir. I mean King Byren!' the player said, then remembered his manners and made a passable bow, proving he must have performed for nobles.

The other two would have followed suit but Byren stopped them. 'Here, none of that. Come down and eat. Then we have to leave.'

Before long they had rearranged the family's belongings and were mounted up on the spare horses, with the scribe and butcher both looking as uncomfortable as Seela had the night before. The dogs barked, eager to get going. Tomorrow, Byren would send men down to the farm to wring the chickens' necks and walk the cows up to the camp. No sense in leaving anything for Merofynians to loot.

For now, Byren saw his old nurse off with a stern warning to watch her back. She travelled on foot, disguised as a wise-woman selling simple remedies. Wise-women were welcomed in every village. They helped with anything from treating bad teeth to delivering babies. It was the perfect way to spread word of the loyalist camp, the Leogryf's Lair.

Seela nodded to the three maimed men, who waited further up the path with Esfira and Tikhon. 'If those three are anything to go by, I'll have no trouble convincing others to join you.'

'And all of them maimed. I'll lead an army of cripples!'

'Take that attitude and you deserve to lose,' Seela told him, tapping his chest with her finger, as if he was ten, not twenty. 'After a bit of training, a man can do wonders with his left hand.'

He laughed and kissed her forehead. 'I'll miss you, Seela. Take care.'

'Don't worry about me. All they'll see is a weak old woman.'

Byren had to be satisfied with that. He let her go and returned to the others, leading Tikhon's horse.

'Will I see Vadik soon?' Tikhon asked.

'Soon,' Byren said, hoping the big brother had not been brought low by his fever. And he plunged up the path, leading the horse with the others following.

FYN BLINKED GRITTY, tired eyes. He'd hardly slept, kept awake by the juddering of the ship's timbers as the *Wyvern's Whelp* tried to outrun the Utland raiders. At the crest of each wave she paused almost as if she'd keep rising. Then she slid down the other side, cutting deep into the upward slope of the next – spray leaping left and right – before clawing her way up the wave's rise.

It was just as well he had his sea legs, for the ship ran before the wind with every concertina-sail fully extended. He looked up, seeing the mid-morning sun gleam through the canvas, the sail's thin wooden ribs illuminated from behind.

They'd been prepared to do battle since last night.

A brazier stood nearby, the coals hot, ready for the stack of tar-dipped arrows.

Fire on a ship at sea? The thought horrified him. If the ship burned to the waterline, they'd drown out here, far from land.

The quarter-master prodded him in the ribs as he passed by. 'Go help Jaku.'

Jakulos sat at the spinning whetstone, sharpening the crews' weapons.

Fyn went over to the big man, who greeted him with a grin. 'Thought so, Bantam can't abide seeing a man idle.'

He spoke the Ostronite trading dialect with the accent of Merofynia, but Fyn knew he had no love for his homeland. He'd been press-ganged to serve the Merofynian navy. With the big man's shirt off, Fyn could see the many criss-crossing scars stretched across the meaty muscles of his back. The blemishes glistened in the sun, silver and slick with sweat. Here, in the lea of the fore-deck, it was surprisingly warm.

Jakulos selected a sword from the pile waiting to be sharpened. The singing of the sword on the whetstone made it impossible to speak.

As there didn't seem to be anything Fyn could do, he looked around. Everyone had a role, everyone knew their place, except him. Even the ten-year-old cabin boy knew more than him and, at nearly seventeen, that rankled.

Back at Halcyon Abbey, he'd completed ten years' training as an acolyte, and been due to get his final scalp tattoo and shave off his top-knot this spring cusp. Now, he suspected he'd never become a monk. To disguise himself, he'd cut the betraying top-knot and his hair was growing out, obscuring his abbey tattoos.

The *Wyvern's Whelp* reminded him of the abbey in some ways. Everyone had a task, from the ship's carpenter who kept her sea-worthy, to the helmsman who handled the wheel, to the navigator, a true artist who read the sea's subtle signs and took the readings to work out their position relative to the sun. They all worked like the clock in the guildhall bell tower, cogs fitting into other cogs to create a greater whole. And, right now, that whole was intent on escaping the Utland raiders.

Jakulos lifted the blade to study it. Satisfied, he placed it on the sharpened pile.

'We're making good time,' Fyn said. 'I don't think they've gained since we put up all our canvas.'

Jakulos sent him a weighing look, then selected a pouch of knives from the table at his side. He ran his finger over each to test their edge, speaking softly. 'They're Utland raiders. We're sea-hounds, their sworn enemies. We've protected merchant convoys. We've hunted down, attacked and sunk more Utland ships than you've had hot dinners. Nothing is going to put them off the chase.' He lifted his head and glanced out to sea. 'And we're too far from Ostron Isle to make it to port. Barring a convenient storm or mist, they'll catch us. Here, take these down to the ship's surgeon.' Jakulos rolled up the leather pouch and handed it to Fyn. 'We're lucky the cap'n believes in keeping a healthy crew. We've a real, Ostron Isle-trained surgeon, nothing like the butchering carpenter who doubled as a surgeon on my last ship.'

Fyn accepted the pouch. Down below deck he found the surgeon's assistant scrubbing the work-table with lye. Its sharp scent stung Fyn's eyes. Meanwhile the surgeon checked his supplies, which were stored in bags or glass jars, labelled in faded, spidery writing.

'Master Jakulos sends your pouch,' Fyn said. The old surgeon took it with an absent-minded nod. Fyn registered no Affinity from him. Nothing to hasten healing. The least of the abbey's healers had Affinity to hasten healing or ease pain or fight festering. Each trained to hone their gift, then worked as a team to save lives. Very different from here.

'What are you staring at?' the surgeon's apprentice asked.

As Fyn opened his mouth to reply, a cry from above cut him off.

'Utlanders to starboard.'

Weren't they to port? For a heartbeat he didn't understand.

Then the surgeon cursed. 'Another scavenger. Just what we need.'

There were two Utland raiders on their tail? Fyn ran up on deck, hurrying up the steps to the rear deck where Captain Nefysto held the farseer to his eye. The wind flung the captain's long black hair over his shoulder.

The younger son of one of the great families of Ostron Isle, Nefysto wore onyx stones threaded through his hair and these glinted in the sunlight. Their countries had never been more than trading partners, but Fyn had more in common with the captain than anyone else. They were both educated men on a ship of scoundrels.

The captain swore softly under his breath, slamming the farseer closed.

'Can we outrun them?' Fyn asked, joining him to watch the converging sails.

'We would stand a better chance if we dumped our cargo over the side. But that would rather defeat the purpose.' He grinned at Fyn. Even on ship, while fleeing Utlanders, Nefysto dressed like the Ostronite noble he was. Velvet knee-length coat, black lace at his throat and boots, when everyone else aboard went barefoot. The light in his dark eyes, however, was anything but civilised.

Nefysto might enjoy the challenge, but Fyn just wanted to survive long enough to get home and find Byren.

Chapter Three

For Piro the day passed in a blur. As a noble from an old family, Dunstany's mansion was built in a prime position overlooking the Landlocked Sea, not far from the king's palace.

His servants prepared a bath scented with rose oil, then led her to a chamber fit for a queen. Chests lay open, heaped with glittering clothes. There were dresses embroidered with gold thread and inset with jewels, wraps of the finest silk from Ostron Isle, slippers of exquisite wyvern skin and bolts of delicate Rolencian lace.

Judging from all this, Dunstany's wealth easily equalled her father's, and the scholar was only a noble of Merofynia. Piro's mother had never said anything, but her old nurse had often complained about the way they lived in Rolenhold, saying they were little better than barbarian spar warlords. Now Piro saw the truth in this.

Servants dressed her in a gown of dark red velvet. It was laced down her back, the bodice embroidered in gold thread. A gold-trimmed cap was pinned to her head and matching slippers tied around her ankles. All too soon she was ready. She sat and waited, gnawing her bottom lip.

A tray of fruit and sweet wine was sent to Piro's room, but she was too nervous to eat or drink. What was Isolt Merofyn Kingsdaughter like? Would she make Piro's life unbearable?

At last the servants came to say Lord Dunstany was waiting in the entrance foyer. Piro paused at the top of the stairs.

The noble scholar looked up and smiled, the corners of his wispy moustache lifting. 'You look every bit a kingsdaughter, Seelon. I suppose I should call you Seela, now that you have resumed your true gender.'

As she glided down the steps, grateful for her mother's interminable lessons in court etiquette, Piro noted that Dunstany had changed out of his usual woollen scholarly attire. For the feast, he wore indigo silk, so dark it was almost black. His robes touched the floor and his iron-grey hair glinted loose on his shoulders. A single pendant, a star-within-a-circle – the Dunstany noble symbol – hung on his chest. She guessed the amber pendant was under his robe, and once again her resentment surfaced.

'Ready, Seela?'

'Do I have any choice?'

'Do any of us?' he asked gently and offered his hand. Surprised by his courtly gesture, she accepted his touch.

They rode in a carriage around the slope of Mount Mero to the palace. Piro was nervous about meeting King Merofyn and his daughter. Isolt had agreed to marry her brother, Lence, with no intention of honouring that betrothal. What sort of people were these Merofynians, who valued their word so lightly?

The walk from carriage to feasting hall seemed endless. Jewel-bright mosaics covered the floor. Piro could feel the heat rising up from the tiles. The palace builders had harnessed Mulcibar's blessing by piping hot water from deep within the earth to run under the floor. Her people used Halcyon's blessing to provide hot bathing water, but they really could have done with under-floor heating, especially during the Rolencian winters.

At last they came to the feasting hall. The air was heavy here with the scent of candles. A lapis lazuli mosaic of a beautifully stylised wyvern glittered on the wall behind the high table. From the king's table, two long tables ran out at right angles. Every seat was taken. Servants scurried about, answering summons.

Piro's first impression was of a cage of exquisite birds, a multitude of chattering people and no forest of columns to obscure the hall's magnificence. How did the roof stay up? She looked up to discover great ribs running from the walls to points above her. The ceiling was so high it took her breath away.

Someone laughed and her gaze was drawn to the feasters. They wore so much glittering jewellery, velvets, silks and feathered headdresses, that Piro felt under-dressed.

She glanced to Dunstany. In his deep indigo robe with his iron-grey hair, he stood out stark and dark. Now she understood why he had dressed so simply.

As they approached the high table, they drew nearer to Palatyne, who stood in front of King Merofyn recounting the battle for Rolencia. He broke off mid-sentence, seeing them.

The noble scholar bowed low with an elegant sweep of his hand. 'My king.'

Piro felt a tug on her skirt and realised she had been staring at the frail old man who had toppled her father's kingdom and brought them such misery. He wasn't at all what she expected, not arrogant, if anything he looked tired and cranky.

Another tug on her skirt. She flushed and bowed her head, hands by her sides in the Rolencian manner, no fancy flourishes.

'Dunstany,' a thin voice spoke. 'Like a black cat, you've returned unharmed.'

The noble scholar lifted his head and so did Piro.

Dunstany shrugged. 'You know what they say, a cat always lands on its feet.'

'But you've been doing that for ninety-four years now.' The old man's eyes blazed. 'How do you do it?'

'A by-product of Affinity, my king.' From his tone, Piro could tell they'd had this conversation before. 'Affinity affects different people in different ways.'

The king sat back with a grimace. Used to being acknowledged by visiting nobles, Piro felt excluded but also relieved, because she could stand back and observe.

Dunstany turned to Palatyne with the barest of nods. 'Overlord.'

'Duke Palatyne,' he corrected, touching a large, official crest on his chest which rested amidst her family's royal emblems. Every time Piro saw the pendants, her stomach lurched as she was reminded of how her mother and father had died. How had Lence died? Would she ever know? He'd been so much larger than life, he and Byren. She could not imagine anything quenching the fire in them.

'You.' Palatyne tugged Piro forwards.

She lifted her chin determined not to let the grand palace, and its even grander people, overwhelm her.

'And this, King Merofyn, is my gift to your beautiful daughter, a Rolencian nobleman's child for her very own seven-year slave.'

Piro glanced to Palatyne, surprised by his easy lie. Then she recalled she wasn't supposed to understand Merofynian.

She let her gaze meet King Merofyn's. This was the man who had assassinated her mother's young brother to steal the crown, relying on his cousinship to legitimise his claim.

Her old nurse had always said you were born with the face the gods gave you, but you ended up with the face you deserved. If this was so, then King Merofyn had been a mean-spirited, angry man and now she thought she also read fear in his frail body. He sat on the great golden throne, behind the royal table, dwarfed by his mantle of office with its gleaming chains and seals.

Originally, she had put him high on her list of people who needed killing. But, since overhearing Palatyne's plan to poison him and now, seeing him in person, she pitied the king.

Next to him sat Isolt Merofyn Kingsdaughter. Her eyebrows had been plucked completely and her face powdered so that she was very pale. Kohl elongated her tilted black eyes and her mouth had been painted a glistening red, like a furled rose bud. With her high forehead and her hair pulled back under a circlet of silver, she looked like a perfect sculpture, not a living, breathing girl half a year older than Piro.

'You do me great honour, Overlord Pal...' Isolt corrected herself, 'I mean Duke Palatyne.'

Piro felt a little kick of delight. If she was not mistaken, Isolt's slip had been deliberate, to remind Palatyne of his origins beyond the Divide. Piro studied Isolt. Was this kingsdaughter a kindred spirit?

No, she couldn't be, not when she held her honour so lightly.

Palatyne's jaw clenched, but he said only, 'The Lady Seela is at your service, Isolt.' No title for her.

'Seela? That is a Merofynian name. Does she speak Merofynian?'

'No. Rolencian only,' Palatyne said. 'These Rolencians imitate their betters but do not have the scholarship to learn another language. How many can you speak, Isolt Kingsdaughter?'

This was a clumsy attempt at flattery and Piro thought Isolt agreed with her, because her answer was barely civil.

'As many as I need to.' She added in only slightly accented Rolencian, 'Come stand behind my chair, lady Seela.'

Palatyne gave Piro a nudge and she climbed the step onto the dais, going around the table.

Isolt did not meet Piro's eyes or acknowledge her and Piro realised that, as a slave, she was invisible, yet right behind the throne. Dunstany was right, she could go anywhere in the palace and all she had to say was that she was on Isolt Kingsdaughter's business for the guards to let her pass.

While Palatyne went on to boast of his success, Dunstany took his seat at the end of the high table. Between the Power-worker and the king were eleven nobles – men and women who had risen to power with the king, Piro suspected, usurping the nobles loyal to her mother's family. This was surprising, as she would have expected the noble scholar to have wormed his way closer into the king's inner circle of advisers.

Palatyne came around to sit on the king's left hand. On his side were three young nobles she recognised from the voyage, and the Utlander. Here was another layer of new allegiances. Clearly, there was a struggle for power between the older nobles who supported King Merofyn and the ambitious young ones who were eager for power at Palatyne's side. And what did Dunstany do?

She glanced his way, catching him watching her.

He sat back and waited. He was a survivor.

During the long meal Piro wriggled her toes in her fancy new shoes, while she observed the nobility and royalty of Merofynia. Now that she was bored, her stomach rumbled and she wished she had eaten earlier.

The king, his daughter and Palatyne all had their own food tasters. They ate nothing that their tasters did not. If this was an elegant high court, then she was glad she had grown up in Rolenhold where King Rolen did not worry about poison and sometimes wandered into the kitchen to help himself to a slab of leftover apple pie.

Sorrow stung Piro's eyes, but grief served no purpose. Revenge was better. She almost laughed. Here she stood, inside the palace, within a body's length of the men who had orchestrated the downfall of her father's kingdom, and no one knew who she was.

Dunstany thought she was spying for him, but she had her own plans.

FYN STUDIED THE sky, hoping for clouds to obscure the betraying multitude of stars.

'No such luck.' Bantam said, voicing his thoughts. 'Under starlight the ship stands out like a cockroach on a silver plate!'

Fyn turned back to the approaching Utlanders. 'They're –'

'Closer still,' Bantam agreed. 'They'll be on us by midnight.'

Fyn swallowed. To die out here, when Byren needed him... 'We're tacking across the wind. Can't we ride before it like we were doing?'

Bantam grinned. 'We'll make a sailor of you yet.

We're tacking because the cap'n's changed course. We're heading towards the Skirling Stones.'

He drew Fyn with him to a better vantage point and gestured by way of explanation.

When Fyn stared in the direction he'd indicated, he was able to make out jagged black rocks, jutting out of the sea. 'What good's that? They'll just follow us.'

'Into the Skirling Stones? Into a maelstrom of seething water, reefs of razor-sharp rocks and whirlpools?' Bantam mocked. 'No one in their right mind would venture into the Skirling Stones.'

Fyn just stared at him. Why hadn't anyone warned him sea-hounds were mad?

'You think we're crazy, don't you, little monk? And we would be, if the cap'n hadn't done this before. He's a true artist, able to feel his way through channels, against tides and over reefs. He knows his way through the Skirling Stones.'

'Why? Why go there in the first place?'

'We're sea-hounds, boy. Ostron Isle pays a bounty for every Utland raider we destroy. But it's hard to catch them unawares on the open sea.' He tilted his head. 'Back home where I grew up, there were spiders big as sparrows. They'd build a trap by digging into the soil and disguise it with bits of twig and bark, so that it looked like a bit of ordinary ground. When an unwary beetle came by, they'd dart out and snatch it. That's a bit like the cap'n's plans. No one expects attack from within the Skirling Stones.'

'That's clever.' Fyn began to hope. 'How many times have you done this?'

Bantam hesitated for a single heartbeat. 'Just the once, to see if it could be done. But the plan's a good one.'

Fyn's heart sank. He'd failed his family, he'd failed the abbot and now it looked like he would die and fail Byren.

BYREN ARRIVED AT the hidden loyalist camp to find another two maimed youths being treated alongside young Vadik. Equal parts anger and frustration boiled through him, making it hard to accept Esfira's thanks as she hugged her crippled son. At least Vadik was no longer feverish.

Leaving the injured men in the care of Dovecote's stable-master, who was the closest thing they had to a healer, Byren went looking for Orrade. This camp had grown around the survivors of Dovecote Estate, people Orrade had led into the hills to escape the Merofynian invasion. Byren needed to know how many more families had arrived since then, how many were warriors and what food and weapons they had.

Clearly reassured to have Byren back, people came up to him, eager for news, eager for words of encouragement. They'd lost homes and loved ones to the invasion and they looked to him to right these wrongs. He felt the weight of their expectation.

Hiding his fears, he paused, exchanging a word here and there as he made his way up to the cave Orrade shared with what remained of Byren's honour guard.

These were the younger sons of lords and wealthy merchants, who had remained true to Byren when Cobalt tried to destroy his reputation by claiming that Byren sought to usurp Lence's claim to the throne. As evidence Cobalt had provided the lincurium rings and pendant, which Byren had found and had made up for his parents and Lence's betrothed. But the really damning evidence was a poem he'd written to Elina, his Dove. Cobalt had twisted the poem's meaning, claiming it was addressed not to Orrade's sister, but to Orrade himself.

Tonight, there was no sign of Orrade in the cave. Winterfall and Chandler greeted him jovially, pulling him over to the fire circle where a thin soup bubbled. Byren felt indebted to his four remaining honour guard, so he sat and chatted about what they'd seen and heard on their way here.

Byren accepted a bowl as they spoke of better times. No one mentioned Cobalt's accusations and, after a while, they fell silent so that only the fire's crackling filled the cave.

'I wish –' young Wafin began, then broke off. He was fifteen, around the same age as Orrade's brother Garzik.

Byren felt a familiar stab of guilt over Garzik's death. It helped him to be patient with the youngster. 'What do you wish, Wafin?'

'I wish I knew if my mother and little brother were all right,' he said.

Chandler made an abortive gesture, too late to cut Wafin off. And everyone winced, glancing to Byren, reminded of his losses.

'I'm sorry –' Chandler began.

Byren silenced him with a wave of his hand as he held Wafin's gaze. 'All you can do is place your trust in the Goddess Halcyon to protect them in this world, or keep them safe in the next.' He said the words, but he didn't believe it. He'd called on Halcyon to help him warn his family, and look what had happened. No, he believed a man made his own luck. Restless, he came to his feet. 'Where's Orrie?'

'Probably up at the Narrows' cave,' Winterfall said. He stood up and walked Byren to the entrance. 'Look, I didn't object when Orrie left Old Man Narrows in charge. He was more experienced than me, but you should do something about that daughter of his. She thinks she's as good as any man.'

Byren hid a smile. 'Up and around the bend, you say?'

Winterfall nodded and went back to the fire circle.

Byren headed off. Florin's unconventional attitude was the least of his worries. With so many people living in close quarters and no proper sanitation, next thing he knew there'd be sickness, claiming the few healthy warriors he had. He could have really used an abbey healer to set up a proper village.

Mind you, with the Merofynians' policy of deliberate cruelty, he didn't know how long he could trust the Rolencian valley people to hide the camp's location. Would the threat of maiming and death succeed, where a bag of gold had failed?

It was all very well to say his people were loyal, but what choice had little Vadik had?

As he approached the cave, he heard Florin's laughter. Pausing in the shadows at the entrance,

Byren spotted Orrade and Florin playing a children's game. Red stones and black moved in patterns on a makeshift chequerboard.

Since Dovecote had fallen and Orrade's father, sister and brother had been killed, Byren hadn't seen Orrade let down his guard like this. Although his friend was now Lord Dovecote and Florin was the daughter of a tradepost keeper, events had stripped them of these distinctions, leading them to a cave in a hidden loyalist camp and a game of strategy.

'There!' With a flourish, Florin cleared the board, winning most of his pieces. 'Next time don't underestimate me.'

'Oh, I'd never underestimate you,' Orrade said, a cheeky grin on his narrow face.

Florin pulled back. 'Are you flirting with me, Orrie? Because I'll tell you now, I don't flirt. I don't play silly games. I say what I think.'

'I know,' Orrade said, lowering his voice. Byren edged closer. If his friend had developed an interest in Florin, it would save them both heartache. 'And that's why –'

So fixed was he on the pair by the fire, that Byren didn't notice the bundle of spare fire wood. He brushed against it, toppling the wood and interrupting Orrade.

Florin turned, saw him and sprang to her feet. 'You're back. I saved you some potato and leek soup.'

Orrade put the game away in the shadows of the cave, where Leif, Florin's little brother, slept.

'Soup sounds good,' Byren said, as though he hadn't just devoured a bowl of the same soup back at his honour guard's cave. He accepted it with thanks and they took their places by the fire.

'When I saw young Vadik and the others...' Florin could not go on, her strong hands clenched on her knees, knuckles white with anger. 'It's cruel. It's wrong –'

'It's war,' Orrade said. 'If you want to win, you can't afford to be soft.'

Florin's gaze flew to Byren's face and he felt moved to protest.

'War doesn't have to turn men into animals, Orrie.'

'Who wins?' Orrade countered. 'The lamb or the leogryf?'

'We're men, not animals,' Byren repeated. 'We make choices. Leaders make choices and people follow them because of those choices. Palatyne rules with fear. I won't be that kind of king.' He dunked the flat bread in the soup, tearing off a chunk and swallowing it. Last season's onions made it tasty. 'If I offered a reward for the head of every Merofynian warrior, I'd be no better than Palatyne. I might win, but I'd start my rule under a shadow of cruelty.'

Orrade met his eyes, deliberately not pointing out that his father, King Rolen the Implacable, had been ruthless, executing the Servants of Palos who had tried to put the king's illegitimate half-brother on the throne.

Unaware of this unspoken interchange, Florin took the empty bowl. 'See, Orrie, Byren's right.'

'I stand corrected,' Orrade said. But there was a smile in his eyes as he met Byren's gaze.

And Byren felt an answering smile tug at his lips. It had always been like this between them. Was he selfish to keep Orrade by him, when he knew his friend's true feelings?

Orrade looked away first. Then he stood and stretched, yawning as he scratched his belly. Florin would see it as perfectly natural. Byren saw it for the act it was.

'I'm for bed,' Orrade muttered. 'Coming, Byren?'

He looked down. Since they were lads on their first spar campaign, they slept side by side, sharing the same blanket. If Byren didn't go back to that cave and stretch out next to Orrade, his honour guard would have reason to suspect there was something in Cobalt's vile accusations. But, now that he knew Orrade's true feelings, he didn't want to sleep, spooned against his friend. 'I'll be down soon as I finish another bowl.'

Florin smiled and served him more soup as Orrade nodded and headed off, leaving him virtually alone with her. It didn't worry Byren, for Florin had spoken the truth. Unlike the girls back at Rolenhold, who had flirted with him and Lence and been only too eager to lift their skirts for King Rolen's twins, Florin didn't smile and cast him coy glances.

Instead, she met his eyes squarely as they discussed the camp and the news from Rolencia. She offered him her observations without reservation, as though it never occurred to her that he would not take her seriously.

The firelight sculpted her strong jaw and long nose, but he saw past her unconventional looks to her mind and liked what he found.

In some ways, she reminded him of Piro. Not in looks, for his sister was small and dainty, piquantly pretty. But Piro had always been impatient with court etiquette, much preferring to say what she thought. He only hoped she was keeping low in Merofynia. Surely, a slave could slip into the background and stay safe?

Chapter Four

PIRO'S FEET ACHED by the time the feast ended and Isolt bid her father and Palatyne good night. The kingsdaughter ignored Piro, who followed her from the hall, up many corridors and stairs until they entered the chambers belonging to the kingsdaughter.

Piro could not tell if they were the same rooms her mother had used. She had become confused since entering the palace, which didn't tally with her mother's stories. Mind you, Myrella had only been eight when she left with her nurse to go live in Rolencia, as surety of peace. Plus King Merofyn had probably made additions. Piro was so tired she could hardly stand.

Scented lamps already lit, several servants waited in the sumptuous chamber to help the kingsdaughter disrobe. A row of doors opened onto a long veranda.

Piro stood just inside the entrance wondering what to do. Impervious to the many people present, Isolt let them strip her and dress her in a soft silk nightgown and matching slippers. Piro found this odd. She always dressed herself, unless her old nurse insisted on helping.

Now in her nightgown, Isolt looked over at Piro and asked in Rolencian, 'Are you really a nobleman's daughter?'

'If you please, kingsdaughter.' Piro decided to stick to her original story. 'I was a maid at Rolenhold until Lord Dunstany took me for his slave. The overlord, I mean Duke Palatyne, claimed me for you.'

Isolt nodded to herself then dismissed the servants. When they were alone, she drew her silk nightgown around her small shoulders and approached Piro. She was delicate, only as tall as Queen Myrella, so her eyes were level with Piro's nose.

Now that her face was washed clean of paint she looked young and vulnerable, but her eyes, when they met Piro's, were keen with intelligence. 'I know you're a spy.'

Piro did not know what to say.

Isolt shrugged. 'It does not bother me. Palatyne will find no secret lovers under my bed.'

'You wrong me,' Piro protested. 'I despise Palatyne. Lord Dunstany thinks I am his spy, but I don't care about their politics!'

A surprised gasp escaped Isolt. She looked at Piro... really looked at her. For a heartbeat Piro thought she saw a flicker of something in Isolt's eyes, a need to believe, then she turned away contemptuously. 'You are either very stupid, or very clever. I can't decide which. You may sleep on the daybed. I care not whose spy you are.'

Obscurely hurt, Piro undressed and stretched out on a narrow, high-backed daybed in front of the fireplace. She stared into the banked coals. Red winking eyes stared back at her, ever watchful, ever wary.

Suddenly, it came to her. Isolt was afraid Afraid to eat, afraid to trust – how awful to live in a state of constant fear!

FYN FROWNED, TRYING to make out the Skirling Stones by the brilliant starlight. Intricate rocky reefs surrounded the stones, and the ship was close enough now for him to see the froth of waves crashing on those reefs. He glanced behind him. The Utlanders had closed in. Now he could just make out their fierce, determined faces.

Putting his back to them, Fyn placed his faith in Captain Nefysto. What else could he do?

One by one, the sea-hounds came on deck. Runt, the little cabin boy, edged close to Jaku. Fyn suspected he would have preferred the captain, whom he idolised, but Nefysto had taken over the wheel.

Now everyone, from the cook to the surgeon, stood on deck. A sea-hound had climbed to the top of each mast, while one waited on the fore-deck with a knotted rope tied to weights, to test the sea's depth.

Bantam caught a nod from the captain and called, 'Trim the sails to one-third.'

The sails contracted like concertinas folding, but the ship still made headway, carried by momentum.

What Fyn had thought was his racing heart drumming in his ears turned out to be the dull boom of the waves crashing on the Skirling Stones. No one spoke.

They passed the first of the outlying rocks. Waves broke, sending spray as high as the tallest mast. A man near him started a chant to Sylion, Rolencia's harsh god of winter and the sea. Soon everyone was whispering to their gods, pleading for safe passage. Some fingered lucky charms, others repeated the actions to ward ill luck.

The man at the prow took a depth sounding and called the number.

Bantam chuckled.

Fyn glanced to him, startled.

He gestured over his shoulder, prompting Fyn to turn. Only a bow shot away, they could clearly see the Utlanders' consternation.

'They're hanging back,' Jaku said.

The news passed along and there was a half-hearted cheer.

To each side of the ship the sea boiled as waves churned over the rocks just below the surface, but the *Wyvern's Whelp* travelled a narrow, dark channel. Fyn wished there was something he could do. He'd rather be up a mast, watching for danger, than helpless here.

Every few moments, the sea-hound called out the depth.

This close, Fyn could see the true height of the Skirling Stones. They reared up, tall as three or four-storey buildings. The first stone the ship passed reminded him of a listing tower, topped by a rakishly tilted beret, where a fuzz of bushes grew, bent with the force of the prevailing wind.

Fyn blinked, his head ached with fear. He was amazed plants could survive out here.

Without warning, the backwash of a wave breaking against the stone's base sent the ship tipping and sliding towards the jagged teeth at the base of another of the Skirling Stones. Sea-hounds shouted and raised oars, ready to fend off just such an event.

Fyn gripped the rail, breath tight in his chest.

And to think, he'd believed wyverns and Utlanders the worst of his worries. His skin prickled. Didn't salt-water wyverns live on islands like this, nesting high in caves, hunting for fish and birds or, failing that, plucking unwary sailors from the decks of passing ships?

Fyn spun to face Bantam. 'What of wyverns?'

'Huh?' He had been concentrating on the ship, watching her sails belly and flap as the wind gusted, then fell, blocked by the towering stones. 'Wyverns? We saw none the last time we came through.'

'Look,' the cabin boy cried. 'The Utlanders are coming after us.'

Fyn spun. It was true. The first of the Utlander raiders followed them, sails at one-third. Would nothing deter these savage men?

He shuddered and felt for the Fate, seeking reassurance. It was warm.

That meant...

Fyn inhaled deeply, opening his Affinity senses. The tension behind his eyes was not a fear-induced headache, but a foretaste of power. Why, if he didn't know better, he would say they approached an Affinity seep.

Could there be a seep at sea? He'd only ever heard of them on land. They were places of power, where Affinity from the earth's heart found its way to the surface.

The Fate felt hot under his hand. Fyn left the rail, edging back to stand beside the captain.

'Busy here, little monk,' Nefysto muttered. 'Are they still behind us?'

Fyn looked over his shoulder, in time to see the first Utland ship pass the leaning stone tower. Then the *Wyvern's Whelp* rounded another pillar, riding the backwash past it, and he lost sight of their pursuers.

'Still following.' Fyn caught Nefysto's eye. 'Captain, I think there's a seep nearby. I can sense it.'

Bantam joined them. 'What's this about a seep?'

Fyn plucked the Fate from inside his vest. The opal, formed from an ancient spiral seashell, glowed. 'The Fate's responding to it.'

'Some kind of sorbt stone?' Nefysto asked, proving he knew more than the average layman about mystical practices.

Fyn went to answer in the negative but he could feel the Fate, even now, eager for the untamed Affinity. The captain's guess might be closer to the truth than Fyn knew, so he remained silent.

The ship had reached the midst of the Skirling Stones, weaving her way through towering black edifices, topped with gnarled trees.

Here, in the centre of the Skirling Stones, the crash of the sea on the outer rocks faded to a distant boom and an eerie wailing came and went, as the wind whirled between the stones, proving someone must have come here at least once, to give them their name.

Fyn frowned. Had something moved on that ledge, three-quarters up the Skirling Stone ahead of them? Affinity attracted Affinity beasts. If it was a new seep, it would attract...

'Cap'n?' A voice called from above, called as if trying to shout softly. 'There are things on the ledges. Lots of them.'

Fyn's hand tightened on the Fate. His teeth tingled and he tasted cold air on his tongue, even though his mouth was closed. The air felt sharp, rich with Affinity.

His mind raced... spring cusp... new seep... Affinity beasts gathering to feast on the power, gathering to mate. Affinity beasts were always dangerous, more so in mating season.

The sea-hound called the depth, his voice pitched to carry above the wailing of the wind.

Fyn clutched Bantam's arm. 'Tell him to be quiet. He'll bring them down on us.'

The captain and Bantam stared at Fyn.

'The seep's attracted Affinity beasts. We're in the midst of a rookery!' His voice rose, and he brought it under control with an effort. 'Tell everyone to be very quiet.'

Bantam tapped Jakulos on the shoulder and the two of them darted off, running the length of the vessel, warning the sea-hounds.

Meanwhile, the cabin boy edged closer, taking Fyn's hand. 'What sort of Affinity beasts, master monk?'

Master monk? How he wished. He wasn't even a proper monk, just an acolyte.

'N-Not wyverns?' The boy's voice quavered.

'I don't know, Runt.' He hoped not. Salt-water wyverns were notoriously aggressive, especially during mating season.

Quick as a bird, something flashed past Fyn, then darted back to hover before him, where it eyed the glowing Fate on his vest.

The creature was as tall as little Runt, but it hovered off the deck so that its head was level with Fyn's. Wings moving too fast to see other than as a blur held it aloft.

Like a bird it tilted its head this way and that, fascinated by the Fate. Its long, sinuous body was marked by scars, possibly from mating fights. While the body was serpent-like, its head was more like a bird's with a long, razor-sharp beak and a crest of brilliant, iridescent feathers behind its neck.

This close, the Affinity beast gave off a pale luminescence and smelled like last week's eel pie gone bad.

Behind it, Fyn saw Bantam and Jakulos return to the rear deck. They hesitated on the top step, both making the sign to ward off dangerous Affinity.

Fyn licked his lips. Runt whimpered.

Fyn squeezed his hand, speaking low and soothing. 'It is a jakulos, lad. Almost as pretty as our own Jakulos. It won't hurt you.' No, not at the moment.

When they attacked, jakulos launched themselves from the sky, flying fast and true as javelins.

'It's nothing like our Jaku,' Runt whispered.

Fyn grinned. 'Perhaps he hadn't seen one when he chose his sea-hound name.' Why the big man had named himself after this Affinity beast Fyn couldn't guess. It was elegant, almost dainty as it hovered to inspect them.

Something moved in the corner of Fyn's vision and he realised another had arrived, and another.

Behind him, Fyn sensed the captain, turning the wheel. A gap appeared between two tall stones, and they saw open sky, heard the growing boom of the waves on the reefs.

'We're almost through,' Runt whispered.

As if this was a signal, the jakulos inspecting Fyn flicked its tail, rose straight up, not at all like a bird, and darted off. Back to its nest, Fyn assumed.

He felt Runt and the captain breathe a sigh of relief, and a laugh bubbled up inside him. Who would have thought?

As he glanced over his shoulder to congratulate the captain on getting through the Skirling Stones, Fyn noticed the prow of the closest Utland ship gliding between the last of the stones behind them. A curious jakulos hovered over its carven head, glowing faintly.

Fyn swore. 'The Utlanders are still coming.' If they got through the reefs, the *Wyvern's Whelp* would be in the same position as before.

They needed something to set off the Affinity beasts' territorial instincts.

His gaze fell on the brazier of hot coals and tar-dipped arrows, readied for the attack. Before he knew it, he'd strung a bow and lit an arrow.

'What're you doing?' Bantam demanded.

'Stirring up the Affinity beasts so they'll turn on the Utlanders.' Fyn ran to the bow rail and took aim, hoping to hit the trees on the crown of the nearest Skirling Stone.

As he let loose, Bantam joined him with another bow.

Fyn's flaming arrow hit the stone's crown and, for a moment, nothing happened. Then flames danced across the tree canopy, driven by the wind.

'I'll go one better,' Bantam muttered. And he aimed at the Utlander's ship which was partially visible as it came from behind the pillar. He let his arrow fly. 'A sailor can't ignore fire at sea.'

His arrow hit the Utlander's sails. Jakulos joined them with a bow. Fyn ran to get another arrow. By the time he'd taken aim, flames were leaping across the Utlanders' deck and the raiders raced about, shouting orders as they sought to save the ship.

A flashing spear of silver shot down from the Skirling Stone. A man screamed. Then another and another.

A cacophony of cries followed, quickly drowned out by the crashing waves, now that the *Wyvern's Whelp* was in the channel between the reefs.

Its crew's cries cloaked by the sea, the first Utlander ship burned. As Fyn watched a wave caught it, driving the ship against the base of a stone pillar and spinning it around so that it blocked the passage, trapping the second ship. Masts toppled, sending flaming sails onto a deck already seething under the Affinity beasts' attack, dropping sails onto the second as yet undamaged ship. The men stood no chance.

Fyn swallowed and turned away, not wanting to witness the manner of their deaths.

Bantam clapped him on the shoulder. 'Quick thinking, little monk.'

Two shiploads of men, dead. Fyn's stomach heaved. He ran to the side and threw up until his stomach was empty. Tears blurred his vision.

By the time he lifted his head, the *Wyvern's Whelp* rode the waves of the open sea. And Runt waited with a mug of watered wine.

Fyn accepted it gratefully, rinsed his mouth, spat and took a gulp. He turned around to see most of the crew watching, waiting. At Bantam's signal, they cheered.

Runt smiled up at Fyn.

And he'd been afraid he would not be accepted.

Still, if they only knew how he had failed the abbey and his family. He'd failed to realise that the seal on the message, supposedly from his father, was a fraud. By the time he had it was too late and the abbey's fighting monks had left, heading into an ambush. He'd failed to save the abbot, when the abbey was attacked. He'd failed to reach Rolenhold in time to save his family. Little Piro...

He mustn't think of Piro.

Feeling a fraud, he shrugged off the sea-hounds' praise, but they broke open a crate of fine Rolencian red wine, stolen from his homeland, and shared it out, insisting he take a drink.

As Fyn lifted the bottle, he met the captain's eye. Here he was, a captive, forced to rob the Merofynians who had plundered his homeland, forced to drink a toast to the survival of his captors.

Well aware of the nuances, Nefysto raised his bottle with an ironic grin.

In defiance, Fyn upended the bottle, gulping its contents. The rich red wine reminded him of evenings in his father's hall. King Rolen calling for stories and songs, his mother's fond smile. Little Piro dancing about, laughing, teasing the storyteller for tales of Queen Pirola the Fierce.

Argh. He must not think of Piro.

He upended the bottle again, seeking oblivion.

Chapter Five

BYREN TENSED. THE shouting came from his honour guard, who were in the next hollow, teaching the fittest of the loyalists the use of the longsword, and the tone was just a fraction too eager. Normally, Orrade would be with them, but he was out checking the sentries on the approach trails.

Byren blew his breath out in a snort of resignation. Judging by those shouts, someone was about to be knocked silly for the entertainment of the lads. And it was up to him to sort it out.

He skirted an outcropping of rock dusted with last night's snowfall, thinking he did not need trouble now.

After breakfast, Orrade had reported on their numbers – the old, the nursing mothers and children, and the able-bodied men. Then, with

Dovecote's redoubtable cook, he had inspected their stores, trying to work out how long they could feed everyone before he'd have to make a trip into the rich Rolencian valley to forage for food. How was he going to pay for this? He didn't want to steal food from his own people.

Normally, the farmers would harvest two crops each summer, but when the Merofynians invaded they'd destroyed the abbey's hothouse-forced seedlings, so the farmers could only hope for one harvest and a lean one at that. Everyone in the valley would have to tighten their belts.

Unless Byren led a successful attack on Rolenhold, recaptured his father's castle, executed Cobalt and retook Rolencia before autumn, there would be deaths from starvation. He needed access to the castle's granary and the abbey's stores.

He needed a lot of things.

Coming around the bend, through the trees, he had a clear view into the hollow below, and paused to take in the tableau.

'Eh, Florin.' He cursed softly under his breath.

The tradepost keeper's daughter swung a staff. It was the traditional weapon of the farmers, who could not afford a sword and armour. She faced Winterfall and, from his expression, he meant to show her her place.

'Now this is why the farmers stay back and let the warriors lead the attack,' Winterfall said, coming in, swinging the sword. He turned the flat for the strike, but even so, Byren knew it would bruise and possibly break a rib.

A cry sprang to Byren's lips, ready to call a halt to the match, but Old Man Narrows stepped out of the trees and touched him lightly on the arm.

'Leave her be. If she's bitten off more than she can chew, it's better she discovers it now, rather than on the battlefield.'

Byren frowned. It seemed a harsh attitude for Florin's father to take, but honest. Female warriors were few and far between. They just didn't have the strength that men had. Queen Pirola had led Rolencia's warriors, but that was different. She'd had to protect her kingdom. Besides, she was safely relegated to history.

Florin was here now, confronting his honour guard. Banning her from these practice sessions would ease the tension, but her father was right, Florin deserved the chance to prove herself, or fail.

He hoped she didn't fail... or did he? He didn't want her risking her life on the battlefield.

'She's her mother all over again,' Narrows muttered. 'I considered myself lucky to win that mountain girl.'

When Byren looked back, Florin was already moving, watching her opponent closely. Winterfall's sword was almost as tall as him. The length meant once he was committed to the attack, if he did not strike home, he had to follow through, adjust his stance and bring the sword around for another strike.

Florin avoided the first blow and took the opportunity to step in. She brought the top of the staff over, clipping him lightly on the head. It was only a tap but the message was there. She could have knocked him out.

Perched on a fallen tree, Leif cheered. Byren's honour guard and the other would-be-warriors were ominously silent.

Florin's concentration didn't lapse.

Winterfall shook his head and gripped the sword more securely, obviously adjusting his attitude as he eyed her warily. He stood half a head shorter than Florin, but with twice the breadth of shoulders, and Byren knew he would hate being bested by her.

Florin waited for his strike, which seemed to infuriate Winterfall, for he glared and took a swing at her that would have knocked her off her feet, if it had connected.

She darted back, brought the end of her staff up, point-on, and thrust so that it darted in, striking him in the chest. If she'd delivered it full strength it would have been enough to wind him. As it was it only angered him.

Byren recognised the signs. Florin thought ahead, while Winterfall was reacting. This was not going to end well for him.

'Perhaps I should call a stop,' Narrows muttered.

Byren touched his arm, giving a slight shake of his head. 'It'll be hard for court-raised warriors to accept a female in their ranks. This isn't the uncivilised spars where women fight alongside their men –'

'Half the time, they have no choice,' Narrows said.

Byren conceded the point. 'But Florin chose this. If she wants their respect she has to earn it. And Winterfall's a good lad. He's big enough to take this.' Byren only hoped he was right.

While they were speaking, Winterfall had attacked

again. Florin side-stepped and, in the same fluid movement, swung the end of her staff down hard on his forearm. Byren could hear the impact as Winterfall's sword fell from his numbed hand.

Then she used the staff to sweep his legs out from under him. Winterfall fell back onto compacted snow, the air leaving his lungs in a grunt of surprise. Florin rotated the staff in her hands, bringing the point to his throat.

Then she lowered the point, grinned and offered Winterfall her hand.

The watchers held their breath. Byren knew this was the real test. His honour guard respected Winterfall, so they would follow his lead.

The youth sucked in greedy breaths, face flushed with exertion and anger. Florin's place in Byren's loyalists hung in the balance. Then Winterfall's expression lightened and he lifted his hand.

Florin hauled him upright, clapping him on the back. But he brushed her hand aside and stalked back to his companions, leaving her alone on that side of the clearing.

As Byren sucked in his breath, he realised Old Man Narrows was doing the same. Winterfall's bruises were not only physical.

Byren tapped Old Man Narrows on the shoulder. 'Here, give me your staff.'

Grabbing the staff, he trotted down the slope to enter the clearing. 'My turn. Let's see if I can get the hang of this weapon.'

Florin turned to him, clever eyes troubled. Clearly, she realised he was trying to smooth things over.

Next thing he knew, her prickly pride would make her refuse his suggestion.

Byren weighed the staff in his hands, addressing the lads behind her. 'A man never knows when he's going to be caught without his sword. If he can pick up a lump of wood and turn it into a weapon, he's always armed.' He met Florin's eyes. 'Come on.'

She smiled, dropping into a bent-kneed, loose-limbed stance.

His honour guard edged back to give them room, shouting advice. Some of it ribald, as one staff reminded them of another. Old Man Narrows came down from the tree line, stepping into view. The bawdy comments ceased.

Byren circled Florin, feeling the length and weight of the staff. As the king's second son, he'd trained with noble weapons such as the sword and shield. A staff was a farmer's weapon, but he was familiar with it, which was just as well because he intended to make a good fight of it... before letting Florin win. His father had always said a good leader leads by example. If Byren Kingsheir could lose to a girl without being belittled, then so could his men.

Florin grinned, her white teeth flashing, long plait swaying as she moved lightly from foot to foot. He knew she would not hold back, would disarm him if she could.

He laughed.

Florin's staff flashed in, testing him.

He met it. The wooden staves clacked, and then slid past each other. She was fast.

They circled each other.

He made a swipe at her legs. She blocked, lifting her staff's end and forcing his up and around so that he was open. He only just managed to duck the head strike that had tricked Winterfall earlier. She was good.

Old Man Narrows chuckled.

Before he could avoid it, she tapped Byren's knuckles. If she'd struck any harder he would have lost the staff. Byren realised he was not going to have to work hard to make his loss look convincing. He glanced up, noting the slope of the gully was crowded with onlookers. Everyone had come to watch their match. Great.

Byren eased his shoulders. It was no good tensing up during a fight. You needed to relax and let your body respond intuitively.

His boot slipped on an exposed rock, his balance wavered and, in that instant, Florin struck. She darted inside his guard, using the force of her rush to disarm him and shoulder him to the ground.

He went down on his back, rolled up onto his shoulders, arched his back and flipped to his feet like an acrobat. It was a trick he had learnt in his early teens. His men cheered.

Florin was surprised to find him facing her and inside her guard. Before she could spring back, he caught her in a bear hug, lifting her off the ground. Since he was half a head taller than her and heavily muscled, it was easy. With her arms and the staff pinned to her side there wasn't much she could do.

But she could kick his shins. He grunted in pain.

She glared at him, eyes laughing. 'You're lucky I don't head-butt your pretty face!'

Byren laughed. Fyn was the pretty one, Lence the handsome one. His mother used to say he had a winning smile. He had no illusions. He tightened his hold. 'You're lucky I don't crush your ribs.'

His men cheered. Byren let her drop to the ground and she sprang away, light as a cat, staff at the ready.

He laughed. 'No, the match is yours. I pity the Merofynian who comes up against you!'

His men cheered again.

Florin's eyes widened in surprise. Then she sent him a quick, wry smile of acknowledgement. No doubt about it, she was sharp. Maybe as clever as Orrade.

Byren laughed and tugged on her plait, just as the cook rattled the lunch ladle. Everyone headed back up to the camp.

But Old Man Narrows caught his arm. 'Eh, Byren? A word.'

'Sure.'

'You've five, no, six maimed men,' Narrows said. 'More will follow.'

'I know. And there's not a thing I can do about it.'

'Don't blame yourself, lad. You didn't give the Merofynians their orders.'

'No, but it's me they're after.'

'So, hand yourself in.'

Byren glared, then snorted. 'You've made your point.'

Old Man Narrows grinned, a flash of white teeth in a dark beard. 'Give the maimed ones to me. I'll train them. I'll give them back their self-respect.'

'How?'

'By not treating them like cripples.'

Byren let out his breath. 'Now I know why Florin is the way she is.'

'And how is she?'

Byren lifted a hand to deflect the father's belligerence. 'Don't get me wrong. She thinks she's the equal of any man. And she may just be right.'

Narrows hesitated. 'She's a good girl, lad. Hurt her and I'll come after you, king or no king.'

Byren shook his head. 'It's not like that. I don't use women like...' he broke off. He'd nearly said 'like Lence.' He started again. 'I gave my heart to Orrade's sister. And she died in my arms. I have no heart. When I marry, it will be to cement Rolencia's alliances.'

'Good, because it's hard for a woman to tell her king no.'

Byren flushed. He was not like Lence.

FYN'S HEAD THUMPED in time to the beat of his heart, his mouth felt like the inside of the captain's bird cage and the midday sun made his eyes hurt. He uttered a silent vow never to drink again.

But Fyn was not alone. The only person on board the *Wyvern's Whelp* who wasn't hungover was little Runt. He went about whistling.

Jakulos winced. 'Eh, lad. Keep it down.'

The cabin boy laughed and came to a stop in front of Fyn. 'Captain wants to see you.'

With a groan, Fyn pulled himself to his feet. He paused halfway across the mid-deck, to swallow a beaker of water.

In the cabin, he blinked and tried to concentrate as he recognised the map spread across Nefysto's desk. The captain was plotting a course for Ostron Isle.

'That was too close a call,' Nefysto muttered, head bent over the map. 'I'm taking her into port to have her hull scraped.'

Fyn said nothing, not sure what was required of him.

Nefysto lifted his head. 'We owe our lives to you. You saw the opportunity to make the Affinity beasts' natural instincts serve us.' He rolled up the map and sat back in his chair, long legs stretched out. 'I know you want to return to Rolencia and I'd like to oblige you, but I have my orders. When we get to port, unless you give me your word of honour to remain with the *Wyvern's Whelp*, I'll have you placed under arrest.'

Fyn wished his head didn't hurt so badly. 'Why? Why do you care what I do?'

Nefysto lifted his elegant fingers in an oblique gesture that told him nothing. 'Orders, little monk. What will it be?'

Anger flushed the stupor from his body. 'I won't give my word.'

'That's what I thought.'

As Fyn turned to walk out, he wondered why he hadn't lied. It would have been so simple to agree, then slip away. It was not as if he owed the *Wyvern's Whelp's* captain a debt of honour. After all, the man had forced him to serve against his will.

'THAT'S A LIE. Take it back!'

Byren tensed, his lunch sitting heavy in his belly.

Not Winterfall again. He peered around the bend to find his honour guard had met up with the maimed on the crossing of two narrow paths.

The player lifted his hands in a no-threat gesture. 'I'm only repeating Cobalt's decree.'

Byren caught Orrade's eye, with a slight nod.

No words needed, Orrade went forwards, while Byren hung back to listen in.

'What decree is this?' Orrade asked.

'Lord Dovecote.' The player acknowledged his rank with a nod. 'It was all over Rolenton. I'm surprised you haven't heard.'

Orrade made no answer.

The player's tone, when he continued, said that he was only repeating what he had heard. 'Regent Cobalt announced that Queen Myrella had untamed Affinity. According to Rolencian law this annuls her marriage to King Rolen, making their children illegitimate. Since Cobalt is the son of King Rolen's older illegitimate brother, this makes his claim to the throne as good as, if not better than, Byren Kingsheir's claim.'

'A lie. A scurrilous lie,' Winterfall insisted. 'If you'd heard the things Cobalt said, the way he twisted words to serve him, you'd –'

'Enough.' Orrade held up a hand. Byren could hear the annoyance in his voice. 'Since Queen Myrella, may Halcyon shelter her, was murdered by Cobalt at Overlord Palatyne's orders, she can't defend herself. And I don't think I'd trust anything Cobalt said. Not when it favours him. Come on, Winterfall, back to weapons practice.'

Orrade led Byren's honour guard off, while Byren held back, cursing Cobalt under his breath. Trust his cousin to muddy the waters. Fancy accusing his mother of untamed Affinity – if ever there was a dutiful daughter and loving wife, it was Queen Myrella.

Later that afternoon, Byren was walking the camp when he heard Old Man Narrows' bellow. As the tradepost keeper had taken the maimed aside to begin training, Byren was curious. He left the track, following the sounds to the hollow where they trained, well apart from the others.

Careful to present no silhouette against the sky, Byren stretched out on a rock scoured clean of snow and watched the clearing below where half a dozen youths watched Old Man Narrows. He held a wooden sword and faced Florin, who was half a head taller. She met his blows with a wooden sword of her own. While she had the advantage of youth, agility and reach, he had experience and formidable strength.

'See, a left-handed man has an advantage against a right-handed warrior, who has only ever fought with a right-handed opponent.' Narrows grunted between blows. 'He won't be expecting attack from this quarter.'

Florin obligingly left her guard down on that side and took a blow to the ribs. Byren could hear the impact of the flat of the sword from up here.

'Now, who wants to have a go? Don't be rough on her, she's only a girl.'

Florin grinned.

One or two of the youths lifted their wooden swords.

That was another thing. Their weaponry consisted of anything they could scrounge, from weapons used in the war thirty years ago, to farmyard implements. Byren didn't have enough swords to arm the warriors Orrade was training, let alone the maimed.

'Come on,' Old Man Narrows urged. 'I'll tell her to go easy on yer.'

They laughed.

'It looks like I'm first,' the player said, stepping forwards. He moved lightly on the packed snow.

Florin nodded and waited.

His first blow was careful, testing his strength and speed, or perhaps testing hers.

Byren frowned as he watched the player deliver his strikes. The man was a dancer. A trickster.

As the player improved, the other maimed warriors straightened up and began calling encouragement. With a feint, the player distracted Florin, swung a leg behind her knee and tripped her.

The maimed cheered as she went down.

She sprang up, ready for more, but Old Man Narrows waved her back.

'Now see that?' His deep voice carried easily to Byren. 'This battle will be nasty. Take every opportunity your enemy gives you. Trip him and run him through, if you can. He'll be underestimating you, because you're one-handed. Use that to your advantage.'

They nodded, looking earnest and eager.

'Right, who's next?' Not waiting for a response he chose the butcher and the scribe, setting one against Florin and one against himself.

Byren slid off his perch and wended his way down to the hollow, coming up beside the player, who stood on the far side of the clearing.

For a few heartbeats, they observed Old Man Narrows and Florin deflect clumsy if enthusiastic blows.

'When are you going to tell them you're left-handed?' Byren asked the player softly.

He grinned and winked. 'No need. Just as there was no need to tell the Merofynians.' He shrugged and nodded to the youths. 'Besides, they need to be inspired.'

'You're not wrong there.'

The others parted and Byren stepped in to offer a word or two of encouragement, before Old Man Narrows called up two more, leaving Vadik for last.

Byren joined the boy, wishing his new-found Affinity could heal wounds other than his own. And he wasn't even sure if it could do that, as it seemed to be tied in with the ulfr pack. 'Show me that stump.'

Vadik complied without hesitation. It was an affront to see a stump where a perfectly good hand had once been, but at least it wasn't enflamed.

'A good clean wound,' Byren told him. 'No more slacking. Get to work.'

Vadik grinned and Byren turned away to hide his pain.

Chapter Six

Piro had endured several miserable days serving Isolt Kingsdaughter as her unwanted, ignored slave. She tried to make herself useful, but the kingsdaughter had a servant for everything.

Every day more ships arrived from Rolencia laden with treasures stolen from her people. Greed rode the city, as wealth was flaunted and gifts exchanged. The greater the gift, the greater the giver. Then, this morning, Duke Palatyne announced he had a special gift for the king.

So the whole court gathered before the evening feast to see this new marvel. Piro looked for Dunstany, but he wasn't present. She hadn't seen him since that first night and she was surprised by the depth of her disappointment.

Standing behind Isolt's chair, Piro watched as

Palatyne's men wheeled in two objects covered by cloth. From their size and shape she knew what they were, and she ground her teeth in impotent fury.

'My king, I bring you a most unusual gift.' Palatyne clearly enjoyed the attention. 'Creatures so cunningly preserved they look as if they could spring to life!'

With a flourish he pulled off the cloths to reveal King Rolen's stuffed wyvern and foenix. The courtiers gasped and clapped.

Piro schooled her face to betray nothing.

A small cold hand closed on her wrist. 'You were not surprised by the duke's gifts, Seela. Why?'

Piro hid her dismay. These last few days had taught her one thing. Isolt was much cleverer than anyone gave her credit for.

'I used to dust them in King Rolen's trophy chamber,' Piro improvised.

The answer satisfied Isolt.

The old king clutched the arms of his chair. 'They are dead, you say?'

'Couldn't be deader, though cleverly lifelike!' Palatyne assured him.

The king stood and walked around the table, but he did not approach the creatures.

'Touch the wyvern, Palatyne. Put your hand in its open mouth,' King Merofyn commanded, voice thin.

His order made no sense to Piro. Although she wasn't supposed to be able to understand Merofynian, the king's fear was clear from his stance, so she asked, 'Why does the king fear a dead wyvern?'

At first she thought Isolt would not reply. Then she sighed and whispered. 'When he was a boy, Father was almost killed by a pet wyvern. His father had all the wyverns on the estate killed.'

While she spoke, the duke placed his hand in the beast's mouth with a flourish, then laughed and bowed to his king. Piro thought the bow a very nicely timed insult.

She glanced to Isolt to see if the kingsdaughter had read the same meaning into this. Their eyes met and they shared a moment's perfect understanding. Duke Palatyne definitely held King Merofyn in contempt.

The king stepped nearer and prodded the stuffed wyvern. He and Palatyne began to discuss the creatures. The rest of the courtiers crowded round and even Isolt left her seat, joining the others.

Unlike the courtiers, she was more interested in the foenix. She stroked its coat, whispering in Rolencian. 'So soft. Surely it cannot be like this in real life?'

'It's even softer,' Piro said, then added quickly. 'The kingsdaughter had a pet foenix. I used to feed it.'

'Father never let me have a pet,' Isolt said, then seemed to regret the admission, for she drew away from Piro.

Feeling lost amidst the pack of overdressed courtiers, Piro followed Isolt and remained by her side. As she watched the nobles chatter to either the king or the duke, depending on their allegiances, Piro felt her lips curl with contempt. No wonder Isolt trusted no one. None of these people were worth trusting, all too eager to flatter and win favour with the king or the duke. Dunstany would have flattered neither.

And, as if her thoughts had called him up, there he was, slipping into the feasting hall and making his way towards the gathering.

Isolt nudged Piro, gesturing to where Palatyne preened, enjoying the attention.

'The duke outdoes himself,' Isolt remarked, putting heavy emphasis on the title. She said the words loudly, as though baiting Palatyne.

Piro did not think Isolt expected an answer from her, but chose to give one. 'Naturally, he sets out to impress you.'

'Naturally?' Isolt looked at Piro. 'You placed extra emphasis on that word. Why?'

With a jolt Piro remembered that Isolt did not know Palatyne meant to marry her. Surely King Merofyn's daughter realised her betrothal to Lence had ended with his death? And, as far as Isolt knew, all of King Rolen's sons were dead, relieving her of any obligation, so that left her free to make a new match. Anger made Piro's pulse race as she hardened her heart towards Isolt. 'It was a word, nothing more. Forget it.'

'I don't know what manner of maids they have in Rolenhold but here, in Merofynia, no one speaks to the kingsdaughter like that.' With a toss of her head, Isolt turned away from Piro.

Just then, Palatyne called the kingsdaughter to take a closer look at the wyvern's sapphire eyes and Piro noticed Dunstany signal to catch her gaze. She wandered casually around the outskirts of the crowded courtiers to join him.

'A fitting gift,' he said, adding softly, 'watch over Isolt. She desperately needs a friend.'

Befriend that treacherous schemer? Piro stared at Dunstany. Was he mad?

'Careful, your face betrays your thoughts. I've come to tell you I must leave Port Mero for a while. If you have any news, or are in trouble, send word to my servants and they will let me know. I have instructed them to obey you.'

This surprised Piro. Then it hit her. Dunstany was going. Without him there was no one she could trust. But then, she reminded herself she should not really trust him either.

Piro swallowed. 'Where are you going?'

'I have a finger in many pies, and one of them is burning.' He gave her a conspiratorial wink and slipped away.

Piro watch him go, feeling bereft. No one else noticed the noble scholar leave, except for the Utlander. Thinking himself unobserved, the Power-worker's expression contained calculating hatred.

The Utlander's eyes narrowed and he turned to stare directly into Piro's face. She'd been mistaken, he knew she was watching him, but he thought her so insignificant he believed he could bully her. Piro swallowed and tried to hide her fear. With a smile that was more a sneer, the Utlander joined his patron, Duke Palatyne.

King Merofyn's palace was a dangerous place to be a slave, let alone a kingsdaughter. Piro's gaze was drawn back to Isolt as she listened to Palatyne, her face a polite mask. Isolt was good at masks and the removal of her eyebrows had made her face harder to read, cloaking those little quirks of expression that conveyed so much.

Piro sighed. Since he'd taken her for his slave, the noble scholar had been nothing but kind to her, if she omitted trapping her essence in the amber pendant. She would watch over Isolt for him, but even he could not force her to be Isolt's friend, not when her dead parents and brother lay between them.

BYREN STOOD ON the edge of the lookout, dragging in greedy lungfuls of sharp mountain air. Orrade had set a bruising pace to reach the outcropping of rock facing down into the valley. In the distance, Byren could see the drift of smoke from Waterford, the closest village, if six houses and a tavern could be called such. Not far away, he could hear the clack of wooden practice swords, as the loyalists trained.

Behind him, Orrade sat, with his back against the rock, legs stretched out. 'Four families in as many days, thanks to Seela. Two maimed, plus nine able bodied men, if you include the fourteen-year-old boy and the gaffer.'

'Accompanied by fifteen women and children,' Byren reminded him. 'More mouths to feed.'

'You weren't always such a grouch.'

Byren sighed. With Orrade he didn't have to pretend a confidence he did not feel. 'I was the second son, the spare heir. All I had to do was stay out of trouble and lend Lence a hand, putting down spar rebellions. I never wanted to be king.'

'We can't all have what we want.' Orrade folded his hands behind his head and let out a sigh. 'I swear I can feel the first touch of spring's kiss.'

Byren laughed. 'You should have been a poet.'

Neither of them spoke. Byren was thinking of his love poem to Elina and its disastrous consequences. He didn't want to know what Orrade was thinking.

'Nine able-bodied men, but untrained,' Byren said as he sat beside Orrade, back to the sun-warmed rock.

'They're willing to learn,' Orrade said.

All well and good, but he did not have long to turn these farmers and shopkeepers into warriors. Because he'd asked them, they'd left their fields unplanted, their shops and farms empty or manned by their womenfolk and children, and crept like thieves across their own country into his mountain hideout. Not because he was the rightful king of Rolencia, but because they believed he could lead a mostly untrained, poorly armed lesser force against his cousin Cobalt.

Byren rubbed his jaw. How many of them would live to return to their farms and shops? As Orrade had said, they weren't here because of some altruistic concept of rightful kingship, they were here because they could not live under an oppressive tyrant.

That reminded him of Fyn, who had suffered under the bullying acolytes at the abbey. There was still no word from his youngest brother, or word of him. It was not looking good. Byren could only hope Fyn was lying low. But surely, if he lived, his brother would come to him?

Byren frowned. 'It's only a matter of time before someone reveals our whereabouts. Then I'll have to lead everyone over the Dividing Mountains onto Foenix Spar.' He was not looking forward to that.

'Warlord Feid is loyal to Rolencia,' Orrade said Then his expression cleared. 'Ahh, it's appearing before him as a supplicant, that's what you can't stomach.'

'Aye, it's that. I have to ask him to shelter a rag-tag mob of old folks, women and children, who outnumber my fighting force three to one. Food's always scarce on the spars.'

'Can't be helped.' Orrade shrugged. 'Feid's one warlord. You can count on Unace, too.'

The warlord of Unistag Spar had sworn her allegiance, after Byren helped her regain her leadership, with a clever ploy that kept his interference secret. Byren trusted Unace to keep her word.

'The warlords of the other three spars won't swallow any of this nonsense about Cobalt being the true heir.' Orrade lowered his arms and sat forwards. 'Was there any truth in the accusation, Byren? I loved your mother, but there were times when she seemed to know what we were thinking before we did.'

Byren laughed. 'No one could ever put anything past her.' At least no one had until Cobalt returned. He'd been the queen's one blind spot. Surely, if she'd had Affinity, she would have seen through Cobalt?

'Pity Seela left so quickly. There's some things I'd like to ask her,' Orrade muttered.

But Byren was off on another train of thought. It wasn't that he had to convince the spar warlords he was the rightful king, but more he had to prove he was the most powerful contender for the title. 'Force is the only thing the spar warlords respect. If the other three don't stand behind me, they could wait for me to exhaust myself defeating Cobalt and his Merofynians, then march over the Divide and attack when I'm weakened.'

A whistling bird cry carried up the valley. Orrade tensed and scurried forwards to peer down at the trail.

'More loyalists?' Byren asked, joining him.

Orrade nodded and pointed. 'Fifteen men.'

Byren sighted along his arm. Each man carried a pack and they marched with their hoods drawn over their heads. Byren tensed. Was this the betrayal he had feared?

'Not our usual desperate families, fleeing Cobalt's bully boys,' Orrade said thoughtfully.

'If they aren't Merofynians foolish enough to try to infiltrate the camp, they're welcome.'

'They must have convinced Longarm they're genuine, else he wouldn't have sent them on. They look like fighting men. A few more of them and we could have a real army!'

Some army. With his twin brother, Lence, Byren had led larger strikes against upstart warlords.

'Come on.' Byren took to his heels, hearing Orrade's light footfalls behind him.

At the base of the lookout they met Florin and her brother coming down the track.

'We heard the signal,' she said.

Byren wanted to tell her to take her brother and head back to camp but, at that moment, the newcomers rounded the bend and looked up to see them. As the first man threw back his hood, Byren knew the face, although he could not place him.

'You don't recognise me, Byren Kingson?' the man asked, his smile flashing white against his beard. They all wore beards now. No time to shave.

'Should I?' Byren's hand went to his sword hilt. There were fifteen of them, but he had Orrade and twenty men within shouting distance. And Florin had her staff, a seemingly innocuous walking aid but deadly in her hands. Somehow he'd have to get Leif out of the way.

'The last time you saw me I had less hair. We all did,' the newcomer said. And, as the others dropped their hoods, he flicked back his cloak to reveal his withered left arm.

'Master Catillum.' Relief flooded Byren, followed closely by fear. Would the abbey mystics master sense Orrade's new Affinity and denounce him? Come to that, would he be able to sense that Byren had taken shelter in a seep and been infected by Affinity? Byren cleared his throat. 'And Halcyon Abbey warrior monks. Welcome!'

So few.

The mystics master bowed. 'At your service, kingsheir.'

'I thought none of the monks had survived. We'd heard –'

'That we were lured into ambush.' Catillum nodded. 'Some of us escaped. We've been hunted across Rolencia. The others will arrive in the next few days. I didn't want to draw attention to your hideout.' He paused. 'There are things you should know.'

'I know the abbey fell. I found out the hard way.' Byren had gone there to call on the warrior monks to help defend Rolenhold, only to find Merofynians held the abbey. He'd barely escaped with his life. 'Are you hungry?'

They grinned.

'Come this way.' How was he going to feed everyone?

Byren left the others in the cook's cave, sent Leif to fetch his father, then walked the mystics master back to Old Man Narrows' cave. Florin strode along beside them, either unaware or deliberately obtuse to the curious glance the mystics master cast her.

They passed the smithy, hammering away.

'You're well set up,' Catillum said, as the noise faded behind them.

'We've been here since Dovecote fell,' Orrade explained.

'Mainly old folks and children...'

'Everyone who can be is out patrolling, hunting for game, or at weapons practice,' Byren said. He gestured into the cave. 'We can be private here.'

Orrade led the way in and took his seat at the empty fire circle, as though he didn't have to worry about revealing his Affinity. Byren sat between him and Catillum, just in case proximity gave Orrade away.

A moment later Old Man Narrows arrived. Byren introduced him to the mystics master and he settled down next to Florin.

Catillum glanced to the cave entrance, as if waiting for someone else.

'What news?' Byren asked.

'Don't you want to wait for Fyn?'

'Fyn lives?'

'He's not with you?'

Byren shook his head.

The mystic let his breath out slowly. 'Fyn lives. Or he did the night we were ambushed. I haven't heard from him since. He kept his head when the abbey was attacked, led the youngsters out of Mount Halcyon, saved their lives and stopped the sorbt stones falling into the hands of the Merofynian Power-workers. You can be proud of him.'

'Fyn...' For a moment Byren could not speak. Then he cleared his throat. 'Where is he?'

'He set off to warn the king, that was before we knew the castle had fallen. I only contacted him the once and a renegade Power-worker severed the connection.' Catillum paused, his dark eyes worried. 'Fyn can't risk contacting me again. His best bet is to keep his head down and stay out of trouble.' The mystics master looked up, summoning a smile. 'He'll come to you when it's safe.'

But Byren was not so sure. What if Fyn went to Cobalt for help? Only Byren and Piro had seen through their cousin. Cobalt had turned Lence and his father against him. And Fyn didn't know what Cobalt had been up to. Their cousin could be very convincing. He might trick Fyn into betraying himself or Byren's whereabouts.

Short of sneaking into the castle and killing Cobalt, there was nothing Byren could do about this. And he had seriously considered assassinating Cobalt, before deciding it was too much of a risk.

Byren poked the ashes of last night's fire. For the time being there was nothing he could do for Fyn or Piro. He had enough troubles of his own looking after an army of loyalists. At least, now he had the mystics master's support, he need not fear Merofynian Power-workers. He did not want to die, as his grandfather and uncle had, in a battlefield tent, killed by unseen Power-workers.

'What news from the valley?' Orrade asked.

'The Merofynians ride across it like lords, taking what they want, searching for you, Byren. They maim all those unfortunate enough to get in their way. It's only a matter of time –'

'I know. I need to move over the Divide, onto Foenix Spar.'

'You haven't heard? The Merofynians have taken over Cedar tradepost and added to the defences, turning it into a fort. They've ordered forts built to block all the spar passes. You won't be able to retreat to Foenix Spar. It may already be too late.'

Orrade cursed softly.

'We can still escape,' Florin spoke up. 'We don't need to take the Cedar tradepost pass. I know a secret pass over the mountain. An old one.'

'There is no secret pass,' Byren said, even as he caught the look Old Man Narrows sent Florin and recalled her mother had been a mountain girl. 'My tutor made me memorise every pass and canal the length and breadth of Rolencia.'

She smiled. 'A king's son would be the last person to know about this pass. It was used to smuggle men and arms over the Divide back when the Foenix warlord was not on good terms with King Rolen's line. It's too steep and narrow for horses, or even donkeys. It takes the better part of two days to walk it.'

Byren grinned. 'What would we do without you, Florin?'

Chapter Seven

Byren stood back from the fire while the monks cooked the food they had brought with them. It would be crowded in Old Man Narrows' cave tonight. Tomorrow he would have to send the mystics master and his monks up the ravine to the higher caves.

He glanced over to Florin, where she was arguing with her brother, insisting he wash in a bowl of warmed water.

'But I'm not dirty,' he protested.

Florin put a finger under his chin and lifted it to inspect his neck. 'Hmm, just as I thought. I could grow potatoes in there!'

Leif grinned and began to scrub. Florin noticed Byren's gaze and rolled her eyes, as if to say *little brothers, what can you do?*

With the arrival of Halcyon's warrior monks the camp was in a good mood. Byren had asked Catillum not to mention the forts in the spar passes.

Orrade had wandered up from the honour guard's cave. He stood at Byren's side watching the warrior monks give thanks before they ate. Sensing that Orrade wanted to speak with him, Byren caught his eye and they went outside where Orrade turned to ask, 'When will we go?'

'Soon. I want to give others time to make their way here.'

'You wait for Fyn.' Orrade knew him too well. There was no censure in his voice. 'The monks' arrival has given the camp hope.'

'Pity there's so few of them,' Byren muttered.

'More will come,' Master Catillum said, joining them.

Byren unfolded his arms. 'How many?'

'Thirty trained fighters, and then there's another twenty boys of fourteen and fifteen. They refused to stay in safety with the abbess of Sylion.'

'Naturally.' Byren smiled. He did not look Orrade's way. His friend would be thinking of his younger brother. At fourteen, Garzik had followed them back to Rolenhold, only to become caught up in Palatyne's bid to take Rolencia. Byren had sent him, along with a dozen youths from Dovecote Estate, to light the warning beacon. That was the last they saw of him.

'Untrained boys, playing at war,' Orrade whispered, disgusted.

'Our acolytes may be unblooded, but they're trained in the use of weapons,' Master Catillum said.

There was nothing Byren could do about Garzik. He sighed, thinking of Piro and Fyn. Two more people he could not help.

The mystics master cleared his throat. 'According to Seela, Piro is guarded by Lord Dunstany's wards. Even if she had an Affinity stone and natural Affinity, I couldn't reach her. Fyn wears Halcyon's Fate. I could try to contact him. But I –'

'Try,' Byren said. If he knew Fyn's whereabouts, he'd know whether it was worthwhile delaying for him.

'There is the matter of the Merofynian Power-workers,' Catillum warned. 'It's dangerous.'

Byren waited, grimly. He knew his request would endanger the mystic, but felt no regrets. He would endanger many more people before this was done.

'I will need a quiet spot,' Catillum said at last.

Byren beckoned Florin, who had followed the mystics master out and been listening unashamedly. 'Is there somewhere private?'

She nodded and led them past the others, deeper into the cave by the light of a single smoking lantern until they came to a large cavern. There was a black gaping hole in the centre.

'Listen.' Florin picked up a pebble and dropped it into the hole. They waited, and waited. Finally they heard the faintest of plinks as it hit the bottom.

'And you must see this.' Florin lifted the lantern to the back wall. Paintings of tall foenixes loomed above them. Across the bottom were little people, men, women and children, all lined up as if they were dancing. But it was the foenixes that dominated the chamber.

Awed, Byren lifted his hand.

Florin caught his arm. 'Nan said not to touch. These are old beyond measure. We must honour the people of the past.'

'Who were they?'

'Nan called them the Foenix Faithful. We don't know what they called themselves.'

'Do you know, mystics master?' Byren asked. He noticed the mystic's expression. 'What's wrong?'

'It's an intermittent Affinity seep.' Catillum's nose wrinkled with distaste. 'I can sense the old residue.'

Byren was relieved. He sensed nothing, and he'd feared his brush with the ulfrs in the seep had made him receptive to Affinity.

'Have you heard of the Foenix Faithful, Master Catillum?' Florin asked.

The mystic shook his head. 'At a guess they predate the ruins on Sapphire Lake and we don't know who made *them*. Some of life's mysteries are too deep even for a mystic.'

Orrade snorted softly.

The mystics master cast him a swift look but did not pursue it. Byren was not sure what was driving Orrade, but he had no time to find out.

'Let's get started, then,' Byren said, turning to the master. 'Do you want us to leave you?'

'You can stay. As long as you are quiet.'

'I'll wait out here.' Orrade went back to the cavern entrance and Byren realised Orrade was uneasy with the use of Affinity. Not because he feared it, but because he had it.

When Byren had begged the old seer to save Orrade's life, she'd said there would be a price and

Byren had rashly agreed to anything. But Orrade was the one who had to pay the price and his friend was not prepared to accept banishment or devote himself to the abbey, not when he was lord of Dovecote and his people needed him.

'Kneel here with me, Byren,' Catillum said. 'As Fyn's kin, you can help me focus on him. Fyn is not experienced with the use of the Fate, but we may still be able to share information before his concentration breaks.'

Hands on his knees, back straight, the mystics master gathered his Affinity and Byren could feel him doing it, which only served to confirm his suspicion. He had been tainted by the Affinity seep after all. Maybe not enough to sense Affinity residue, but enough to sense the mystic at work when they were side by side.

Master Catillum stared fixedly across the chamber at the far wall with its ancient paintings. By the flickering light of the lantern they seemed to be moving in the shadows. Byren's hand went to the foenix spurs he wore around his neck and he felt a pang of guilt at having killed the mother foenix when she had only been trying to protect her nest.

Once these mountains had been filled with the beautiful but deadly birds. Now, few were left, and his father had tried to preserve them.

What had the Foenix Faithful done in this cavern with its deep pit? In his mind's eye Byren saw leaping flames. Men and women dressed in foenix crests confronted a wretch who fell backwards into the pit, his piercing scream going on and on, before it cut out suddenly.

Catillum cursed then lurched like someone waking from a bad dream. He shook himself and Byren jerked, his heart thumping. Byren glanced over his shoulder to Florin and Orrade at the cavern entrance, seeing them only as dark shapes. Now he wished he was with them and not close enough to the mystics master to be swept along in his Affinity-induced visions. The mystic was supposed to be contacting Fyn, anyway, not recalling the past.

'I'm sorry, kingsheir. This place carries powerful memories,' Catillum whispered. He looked a little grey in the lamp light. 'Let's try again. Concentrate on your brother.'

So Byren closed his eyes and thought of Fyn, as he had seen him at the Proving, ready to battle for his place in Halcyon Abbey.

FYN SWAYED IN his hammock, listening to one of the sea-hounds sing a mournful song about love gone wrong. For ruthless pirate-hunters they were surprisingly fond of the old romances, tales of adventure and love from before the unifying of the Twin Isles under Kings Merofyn and Rolen.

Fyn yawned and rubbed his face, feeling the calluses he'd developed splicing ropes under Jakulos's watchful eyes. At least he was not a dead loss now, and they were on course for Ostron Isle. Why hadn't he agreed to serve on the *Wyvern's Whelp*, and then jumped ship so he was free to barter a berth back to Rolencia?

The Fate rested on his chest, much as the royal sigil had. He was glad he'd hidden the emblem far below the abbey in Halcyon's Sacred Heart.

The Fate felt heavy and warm. Fyn's fingers settled around it and the singer's voice faded. He swayed in the hammock... no... he was floating above it, rising above the ship, which lay as a shadow on the pewter sea.

This feeling of disembodiment did not surprise him. It had happened once before, back in Rolencia when he had seen Byren. Now his thoughts turned to Byren.

He knew he should he afraid of the Fate's power. Much could go wrong, but the sea was so beautiful that, for the moment, he felt only wonder. It stretched out below him, glistening silver in the starlight. So much empty sea.

Did physical distance matter when he was in this incorporeal state? He vaguely knew they were on an easterly bearing, which meant Merofynia lay due west and Rolencia lay beyond that. Dare he try to reach out to Byren? What if he couldn't find his way back to his body?

While he agonised over this, he spotted another ship – far across the sea – and arrowed over to it, faster than any sea-eagle. This was a merchant ship, Ostronite by the flag, so the sea-hounds were honour-bound to protect it. One of them accompanied it.

Uninterested in the ship, Fyn looked further afield. His home lay so far away. Dare he try to reach Byren?

Fear made his stomach lurch and he dropped towards the Ostronite ship. Before he could save himself, he felt a force surge out of the ship towards him and recognised the essence of the dark-eyed noble Power-worker who had captured him back in Rolencia.

Instinctively, he pulled back. Back across the silver waves, back to the *Wyvern's Whelp* below decks with its soft singing. Plunging back into his apparently sleeping body, he jerked awake, heart racing.

With a curse he let the Fate go and licked his burned palm, blowing on it to ease the stinging. When would he learn to stop fiddling with things he did not understand?

BYREN WATCHED SWEAT bead on the mystic master's face, noting that his breath had slowed until he seemed to have stopped breathing all together. Byren had not been born with Affinity like Fyn, but he had become attuned to it and he could feel a building oppression now. Something was wrong.

'Orrie?'

His friend did not hesitate, hurrying to kneel at his side.

Byren snapped his fingers in front of the master's blank eyes. Nothing. Not even a blink. He remained rigid, hands clasped on his knees.

'Maybe a renegade Power-worker's got him.' Florin voiced the fear they all shared as she came closer.

Byren looked to his friend. 'Can you help him, Orrie?'

'If a renegade Power-worker does have him and I touch him, it'll claim me too.'

Florin said nothing. She already knew about Orrade's Affinity. He'd revealed his vision of Byren bleeding in the seep so she could guide them there.

Byren understood Orrade's hesitation. Even he, with just an awareness of Affinity, struggled against the oppressive, unseen force.

'Byren?' Florin turned to him.

'Ever since I lay in the seep...' He did not go on, ending with a shrug. The flickering lamplight made their eyes glisten. He looked for condemnation but did not find it in Florin's gaze.

'I guess that leaves me,' she muttered, kneeling in front of the mystic master. 'Hey?' She prodded his chest. 'Hey, master monk, wake up.'

Nothing.

Florin bit her lip. 'I don't think I can reach him.'

Head thumping with tension, Byren did the only thing he could think of. He jabbed the master's hand with his dagger, not holding back. Blood flowed from the broken skin.

Luckily, pain did the trick.

With a shuddering breath, Catillum collapsed. Byren caught him.

'Remind me not to ask for your help,' Orrade muttered.

'It worked, didn't it?' Florin countered, pulling a kerchief from her pocket and wrapping it around the mystic's bleeding hand.

'I was desperate,' Byren admitted.

'And desperate measures were called for,' Master Catillum whispered, his voice cracking. He tried to sit up and failed. Byren helped him. With a shaking hand, Catillum massaged the bridge of his nose.

'What happened?' Byren asked. 'Did you reach Fyn?'

The mystic's gaze strayed uneasily to the painted wall. 'No. Before I could, an enemy found me. A powerful renegade, with the taint of Mulcibar...' He shuddered and swallowed. 'He was searching for you, Byren. I held him off, but I couldn't get away. If you hadn't...' He lifted his injured hand. Blood had seeped through Florin's makeshift bandage.

'I didn't know what else to do,' Byren admitted.

'Brutal but effective. You saved me. Saved us all.'

There was silence for a few heartbeats as they digested this.

'Then you'd better not try to contact Fyn again,' Byren said.

'I couldn't right now. Not for several days. I'm drained.' The mystics master grimaced as he pressed his injured hand to his chest. 'Fyn has no defences. I can only pray he won't try to use the Fate.'

'Well.' Byren stood. Still no answers, and time was running out. He offered Master Catillum his hand, helping him to his feet. 'I thank you for trying.'

Catillum swayed but stayed upright.

'We can't stay here much longer,' Orrade said. 'What will you do?'

Byren didn't answer, because he didn't know.

'Come on.' He offered Catillum his arm. Florin collected the lamp and they headed back to the outer cavern, where they left Catillum with the monks.

Florin walked Orrade and Byren outside to see them off, back to their cave.

But before they could go, Leif came scampering to find them. 'Someone's come from Waterford. Lord Cobalt will be there by tomorrow evening.'

'Cobalt?' Byren stiffened. This close?

'Byren...' Orrade muttered. 'Don't fall for it. He's trying to draw you out.'

'I know, but it's too good an opportunity to miss.'

'If you go after him, I'm coming,' Florin insisted. 'I know Waterford and I know the foothills.'

'Too risky.'

'And living in the loyalist camp isn't?' Florin countered. 'You're too important to the loyalist cause, Byren. If you suspect a trap, you shouldn't risk yourself. Send Orrie.'

'Yes, send me.'

Byren shook his head. He'd already sent Garzik to his death and held Elina while she died. He wasn't losing Orrade. Besides...

'You don't understand, Florin. I'm a king without a country. If I want the people of Rolencia to follow me, I must inspire them. Sitting safe up here in the caves while someone else risks their life to kill Cobalt will not win me their trust!'

Chapter Eight

FYN SAT ON the window seat of the captain's cabin, trying hard to contain his resentment and frustration. Here he was, a prisoner, as far east of his homeland as he could be.

Their ship had just entered the Ring Sea. Ostron Isle was actually two islands, a larger circle of steep peaks called Ostron Ring, with one break that led through towering headlands. On the inside the peaks sloped away more gently, down to the Ring Sea and Ostron Isle itself.

As the *Wyvern's Whelp* sailed the Ring Sea, famous for its perfect blue-green shade, the water reflected the terraced slopes of the outer island, Ostron Ring.

Ostron Isle was completely cultivated, dotted with pleasant villas and terraced fields. The Ostronites believed their inner island and city, with its boulevards and parks, was the most beautiful place in the known world. Watching these glide past, Fyn could almost agree.

'How many days before we head out again, cap'n?' Jakulos asked. 'We're missing those fat Merofynian merchant ships full of Rolencian booty.'

Fyn turned away from the windows.

Jakulos had lathered Nefysto's face and now sharpened the razor on the strop. The captain's finest clothes were laid out on the bunk. Runt sat cross-legged on the floor polishing the captain's knee-high boots. Fyn suspected Nefysto was going to report to the elector's spymaster.

Across the cabin, by the door, Bantam cleaned his nails with his dagger, saying nothing, watching everything.

Nefysto caught Jakulos's hand as he went to scrape off the bristles. 'We're returning with a full hold and our lives, thanks to the little monk. Your share will be more than you would have earned in a lifetime serving the Merofynian navy. Why the urge to make more?'

'There's a pretty lass I mean to marry, but not before I set myself up like an Ostronite noble.'

'Is it the seamstress, the lace-maker or the hat-shop girl?' Bantam asked.

Jakulos smiled and shook his head.

Nefysto gave a shout of laughter. 'Well, Jaku? He has you there.'

'I'm not about to bandy about the name of the lass I mean to marry.'

'Then it's none of them,' Bantam said.

Fyn felt a smile tug at his lips. He liked these men. He didn't want to have to kill them to escape.

'So you're motivated by true love, Jaku?' Nefysto teased. He sent Fyn a sly glance. 'The little monk here is motivated by revenge.'

Bantam returned his knife to his belt. 'And what's wrong with that?'

Fyn watched the interplay, torn between curiosity and resentment.

'What can one man, even an abbey trained warrior such as Fyn, achieve?' Nefysto said. 'Palatyne has gone back to Merofynia. Our monk could assassinate Cobalt but the Merofynians would just send another puppet ruler.'

Nefysto was right, but Fyn did not intend to kill Cobalt. He'd promised to help his cousin find Byren so they could retake Rolencia.

Byren did need allies. Even if Fyn could slip back into Rolencia and reach Cobalt without the Merofynians capturing him, his cousin was little better than a prisoner and his brother hid in the hills like a common brigand. Byren needed powerful allies.

'There's the warlords of Rolencia,' Nefysto said, as though following Fyn's line of thought. 'The monk could call on them for help. But, knowing them, they'll sit back and see which way the wind blows. To really strike at Merofynia he needs a powerful ally.'

'Like the elector?' Runt said, proving he was listening and learning.

Nefysto's eyes smiled as Jakulos scraped his bristles off under his nose. Fyn waited.

As Jakulos turned away to wipe lather off the blade, Nefysto answered. 'Normally, you'd be right, Runt. But the elector's health is failing and, until a new elector is chosen, Ostron Isle will make no new alliances. I was thinking of Mage Tsulamyth.'

'A mage?' Bantam's tone echoed Fyn's feelings of distaste.

'A desperate man must take allies where he can,' Nefysto said.

Even living the life of a secluded acolyte, Fyn had heard rumours of the mage of Ostron Isle. He was said to be all-powerful and over two hundred years old. Obviously, stories put about to scare off other Power-workers. Even so...

'According to the abbey mystics master, Tsulamyth is the most powerful living Affinity renegade,' Fyn said, choosing his words carefully. 'That makes him a very dangerous man.'

'To his enemies, yes.' Nefysto smiled. 'The same is said of me. Besides,' he shrugged, 'whatever you may have heard, Tsulamyth is an honourable man. As the most powerful living mage he could rule the known world, but he sits on his island, collecting and breeding harmless abeilles.'

The mage collected harmless butterflies? Well, not entirely harmless, no Affinity beast was. But the abeille was close to harmless. The Ostronites had adopted it as their symbol because they were both beautiful and industrious. An Affinity cousin to the bee, with the double wings of the butterfly, abeilles farmed the cinnamome trees for which Ostron Isle was famous, harvesting the pods and turning them into the fine powder. This cinnamon was prized across the known world for its restorative powers.

'Done.' Jakulos stepped back with the razor and reached for a hand mirror.

Nefysto wiped his chin, inspecting the big man's handiwork. 'A close shave. Now I'm fit to be seen by Ostronite society.'

By mid-afternoon, the *Wyvern's Whelp* had docked and been unloaded before being moved to a dry dock, with the efficiency of a people dedicated to making money. The crew had dispersed, all but for Bantam and Jakulos, who escorted Fyn up the hill to a cinnamon-tea house where he would be their prisoner.

It was the most beautiful city Fyn had seen. Because land was limited, the people built up. Seven storeys was not uncommon. It might have felt cramped but for the wide boulevards and palazzos. Every Ostronite took pride in their little piece of the island. Minuscule balconies were strung with washing and housed tubs filled with vegetables and flowers. Even the weather on Ostron Isle seemed kinder. There was a saying, *Spring comes early to Ostron Isle*.

He could well believe. If his reckoning was right it was twelve days until spring cusp, but already the air was warm. People crowded the streets. Stalls set up under awnings did a brisk trade. Children chased each other, or herded geese and goats to market.

The buildings were more open than those in Rolencia. He heard laughter and music coming from behind delicately patterned lattice-shielded windows and verandas. It felt strange until Fyn realised the place had not been built for defence. Since the high peaks of Ostron Ring defended the Ring Sea, and its only entrance was guarded by two towers and a chain that could be drawn up to close off the passage, the people of Ostron Isle considered themselves safe from invasion.

He could see many terraces on the inner slope of Ostron Ring, already tinged with green growth of spring planting. Why was Sylion's hand so much lighter here than in Rolencia?

Fyn no longer looked like the acolyte of Halcyon who had fled for his life. His acolyte's plait had been cut and his head was now covered in a crop of fine, dark hair, which obscured his tattoos. He wore a sea-hound's calf-length trews, a knitted vest and a light coat. As a concession to the hard cobbles they all wore boots. Even after so short a time at sea, Fyn found the shoes restrictive.

They reached a palazzo with a clear view down a long sloping road to the Ring Sea. At the end of the road, Fyn could see a tall tower, which was built on an island in the Ring Sea itself, connected by a narrow causeway to Ostron Isle. The tower was so tall, the royal ingeniator would have been envious. The man had spent his time building canals across Rolencia, but he'd shown Fyn drawings of wondrous things including towers. Did he still live? Fyn had no idea.

'That's the mage's tower,' Bantam said, noticing his interest.

Around the high tower's base, four and five-storey buildings clustered. Which meant Mage Tower was taller than Eagle Tower at Rolenhold.

'How high is it?'

'Highest in the known world!' Bantam said with a touch of pride. He came to a stop in front of a white stone building, from which came singing and laughter and the scent of rich cinnamon-tea brewing. 'Here we are.'

Fyn's prison. He looked up. Seven storeys. Knowing his luck, they would be on the top floor.

They were.

FROM THE WINDOW tucked into the roof of the tavern, Byren studied Waterford's twilight-shrouded square. The village consisted of six houses, a tavern and a building that doubled as Sylion's oratory in winter and Halcyon's chantry in summer, probably to the disgust of the visiting nuns and monks. The place was too small to have permanent abbey representatives.

And it was too small to attract Cobalt, unless he'd heard rumours that Byren's camp was nearby and was using himself as bait to draw him out.

So be it.

Byren had chosen twenty men, mostly experienced warriors, among them Orrade and the honour guard. He'd hidden them around the outskirts of the village, choosing to hide in the tavern's best room himself, in the belief that Cobalt would claim it. When he did, Byren would be waiting.

'What if he rides in here with fifty men?' Orrade asked, keeping his voice low.

'Reports said he had thirty. Besides, it won't matter how many men he has if we kill Cobalt and get out quickly over the roof. The villagers will run to the hills on our signal. When the Merofynians discover Cobalt dead in bed, they'll go back to the castle. Without a leader, they'll be vulnerable. I can nip over the pass into the spar, convince Feid to support me and be back before they can get word to Merofynia. We'll attack while they're disorganised. If I can retake the castle, we'll –'

'You know what they say about plans?' Orrade interrupted. 'They're only good if the enemy follows them.'

Byren grinned. 'It was mostly your plan.'

Orrade grinned back. 'It was mostly to convince Florin we knew what we were doing. Convince her to stay behind.'

Byren rubbed his top lip, hiding a grin.

Orrade stiffened. 'They're coming.'

Byren joined Orrade on his side of the window. Waterford's tavern faced the stream from which the town took its name. Dark horses and riders flowed across the shallow ford in pairs, riding up into the town square in front of the tavern. Byren counted sixteen pairs. Cobalt was not in the lead pair, or the second pair. After that the space in front of the tavern became too congested to get a clear view as they arrived.

The keeper came out with a lantern. There was much shouting as the men dismounted and the horses were led around back to the stable, which would not be large enough to cope.

Byren searched the milling men for Cobalt's profile. Last time he'd seen him, his cousin had affected the

Ostronite style of clothing, with padded shoulders, a nipped-in waist, and his hair loose, curling down his back. Cobalt probably wore Rolencian clothes now – or, more likely, Merofynian.

The men parted, shoving two youths forwards to confront a tall, dark-haired man, who stood with his back to Byren.

Since everyone was black-haired Byren could only go by the man's height and bearing. It could be Cobalt. The right sleeve swung loose.

'Prisoners,' Orrade whispered, disgustedly. 'This is going to get ugly.'

Byren agreed, as a sick feeling of dread settled in his stomach. 'Boys of no more than sixteen by the look of them.' He frowned. 'The one on the right is familiar.'

'Probably served you wine or held your horse in Rolenton,' Orrade said.

As they were shoved to their knees, the tall skinny youth's fur cap fell off, revealing a head with no more than a finger joint's length of dark hair. Unless he'd been shorn because of fever, he was a monk.

Byren shifted uncomfortably. This could be Fyn's fate if he tried to reach the camp.

With a gesture, the man who could be Cobalt indicated the second youth's cap was to be removed. His hair was also cropped short. One of the men parted his hair, looking for abbey tattoos.

'They're monks, alright,' the man reported, his voice carrying easily to Byren.

'Perhaps they know where the other kingsheir is,' the leader said. 'Bring them inside.' As he turned to walk into the tavern, his features were clearly revealed for the first time. But Byren already knew by his voice that he wasn't Cobalt, just a Merofynian masquerading as his cousin.

Orrade swore. 'It's a set-up to trap you, and they're going to torture the boys.'

Byren swallowed. He should leave now, but he could not abandon the youths. 'Besides,' he said. 'It's clear the boys were headed this way to join me. They must know the camp's whereabouts. We have to –'

'Kill them or rescue them,' Orrade finished for him.

Byren met his eyes. 'I'm not killing them.'

'I know. So how do you propose we rescue them?'

'A diversion.'

'The horses?' Orrade's eyes gleamed. 'There's too many for the stable. They'll be in the holding yard. We could turn them loose and set fire to the stable.'

'The tavern keeper won't be pleased.'

'When you're king you can build him another stable.' Orrade opened the window. Night had fallen while they spoke and stars silvered the thatch. 'Don't make your move until I come back.'

Byren nodded, fully intending to slip down the stairs and watch from the shadows. He didn't want the boys killed before he could rescue them.

Orrade frowned. 'I know you, you'll –'

'Just go. Time's a wasting. They could be losing fingers while we talk.'

With Orrade gone, he went to the door. No one had brought the Merofynian leader's travel kit upstairs. They were probably too intent on the prisoners.

Opening the door a fraction, Byren peered down the short hallway. Only two other rooms gave off it on the other side. When they didn't have customers, the tavern keeper and his family slept up here. Tonight they would sleep under the kitchen table, if they slept at all. Byren hoped they and the other villagers escaped this night unscathed.

He went to open the door fully, just as the tavern keeper's son came up the stairs with several travel kits slung over his shoulders.

The boy caught Byren's eye, stiffened, then kept coming. He slipped into the room, divesting himself of the largest travelling kit.

'Lord Cobalt has two prisoners, both monks,' the boy reported, then shuddered. 'He's ordered the tap-room fire built up.'

'That's not Cobalt,' Byren said. 'And don't you worry about the monks. When the fighting starts, get out. Hide in the hills. Tell the villagers.'

He nodded and left. Byren waited for a moment, then headed for the stairs. Voices speaking Merofynian drifted up to him. He silently thanked his mother for making sure he spoke the languages of both Rolencia's trading partners.

From what Byren could hear, the Merofynians had begun drinking already. Pity they weren't about to drink themselves senseless. No, they'd be too eager to discover what the monks knew.

He shuffled lower, coming to the last bend, only six steps stretching below him to the tap-room. From up here, he couldn't see much, mainly men's backs. They faced the open fireplace. Presumably the monks were being held in front of it. The men-at-arms' rough, mocking voices told him they enjoyed baiting the two youths.

How long must he wait for Orrade to organise the others?

Byren fingered his sword hilt, reminded of how he'd had to leave Elina in Palatyne's bed while Dovecote's defenders prepared to strike. That had sorely tested him, and even though he did not know the monks this was no easier.

A shout from the rear of the tavern reached Byren, but the Merofynians were too engrossed to notice.

'Lord Cobalt, Lord Cobalt?' The tavern keeper himself came running in. 'There's a problem with the horses. Something spooked them. They've broken through the fence!'

Byren could imagine the Merofynian leader's annoyance. The man masquerading as Cobalt sent half the men out to catch the horses. It was clear from his voice that he did not realise this was an attack.

Now that there were fewer men, Byren could see the Merofynian leader seated on the end of a long table, one boot swinging, as one of his men added fuel to the fire. 'Yes, build it up. Get that poker nice and hot. I want it glowing.'

The shouts from outside changed tone, becoming more frantic. A man came running into the tap room. 'The stable's on fire.'

The Merofynian leader shoved himself to his feet. 'The kingsheir has made his move. Come on.'

All of them raced out, leaving Byren a clear view of the two monks tied to chairs in front of the fire.

The moment the Merofynians left, the monks began to struggle against their bonds. They broke off to stare at Byren as he came down the stairs, crossing the tap-room.

'Byren Kingsheir?' the familiar one gasped. 'Am I glad to see you!'

Byren grinned and knelt beside him to cut the ropes, then dealt with the other one's bonds.

Someone charged through the kitchen, throwing the door open.

Byren spun to his feet, sword drawn. He couldn't believe his eyes. 'Florin?'

'There you are!' She darted between the tables and scattered chairs, unabashed. 'Quick, out the front door. Orrie has sent them on a mad goose chase, so our people can ambush them in the trees, but some stayed behind to rescue horses from the stables, and the leader took some men and went in search of you. He'll be back when he can't find you.'

'Right.' Byren turned to the two monks. 'Can you run?'

'We ran behind the horses since lunch time,' the skinny one with a protruding Adam's apple said. 'But we can run if we have to.'

Byren headed for the door, throwing it open, only to find Cobalt's imposter there with a half a dozen men at his back. He slammed it shut, but not before one of them got his shoulder into the gap.

'Out the back,' Byren yelled.

But before Florin could get the monks out the kitchen door, it opened and several soot-stained men came running in. Seeing the monks free, they charged.

'To the stairs,' Byren yelled.

Florin ran, the Merofynians at her heels. Byren followed, slashing at the nearest warrior, who tried to block his way. Then he was running up the dim stairwell, expecting a knife in his back at any moment.

At the top of the steps Florin ran down the hall, thrusting doors open.

'The one on the right,' Byren yelled.

She darted inside, followed by the monks. Byren joined them, slamming the door shut, cutting off the vision of Merofynians tearing down the narrow hall towards them.

'Help me drag the chest of drawers,' Florin gasped.

The monks took over and she directed them to shove it against the door. Meanwhile, Byren thrust the window open.

The yard was empty.

The chest of drawers jerked as men threw their weight at the door.

'It's not going to hold,' Florin said.

Byren beckoned. 'Over here. Quickly.' The monks joined him. 'Out the window, slide down the thatch, jump to the ground.'

They nodded, the skinny one going first, then the other. The chest of drawers screeched as it was shoved aside.

Florin glanced back to Byren. 'You go. I'll cover you.'

But Byren wasn't having that. He swept her off her feet and dropped her out the window, onto the roof. She slid down and off the end with a cry of annoyance.

The door burst open behind him. Byren swung his leg over the sill and let go. The last thing he saw was five men racing into the room, swords drawn. Then he was sliding down the thatch. He hit the ground with his knees bent. His stomach protested, reminding him it wasn't so long since he'd been wounded.

Orrade rode up bare-back, leading three horses. The monks clambered onto one, riding double. Florin scrambled atop another horse. Byren reached for the last one, but it danced away, frightened. Someone crashed off the roof behind him, crying in pain as he landed badly. Another followed. By then, Byren was astride the horse and headed across the ford, into the forest.

From there, it was a mad dash through the night on starlit tracks, as the sounds of pursuit faded. Twenty minutes later, Orrade called a halt and the horses snorted and stamped, shivering with excitement.

Byren met his friend's eyes with a laugh. 'Your arrival was well timed.'

'The whole thing was a disaster!' Orrade muttered. 'I don't know where our people are. Hopefully, they ambushed a few Merofynians, then melted into the trees.'

'We're safe for now,' Byren said. 'Their horses are scattered. But they'll be furious. I hope the villagers got away...'

He craned his head. They were on the crest of a ridge. Through the tree canopy, he could see the glow of flames. More than just the stable was burning. 'I think the Merofynians have taken their anger out on Waterford itself.'

Orrade urged his horse closer. 'You're right. Nothing will be left standing. Which means...'

'Another thirty hungry mouths to feed, if they get away safe. Mostly women and children.' Byren sighed. 'Can't be helped. The Merofynians will be searching the foothills but they don't know the tracks like the locals do.'

'Still, this was too close.' Orrade swung his leg over his mount and slid to the ground. 'We don't want the horses. Much better to go on foot. Hide our trail.'

Byren dismounted and went to offer Florin his help before he could stop himself. It was his mother's courtly training. Not that Florin knew that. She saw it as an insult. With a toss of her head, she leapt lightly to the ground.

For some reason this annoyed Byren. 'You nearly got yourself killed back there. Since when does a mountain girl know better than her king? What were you doing, disobeying a direct order?'

Startled by his anger, her eyes widened. Then she tilted her chin and he just knew she was going to back-chat him.

He wanted to grab her and shake her. 'If I give an order I expect it to be obeyed.'

For a heartbeat she stared at him, defiance in the line of her mouth. Byren feared she would openly defy him and then what would he do? Her pride was so prickly. He shouldn't have pushed her.

Before Florin could overstep the line, Byren turned around... to find the two monks kneeling at his feet.

'Byren Kingsheir,' they chorused, slightly out of time. 'We come to serve –'

'Yes, yes. No time for that now.' Byren took their arms and hauled them to their feet. 'You're lucky we were there...' He broke off, because he didn't know their names.

'Feldspar,' the skinny one supplied.

'Joff,' the other said. 'You were at the Hearing, back at midwinter, when –'

'Now I remember. Your Affinity came on you late, and the villagers were angry with your father for keeping it hidden.' He hesitated. It had all seemed so cut and dried then. Now he worked alongside Catillum and dreaded discovery. 'Have you heard from Fyn?'

The two monks exchanged looks.

'We thought he'd be with you,' Feldspar said. 'He left us at the base of Mount Halcyon, headed back to Rolenhold to warn your father that the abbey had fallen.'

'Same old news,' Orrade muttered.

Byren hid his concern. 'Right, we'd better get moving. Orrie, you bring up the rear. Florin, you take the lead. You know the paths.'

Her eyes glittered strangely in the starlight and, when she spoke, her voice was husky. 'Of course, my king.'

She'd never called him that before.

With a jolt, Byren realised she meant it as an insult. Before he could think of a thing to say, she turned and strode off, long legs eating up the distance. At Byren's signal, the two monks hurried after her.

Byren met Orrade's eyes.

'Looks like you've angered Mountain-girl,' Orrade muttered.

'Don't you start. If she wants to be treated like a warrior, she has to act like one.'

Orrade raised one eyebrow.

Byren stomped off after the others. He was justified. If any of his honour guard disobeyed a direct order, he'd discipline them.

But Florin wasn't like his honour guard. There was only one of her and he hadn't handled her well at all.

Chapter Nine

PIRO WATCHED ISOLT as servants fussed over the kingsdaughter arranging her hair in an elaborate coiffure. Since Dunstany left, she'd been trying to see behind the court mask to the vulnerable young woman who, according to the noble scholar, needed a friend. But Isolt had her flawless mask securely in place.

When they woke this morning, a servant had delivered the message that Duke Palatyne requested a meeting with the kingsdaughter. Isolt had set a time, making him wait until mid-afternoon.

Presented in the height of Merofynian fashion – her face powdered pale, her eyes and lips painted, her hair pulled back to reveal her high forehead, a circlet of sapphires resting on her head, one large sapphire hanging on her forehead – Isolt regarded Piro coldly. 'Do you have anything to say, slave?'

Yes – unspoken words jostled to be unleashed – *you let your father betrothe you to my brother so he could invade our kingdom while we were unprepared. Now, half my family are dead and the other half are missing.*

There were so many things to say, Piro could only shake her head. Since the stuffed wyvern and foenix had been presented, Isolt had withdrawn, as though she regretted letting her guard down with Piro.

After Isolt dismissed her other servants, they waited for the duke in silence.

When they heard Palatyne's boots in the corridor, Piro noticed Isolt's hands tighten on the arms of her chair and she felt an unwilling sympathy.

Palatyne made Piro's skin crawl. He swept into the room, a servant following him with a cage covered in silk.

'Isolt Merofyn Kingsdaughter. You may wonder why I have presented your father with many gifts but you with only the one slave. I was waiting for the most precious of gifts to arrive. Behold!' And he pulled the silk off the cage to reveal Piro's foenix. 'The only living foenix in captivity!'

Piro bit back a gasp. Her heart went out to her pet.

The foenix's usually brilliant red vest of scales was dulled and its tail feathers drooped. Its emerald eyes searched the room until it spotted Piro, then it gave a happy cry.

'A gift fit for a queen,' Palatyne said, bowing over Isolt's hand. He kissed her fingers as though she was the most precious thing in the world. Isolt remained stiff and distant, hiding the distaste Piro was sure she felt.

'You are most kind, duke,' Isolt said, but her eyes were on the foenix. 'It is much smaller than the stuffed foenix. Is it a baby?'

'Two years old, hand-raised by the daughter of the Rolencian king.'

'Bring it here.' Isolt came to her feet, approaching a step, as though she couldn't help herself. This did not go unnoticed. Piro hated Palatyne's gloating smile. 'I wish to hold this foenix.'

Palatyne frowned. 'It's too wild. No one has been able to get near it.'

'I thought you said it was hand-raised by the kingsdaughter?' Isolt did not miss a trick. She frowned. 'Perhaps your men frightened it. I will win its trust.'

'I'm sure you will,' Palatyne agreed smoothly, then hesitated. 'But I must warn you against placing your hand inside the cage. One of my men has already lost a finger.'

Piro hid a smile. She would reward her foenix handsomely for that finger. What a pity it hadn't been Palatyne's eye!

Isolt returned to her chair, arranging her gown over her knees. 'It was so kind of you to deliver the foenix in person. Thank you.'

This was dismissal. Palatyne could do nothing but grit his teeth and depart. Piro did not bother to hide her smile.

As soon as he was gone, Isolt slipped out of her chair and ran across the tiles, her silk under-skirts swishing. She knelt on the floor next to the cage, oblivious of the damage to her gown.

'The only living foenix in captivity,' she whispered, marvelling. 'Are you a boy or a girl, my pretty? Seela, run to the kitchen and fetch some food. I will win this bird's trust. Truly, he is fit for a queen!'

'Palatyne's queen!' Piro snapped.

Isolt sat back on her heels, looking up at Piro. 'I'm not betrothed to Duke Palatyne. Nor will I –'

'Just like you weren't betrothed to Lence Rolen Kingsheir?'

'I was never betrothed to him.'

'How can you say that? You sent him your portrait, a miniature!'

Isolt sprang to her feet, naked brows drawing together in a frown. 'I had a miniature painted as a gift for my father last spring.'

A servant entered the chamber.

'Yes?' Isolt tapped her foot impatiently.

The poor servant bowed and spoke with his head down. 'Your father wishes to speak with you, kingsdaughter.'

Isolt turned to Piro, holding her eyes. 'I will be back and I will get the truth from you.' She barely glanced to the servant. 'Where is my father?'

'In the throne room, with Duke Palatyne, kingsdaughter.'

Isolt stiffened, casting Piro a swift look. Suspecting the worst, Piro wanted to warn her but the servant was present and Isolt offered no hint that she would welcome advice. Lifting her chin, the kingsdaughter smoothed down her gown and left.

Alone with her pet at last, Piro knelt by the cage, reaching in to stroke the foenix's satiny scales. He cooed deep in his throat and looked reproachfully at her when she did not let him out to play.

'My poor boy,' she crooned and, as if that was a signal, her Affinity welled up, travelling down her arm to make her fingers throb with power. The foenix uttered soft, delighted noises in his throat as he rubbed his head and neck on her skin, absorbing her excess Affinity. It felt good. Only now could Piro admit that the build-up of power was making her edgy.

When the pressure eased, she sat back on her heels, to tell the foenix, 'be good and I'll fetch food.'

She went straight to the kitchen where she ordered a tray prepared for Isolt's new pet.

By the time she got back it was nearly dark. Palace servants were running a hot bath and stripping the royal bed. After replacing the bed's silk covers, they sprinkled rose petals on the pillows and lit two starkiss-scented candles. This reminded Piro of Dunstany. Despite his trickery, she missed him.

Being above a mere Rolencian slave, none of the servants spoke to her, but they did talk in front of her. The palace was alive with rumour of Isolt's betrothal to Palatyne.

For privacy, Piro took the foenix's cage through to the bathing chamber, where the warmth from the steaming sunken tub would make him comfortable, and opened the latch. The foenix stepped out disdainfully, as if being caged had been beneath his dignity.

Piro smiled as she rubbed his crest. Speaking nonsense words of love, she fed him, holding strips of meat up so that he took them from her fingers, laced with her Affinity.

Lence had mocked her, insisting the bird was no more intelligent than a chicken. If only he could have seen how the foenix recognised her... but now he never would. Piro felt the bone-deep ache of Lence's loss and prayed that Byren and Fyn were safe.

When the bird had satisfied his hunger, Piro let him play tug-of-war with her sleeve. For the first time since arriving in Merofynia she did not feel so lonely.

Then she heard the outer chamber door close and running steps. Piro went to pick up the foenix to put him back in his cage, but he darted away from her.

'Seela?' Isolt cried. Footsteps headed for the bathing chamber door.

Piro scooped up the bird, just as Isolt threw the door open. The foenix gave a little cry of fright and she soothed him, watching Isolt warily.

'You knew Palatyne wanted to marry me!' Isolt accused.

Piro cradled the bird. 'It was not hard to guess, kingsdaughter.'

'Ahh. How I hate that title! My father has betrothed me to Palatyne, but I will not be his prize. I will escape the cage just as my mother did.'

Isolt ran around the bath, towards the balcony, which reminded Piro that King Merofyn's wife had killed herself by jumping to her death.

'Isolt!' She dropped the foenix. He flew to the tiles with a cry of protest. Piro ran after Isolt, just managing to grab her before she could unlatch the door to the balcony.

'Let me go. I command you!'

Piro laughed. 'What sort of a friend would I be if I let you kill yourself?'

Isolt stared at her.

'I know how you feel,' Piro said. The foenix flew to land beside her, giving a soft cry of query, almost as if he was asking what was wrong. She took him in her arms. 'My father was going to betrothe me –'

'You, a serving maid?' Isolt looked at the foenix, then back to Piro's face. Her beautiful tilted eyes narrowed. 'You're no servant. You're Piro Rolen Kingsdaughter!' Her mouth hardened. 'And you're here to kill me!'

Isolt backed off, turned and ran around the far side of the tub, but Piro was quicker. She put herself between Isolt and the door.

The Merofynian kingsdaughter came to a stop, alert as a trapped wild creature.

'Don't be ridiculous,' Piro snapped. 'If I was going to kill you I could have done so a hundred times since I arrived.'

Isolt's eyes widened. 'You're supposed to be dead.'

'I very nearly was.' Piro shuddered. 'I saw Palatyne murder my mother and father. He had my eldest brother killed. He would have murdered me but I let him think another girl's body was mine.'

'If you don't mean to kill me, why did you come here?'

'I didn't have any choice. Lord Dunstany claimed me for his slave, then Palatyne wanted to give me to you.' She shrugged. 'So here I am, one kingsdaughter slave to another.'

They stared at each other across the steaming rose-scented water and the immensity of it struck

Piro. Now that Isolt knew who she was, one word from the kingsdaughter and she would be dead. It was on the tip of her tongue to ask for reassurance but, because she did not trust Isolt, she did not want to show any weakness.

'I thought you were different, but I didn't realise how different,' Isolt whispered. She skirted the tub, halting an arm's length from Piro, her gaze on the foenix which nestled in Piro's arms. Isolt lifted one tentative hand and looked at Piro. 'May I?'

'Move slowly. He's shy of people he doesn't know.'

Isolt stroked the bird's back, then smiled. 'You were right. He's so soft, his feathers feel like fur.'

'He doesn't like being in a cage either.'

'I can understand that.' Isolt's voice cracked and when she looked up into Piro's face, tear tracks marred the white powder on her cheeks. 'Palatyne gets what he wants, and he wants the throne of Merofynia.'

'That's not all he wants. He plans to be emperor of the known world,' Piro revealed.

A bitter laugh escaped Isolt. 'And he may just do it!'

Piro didn't think so, not if Byren had anything to say, but she kept her tongue between her teeth. She wasn't about to tell the daughter of the Merofynian king that the rightful heir to Rolencia still lived.

'What will you do?' Piro asked. 'You can't trust Palatyne. He means to kill King Merofyn. He killed my father under a flag of truce.'

Isolt pulled back. 'Of course you would say that.' Her eyes narrowed thoughtfully. 'It is well known the Rolencian royal family can't be trusted. They are tainted with a streak of aberrant Affinity. Everyone knows King Byren the Fourth could talk to animals, which makes him little better than an Affinity beast himself!'

Piro's mouth dropped open. Was her strong Affinity the product of mixing her mother's blood with her grandfather's? Talk about the pot calling the kettle black, but then Isolt didn't know Queen Myrella had been cursed with Affinity.

Isolt stepped away from Piro. 'Return the foenix to his cage. You are dismissed for tonight.'

'But... what will you do about Palatyne? He can't be trusted.'

'So you say, yet you are the enemy. We were warned that your army was massing. That's why Palatyne attacked.'

'Not true!' Piro protested. 'At least, no more than usual to keep the warlords in line. We have honoured the treaty with Merofynia these past thirty years. It was Palatyne who broke it, just as he murdered my father under a flag of truce!'

From Isolt's expression, it was clear she did not believe Piro. 'Palatyne is a crude barbarian who has conquered Rolencia in my father's name. He looks too high if he thinks to marry into royalty. I asked for time. I mean to go to Father and plead my case. He cannot force me to marry Palatyne.' Isolt gave an unsteady laugh. 'After all, I am a kingsdaughter!'

Piro eyed Isolt uneasily. The kingsdaughter had rallied after trying to throw herself off the balcony, but what were her options really?

While Isolt bathed, Piro made a nest for the foenix in a linen basket and sat it beside the daybed. She lay down but could not sleep. Instead, she fumed silently. Aberrant Affinity, indeed. King Rolen's army massing to attack Merofynia. Rubbish!

What other slander had King Merofyn been spreading about her family to justify his own treachery?

When Isolt returned to the main chamber, she knelt beside Piro's daybed to stroke the foenix and Piro pretended to be asleep. With a sigh, Isolt returned to her own bedchamber, putting out the light.

Piro rolled over, thumping the duck-down pillow. Well, if Isolt did not believe Palatyne was equally treacherous, there was nothing Piro could do. She had troubles enough of her own. One word as to her true identity and she would be executed. Fear sat like a coiled snake in the pit of her belly, waiting to strike.

She would never sleep.

Freezing Sylion take Palatyne!

BYREN TRIED NOT to watch Florin's bottom as she climbed the trail ahead of him. Her shoulders were broad and her legs long, with a stride that almost matched his. But her narrow waist, the curve of her behind and the sway of her hips proclaimed her femininity. And wouldn't she hate it if he told her so?

Ostensibly, he'd suggested they scout the trail to the secret pass over the mountain, in case they had to make a hasty retreat. This was true as far as it went, but he also wanted to make things right between them.

Since Waterford Florin had been avoiding him, quite an achievement in a camp that consisted of four caves covering a space not much bigger than a ploughed field. When she did speak to him, it was all 'Yes, my king, no, my king.'

It was driving him crazy.

She came to a stop on a patch of snow barely big enough for the two of them to stand side by side, in the gap between two rocks large as houses. He opted to stand with his back to one of the rocks.

Dusk had fallen while they climbed and now only starlight illuminated the night.

'These.' Florin reached past him to pat the rock by his shoulder. 'I recognise these, my king. I haven't forgotten the trail to the secret pass.'

'Just like you don't forget to hold a grudge?'

She blinked and frowned at him. In daylight he suspected he would have seen colour in her winter-pale cheeks.

'Have I offended you, my king?'

'No. I've offended you.'

The silence stretched. He'd been wrong about Winterfall. The noble youth had not had the strength of character to admit his fault. For some reason, Byren did not want to be wrong about Florin.

His voice dropped. 'I called you a mountain girl. Was that the last straw?'

She looked away, jaw clenched. 'No. You were right. If I want to be treated like one of your honour guard, I have to accept orders like they do.'

He hadn't actually said that, but he wasn't surprised that she'd made the leap.

'But you're not one of them. They're a bunch of untried youths, eager to win honour on the battlefield. You're more like Orrade. You see through things.' He hesitated as she cast him a swift, inscrutable look. Should he explain that there was nothing between him and Orrade? Nothing on his side, at least. He was on the verge of telling her, but he could not bring himself to reveal his best friend's vulnerability.

In that moment, he saw he had been right about Florin. She was like Orrade. She was clever and pragmatic, but she was also vulnerable. It was her pride, her insistence on being as good as any man that left her open to ridicule.

'You don't have to prove anything to any one, Florrie.'

'Don't call me that,' she snapped.

A grin tugged at his lips. 'Mountain-girl?'

Her eyes widened as she stared at him like she was trying to work something out.

His heart picked up a notch and he felt his body tighten unexpectedly. Hold on. He did not fancy boyish women who could just about look him in the eye, no more than he fancied Orrade.

He blew his breath out, at the same time as Florin blew hers out in a huff of annoyance.

'Mountain-girl it is then.' She thrust past him, heading back the way they'd come. 'I'll answer to that, my king.' The last was thrown over her shoulder, a challenge if he ever heard one.

Damn, he did find her fascinating. Now that was inconvenient. Luckily, Florin didn't have a clue.

Chapter Ten

POSSIBLY BECAUSE SHE was thinking about him, Piro found herself dreaming of him. Palatyne and the Utlander crept through the palace courtyards, keeping to the shadows cast by the brilliant stars. Palatyne was in such a hurry, the short Power-worker had to take running steps to keep up.

'You've seen to the guards?' Palatyne was saying.

'Yes, my duke. There is only the slave, Seela.'

'And she won't object, if she knows what's good for her.' Palatyne gave a bark of angry laughter. 'How dare that little bitch ask for time? She means to refuse me, I know it. I could break her neck with my bare hands. One snap, like a chicken!'

'But that is not why you are going to her,' the Utlander warned.

Palatyne came to a stop and looked up. Piro recognised the private veranda that all Isolt's chambers opened onto.

'Do not fear, Utlander. I won't let my temper get the better of me. I will woo her with sweet words, tell her I cannot wait for our wedding day, that her beauty has enflamed my passion. And if that does not work, I will force myself on her. After one night in my arms she will wed me to avoid disgrace.' He gave a nasty grin. 'Who knows. She might even enjoy it!'

He took several steps back and the Utlander handed him a grappling hook and rope. Palatyne swung it expertly, letting it fly. It hooked over the balcony rail and held. He clambered effortlessly up two storeys and over the balustrades.

Piro woke, her heart pounding. Starlight cast long oblongs of light through the balcony doors.

With a certainty that went core-deep, she knew this was not a dream. Her Affinity was trying to warn her. Palatyne was about to break into Isolt's chamber.

Barefoot and terrified, Piro ran to open the door to Isolt's bedchamber. The shadow of a broad-shouldered man appeared on one of the balcony doors.

Piro scrambled onto the bed to shake the kingsdaughter, whispering fiercely, 'Isolt. Wake up. Palatyne's trying to force the balcony doors.'

'What?' Isolt was instantly alert. 'What trickery is this?'

'No trickery.' Piro pointed to the balcony, where Palatyne's form was silhouetted against the starlight. The catch rattled. Her breath caught in her throat.

Isolt gasped, rolled out of bed and ran through to the next room, with Piro at her heels. Isolt tugged on the door to the corridor. When it refused to open, she gave a little moan of fear and frustration.

'Locked!' She thumped the door. 'Guards!'

The guards did not respond.

Piro was not surprised. 'The Utlander said he'd dealt with them.'

The foenix raised his head to give a querying call, feathers ruffled, foreleg lifted to strike. But he was only a juvenile and his spurs hadn't grown yet.

'Oh, good boy.' Piro ran back and scooped him up. Under her hand his heart raced with fear.

A soft tinkle of broken glass told them Palatyne had given up trying to force the door and had broken the pane instead. The hinge on the balcony door squeaked.

Isolt cursed and glanced to Piro.

'Where can we hide?' Piro searched the room, illuminated by the faint glow of the banked fire. Behind the couch? Too obvious. Under the bed? Again too obvious.

'I know.' Isolt tugged her arm, dragging her over to the writing-table nook which was walled on three sides by bookshelves and illustrations.

Isolt swung a large framed map of the known world aside. Behind it was a waist-high dark gap. She shoved Piro forwards. With the foenix in her arms Piro was off balance and hit her toe on the bottom lip of the opening. Biting back a yelp of pain, she crawled on her knees into the darkness until her forehead hit the back wall. A bolt hole. Her mother had described such things in stories.

Piro turned around, pressing her back to the wall, hugging the foenix to her chest. He seemed to understand that they must be quiet. Isolt had climbed in after her and now pulled the map down, hiding them. It was dark, but for a faint glow which came through the map's fine vellum. Piro could see Isolt only as an outline as she sat hugging her knees.

Neither of them made a sound. They hardly dared to breathe. Piro's toe throbbed in time to her heart beat. If a stubbed toe was the worst she got out of this night, she'd count herself lucky.

There was no noise for such a long time, the temptation was to venture out.

After a while, they heard a muffled exclamation and a golden glow appeared on the other side of the map. Palatyne must have lit a branch of candles to search for Isolt. He strode around the room, slowly at first, his boots hardly making a sound, then more loudly as he realised the kingsdaughter wasn't present.

He left the room, returning to Isolt's bedchamber.

In the dimness, Piro felt for Isolt, her hand coming to rest on the kingsdaughter's knee. She squeezed. 'Don't move. It might be a trick.'

Isolt's hand covered hers to return the pressure.

They waited. Piro counted to twenty-five, then the glow came back. This time there were two sets of footsteps.

Isolt's eyes were dark pools of fear as she stared across as Piro. *Who?* she mouthed. But Piro had no time to reply. She tensed as she felt the foenix shiver with fear and hunch down even further in her arms.

'See? Empty. I told you I searched all Isolt's chambers. Where else could she be?' Palatyne demanded.

'The kingsdaughter must be here. My spies did not see her leave,' the Utlander insisted. 'She's hiding.'

Isolt's hand closed tightly over Piro's.

'I've looked,' Palatyne snarled. 'By the fires of Mulcibar, why couldn't the little bitch agree to marry me!'

'She'll agree quick enough once you've had her. Now hold your tongue and give me the candles,' the Utlander snapped. 'I'll soon find her.'

Mouth dry, Piro met Isolt's eyes. She felt sick to her stomach. The Utlander was sure to find them using his Affinity. And then Palatyne would rape Isolt, claiming her for his own. It was the way of the Utlands, and the spars weren't much better.

Silence stretched. The air grew heavy and oppressive with Affinity. Piro's teeth ached.

'Well?' Palatyne demanded.

'She's here somewhere, all right. Her essence is still on the air.' The Utlander was hatefully pleased with himself.

Piro caught her breath, then remembered to let it out silently. The glow grew stronger as the renegade Power-worker walked slowly across the room, drawing nearer.

The Utlander must not find us Piro prayed. *He must not.* It became a litany in her head. She remembered hiding in the loft over the stables while Byren and Fyn looked for her last midsummer. They never found her, not even when they glanced into the loft. She'd willed herself unremarkable.

The glow grew brighter and, for a heartbeat, she saw the Utlander's thin arm silhouetted against the vellum. In her mind's eye she saw him triumphantly pull the map aside, saw Palatyne drag Isolt out by her hair.

No. It would not happen.

It would be just like in the stable. They would pass over her. Piro concentrated all her will, harnessing her Affinity as she stroked the foenix. She and Isolt weren't even here. They were hiding in the stable back home.

'Well?' Palatyne repeated.

The Utlander sniffed. 'Strange, I smell horses.'

'Horses in a royal bedroom? Your Affinity's playing up.'

'More like someone else's Affinity is playing tricks on mine,' the Utlander muttered. 'A curse on Dunstany. I cannot sense her at all now. He's put some sort of protective ward over the kingsdaughter.'

'Dunstany is on the other side of Merofynia at his estates. He could not know I planned to seduce Isolt tonight. No one but you and I know.'

'Someone with Affinity has warned her. The bird has flown the coop.'

'I thought you said you sensed her essence,' Palatyne countered.

'Well now all I sense is horse shit!' The Utlander snapped. 'We've been out-manoeuvred. Someone knows about us. They could be on their way right now, or... worse. I don't recognise the style of this Power-worker. They may have left a trap.' His voice rose. 'We've got to get out of here, now!'

'A trap?' Palatyne echoed. Piro could hear the fear

rising in his voice. 'I won't be tainted by Affinity. Come on.'

The glow faded as they returned to Isolt's bedroom, presumably to climb over the balcony.

But Piro and Isolt sat in the dark, knees wedged together for a long time. Every now and then a shiver ran through Isolt. Gradually, the foenix's body relaxed and Piro felt him vibrate with the cat-like purr that meant he was happy.

She cleared her throat. 'I think they've gone.'

Isolt nodded. Shuffling onto her knees, she moved one side of the map a little and peered through.

Meanwhile, Piro quested with her Affinity-enhanced senses. The room felt empty and, now that the crisis was over, she trembled with exhaustion.

'I think you're right,' Isolt whispered. She lifted the map aside and slid her legs out, dropping to the floor.

Piro followed her, the sleeping foenix in her arms. He seemed as exhausted as she was. Limping a little due to her sore toe, she put the foenix in his basket then crept across to the entrance of Isolt's bedchamber. The balcony doors were closed. Only the broken glass panel was evidence of Palatyne's treacherous plan.

Isolt stood in the doorway.

'They've gone, but I can't sleep in here.' Isolt closed the door to her bedchamber and wedged a chair under the knob.

'I don't think they're coming back,' Piro whispered. She felt dizzy, and flecks of light danced in her vision. 'I have to sit down. I think I might be sick.'

Isolt drew her over to the daybed, propping a

pillow behind her back and wrapping the silk-covered eiderdown around her. The kingsdaughter lit a branch of candles and made up a tray of sweet wine, fresh fruits and nuts from the side-board.

Piro watched, her tired brain struggling to grasp the significance of this. But, when Isolt brought the tray over, her stomach revolted.

'At least have a sip of sweet wine,' Isolt insisted.

Piro took one mouthful, then another, nibbled some salted cashews and discovered she was ravenous.

Isolt sat at the other end of the daybed, resting against the carved footboard, and watched her eat with satisfaction. 'You could have left me to my fate but you saved me, Piro.'

'Of course.'

'I misjudged you.'

Piro shrugged as she peeled a honeydew melon, sucking the sweet pulp.

'What? Aren't you going to make me sorry?' Isolt prodded.

'No point,' Piro mumbled, mouth full.

Isolt eyed her for a moment. 'The Rolencian court must be very strange –'

'Strange?' Piro laughed. 'The Merofynian court is strange. Everyone holding their breath, too scared to say what they really think.'

'So you understand why I doubted you? And you won't hold it against me?'

Piro picked up another honeydew melon. 'These are very good. Want one?'

'Yes.' Isolt gave the first genuine smile Piro had seen from her.

As they ate, she studied Isolt surreptitiously. The Merofynian kingsdaughter licked her fingers and stared into the fire. She was still the same girl, beautiful as a porcelain doll, but the muscles around her mouth had relaxed. She looked somehow different.

Her face was no longer a mask.

Piro must have made some small sound because Isolt looked over to her. 'What?'

'I'm glad I grew up with a mother who adored my father and three brothers, even if they loved to tease me,' Piro said.

Isolt's eyes widened. 'You read my mind?'

'No. I don't –'

'You do have Affinity. Don't deny it.'

Piro nodded. 'But not much. If I could, I would have saved my father.'

'You are Affinity-born, just like Lord Dunstany. That's why he chose you for his slave.'

'I suppose so.' Piro hadn't thought of it that way. She licked her fingers and took another sip of wine, her thoughts returning to what was worrying her. 'I don't think this setback will stop Palatyne. Marrying you will make him the legitimate king-in-waiting.'

'After tonight nothing will convince me to wed him.' Anger sharpened Isolt's features, making her beauty more interesting. 'I'll tell Father how he broke in here and what he intended.'

'Your father is afraid of Palatyne, for good reason. I fear you'll get no help from him. When was your betrothal to be announced?'

'Spring cusp festival. He wanted to wed me on midsummer's day or sooner. But I can't marry him.

I'd rather die!'

'Better that he dies.'

Isolt went very quiet. 'Palatyne is surrounded by loyal followers, plus there's the Utlander. Can you –'

Piro shook her head swiftly. 'Lord Dunstany said my Affinity visions are triggered by nexus points, moments when events hang in the balance. Most of the time I can do no more than guess a card.'

'Then I must run away. But they'll be watching me.' Isolt's frown cleared. 'I know. Every spring cusp I go to Cyena Abbey to receive the offering for the festival. I'd planned to leave in a few days anyway. I'll leave tomorrow. The abbess will give me sanctuary. She's very powerful. Palatyne will not dare invade the abbey to take me by force!'

Piro considered this. 'Normally you should be safe behind the abbey walls, but what if the king demands your return? An abbess cannot refuse a king.'

'Then I will renounce the world and become a nun. A king cannot command the goddess!'

Piro laughed softly, then sobered. 'When you are safe with the abbess, you must free me.'

'I free you now.'

Piro gasped. 'Just like that?'

Isolt nodded.

'Then I misjudged you,' Piro conceded. 'Back home, they said you were like your father, cunning, not to be trusted...'

Isolt sat forwards. 'Oh, Piro. I'm not –'

'I know.'

'I'm not like Father at all. I'm more like Mother, but she was weak. I'm not.' Tears glittered in Isolt's slanted black eyes. 'I'm strong. And, if I've become hard and cunning, it's because I've had to.'

'To survive.' Piro nodded. That made sense. 'But you can't free me yet. Not officially. I can't leave you suddenly. Palatyne would be suspicious. I'll stay with you until we reach the abbess. All I ask is passage on a ship to Rolencia.'

'You have it.' Isolt hugged her knees. 'When he came in here with that evil-smelling Utlander... I've never been so afraid in my life. Without your Affinity...'

Piro nodded. She tried to hold back a yawn and failed. Now that she had eaten, she wanted nothing more than to fall asleep.

Isolt smiled. 'Sleep, Pi– *Seela*. I'll keep watch.'

Piro snuggled down, marvelling how her position had changed from slave to trusted confidante in just one day.

Dunstany had been right. Isolt was the innocent pawn of her father, King Merofyn. Piro had to let the noble Power-worker know Isolt's plans. They would pass his mansion on the way out of Port Mero. She could leave a message there. The sooner they were out of the palace and beyond Palatyne's reach, the better.

BYREN WOKE TO find his back felt cold. Where had Orrade gone? He sat up. The cave's ceiling glowed with reflected light from the snow outside. And it was silent, other than the snores of his honour guard and the several monks. After filling Catillum's cave, the newest arrivals had taken up residence in this one.

What if Orrade had felt another Affinity vision coming on? The monks would report it to the mystics master and his best friend would be unmasked, forced to leave Rolencia, just when Byren needed him most.

Whatever the cost, he had to protect Orrade. Heart thudding, Byren rolled to his feet, slinging his cloak around his shoulders. Carefully, he stepped over the sleeping bodies that were packed tight as a litter of puppies. It was like this in all the caves.

With his eyes adjusted to the darkness of the cave, outside the starlight seemed bright. He blinked and lifted his head, listening, smelling the crisp mountain air.

'Over here,' Orrade's voice reached him, no more than a whisper.

He headed that way and found his best friend just around the bend in the trail, wrapped in his cloak.

'What's wrong? Is it –' Byren broke off, not wanting to speak of Orrade's Affinity when one of the monks might step outside to relieve himself and overhear them.

Without a word, Orrade turned and strode up the path. Byren followed. As they passed Florin's cave Byren glanced in, but it was too dark to see anything. Soon they left the caves behind and came to a spot where they would not be overheard by any lookouts.

Orrade turned to confront him. 'I didn't ask for this Affinity. I don't want it, I'd rather not...' He broke off and let his breath out in a rush. 'No, that's not true. It's been useful. I wouldn't have found you in that seep if I hadn't had the vision.'

'I'm sorry, I didn't know asking the seer to heal you would trigger Affinity.' No, but she had warned him Orrade would never be the same and he'd been too selfish to consider what this meant.

Orrade brushed his apology away. 'You did what you thought best and I'd be dead if you hadn't.' He turned away, strode to a flat stone, jumped onto it and kicked heaped snow aside, then sat with his back to a rock, staring out into the night.

Byren joined him. Shoulder to shoulder, arms resting across their raised knees, they stared out across the foothills. Amidst the pines, silhouetted winter-bare trees stood stark against the stars.

'I won't leave,' Orrade said softly. 'When Dovecote fell, Father's people looked to me to save them. I was half-mad with grief...' He took a shaking breath. 'You know what it's like.'

Byren nodded, unable to speak for the lump in his throat. But his grief was mixed with a bitter dollop of relief. With Lence gone he no longer walked on eggshells, trying to appease his twin, trying not to offend him, unwilling to see the man his twin was becoming.

Orrade rubbed his face vigorously, finally dragging his hands down over the wispy ends of his beard.

Byren shifted on the cold hard stone. 'I told you, when I'm king I'll rescind Father's law. You won't –'

'The abbeys won't like it. In the last thirty years they've grown in size. Every child detected with Affinity has been gifted to the abbey, along with a payment. Wealth and willing workers. How do you think the abbeys will react if you rescind your father's law?

'Also, while Halcyon's monks and Sylion's nuns are the only source of Affinity knowledge and control, they have the ultimate power over seeps, ceremonies, Affinity beasts – both the dangerous and the useful – not to mention protection from foreign Power-workers. You can see why they don't want the ordinary folk able to take care of these things themselves.'

Byren nodded, seeing why he needed Orrade's sharp mind. 'Although ordinary folk are glad enough to call on the abbeys for protection.'

'They used to handle the small things, up to a renegade Power-worker or a seep, by calling on someone from their own community who had Affinity. Ever since Florin's grandmother told us how it used to be, I've been asking other old folk,' Orrade revealed.

They lapsed into silence. Byren saw a shooting star and nudged Orrade. 'My wish.'

His friend grinned. 'What do you wish for, Byren?' His voice dropped, growing serious. 'If you could have anything you wanted, what would it be?'

Byren opened his mouth to say he wanted things back the way they were, Mother and Father alive, Piro and Fyn safe, Lence...

The smile left his lips. 'An end to this war with Merofynia. Me, the kind of king Rolencia needs. You, happy and safe from persecution.'

When Orrade said nothing, he glanced to him, noticing the sheen of unshed tears in his eyes.

'Orrie?'

His best friend shook his head and lifted his hands so that they hid his face. When he spoke his voice was the barest scrape of sound. 'Go back to bed, Byren.'

'I've offended you.'

'No.' His hands dropped and he stared away, so that all Byren could see of him was the line of his lean cheek and jaw, lightly dusted with a wispy black beard. 'No, you haven't offended me, quite the opposite. But you don't want what I want. And tonight I can't pretend I feel only friendship for you.'

Byren swallowed. 'You are my best and closest friend. I trust you with my life.'

Orrade nodded, voice thick. 'And I, you.'

'But it's not enough. I'm being selfish keeping you with me.'

Orrade snorted. 'I'm not going anywhere. The people of Dovecote need me.'

'I need you.'

Orrade let his breath out slowly. 'You can trust me, Byren. I'll never betray you.'

'I know.'

'Go now. I'll be down soon.'

Byren felt he should say something more, but... He came to his feet, adjusted the cloak and jumped off the rock. Orrade continued to look away, arms clasped tightly around his bent knees.

Alone.

If he could, Byren would, but he couldn't.

So he turned and walked away.

* * *

THE NEXT MORNING Piro watched as Isolt ordered servants about imperiously as they scurried to pack for her annual pilgrimage.

While the servants worked, Piro and Isolt took their breakfast on the veranda – fresh fruit, tiny sweet pastries, rich hot drinking chocolate. It was the kind of breakfast Piro had never known until she came here, the kind her mother had known until she came to Rolencia to live.

Isolt had told the servants her clumsiness broke the window, and an industrious youth was repairing it while they ate.

'Nine days until spring cusp,' Isolt said. They were both aware of their audience. 'I'm looking forward to it. We'll travel slowly so it will take several days to walk to the abbey.'

'Walk? Can't we ride or sail?'

'Walking is part of my penitence. I am allowed servants and several donkeys to carry the tents and provisions, but we all walk. As Isolt Merofyn Kingsdaughter, I represent the land and her people. I go to plead with the Goddess Cyena to free us from her cruel, wintry grasp, or the farmers won't be able to sow their crops.'

This talk of a wintry goddess confused Piro, who was used to the Goddess Halcyon ruling over summer.

'Don't worry, Seela.' Isolt gave a determined smile. 'We will reach Cyena Abbey safely.' The unspoken – *and then we'll both be free, you to go home, me of Palatyne* – reverberated between them.

Isolt selected some choice slivers of fruit. 'Now,

let's see if the foenix will take the food from my fingers. Come, my pretty boy.'

His cage had been placed on a low table beside theirs. Piro watched as the Affinity beast daintily took the fruit from Isolt's fingers.

At two years of age his beak could slice flesh. One day he would be as tall as a man and his leg spurs would contain deadly poison. If only he were full-grown now and she could turn him on Palatyne!

Chapter Eleven

FYN COLLECTED THE cards and shuffled them expertly. He'd grown adept in the last few days. This evening, he and Bantam were alone. Jakulos had gone down to buy another bottle of wine. It would have been the perfect opportunity to escape, but the sea-hound was on his guard.

'Go on.' Bantam indicated Fyn should deal the cards.

At that moment, they heard the heavy tread of Jakulos's return. The big man entered, plonked two bottles of Rolencian red on the table and dropped into his chair with the air of one who is well pleased.

'Look what I've just bought.' He pulled a drawstring bag out of his vest and undid it to reveal a small piece of fabric so fine it was almost see through.

'A caul,' Bantam whispered. 'Bet you paid the midwife a fortune for that.'

Fyn blinked. It was not fabric at all. Sailors believed those born with a caul, a piece of the birth sack over their face, could not drown. Fyn had not known they also believed the caul itself could prevent drowning. Back in Rolencia it was thought to be a sign that the baby would develop Affinity.

'Worth every silver.' Jakulos folded the caul carefully and slipped it into the bag, tucking it safely inside his vest.

Bantam uncorked one of the bottles. 'Don't supposed she had another one?'

Jakulos shook his head. 'Tell you what, if the boat sinks, hold onto me. I'll keep you afloat.'

The big sailor looked so pleased, Fyn didn't have the heart to point out that he had parted with good silver on the strength of an unknown midwife's word.

'Go on, pour the wine.' Jakulos gestured to Bantam. 'Guess what? Palatyne's been made a Duke.'

'You don't say?' Bantam muttered. 'That jumped up spar warlord?'

A roaring filled Fyn's head. To think, the man who had murdered his family had been rewarded with a dukedom.

Jakulos nodded. 'When I left Merofynia six summers ago, there were rumours about the warlord from Amfina, as he was known in those days.' He grimaced. 'Never thought to see Palatyne made a duke.'

There was a knock at the door as the serving boy delivered their evening meal. And a fine meal it was too. If Fyn hadn't been eaten up with outrage and the need to get home he would have been enjoying himself.

He glanced out the window behind Bantam. The last rays of the setting sun picked out the tip of Mage Tower, making the white stone glow salmon-pink. He'd had time to think over what the sea-hounds' captain had said. Nefysto was right. Byren needed allies, strong allies, and the elector was no use to him.

But a renegade Power-worker like the mage?

Since arriving in Ostron Isle the arguments had gone around and around in Fyn's head until he was dizzy. Having Affinity of his own meant he was open to those who used Affinity for evil purposes. But he had been abbey-trained, and knew the wards to protect himself. He was ideally suited to meeting the mage and at least sounding him out.

But it would depend on what the mage wanted – no one offered an alliance without asking for something in return. Fyn could always refuse and walk away. He'd be no worse off than he was now.

And there it was. He'd decided to go against the teachings of Halcyon Abbey and seek out Mage Tsulamyth. Nefysto had been right, a desperate man couldn't afford to be picky. Besides, forewarned was forearmed.

'Another hand of cards before dinner?' Bantam asked.

'Food,' Jakulos said, the same as he'd done every night.

They laughed.

If there was a way to leave without killing at least one of these two, Fyn had yet to find it.

*   *   *

'BYREN?' ORRADE MET his eyes across the fire circle, his mouth grim.

Rather than leap up and worry the others, Byren said, 'Watch this, Orrie. Go on, Vadik.'

The boy beamed and did the dancing-coin trick, running the coin over the fingers of his left hand, as if he'd been born left-handed.

Orrade laughed and clapped.

'My best student,' the player said. He'd been teaching all the maimed his tricks, to train their minds and coordinate their fingers.

Byren clapped his hand on the lad's shoulder then stood, wandering outside with Orrade. After their talk last night, he had barely seen his friend that day and now it was dark.

When they stood under the stars, out of hearing distance of those in the cave, Orrade turned to face him, voice low and tight. 'Word's come of a large force of Merofynians camped in the burnt-out remains of Waterford. Either the raid gave us away or they've had a tip-off.'

'Bound to happen eventually.'

'You can't wait for Fyn any longer.'

Byren nodded, mind racing. The last of the monks had reached them. Twenty-two of them boys under sixteen. He didn't want to send children into war. Neither did he want to appear before Warlord Feid as a supplicant, but he had no choice. 'With so many elderly and children, we can't travel fast.'

'There's no cloud cover to cloak the starlight. Send them over the Divide tonight with an escort. Keep your best warriors here. Buy time.'

Byren nodded, not happy with sacrificing his best to save non-combatants. But what kind of a leader would he be, if he left the defenceless behind?

'I know,' Orrade began. 'I'll take a dozen, lay a false trail and lure the Merofynians away. Maybe I can take out a few stragglers, make them suspicious of an ambush.' He grinned. 'That should hold them up for a day or two.'

Byren didn't want to put Orrade in danger so he didn't agree to, or refuse, his friend's plan. Instead he played for time, hoping something would come to him. 'Let the camp know. Oh, and Orrie, tell Florin I'm relying on her.'

In no time at all the camp was abuzz with movement. Since most people had carried their belongings on their backs, there was not much to pack. Adults hurried about, efficient and focused, while small children darted round them, excited for now. Soon they would be tired and grumpy.

Byren watched the proceedings. He had to leave the horses behind, turning them loose to fend for themselves. He regretted this, fearing Cobalt's men would recapture the animals and use them against him. There was an alternative, but it went against the grain to order the killing of good animals just to prevent them from falling into the enemy's hands.

Lence and his father might have done it, but not him.

Again the old seer's words came back to Byren. And he'd thought it simple to tell right from wrong.

As the last of Halcyon's monks shouldered their

packs and buried the hot coals of their cooking fires, Byren wondered if he had what it took to be a leader in these desperate times. Was he ruthless enough?

Coming around the bend from the cave his honour guard shared, Byren met up with Florin on her way down, her travelling bag slung across her shoulders. There was a smudge of soot on one side of her nose. He wondered if he should tell her.

'Nearly, ready to go?' he asked.

'Aye. You know the way as far as the big boulders.' She pulled several pieces of charcoal from her pocket with blackened fingers. That explained her nose. 'After those stones, I'll mark the trail so you can find it. Be sure to obscure the marks as you pass.'

He nodded. He wanted to take her chin in his hand and clean off her nose. But the very fact that he wanted to, meant he couldn't. 'There's a smudge on your nose.'

'Oh.' She hitched the sleeve of her jerkin over the heel of her hand and rubbed at her nose, then tilted her face for his scrutiny. 'Did I get it?'

'Yes.' He was right. She felt nothing for him and it caused him a wry pang, because so many girls in the past had been quick to lift their skirts and profess undying love, and he had accepted it as his due. That was before he realised how much Elina meant to him. Come to think of it, how could he even feel this way about Florin, when Elina was dead? He cleared his throat. 'Take care, Mountain-girl, I'm relying on you.'

'Eh, Da will be bringing up the rear. We'll be fine. It's you that has the dangerous job.'

He shrugged this off, thinking there had to be a way

he could circumvent Orrade's plan. His best friend didn't know the secret way over the mountains. He'd be trapped on this side, forced to play cat-and-mouse with Cobalt until Byren returned with the warlords.

'I'm off then.' Florin left him. Not long after that, she led the way out of camp with Leif, the elderly, nursing mothers and children following. They were escorted by the majority of the able-bodied men. The path was narrow and they had to go in single file, so it was late by the time the last of them went. Luckily, it was a clear night. Above them a sky of blazing stars cast shadows on the silvered snow.

That left Byren with Orrade, his four honour guard and the mystics master plus a handful of battle-hardened monks. Byren looked around for the mystic.

'Where's Catillum?' Byren asked one of the monks.

'He and Orrade went to check the approaches.'

Byren nodded and headed down to the lookout, where he found the mystics master lying on his belly alongside Orrade as they both peered out over a cliff. Something about their concentration and stillness warned Byren. He crawled up to them, keeping low so as to present no silhouette.

'What is it?'

'An advance party, too many for scouts. I think some Merofynian captain's eager for glory,' Orrade whispered, pointing to several dark moving patches, seen clearly against the pale snow. Then they blended into shadows under the pines. 'I counted fifteen of them. They'll be up here in twenty minutes at least.'

Byren cursed. The last of the others had only just left. They needed more of a head start than that. 'No time to erase the trail properly. No time to lay a false trail.'

He eased back from the lookout lip, crouching low. The other two joined him.

'We could lead them off, making just enough noise to make it seem like we were fleeing in panic,' Orrade suggested. 'The numbers are about even.'

'My monks have seen battle,' Catillum offered. 'We'll have no trouble handling them.'

Byren knew it was true. But... 'What if we could lead them into a trap somehow? Make it look like the Merofynians had been killed by renegade Affinity. Make them so scared they'll be afraid to follow?'

'Subterfuge is always good.' Catillum's voice held cautious approval.

'How?' Orrade asked.

Byren fingered the foenix spurs he wore around his neck. 'There's that hole in the cavern of the Foenix Faithful.'

'Tip them in?' Orrade smiled. 'I love the way your mind works!'

Byren grinned, then glanced to the mystic to see if his friend had unwittingly revealed himself.

But Catillum was thinking. 'If I could use the foenixes, somehow creating an illusion –'

'You can do that? Then we'll leave one Merofynian alive. He can take the tale of rabid foenixes back to his commander.' Byren came to his feet. 'Come on.'

Twenty minutes later, the Merofynians found Byren's camp. They entered with weapons drawn and caution in every step, but this soon disappeared as it became evident the camp was empty.

One man knelt over the fire circle, stirring it with his sword tip. 'Coals are still hot. They left in a hurry.'

'Find their trail,' the leader ordered, his voice sharp with barely contained impatience. He stood with his back to the cave where Byren hid, one boot resting on a stone of the fire circle.

Byren watched from the darkness, grateful yet again that his mother had tutored him in Merofynian.

After a few moments, the men returned with news. One reported, 'There's another cave, around the bend. From there, a trail leads up into the hills.'

Their leader laughed. 'He's not thinking, he's reacting. There's no pass that way. We hold the only pass to Foenix Spar. We'll have him in a day or two. But I'd rather catch him tonight and split that bag of gold among us. So, who wants to come with me now?'

Judging the moment right, Byren let two stones click together. The leader glanced into the cave. Byren made a soft scuffling noise, leather on stone. It was just the kind of surreptitious sound that someone might make while trying to move quickly, but quietly.

The Merofynian leader lifted his hand for silence, listening. 'The clever cock. He's split his forces, sacrificed some to lead us off, while hiding in the caves, waiting till we pass.'

Here was the weakness of the plan. A sensible leader would wait for reinforcements, but Byren wanted to lure them in. Would he have to reveal himself or would greed do the trick?

The one who had poked the fire wrapped a piece of cloth around his sword, poured a little something from a vial onto this and dipped it in the coals. Flames sprang from the makeshift torch.

The others edged nearer the entrance.

'Could be the caves join up and lead out somewhere else,' one of the men said. 'Could be they're getting away.'

'Could be,' the leader conceded. 'And we can't have that, can we lads? Come on.'

The man with the torch went first, sending shadows skittering up the walls of the cave and across the ceiling.

Byren sprang to his feet and took off, running towards the passage at the back, past a side passage where Orrade and the others waited.

'A piece of gold to the man who takes him alive,' the leader shouted. The Merofynians gave a roar and charged.

Byren ran, leading them on. He knew the way and, once around the next bend, the glow coming from the foenix cavern reached him.

His pursuers howled like dogs catching the scent.

As soon as he entered the foenix cavern Byren darted to one side. Avoiding the place where the floor appeared to be solid stone, he ran around the hidden central pit, towards the back wall. A single torch lit the paintings. By its flickering light the foenixes shimmered and danced in unison. Even blinking did not dispel the illusion. Byren's teeth hurt and his skin prickled with Affinity.

Of course – Catillum was casting an illusion from

his hiding place in the shadows of a crevice.

Byren took up his place in front of the paintings. Apparently trapped.

The Merofynians ran into the cavern and hesitated, looking for hidden threats. He had to lure them on.

'I am Byren Kingsheir, son of King Rolen the Implacable. Come and get me if you can.' Byren lifted his hands, holding a foenix spur in each one so that his arms ended in long claws. 'The royal foenix will protect me.'

'He's stark raving mad!' the one with the makeshift torch muttered.

'Mad or not, he'll die by the sword,' their leader yelled. 'Get him.'

Several of his men charged across the floor, swords raised. When they reached the pit, they plunged so suddenly through the apparently solid floor that they seemed to disappear. Only their startled cries hung on the air, fading away.

The others made the sign to ward off evil and looked around uneasily.

But the trap closed as Orrade led the honour guard and monks to attack from behind. They cut down two men before the others realised the source of the threat.

Yelling orders, the Merofynian leader backed up, feeling the floor of the cavern with his sword tip. A wise move, but ultimately pointless, because one of his own men cannoned into him to avoid a monk's blow and the pair of them staggered backwards. They dropped through the floor.

Orrade's men beat the Merofynians back, the last

few making desperate attempts to hold their places as their companions disappeared behind them.

When only one man remained, Orrade called his warriors off.

The last Merofynian was a small man who Byren suspected survived on his wits, rather than strength. The Merofynian let his sword drop and raised his hands with little hope.

In the sudden silence the very air of the cavern seemed to throb.

Byren strode around to the crevice to where the mystics master hid. 'Drop the illusion, Catillum.'

Grey-faced, the mystics master stumbled from his hiding place and leant against the wall, lifting his good hand to his face, fingers trembling.

When Byren glanced behind him, the black maw of the hole was revealed.

The surviving Merofynian cursed under his breath.

Byren turned back to Catillum. 'Holding the illusion weakened you?'

He nodded. 'People see what they expect to see. In this case a flat floor. But yes, it weakened me. My presence has awakened the seep and I had to fight the urge to draw on it. Untamed Affinity leads to evil.'

Byren no longer believed this, but he was not about to argue the point.

A shout made him spin. The Merofynian had tried to plunge through the others in a bid to escape. The scuffle ceased as suddenly as it had begun.

Orrade knelt next to the collapsed man. 'Dead, I'm afraid. Broken neck.'

Byren swore. They had been going to leave the

man with a false memory of foenixes driving his companions into the pit, but that would not work now. Byren would have to improvise.

'Bring him here.' He indicated a spot under the tallest foenix painting.

Byren took one of the foenix spurs and slashed it across the dead man's throat, leaving it hooked in his flesh.

He stood back as blood flowed across the man's chest. With no heartbeat to pump the blood, it soon stopped. Byren wiped his hands, fastidiously. 'Best I can do. Foenixes can grow a new spur if one snaps off in combat. Unless they look closely it will appear that he was killed by the kick of a foenix.' Byren removed the burning brand from under the foenix paintings. 'Right. Everyone out!'

Two monks hurried around the pit to help Catillum, while the others filed out. All but for Orrade, who stayed back to help Byren complete their illusion.

Knowing the distinctive sign of a foenix's tracks, Byren had no trouble making a few fake prints on the floor. Then he partially scuffed the tracks as if there had been a struggle.

That done, he and Orrade prepared to leave, but hesitated over the deep pit. Far below, a pinpoint, the remains of the Merofynians' makeshift torch, glowed.

'Hope they're all dead,' Orrade said softly, voicing Byren's thoughts.

'Come on.'

In the entrance to the caves they removed all signs of their men leaving, while making sure the signs left by the Merofynians' entrance remained. A boot mark on the soft earth here, a scuff mark there.

When Cobalt's main body of soldiers found this cavern and followed the trail into the far chamber they would find one dead man, no sign of the other bodies and the prints of the foenixes. Since they knew of no pass in this valley, they would turn around and leave, carrying tales of phantom Affinity beasts coming to defend the royal house of Rolencia.

At least, this was what Byren hoped to achieve. It was the best he could do.

He checked the stars. Barely an hour had passed since they had first spotted the Merofynians. If they hurried they could catch up with the tail of the army.

The ravines were covered in new trails, caused by the men coming and going from cave to cave. If Byren's group covered their tracks well, Cobalt's men would never find the beginning of the secret trail. They might even think he had spirited them over the mountains with the Goddess Halcyon's intervention.

Once they got over the Divide and into Foenix Spar, he had a whole new set of problems. Unace would be true to her word, but would Warlord Feid remain loyal to King Rolen's kin? And even if he did, would the three remaining warlords support Byren?

Chapter Twelve

FYN YAWNED AND scratched his tummy as he sprawled across the window seat. To anyone observing him, he was idly watching the comings and goings on the long road down to Mage Isle. In fact, he was waiting for Jakulos to slip off to the privy at the end of the hall.

The big sea-hound went every morning around this time. Sure enough, he stood, stretched and headed off.

Fyn's heart rate picked up a notch, but he continued to casually swing his bare foot. Bantam sat at the table, practising card tricks. His nimble fingers flew as he made the cards dance. Then he reached for another sticky date bun.

'Hey, leave one for me,' Fyn protested. He stood and came towards the table, passing behind Bantam to reach for a bun.

But his hands went for the man's neck instead. One arm slipped around Bantam's throat, the other applied pressure directly to the artery on the side of his neck and, at the same time, Fyn pulled him backwards off the chair, so that he was unbalanced, his legs scrambling for purchase.

He'd seen the weapons master knock out an acolyte in a matter of heartbeats like this. The youth had woken soon after with a thumping headache, nothing more.

Bantam's fingers went for Fyn's arm, trying to pry him off. This was the mistake of the untrained. The weapons master had shown the acolytes how to break this hold. You had to turn your throat into the crook of the elbow, giving yourself a little more room and time, then go for your captor's fingers, bending them back and breaking them.

Fyn applied even more pressure to the big vein that ran up Bantam's throat. Soon the little sea-hound's struggles slowed.

Fyn held on, counting to twenty. When he was sure Bantam was out cold, he released him, carried him to the bunk, and left him safe.

Quickly, Fyn grabbed his boots, not yet slipping them on. Then he went to the door. No sign of Jakulos, he'd be a while yet.

Pausing, he glanced once more around the room, then darted through the door, closing it softly after him. He headed down the stairs, all seven flights, bare feet flying almost soundlessly.

At ground level he slipped on the boots and walked casually out through the cinnamon-tea room, as though he hadn't been a captive here for the last three days.

Out on the street, he blended with the busy Ostronite people, making his way down the road towards Mage Isle. Just another sailor on shore leave. No one gave him a second glance.

Twenty minutes later, as Fyn crossed the causeway to the island, he noted the solid gate tower. These were the first strong defences he had seen on Ostron Isle. Tsulamyth's miniature island kingdom would not be taken easily.

At the gate, he knocked and waited. A slot opened and someone peered out.

'I wish to speak with the mage,' Fyn said. Would Tsulamyth deign to see him? Back in the room it had seemed so simple.

'And who are you?'

'I can tell only the mage.' Without his royal emblem how could he prove his claim to the throne? Fyn expelled his breath in annoyance. He'd been so intent on getting away from the sea-hounds, he really hadn't thought this through. Maybe he should give up and go barter his way onto a merchant ship headed for Rolencia.

'Why should I let you in?' the gate-keeper asked.

Was he angling for a bribe? Fyn wondered. The abbey hadn't prepared him for this.

Of course...

Wordlessly, he tugged at the Fate's chain, pulling it free. As it swung in front of the gate-keeper's gaze, Fyn focused his Affinity and the opal began to glow.

The slot closed abruptly and, after some clanking, the small postern gate swung open. Fyn tucked the

Fate away and entered a dark tunnel that gave out onto a leafy courtyard. With the Fate, he'd have no trouble convincing the mage he was from Halcyon Abbey. But how was he going to convince him he was Fyn Rolen Kingson?

As the gate-keeper trotted ahead of Fyn, leading him out into the sunlight, Fyn's step faltered. What if he did convince Tsulamyth of his identity, and the mage betrayed him to the Merofynians?

Too late to back out now. He would just have to keep his wits about him.

In the centre of the courtyard was an ancient peppercorn tree. Willow-like, its long, fine branches trailed almost to the paving. The smell of horses came from an open double door and light came through from another courtyard beyond this. Washing, strung from one corner of the courtyard to the other, flapped in the light breeze. A flute's rippling tune flowed from an open window somewhere above. Buildings of between two and four storeys surrounded them but did not crowd the courtyard. Permeating all was the sweet smell of baking bread. It hung on the air, making Fyn's stomach rumble.

A boy of about eleven threw a rag-ball for a puppy, while a smaller lad cheered them on.

The gate-keeper turned to Fyn. 'Wait here. I'll see if one of the mage's agents will meet you.' He went over to the boys and sent the older one off with a message, before going back to his post.

Fyn leant against a mounting block, crossing his legs at the ankles. Here he was, about to walk into the spider's web. The mystics master would be horrified.

*   *   *

PIRO NUDGED ISOLT. 'See that man? I think he's one of Palatyne's spies.'

They sat on travelling chests, waiting while the servants set up Isolt's tent. Other servants had already started the cooking fires. Because the kingsdaughter was on a pilgrimage, she could not stay with any of the nobles. She had to walk and sleep on the ground. This was interpreted to mean servants carried her things and set up a tent with carpets and every luxury she could ask for. Piro found the Merofynian interpretation amusing.

Estates and farms they passed along the way had only been too happy to give them fresh bread, eggs and a chicken or two.

'The man who's missing most of his left ear?' Isolt whispered.

Piro nodded. 'I think I remember his ugly face from the ship.'

'Well, it won't do him any good. The abbess allows no men past the abbey's outer courtyard.' Isolt squeezed Piro's hand. 'Only another six days. And once I take the acolyte's vows, we'll be safe. No one, not even Father can touch us.'

Piro smiled, but she was not so sure. Palatyne struck her as a man who would not be thwarted.

BYREN SURVEYED THE hasty camp, set in the Foenix Spar foothills. Thanks to the elderly and the mothers with small children it had taken the better part of three days to make it over the pass. Byren had left

Catillum and his monks to defend the rear, while forging ahead to catch up with Florin and the others.

First he caught up with Old Man Narrows, who said they'd been sighted as soon as they came down out of the pass, which meant word would have reached the warlord.

Good. He did not want his people having to spend another night in the open. This was not an invasion, so they did not attempt to hide their camp, but he felt vulnerable, with makeshift shelters spread out over the only patch of relatively flat land they could find.

Now he went in search of Florin.

Leaving the path, he climbed across boulders to reach the lookout where she watched for signs of Foenix warriors or messengers. It wasn't because he wanted to stretch out on a rock in the sun with her... well, only partly. No, he wanted to thank her for bringing his people safely over the Divide and share details of how they had tricked the Merofynian advance party. She'd enjoy hearing about that.

Old Man Narrows had said to follow this path and just around the bend he'd find...

'Come on,' a male cajoled.

Byren froze. He'd thought Florin was alone. He knew that voice, Winterfall. Since when did he fancy Florin? And Byren thought he'd made it clear she wasn't to be treated like a camp follower, but one of his warriors.

'Just one kiss.' Impatience drove the voice.

'Get your hands off me,' Florin muttered, annoyed rather than frightened.

Scuffling.

'Come on.' Rough now. 'Why are you playing

hard to get?'

Byren didn't like the growing anger in Winterfall's voice. He started forwards. They'd be in sight once he rounded this bend.

'Ah, I see,' Winterfall mocked. 'You're saving yourself for him. He'll never bed you. If he'd wanted a quick tumble, he'd have had you by now.'

Byren hesitated. Florin had her eye on one of his men? Why should he feel betrayed?

'I don't want him,' she protested. 'I don't want any man. I've sworn my service to Sylion.'

Winterfall laughed. 'Don't lie. I've seen the way you look at him, when he's not watching. You're sick with love for –'

'You two up there,' a voice shouted from far below. 'Let your master know Warlord Feid approaches.'

Byren backed off, turned and ran lightly down the slope, then pretended to be making his way up to the lookout.

Winterfall and Florin nearly barrelled into him as he rounded a large, rocky overhang.

'Feid's coming,' Winterfall gasped.

'Good. You lead him up to meet me. I'll go back to the edge of camp. Come on, Florin.'

She fell into step with him as Winterfall veered off. Byren didn't know what to say. He could hardly admit to overhearing.

'Will Feid support you? Can we trust him?' Florin asked. No hesitation, no awareness of him as anything other than her king.

'Apart from the occasional hot-head, the warlords of Foenix Spar have always supported Rolencia's kings. But the people of the spars respect strength, and...' Byren wondered if news of Palatyne's elevation to duke of Merofynia had reached the warlords yet. If one of their Merofynian counterparts could conquer Rolencia and rise so high, why should the warlords honour an oath of fealty?

'And you come to him, laden with more families than warriors,' Florin finished for him.

Byren nodded. They'd reached the camp. 'Find Orrie and your father. I want them at my back when I meet him.'

She hurried off. What was he going to do with her? How was he going to protect her from the likes of Winterfall?

In a short time, Byren had gathered his honour guard and chosen supporters for when he would meet the warlord. The trail opened up briefly. Amongst the rocks and patches of snow grew bright green grass and spring wild flowers. Most were still buds, but a few had bloomed, their scent piercingly sweet on the cold air.

He watched the sloping path.

Winterfall rounded the bend first, followed by Feid and five of the spar warlord's honour guard astride wiry mountain ponies. For all Byren knew, Warlord Feid might have a hundred warriors waiting around the bend to slaughter his people.

Feid came to a stop while Winterfall stepped past Byren and joined the others.

'Wait here,' Byren told his honour guard as he walked forwards alone, displaying a confidence he did not feel.

Warlord Feid and his five warriors waited at the end of the open ground, making Byren come to them. As he approached, he studied their faces, trying to gauge their mood. Only last midwinter he had drunk at the same table as Feid and arm wrestled him, beating him two times out of three.

Then the warlord had laughed and drunk to his health, but now he watched Byren coldly, one hand on his sword hilt. Feid was in the prime of life, perhaps eight years older than Byren, and he had always kept his own counsel when visiting Rolenhold to give his oath of fealty, unlike some of the other warlords who blustered and crowed like roosters squaring off.

'Warlord Feid,' Byren greeted him. 'I see a man who stood before my father last midwinter and swore fealty.'

'I see a man with a couple of hundred hungry, footsore followers. I see a king without a kingdom,' Feid said.

'I see a warlord who is a prisoner on his own spar,' Byren countered. 'I see a warlord who must pay taxes to our ancestral enemy. Is the warlord of Foenix Spar a servant of Merofynia?'

Feid's honour guard shifted angrily. Responding to this, their ponies whickered and shuffled until the riders brought them under control. Fury tightened the warlord's features. Byren wondered if he'd pushed too far.

'My enemy is your enemy,' Byren said.

The five warriors looked to their leader.

The warlord of Foenix Spar swung a leg over his pony and dropped to the ground, marching forwards to meet Byren, who wasn't sure until the last moment if Feid was going to draw his sword and gut him, or hug him.

Enveloped in a hug, Byren felt a rush of relief. He had his first ally. Tonight his people would eat and sleep in warm beds. One obstacle down. More to come. While he had Foenix and Unistag Spars' support, he still had to convince the other warlords to back him. Even with all the spar warlords behind him, his army would be outnumbered.

Feid stepped back and his warriors relaxed, greeting Byren like a long-lost brother. If Feid had ordered it they would have slaughtered him with as much enthusiasm.

'You came over the old pass,' Feid said, as Byren's honour guard approached. 'Now Rolencia knows all Foenix Spar's secrets!'

He grinned, but Byren realised there was truth to what he said. He put a hand on Feid's shoulder. 'There should be no need for secrets between a king and his warlords.'

'Then let us hope you live long enough to be king,' Feid said softly, before raising his voice. 'Welcome to Foenix Spar, Byren Kingsheir. Tonight we feast!'

LEANING AGAINST THE mounting block, Fyn fought a growing sense of oppression. His heart picked up speed, beating in time to the tempo of the flute's tune. What if he was walking into a trap? The flute music seemed to swirl down from above, stirring the washing on the line, stirring the air around him, beating against him.

A headache built behind his eyes, beating in time to his racing heart. What if the mage turned him over to the Merofynians?

Someone knocked on the gate – a messenger, going by the gate-keeper's greeting. The gate opened and the man entered the long dark tunnel that led to the courtyard. He exchanged a word or two with the gate-keeper in the Ostronite tongue but that didn't mean he wasn't Merofynian. The sound of his horse's hooves echoed down the passage as he approached. Each clip of the hooves made Fyn's head hurt more.

As Fyn watched the entrance to the courtyard, tension coiled in his belly. This was a mistake. He shouldn't have come here.

Meanwhile, the scruffy little lad picked up the rag ball and, with his equally scruffy puppy trotting at his heels, walked around Fyn, studying him. The lilting flute seemed to follow him, plucking at Fyn's peace of mind, urging him to flee while he still could.

'What happened to your hair?' the boy asked. His Ostronite accent was that of the streets, but Fyn had no trouble understanding him. 'Did it get cut off because you were sick?'

This was as good an explanation as any, so Fyn nodded, while keeping an eye on the courtyard entrance. If only his head would stop hurting, then he'd be able to think clearly. When the flute's tempo rose, his headache went up a notch. The messenger was almost out of the gate tunnel. Fyn could still escape.

The boy scooped up his puppy, thrusting the

ungainly creature in Fyn's face. 'Do you like him? I named him Rolen. But now that the king is dead I might name him Merofyn.'

Fyn summoned a smile he did not feel. 'You must have high hopes for that scruffy pup, if you name him after kings.'

'He's going to be a guard dog. He's already a great ratter!'

Amused despite his fears, Fyn gave a soft snort of laughter. 'He's not much bigger than a rat.'

The boy looked offended and turned to go, putting the pup down just as the messenger rode in. He wore no Merofynian insignia, but then a spy wouldn't.

The flute struck a high note. The horse took offence to something – the flapping washing if not the flute, for it was far too shrill.

The messenger's mount reared. The puppy panicked, running under the horse. The boy cried out and ran after it. Fyn grabbed the lad, dragging him from under the hooves, and they were both knocked off their feet.

As he tried to control the frightened horse, the man cursed roundly in Merofynian, confirming Fyn's fears.

Fyn should leave now, while he still could.

Quite unhurt, the puppy came back to the boy and the music dropped to a teasing background whisper. Fyn sat up, his sailor's breeches muddied, his boots scuffed, his heart still racing. Meanwhile, the man dismounted, trying to soothe his horse as it danced away, hooves clattering on the paving.

Once the horse had calmed, he strode over, clearly furious. Fyn felt exposed, but even if this was a

Merofynian spy, the man could not know who Fyn was, so he held his ground.

The messenger loomed over him and the boy. 'Watch it, brat. You're lucky the dog isn't mince meat.'

'He's a good dog,' the boy protested.

Fyn hushed him. The man sent them both a contemptuous look before leading his mount into the stables.

The puppy licked the boy's face and made a swipe at Fyn.

Fyn came to his feet. 'Are you hurt, lad?'

'No.' But when the child tried to stand, he clutched his foot whimpering. Fyn could see a nasty bruise developing.

'I want Ma,' the boy wailed.

Fyn looked around, hoping the boy's mother would hear him, but no one came. There was no sign of the gate-keeper or the older brother, either. If Fyn slipped away now the Merofynian would never know, but he couldn't leave the boy like this.

'Where's your mother?'

The child pointed up, to where the music came from. It appeared his mother was the minstrel, a very accomplished one if the complexity of the tune was anything to go by. Fyn lifted the boy.

'Don't forget my puppy.'

With a sigh, Fyn bent down and the boy scooped up the pup, hugging him to his chest, covering Fyn in shaggy dog hairs. Following the child's directions Fyn carried him across the courtyard to a small door and up a narrow flight of steps, all accompanied by the flute. Only now the lilting music seemed friendly rather than disturbing.

The door opened on a small room with a steep ceiling and a single window. A shaft of sunlight came through the window, hitting the floor and reflecting on the ceiling. The sun illuminated a low foot-stool, where a fancy silver flute sat.

As Fyn stepped into the doorway the last flute note faded softly. No, that couldn't be right. Unless the flute was much more than it seemed.

Fear made Fyn's skin tighten as he opened his senses to Affinity. Power emanated from the person who sat in the only chair beyond the patch of sunlight, face hidden in shadow. The older boy crouched by the chair, eyes glistening, reflecting the sunlight, his gaze curiously blank.

Fyn's chest felt tight and his breath solid. Somehow, he managed to swallow.

As if waking, the older boy focused on his little brother. 'Ovido.'

He sprang to his feet, crossing the patch of sunlight to join Fyn. The puppy barked a greeting.

The boy wriggled in Fyn's arms, indicating he wanted to be put down. He hugged his brother. 'My head was hurting but it's stopped now.'

Head hurting? Fyn winced at his blindness as his own headache still thundered behind his eyes. The classic sign of an Affinity assault. Why hadn't he recognised it for what it was? And he'd thought himself well trained to resist an Affinity renegade's attack.

'Silly Ovido,' the brother said fondly. 'You and your headaches. Come on.'

As they darted out the door, Fyn noted that the little boy no longer limped.

Silence settled in the room. Fyn stared, trying to make sense of the person seated beyond the shaft of sunlight, wrapped in shadows that seemed to resist his gaze.

Fyn's teeth throbbed and his headache eased, as the silhouette resolved itself into a masculine outline. Everything all fell into place. He and the boy had been manipulated. By this man.

He might not have sensed the Affinity attack when it first started, but he had fought it all the same. By resisting it and the urge to run, Fyn had done what he believed to be right, despite the risk to himself. This had been a test, a very subtle test of his mettle.

Fyn might not have a strong Affinity but he could sense the force of it coming from the stranger now. It reminded him of Palatyne's Utland Power-worker, who had radiated ice-cold Affinity like a forge radiated heat. But the Utlander had been bluffing and had dropped the pretext the moment it was no longer needed.

If this stranger was trying to impress Fyn, he had.

The stranger stood, reaching for the flute, which leaped off the foot stool and into his hands. He tucked it under one arm as he stepped into the sunlight, but only far enough to reveal his elegant clothes. His face remained in shadow. 'I am one of Mage Tsulamyth's agents, and you were told to wait.'

'Some things cannot wait,' Fyn said slowly. 'Besides, you were testing me. Did I pass?'

The other stiffened slightly.

Fyn allowed himself a small smile.

'You must forgive me,' the agent said, though it was more of an order than an apology. He stepped closer. 'The mage likes to know what manner of man he deals with.'

Now that Fyn could see the stranger's face, he was startled. Since Tsulamyth was so old and powerful, Fyn had expected his agents to be at least as old as his father, but this man looked about Byren's age, only his eyes were older. 'You're the mage's agent?'

'One of them. You can call me Tyro.'

He was taller than Fyn, but who wasn't? His body held a wiry strength, different from Byren, who was more densely muscled. Fyn guessed the agent would move fast if attacked.

He swallowed. If the mage's agent was this powerful, the mage himself must be truly impressive, which meant Fyn was out-classed. But he had known that when he decided to approach Tsulamyth.

'Come this way.' A section of the plastered ceiling swung down to reveal stairs. Fyn followed the agent up the narrow steps into what had to be the roof cavity. This opened into another building entirely.

They went down corridors and around corners until, finally, double doors parted to reveal a large, circular chamber. At the far end, through a set of doors, inset with glass panels, Fyn could see a balcony that looked out onto the distant inner slope of Ostron Ring.

Sunlight reflected from the Ring Sea below, ripples dancing across the chamber's white ceiling. Combined with the blue-green floor tiles this made Fyn feel as if he was beneath the waves.

In the centre of the room was a war table similar to his father's, only this one was twice the length of a tall man. Down the end nearest to Fyn was Ostron Isle, and about halfway along came Merofynia with its crescent opening to the south, then the Snow Bridge, its mountains taller than anywhere else, and then Rolencia with its north-opening crescent.

On the blue, ripple-glass sea were miniature boats, just as there were miniature buildings on the land masses and quite a few carved people. They were out of proportion, as tall as the model ships' masts. Fyn guessed they were pieces from the game of Duelling Kingdoms, but there were more of them than in a Kingdoms game. Everything else was to scale and cleverly made. Fyn went to pick up the nearest boat, to admire its workmanship.

'Ah, I wouldn't do that if I were you,' Agent Tyro advised then turned to face him. 'You impressed the gate-keeper with an Affinity tool. Show me.'

What if the agent demanded he hand over the Fate?

It wasn't his to give. Nevertheless, Fyn tugged on the chain, bringing it up for the agent to see. Would Tyro recognise it?

'Halcyon's Fate. How did it fall into the hands of a sea-hound?'

'I'm not a sea-hound. I'm...' Fyn hesitated, not sure if he should reveal who he really was. 'I'm from Halcyon Abbey and I'm –'

'Here to see Mage Tsulamyth. Why, if not to ask for his help against Merofynia?'

Fyn nodded, almost wishing it unsaid. What if the

mage refused to help him? Worse, what if the mage agreed, but his terms were impossible? Would the agent let Fyn leave? He doubted he could even find his way out.

'Why should the mage help a penniless monk?' Tyro asked. 'Do you offer the Fate?'

'It's not mine to barter with.'

'Good. The mage would have turned you down. He has Affinity tools aplenty.'

The silence stretched. Fyn wondered what came next. Should he plead his case?

'Perhaps the mage knows more than you think,' Tyro said, voice silky. Fyn mistrusted his shrewd black eyes and felt a moment's disorientation as the agent picked up a Kingdoms piece. 'Here's a cunningly wrought piece, King Rolen's third son, masquerading as a lowly monk. Many believe him dead. This means he can go places no one expects.'

Fyn hid his surprise. Had he given himself away or was it a guess? Whatever happened, he had to keep Byren safe.

Tyro studied the carving. When he tilted the Kingdoms piece this way and that, Fyn felt the room sway. No, he was disoriented by the rippling light dancing across the ceiling.

'Now what would King Rolen's youngest son want, I wonder,' Tyro whispered. 'Vengeance?'

'I don't know. I can only speak as a monk.'

The agent's black gaze flew to his face. Then, as if he had come to a decision, Tyro put the piece in his pocket. 'The mage might have a use for one of Halcyon's monks, trained in the martial arts. If this monk proved loyal, the mage would look more kindly upon his request.'

He beckoned Fyn and walked to the far end of the war table.

Tyro pointed to ships making their way through the Rolencian Straits past the warlords' spars, weaving through the Utlands around to Merofynia. 'These are merchant ships returning to King Merofyn with the stolen wealth of Rolencia. Before leaving Rolencia, Palatyne ordered forts built on the passes over the Divide to keep the warlords in line and he has crushed the might of Halcyon Abbey.'

'What of Sylion?' Fyn asked.

'They had warning and sealed their gates. Palatyne is not worried about them as their power wanes with winter's passing. But the valley merchants, the fisher folk and farmers are vulnerable.'

Fyn felt this as if it was his personal failing. His family had a duty to protect the people of Rolencia.

'Palatyne has appointed Cobalt as his puppet king. Cobalt has declared Rolen and Myrella's marriage illegal because, according to him, the Merofynian kingsdaughter had Affinity. This makes his claim to the throne as good as any of King Rolen's kin.'

Fyn blinked. Cobalt had done this? It made no sense, not when he'd asked Fyn to find Byren so they could defeat the Merofynians. But he'd also warned Fyn, he would have to do things that made it appear he was Byren's enemy.

The agent continued. 'Palatyne has been rewarded with a dukedom but this does not satisfy him. He plans to wed –'

'King Merofyn's daughter,' Fyn guessed.

'Exactly.' Tyro strode past the Snow Bridge until he reached Merofynia. 'According to my sources, she is travelling along the coast road to Cyena Abbey. It would interfere greatly with Palatyne's plans if someone prevented this marriage.'

Murder a girl hardly older than Piro? Fyn took an instinctive step back, hands lifting in denial. 'I won't do it.'

The agent was silent for a moment, watching him from eyes that seemed to weigh his soul.

'Why not?' the agent countered. 'Her betrothal to Lence Kingsheir lulled King Rolen into a false sense of security and gave Palatyne his chance to invade. Surely, she is as false-hearted as her father? Agree to serve the mage and he will place a ship at your disposal, as well as trained men.'

Fyn knew that without the mage's help he could not hope to aid Byren. Yet... his brother would not ask him to murder Isolt, who could yet prove to be innocent.

He could not do it. Best to be honest.

'Back in Port Marchand, I had Palatyne defenceless under my knife and I could not kill him. If I could not kill an ambitious murderer to avenge my family, I could never kill a girl who might be innocent.' His mind raced as he tried to come up with an argument to convince the agent.

Tyro's face remained impassive. Fyn wondered if he was communicating directly with the mage. There had been hints of this sort of thing in the abbey scrolls.

'What do we know about Isolt? King Merofyn might have arranged the betrothal without her knowledge.' Fyn met Tyro's eyes and held them. 'I will not become an assassin, not even for the mage's goodwill.'

'Excellent.' Tyro smiled slowly, the skin at the corner of his eyes crinkling. 'How are you at abduction?'

A weight lifted from Fyn.

Chapter Thirteen

THAT EVENING IT rained heavily, so the mage's agent sent Fyn in a closed carriage, through the streets of Ostron Isle to the dock where a ship waited.

Fyn glanced through the downpour, spotting three sails, and knew it was a fast-moving sloop like the *Wyvern's Whelp*, probably a sea-hound. Grabbing his borrowed bag with a change of clothes, he ducked out of the carriage, head down, and ran up the gangplank, across the deck and into the captain's cabin.

Where Nefysto awaited him.

Blinking rain from his eyes, Fyn spun around to find Jakulos and Bantam on either side of the door.

The little quarter-master rubbed his throat. 'I had a thundering headache, thanks to you.'

'You made us both look fools,' Jakulos said.

Fyn stiffened. 'I swore no oath to the sea-hounds, my loyalty lies elsewhere.'

'See, revenge motivates him,' Nefysto said. 'If you know what a man will die for, you know him.'

Fyn spun to face the captain. 'You let me think you reported to the elector, but you report to the mage. Why didn't you tell me?'

Nefysto grinned and tapped the side of his nose.

Ostronites were known to play their cards close to their chests. Fyn felt the ship shift, as the oars pushed them away from the dock, and automatically adjusted his stance.

'Let's see what our orders are.' Nefysto unrolled a message and appeared to read it, but Fyn knew it was all an act.

'It seems I am to offer the mage's new agent all assistance.' Nefysto rolled up the message. 'Runt, take Agent Monk's bag and show him to his cabin.'

Fyn didn't know what to say. The captain threw back his head, laughing. Bantam and Jakulos joined in. It was true, sea-hounds were half-crazy.

With their hilarity echoing in his ears, Fyn followed the cabin boy down below to one of the little cabins tucked under the captain's. It was only as he lay down to sleep that he remembered Nefysto had said his original orders were to keep Fyn captive.

Why would the mage want him locked up?

The same reason he wanted Fyn to abduct King Merofyn's daughter. The more Kingdoms pieces the mage had to play with, the more chance he had of winning. But what prize was Tsulamyth playing for?

Fyn let out his breath. What did it matter, as long as it helped Byren recover Rolencia?

* * *

BYREN WENT IN search of Florin.

He and his honour guard had been given the warlord's best chamber, reserved for visiting royalty. His head rang with voices and noise. From one end of the warlord's stronghold to the other, people packed every available space. Many of Byren's company had been taken into the homes that dotted the slope down to the fjord, and the rest tried to squeeze into Feid's stronghold, crowding the warlord's own honour guard.

The majority of Feid's men were still out on their farmsteads, awaiting the call to arms. By spar custom, his honour guard numbered over ninety, which meant the stronghold was filled to capacity with men. And these men would see any unattached woman as fair game. After Winterfall's none-too-subtle attempt to seduce Florin, Byren wanted her safe.

Not that she would thank him.

He should be upstairs, enjoying a hot bath with the offer of a willing serving girl, before dressing for the feast. Instead, he was searching for the ungrateful mountain girl.

He found Old Man Narrows in the stable, sorting out a fight between a couple of lads who should have known better. A quick clip over the ear and both were sent about their business.

'At the feast tonight, I want you at the warlord's table,' Byren said, 'where you can listen in to what we're planning and give your opinion.'

Old Man Narrows rubbed his thick fingers. 'Eh, I'm flattered, lad, but wouldn't you rather I'm down with the men, where I can keep an eye on the hotheads and listen in to what's being said? You've got Orrie at the table, not much gets past the young Dove.'

Byren grinned. He wondered if Orrade was aware that he had inherited his father's nickname. And Old Man Narrows had a point.

The former tradepost keeper beckoned Leif and rested his hands on his young son's shoulders. 'From the stables and the kitchen I'll hear things you wouldn't hear otherwise.'

'You're right.' Now to what was really worrying him. 'Where will you be bunking down?'

Old Man Narrows nodded to the stable loft. 'Here, where I can keep an eye on the lads.'

'Fair enough.' But what about Florin? If she wandered the stronghold with the freedom she was used to back at camp, Feid's warriors would consider her fair game. He didn't want her having to box some lout's ears, or worse, to convince him to leave her alone. 'Where's Florin?'

'Over back.' Narrows gestured.

'No, Da,' Leif said. 'She went up the loft to make up our beds.'

So Byren climbed up to find her in the sweet-smelling hay, making up beds in the dimness. He did his best not to think about the last lass he'd tumbled in Rolenhold's hayloft. 'Eh, Mountain-girl.'

Florin turned. 'Yes, my king.'

He didn't think she was still angry with him. It had become a nickname now, like his use of Mountain-girl. Both of them had to duck their heads to avoid the beams. He rested his forearm on one. 'You're not sleeping here.'

'Here's fine by me.'

It was too dim to judge her expression, but her tone said she'd enjoy an argument, especially with him. Why couldn't she be more like his mother, and bend before the wind? He needed a reason for her to cooperate, after all he was only trying to look out for her. And it came to him.

'I didn't come here to argue. The warlord has a pretty new bride. Someone has to get close to her, to find out what he's telling her.'

Florin looked uneasy. 'I know nothing about courts and courtiers.'

'Neither does she. They say he found her in the kitchen of a merchant house last trip he made to Ostron Isle.' Orrade had reported this choice gossip to Byren. Along with the news that the warlord's new lady was lonely, since she wasn't used to spar customs. Why Feid had married outside of his spar, Byren didn't know, although going by the way the warlord's eyes lit up when he said her name, it was a love match. 'She's as much out of her depth as you. She's only been here since late last summer.' And already swelling with child. Life was short on the spars, and they bred fast. 'Will you befriend her for me, share the secrets women share?'

'I don't know.' Florin brushed her hands down her thighs. 'I've never had a female friend, but I can try.'

So he explained the gist of what he needed to her father and took her up to the warlord's private chambers.

After rapping on the door, he turned to Florin,

noticed a piece of straw in her hair and reached to pluck it out. Her hand lifted to fend him off. He caught it. 'Eh, lass. I'd never do wrong by you. You had straw in your hair.'

She blinked, then flicked free of his touch and ran her hands through her hair, plucking the straw free. Byren wanted to say something about Winterfall but just then the warlord himself opened the door.

There was laughter in his voice and a smile on his face. 'Byren?' He glanced curiously to Florin.

'Feid, this is...' Now that he came to it, how was he going to introduce her? He could not say, this is the lass I want, but I can't have her, so I don't want anyone else to have her. 'This is Florin. She saved my life and, when I'm king, I mean to see her set up for life.' As he said it, he realised this much was true. He hadn't been able to save Elina or his mother, but he would make sure that Florin was safe.

'Cinna, come here,' Feid called.

A pretty lass, with her hair all atumble, peered around the door. Feid dragged her against his body with a possessive air. Byren held his breath as Feid's lady looked Florin up and down, taking in her men's clothes and her dirty face. A kitchen maid, elevated to the status of a lady, might just turn her nose up at Florin. Many would.

'You poor thing,' Cinna exclaimed in Ostronite. As she drew Florin into the chamber, she switched to heavily accented Rolencian, talking about a bath and clothing altered to fit.

Florin cast a desperate look over her shoulder, but allowed Cinna to lead her off, and all Byren could hear was the lady's happy chatter.

Feid stepped out of the chamber, closing the door after him. 'She's got a kind heart, Cinna. She'll find a husband for your lass, if you want.'

'No.' Byren spoke too quickly. 'At least, not just yet. I'm going to clean up for the feast. You know, I won't forget this, Feid.'

He grinned. 'That's what I'm counting on.'

Much later that night, Byren stood on the stronghold's tallest tower, watching the stars.

He grinned to himself.

Florin had come down to the feast in a borrowed gown, one made for someone a head shorter – it revealed her calves rather than her ankles, but it clung elsewhere, being laced around the waist. When he'd asked her to dance she'd refused, saying she didn't know any dances fit for court. Byren would hardly call Feid's great hall a fancy court, but he'd told the musicians to play a country dance. To which she'd insisted she never danced. He'd told her she did now because it was the only chance she'd have to report what she'd learnt so far.

He smiled, remembering how quickly she'd picked up the steps and how earnestly she'd related her observations of Lady Cinna. All of which had been quite innocent, if revealing of Florin's discomfort with her current situation.

But the smile soon left his face. Though he was exhausted, Byren could not sleep. He paced the tower. Tomorrow Warlord Feid would send four swift boats to the other spars, calling on the warlords to support the rightful king of Rolencia.

All Byren could do now was wait, and he hated not being in control. Give him a fort to take, a beast to kill or a border to hold and he would, but this waiting stole a man's spirit.

Someone pushed the trap door open behind him.

'Orrie,' Byren greeted him with relief. 'What brings you up here?'

He was followed by one of the young monks.

'Feldspar has something to tell you,' Orrade said and stepped aside. 'Go on, lad.'

The youth hesitated.

A cold wind cut through Byren's jacket. 'Spit it out.'

'It's the mystics master, kingsheir. Even though he drugs himself each night with dreamless-sleep he moans in his sleep.'

'A man can't be responsible for his nightmares,' Byren said.

'If they are only nightmares,' Feldspar whispered.

'What are you saying?'

'By creating the illusion in the foenix cavern Master Catillum laid himself open to untamed Affinity. I know. I felt him fight it.' Feldspar let out his breath with a shudder. 'I fear he fights it still.'

Byren noticed Orrade touch his sword hilt, and shook his head swiftly. 'We each fight our battles in our own way. The mystics master has proved his loyalty to me, Feldspar. I want you to watch him. If it looks like he's failing to win his private battle, let me know.'

'You can't ask this of me,' Feldspar blurted, backing up a step. 'I'm not trained.'

'Who else can I ask?'

Feldspar gaped.

'Bring word to me, not to Byren,' Orrade said. He caught Byren's eye. 'Catillum might grow suspicious if one of his monks seeks you out.'

Byren nodded, then took pity on the youth. 'Go down to bed, lad.'

When he slipped away, Byren paced and Orrade walked with him.

'I swear it's colder out here on the spar than in Rolencia.' Orrade pulled his cloak more closely around his shoulders. 'Sylion knows, I feel for the mystics master but it'd be safer to kill Catillum now.'

'Safer, but would it be right? A man should have the chance to prove himself. Besides, I'd lose the support of his monks.'

'His death could be made to look like an accident.'

Byren stopped. 'Since when were you so quick to deal in death?'

'Since I became your spymaster.' Orrade faced him. 'I will always tell you the truth, whether you want to hear it or not. If Catillum's Affinity is compromised and we wait too long, it may be too late to contain him. He's powerful, Byren.'

'You're right. But I won't be that kind of ruler, Orrie.' Byren hid his disquiet. 'Catillum's loyal for now. Let's not borrow trouble. We have enough of our own.'

'You stayed your hand the night Dovecote fell. You let Palatyne rape my sister, so the others had time to escape. I thought you hard then –'

'And you think me weak now?' Byren asked, his voice growing tense. The memory of that night still tortured him. It would as long as he lived.

'No...' Orrade admitted. 'I think you've made another hard decision, for the right reason. You see clearly, Byren. Further than me.'

He shook his head. 'Your mind's sharper than mine.'

'Maybe, but perhaps not as...' he shrugged, 'honourable.'

Byren snorted.

'I would kill for you, Byren. Willingly kill to protect you.'

It came to Byren then that Orrade made the best kind of spymaster, ruthless and utterly devoted. 'I'm lucky to have you. Orrade shrugged and resumed pacing. 'We should hear back from Leogryf and Unistag Spars soon. But it will take Feid's messengers longer to reach Manticore and Cockatrice Spars.'

'And who knows if Cockatrice has settled on a warlord, since you killed Rejulas?'

The night Dovecote fell, Orrade had killed the Cockatrice warlord. He'd had no choice for, in the mistaken belief that he was helping Lence seize the crown, Warlord Rejulas had opened his pass to Palatyne, giving him access to Rolencia's soft underbelly.

'The new Cockatrice warlord should be eager to prove his spar's loyalty,' Orrade muttered. 'How long will you wait for the last two warlords' responses? The longer we delay, the more defences will be added to the new fort over Foenix Pass.'

He was right. More decisions. 'Ask me tomorrow.' Byren faked a yawn, which turned into a real one.

'I'm for bed.'

But, even in his bed, he could not sleep. For once, Orrade did not stretch out beside him and Byren missed his presence. His friend was stretched out on the floor, along with the rest of Byren's honour guard. Beyond the bed's rich drapes their snores filled the darkness.

Byren lay on his back, staring up at the canopy, which was all but lost in the darkness, as he wrestled with the decisions he'd made and had yet to make. He wished he had as much faith in himself as Orrade had.

These moral dilemmas were why he had not craved the kingship. How did he know what was the right decision? The crazy old seer had known what she was talking about.

Pity she was long dead.

DUSK, TWO DAYS later, Byren met with Warlord Unace's representative. The uprising had decimated her forces, so she'd sent one of her few surviving kinsmen, an old man with white hair and a tendency to shout due to his deafness. Consequently the meeting was short.

As Master Catillum and Feid escorted Unace's kinsman out of the war table chamber, Byren caught Orrade's arm and they fell behind.

The mystics master glanced over his shoulder, noticed and sent Byren a look of query. Bearing in mind Feldspar's warning, Byren gave a slight shake of his head. The door closed on the others and

Byren wandered over to the window where Orrade joined him. Byren barely noticed the activity in the courtyard three floors below them.

'Unace will send four hundred warriors, mostly untried youths.' Byren rubbed the bridge of his nose. He did not want to send boys to their deaths.

'And no word from Leogryf Spar,' Orrade said.

'Not surprising. He has farther to sail.' Feid's stronghold was on the east coast of Foenix Spar and, on a clear day, they could see the peaks of Unistag Spar. Leogryf Spar was further away, to the west. 'I don't expect to hear from him for a day or two.'

Orrade leant closer to the window, to look down into the courtyard. 'I knew it wouldn't last.' There was a smile in his voice.

Byren followed the direction of his gaze. His people filled the courtyard, sharpening weapons, repairing tack, laughing and talking. Florin moved through, heading for the stables to see her father and brother, no doubt. Byren should have known he couldn't keep her out of harm's way, but still it made his body tense.

'Florin's back in her trews.' Orrade grinned. 'I knew the dress wouldn't last. Mind you, it did look good. I'd no idea she hid a woman's curves under her men's clothing. Maybe I'll ask her to dance tonight.'

'Go right ahead,' Byren said, surprised by the pang it caused him.

But it would be the perfect solution to his problem. With Orrade in Florin's bed, no one would suspect his friend's preference for men, for Byren specifically. The thought of Orrade and Florin together left a bitter taste in Byren's mouth. Since he had no intention of attaching himself to a mountain girl without useful connections, he could not satisfy his itch and besides, Florin deserved more than a tumble in the hay.

With that realisation, Byren wanted to warn Orrade off, unless his intentions were honourable, but his friend was far too perceptive. So he kept his silence.

And he tried not to recall the feel of Florin's waist in his hands as they danced.

Chapter Fourteen

DISGUISED AS A Merofynian merchant ship, flying the azure and black flag, the *Wyvern's Whelp* lay at anchor in a secluded cove not far from Cyena Abbey. Fyn perched on the window seat of the captain's cabin, fingering his dagger hilt. It felt strange having the captain answer to him.

Nefysto had confirmation that Isolt Merofyn Kingsdaughter was making her last camp before reaching Cyena Abbey. Fyn had to act tonight, to save this girl from Palatyne.

If only he'd been in time to save Piro. Despite his best efforts not to, he imagined Piro's last terrifying moments and his stomach churned.

At least he could save this young woman whether she wanted it or not.

Perhaps Isolt thought marriage to Palatyne would make her empress of the known world one day.

She should have been married to Byren.

Fyn sat up.

His mind raced as he made the connections. Isolt had been betrothed to Lence, so his death meant she was betrothed to Byren. His brother needed allies to win back Rolencia. If Fyn subdued Isolt and whisked her back to Mage Isle, then took her to Rolencia to find Byren, his brother could marry her.

Surely, if Byren and Isolt were married, King Merofyn would negotiate peace with his own son-in-law? But that didn't take into account Palatyne.

'Ready, Agent Monk?' Nefysto asked.

Fyn heard mockery every time the captain used this new title, but it was affectionate teasing.

'Ready as I'll ever be.' He came to his feet. Tonight he'd abduct Isolt. Tomorrow, he'd worry about Palatyne.

Dressed in a sailor's rough leggings and jerkin, Fyn stepped onto Merofynia's shore. Bantam and Jakulos pulled the row boat up onto the shingled beach under an overhang, where the stars cast a deep shadow.

'Sure you don't want us to come?' Bantam asked.

Fyn shook his head. Alone, he could slip into the camp, knock Isolt out and get away. He hoped. But with two sea-hounds in tow, the chance of discovery grew and the any ensuing altercation would make success less likely.

After a whispered word of luck from Jakulos, Fyn climbed the slope. He found Isolt's servants had already made camp. Oblivious to threat in their own kingdom, her attendants were relaxed as they wandered through gaily coloured tents and chatted around the cooking fires.

When the camp had settled for the night, Fyn crept stealthily towards the largest tent. The smells of Merofynian cooking still lingered on the night air, reminding him of his mother. Reminding him painfully that he'd lost her.

Dagger ready, Fyn hesitated at the rear of the tent. A knot of tension formed in his belly and fear made his mouth go dry. One outcry and he was dead. Fyn swallowed and tightened his hold on the knife. He would slit the canvas and go in, hold the girl's throat until she passed out, throw her over his shoulder and slip out the same way he'd come in.

His plan clear, Fyn lifted his dagger and slit the tent canvas. It sounded horribly loud in the still night air, but there was no outcry as he slipped inside. The interior was illuminated by the red glow of a brazier. Someone slept on a richly draped, low bunk. Creeping across the carpets, Fyn knelt and looked down on Isolt Kingsdaughter, schemer, betrayer.

In his vision he had seen her speaking, in the portrait he had seen her composed, now he saw her sleeping and his heart contracted. Why, she was smaller than Piro and, without her eyebrows, seemed even younger. Her black hair spread across the pillow, fine as silk, framing a face vulnerable in sleep. Her pale skin was so translucent he could see the tracery of veins on her eyelids. She gave a little moan, as if her dreams were troubled.

How could this innocent-looking young woman be the conniving daughter of King Merofyn, partially responsible for the fall of Rolencia and the death of most of Fyn's family?

Without warning, a small woman tackled Fyn and they fell forwards over the sleeping Isolt. She gave a muffled cry as the travelling bunk collapsed. Desperate not to alert the sentries, he struggled to subdue his attacker, while Isolt writhed to free herself from under him and the tangled bedclothes.

Sharp teeth sank into his forearm. Cursing, Fyn came to his feet. Manoeuvring his attacker so that her back was pressed to his chest, he held his dagger to her throat. His forearm stung with the imprint of her teeth. Silky dark hair tickled his nose and he could feel his captive's heart hammering, but he concentrated on Isolt, who stood on the far side of the splintered bunk.

Her frightened eyes darted from his face to the entrance beyond, as she calculated the odds of help coming before he killed them both. 'Don't hurt her,' she pleaded.

The serving girl jerked her head back, striking Fyn's nose. Tears of pain filled his eyes but his hold didn't weaken.

'Little wyvern!' Blinking to clear his vision, he spoke thickly through his throbbing nose. 'One word, kingsdaughter, and I *will* slit her throat!'

'It is a brave man who kills sleeping women,' Isolt told him haughtily. 'Strange. I thought Palatyne would wait until after we were married and I had given him an heir before having me murdered.'

Fyn gasped. 'If you believe he plans to kill you, then why are you marrying him?'

She glared at him. 'I will not debate marriage with a treacherous assassin!'

Anger flooded Fyn. 'That's right, you are an expert at treachery. You betrothed yourself to Lence Kingsheir, while sending an army to crush Rolencia!'

'I didn't know anything about that betrothal.'

'You sent your portrait on a pendant.'

'A portrait meant for my father.'

It could be true, but his brother was still dead. The pain of loss tore at Fyn, making his voice ragged. 'Lence gave his betrothal vows in good faith and now he's dead.'

'And I'm sorry for it,' Isolt insisted. 'But truly, I did not know.'

Fyn hesitated. Had Isolt been an innocent piece in a game of Duelling Kingdoms she knew nothing about?

'Fyn? Is it really you?' Isolt's maid craned her head to see his face. 'Don't you know your own sister?'

'Piro?' Disbelievingly, he released her and his sister turned to face him. 'Piro... They told me you were dead.'

She laughed, but pain haunted her eyes. Then she noticed his swollen nose. 'You're bleeding.'

'Find something to clean him up,' Isolt ordered, but Piro had already darted across the room to a pitcher of water.

Delighted and a little stunned, Fyn watched his sister return with a bowl of water and a cloth.

'Sit down,' Isolt said, pushing his chest. He dropped onto a stool. Isolt lit a candle then turned his face to the light. A pucker of concern between her plucked brows, she cleaned the blood from his mouth and chin.

'Did I break his nose?' Piro asked, as she went around behind him, standing with her hands on his shoulders.

'I don't think so,' Isolt said. 'But it must hurt.'

'Only a little,' Fyn lied.

Isolt ignored him and rinsed the cloth. Folding it, she pressed it to his nose. 'Tilt your head back.'

'I am sorry, Fyn.' Piro's eyes twinkled above, as she supported his head. 'At least I didn't forget what you taught me.'

He grinned weakly. 'You're a sight for sore eyes. Why does everyone think you're dead? How did you come to be maidservant to King Merofyn's daughter?'

'I let them think another girl's body was mine and Lord Dunstany, the king's Power-worker, claimed me for his slave. Then Palatyne asked for me and gifted me to Isolt. How did you escape?'

'No time now,' Fyn told her, focused on his mission and Isolt. 'I've come to rescue you. My ship is waiting.' He could not help searching Isolt's face to see if she was impressed.

She removed the cloth. 'Good, the bleeding has stopped.' After dropping the bloodied cloth in the bowl, she turned away without meeting his eyes or commenting.

'This is perfect, Isolt,' Piro said. 'My brother can get us away from Merofynia. I didn't say it before, but I think King Merofyn and Palatyne could force the abbess to hand you over even if you became a nun.'

'We can't go to Rolencia,' Isolt said. 'We'd have to go to –'

'Ostron Isle. The elector always remains neutral so he can profit from our wars,' Fyn said, as he came to his feet. The longer they delayed, the more chance there was of discovery. 'If Palatyne gets his hands on Piro or me, our lives are forfeit. Come with me, Isolt, and I promise you'll be safe from Palatyne.'

'It means placing myself under the elector's protection and becoming a pawn in his power games.' Her black eyes blazed. 'But it's better than becoming Palatyne's trophy queen!'

'Good. Now, all we have to do is get out of here.' Piro turned expectantly to Fyn.

This was better than Fyn had hoped, his sister back from the dead and Isolt Kingsdaughter cooperating in her own abduction. Only now he wasn't kidnapping her, he was rescuing her. 'We'll slip out the back of the tent and down to the... What are you doing?'

Isolt and Piro had begun sorting clothes.

'I can't go dressed only in my night gown,' Isolt pointed out.

It was rose-coloured silk, so fine it was almost transparent. Fyn looked away quickly and cleared his throat. 'You must leave everything. Make it look like you were taken against your will.'

'Good idea. That will confuse Palatyne's spy,' Piro said, tipping over a chest and spilling its contents to make it appear there'd been a struggle. She tipped the water from the bowl and draped the bloodied cloth artistically on an upturned stool. 'This will convince them!'

'Excellent.' Isolt beamed, then turned to Fyn. 'What about shoes? And a cloak to keep out the chill?'

'Take nothing. I have a boat waiting, a ten minute walk from here. On second thoughts, you will need shoes, but nothing else.'

Isolt knelt to lace up delicate jewelled sandals.

Fyn glanced to Piro, who had slipped on shoes and was about to pick up her foenix. How did it get to Merofynia? He stared at the sleepy bird in his ornate cage. That was all they needed, pet birds. 'Piro, I...'

Her chin lifted.

He sighed, recognising defeat when he saw it. 'All right, but keep him quiet.'

'Come, my pretty.' Piro lifted the cage. 'Ready.'

His sister and the kingsdaughter followed Fyn from the enemy camp. A blaze of starlight illuminated the night, bright enough to cast shadows. It was a pity it was not cloudy. Fyn hesitated in the tent's shadow. Now that he had two lives in his care, fear almost paralysed him. How could he protect these trusting girls?

He tapped Piro on the shoulder and pointed to a thicket. He had not come in that way, but it was a quicker path to the boat and escape. She nodded her understanding and ran across the open ground into the shadow under the trees. The foenix did not cry out. No alarm was given.

Fyn caught Isolt's hand and set off. Entering the shadow he smelled horses – no, donkeys. They stirred, reacting to the scent of the foenix. Fyn cursed silently. The bird made an interrogative sound.

'Hush, my pretty,' Piro whispered.

'Come.' Fyn turned to lead them on.

A broad-shouldered outline detached itself from the night, cutting off their escape. They had only a heartbeat before the camp was alerted. A donkey, sensing their fear, gave its strident bray.

The sentry drew his sword. 'Who goes there?'

As the man stepped forwards to strike, Fyn darted in and caught his sword arm. Pulling him off balance, Fyn swung the man around and snapped his neck without making a sound.

The sentry's body collapsed.

Fyn straightened up. Both Piro and Isolt stared at him.

A muffled query came from the next sentry. Another donkey brayed with fright and the others shifted, pulling at their ropes.

'Run for it!' Fyn pushed both of the girls ahead of him.

A shout told them the sentry's body had been found. More shouts followed as the alarm was raised.

Fyn ducked to avoid low branches, praying none of them would fall and twist an ankle on the shadowed, uneven ground.

The reached the dunes. Soft sand slid away under their feet, impeding their progress. The girls floundered. Breath rasping in his throat, Fyn caught both their arms and dragged them up the steep rise to the crest of the next dune. From here they could see the small cove, its pale sand gleaming in the starlight. Piro gasped, struggling with the weight of the foenix in its cage.

'There's the ship.' Fyn pointed to the *Wyvern's Whelp*, a dark shadow on the glittering sea. 'We're nearly safe.'

He glanced behind him. Pursuers lumbered up the sand after them.

He shoved both girls down the steep dune. They skidded through deep sand drifts, sliding to the base, the cage swaying wildly. He followed.

He pulled Piro upright, pointing to where Bantam had dragged the row boat into the shallows. 'Run.'

Then he pulled Isolt to her feet.

She stared at him. 'You killed that sentry quicker than a striking snake. What are you, an assassin?'

Fyn went to deny this, but someone shouted from the crest of the dune behind them. 'To the boat.'

Piro was already running. Isolt took off. Fyn ran after her, ready to stop and fight to ensure they got away safely if need be.

They made better time on the hard sand left by the retreating tide. As they ran towards the boat, the large figure of Jakulos charged past Fyn to defend their backs. Metal rang against metal. A man cried out.

Bantam already had the boat in the shallows, his hands on the oars. Fyn caught up with the girls, took the foenix's cage while Piro scrambled into the boat, then returned the cage. Next he caught Isolt around the waist and threw her in, shoving the boat into deeper water. When he was thigh-deep, Fyn turned to look for Jakulos.

The big sea-hound charged through the water towards them, sending spray flying. Jakulos grabbed

Fyn by the collar and shoved him into the boat, driving it even further from the shore, before he rolled his weight aboard, splashing everyone and making both young women cry out. The foenix gave a shriek of warning as the boat rocked alarmingly before settling.

Bantam resumed rowing, hardly breaking his rhythm, and they picked up speed. Fyn scrambled to the prow to balance Jakulos's weight. Their pursuers on the shore shouted and cursed, but could do nothing.

The boat reached the ship and the rope ladder rolled down. Piro handed the bird's cage to Fyn, then clambered up. He passed the cage to someone above before turning to help Isolt, but she brushed his hands away and made the climb ahead of him. He tried not to watch her lithe legs through the thin silk of her night gown.

Fyn climbed the ladder, leaving Jakulos and Bantam to fix the hooks to the boat's prow and bow so that it could be winched up.

The ship's anchor had been raised. The sails rose, unfolding, each segment gleaming in the starlight as they opened. The ship soon made headway out of the inlet.

He glanced up to see Captain Nefysto at the helm, steering through the sand bars that guarded the inlet. As the sea-hounds took depth soundings and secured the boat, the sailors watched Fyn escort Piro and Isolt into the captain's cabin. It wasn't every day their ship hosted a kingsdaughter – two kingsdaughters, if they only knew.

* * *

FYN LIT THE second lantern in the captain's cabin and looked around. Isolt shivered. Her fine silk night gown clung to her, ruined by the salt-water. She might as well have been naked. He opened a chest, taking out a blanket and averting his eyes as he handed it to her.

Looking in the other direction, he saw Piro place the foenix cage on the floor. She peeped behind the screen to investigate the captain's Affinity birds.

'I've always wanted to see a pica pair,' Piro said.

A tray of wine, bread, cheese and fruit sat on the desk. Fyn gestured to it. 'Help yourselves.'

Piro came over to pour wine and slice cheese. Her musical voice rose and fell as she relived their close escape. Isolt ate, saying nothing. They were opposites, Piro all light and laughter, Isolt dark and troubled. He wished he could banish Isolt's fear.

'A pair of pica birds?' Isolt asked. Her gaze slid to Fyn. 'So you serve the elector?'

'Mage Tsulamyth, as does Captain Nefysto,' Fyn answered. He was in the mage's debt and power, but to ensure Tsulamyth did not have the same power over Piro he would introduce her as Isolt's maid.

To think, he had been ready to renounce the world and live a monk's life. He looked up. 'We three must make our plans now, before the captain comes.'

Piro had been on her knees, slipping grapes through the bars of the foenix's cage. At his tone she turned with a questioning look, and Isolt put her wine goblet down.

Fyn decided to be frank. 'Piro and I are worth more dead than alive to our enemies, and I don't know who we can call friend.'

'The mage sent you to save Isolt. Surely he is our friend?' Piro asked.

Isolt made a rude noise. 'From what I've heard Mage Tsulamyth is his own best friend.'

Piro looked to Fyn.

'He is an Affinity renegade, Piro. The abbot would say we can't trust him at all. I haven't met him, only one of his agents, so I can't judge. The mage is the force behind the elector of Ostron Isle, in some ways more powerful than a king, and we are at his mercy. That is why we must make a pact.' He placed his hand palm-down on the table. 'I swear to protect both of you with my life, and to see that you are restored to your rightful places.'

Piro walked over to the desk, placing her hand on Fyn's. 'I swear to protect you two by whatever means I can.' She smiled. 'It's good to have you back, brother, but I fear just surviving may be hard enough without trying to win back Rolencia.'

Fyn smiled. 'Maybe not. We have a secret ally inside Rolenhold.'

Piro's eyes widened. 'Who? Tell me.'

'Cobalt. He's promised to help restore Byren...' Fyn broke off, seeing Piro's expression. 'What is it?'

She pulled back. 'You haven't told Cobalt where Byren is, have you?'

'Not yet. Piro, I know it appears that Cobalt is Merofynia's puppet king. But he told me to bring Byren to him, so –'

'So he could kill him!' Her pretty mouth twisted with grief and anger. 'You went back to the abbey after midwinter, Fyn. You didn't see what our cousin did. I watched it all unfold and there was nothing I could do. First Cobalt turned Lence against Byren, then he turned Father against Byren, claiming that Byren was Orrade's lover and the Servants of Palos meant to put him on the throne. Then he turned Father against Mother and broke her heart. And it was he who ordered the postern gate opened to let Palatyne in.' She raised tear filled eyes to Fyn. 'All the while, he smiled and made everyone love him. I swear he's the two-headed snake, not Palatyne.'

Fyn sat down abruptly.

'Fyn?' Piro leant closer. 'You didn't give Byren away to Cobalt did you?'

'No.' He repressed a shiver then lifted his head. 'No. I didn't have a chance. But I meant to... Cobalt was so convincing, Piro. I found him lying there in Rolenhold, Palatyne's captive. He was injured, bearing his pain with great fortitude.'

She nodded. 'That's why he's so dangerous. With Palatyne you know he's your enemy. With Cobalt, he'll smile as he slides the knife in.'

Fyn shook his head. 'I can't believe I nearly –'

She touched his hand. 'It's all right, Fyn. He had Mother fooled until just before the end. She tried to kill him with his own sword.'

Fyn couldn't imagine his elegant mother swinging a heavy sword. 'When the abbey fell, I tried to reach you. If only I'd been in time.'

'Don't blame yourself, Fyn.' Piro eyes searched his face. 'You couldn't have saved us. It was a two-pronged attack. Cobalt betrayed the stronghold, even while the abbey was under attack.'

Fyn felt a great weight lift from him. He hadn't failed his family. Tears stung his eyes and he lifted a hand to his face, trying to catch his breath. Piro squeezed his shoulder.

After a moment she turned to the kingsdaughter. 'Are you with us, Isolt?'

Isolt looked from Piro to Fyn. 'You want me to make a pact that will see my father dead? He might be a ruthless man, but he is still my father. I won't stand by while someone plots his death.'

'Palatyne plots his death,' Piro said. 'I heard him ask Lord Dunstany for a poison that mimicked natural death and Dunstany provided it – he had no choice. Palatyne would have ordered him killed if he hadn't.'

Isolt's eyes widened. 'Why didn't you tell me? I could have warned my father.'

'I tried to tell you,' Piro said. 'But you didn't believe me. And your father is safe until you marry Palatyne. He planned to kill the king after he had you safely wedded and bedded. And he wasn't too fussed about the order, if you remember.'

Isolt blanched.

The thought of Isolt in Palatyne's hands made Fyn's stomach revolt. He came to his feet. 'Your father has many enemies, Isolt.'

She stared across the desk at him, the lantern's glow pooling in her troubled eyes.

'I can promise that I will not kill King Merofyn.'

Isolt considered this. Then she leant across the desk, offering her hand. 'I cannot ask for more.'

Piro caught her hand and Fyn covered them both,

then gave them a squeeze. They all took a step back.

'Now we must decide what to tell the mage,' Fyn said. 'You must pretend to be Isolt's maid, Piro. I don't want him realising he has two of King Rolen's heirs in his power. I'll leave you on Ostron Isle and return to find Byren. I intend to be with him when he wins back Rolencia.'

'I'm coming too,' Piro said.

Fyn shook his head. 'It is safer for you on Ostron Isle.'

'With someone you regard as an Affinity renegade?' Isolt countered.

Fyn smiled, acknowledging her point. She was clever as well as beautiful and he could tell she did not like him, though he did not know why. 'We don't have a lot of options. I need a strong ally to help win Byren his kingdom. That's where you come in, Isolt. The Merofynian ambassador said the words of betrothal on your behalf. Since Lence is dead, you are betrothed to Byren according to both Merofynian and Rolencian law.'

'I don't want to be betrothed to anyone. I'm not some king's trophy.'

'Well said.' Piro applauded. 'I never asked to be betrothed to Rejulas. Why should we kingsdaughters be married off as prizes?'

They both glared at Fyn, righteously indignant, itching for a fight.

'You're right,' he said, sitting down and popping a grape in his mouth, as though he didn't care how they responded. 'When we get to Ostron Isle, leave this ship and walk away. Earn your bread as maids in a bakery for all I care.' He paused to let this sink in, then leant forwards, his voice growing hard. 'But if anyone discovers who you are, you will be killed or transported back to Merofynia. You can't deny your standing and you both have a role to play in this game.'

'Curse the game of Kingdoms!' Isolt whispered.

'It's not so bad being a maid, when you've been a slave,' Piro said. 'At least I'd be free.'

Fyn had never thought she would take his suggestion seriously. He reached for her hand across the desk. 'Stay with me, Piro. I've lost you once already. I couldn't bear to lose you again.'

Piro smiled and came around to stand behind where he sat. She hugged his shoulders and kissed the top of his head, then laughed, rubbing his hair. 'I can't get used to seeing you with hair. You should be bald and tattooed!'

Fyn grinned self-consciously.

'You two are lucky,' Isolt whispered. 'You have each other. I have no one. Even my mother hated my father more than she loved me.'

Fyn's heart went out to her.

Isolt met his eyes. She glanced away suddenly and pulled the blanket more tightly around her shoulders. 'I'm tired. Where will I sleep?'

He should have thought of that. 'I'll ask the captain –'

'It's as cold as Cyena's breath out there!' As if speaking of him had called him up, Nefysto thrust the door open. He spoke Merofynian out of courtesy to Isolt as he gave her a flamboyant Ostronite bow. 'Welcome aboard, kingsdaughter. We won't be taking the trade route back to Ostron Isle. Don't want anyone coming after us. We'll veer out to sea and plot a path back by the stars. If we avoid the Utlands and the trade routes we'll be safe from raiders, and any wyverns bold enough to climb on board for a snack better beware!'

Nefysto laughed. Pulling off his fleece-lined weatherproof, he dropped it onto a chair and turned to Fyn. 'Now what's this, Agent Monk? You go off to rescue a kingsdaughter and come back with her, her maid and a pet bird?'

'We couldn't manage the rest of her luggage,' Fyn said.

Isolt giggled then covered her mouth, as though surprised at herself.

At that moment, Runt came in and darted around the cabin, gathering the captain's clothing and personal items.

Nefysto's gaze returned to Isolt, and his lips parted in a smile of appreciation. 'Allow me to offer my cabin, such as it is. And allow me to introduce myself, since Agent Monk's manners are sadly lacking.' He gave another elaborate bow. 'Captain Nefysto, of the *Wyvern's Whelp*, at your service, Isolt Merofyn Kingsdaughter.'

Fyn was certain Nefysto came from one of the great merchant families of Ostron Isle, but for whatever reason, he chose to keep his true identity a secret. When the opportunity arose, Fyn introduced Piro as Seela, the maid.

'Grab a blanket, girls,' Nefysto said. 'Come with me now and I'll show you Mulcibar's Gate. It's at its best at night. A fine way to farewell Merofynia.' And he swept them out to see the river of slow-moving liquid rock that bubbled up from deep inside the earth before flowing down one of the headlands that guarded Mero Bay.

Fyn waited until they were gone, then he knelt on the cabin's floor, facing east, as best he could judge. East was the goddess's direction. He had not prayed to Halcyon since the abbey fell, but tonight he felt he needed her forgiveness.

Tonight he had killed.

It had been a conscious decision to permanently silence the sentry. The man had been armed, he had been about to alert the others, but Fyn still felt for him. The man had a mother somewhere, perhaps a wife and children. After all, the sentry had only been doing his job.

Tears stung Fyn's eyes and he welcomed them. He would not become a callous killer like Palatyne.

Fyn folded his hands in his lap and cleared his mind, seeking the solace of Halcyon's blessing. He sat there for a long time but the mental state he used to be able to achieve back at the abbey eluded him. Eventually, a soft noise broke his concentration. He looked up to see Isolt in the doorway.

'I'm sorry. I did not know you were praying. I'll go.'

'No.' Fyn rose. 'This is your cabin, you must be tired. I'll go.'

'There are tears on your cheeks.'

'Tonight I killed a man.'

'The sentry? But –'

'I know. I know...' Fyn sighed. 'I was raised to believe life is precious. Every time I kill, it kills something in me. A single death here, a few more there. Every time it will get easier, until the day I order the execution of an innocent man because he is in my way.' He hesitated. He'd almost mentioned his mother's brother, Sefon, but held back since it had been Isolt's own father who'd ordered the young king assassinated. 'I will not become that man.'

Isolt frowned. 'Then why do you serve the mage?'

'I must, to win back Rolencia and restore Byren to the throne.'

'What about you? If Byren died you would be the uncrowned king.'

Fyn stepped back, revolted by the thought. 'He's my brother.'

Isolt studied him, beautiful eyes thoughtful. 'Then Byren is a very lucky man.'

That was when Fyn realised Byren was a very lucky man indeed. Not because Fyn knew his duty but because he was betrothed to Isolt.

Startled by this revelation, Fyn took another step back and bowed stiffly. 'Goodnight, kingsdaughter.'

Chapter Fifteen

FYN SMILED AND stretched. It seemed like he had been running, living on his wits, avoiding death since the abbey fell. It was good to be safe. They'd left the shipping lanes and been sailing east all morning, picking their way through the islands too barren for even the hardy Utlanders to settle. These islands were nothing more than spires of rock. Now that it was spring, it was warm enough to stay on deck without a fleecy jacket.

'Good boy,' Piro cried as she scooped up the foenix and rewarded him with a morsel of meat. She was teaching her pet to come when she called by giving him dried fish scraps.

'You'll make that bird too fat to fly,' Fyn teased.

Piro just tossed her head and crossed to the far rail of the ship to put the foenix down, then returned to Fyn, to call the bird gain. The man at the wheel watched her. All morning he'd been dividing his time between watching Isolt and Piro. He'd made no secret of his appreciation of them both and Fyn could not help bristling.

The foenix had grown since Fyn last saw him. With his long legs and elongated neck, his head now came up to Piro's waist. And he was beginning to grow the elaborate comb on his crown, but he was still only an infant. The foenix lifted one wing, preening and ignoring Piro's soft calls.

'That Affinity beast is more like a cat than a dog. He only comes when he wants to,' Fyn said, and although he was not watching her face, he knew Isolt smiled. He was deeply aware of her, standing by his side as they leant on the rail. His body ached with the knowledge that he could simply reach out and touch her. If he dared. If she was not betrothed to his brother.

Isolt turned to look down onto the sparkling sea. 'I always wanted a pet, but father would never let me have one. He said pets made you weak, that caring for things made you weak. No one could accuse him of that.'

Fyn didn't know what to say. He watched as a cold mask settled on Isolt's face.

'My brother's not like that,' Fyn assured her. 'Byren's kind. He found the foenix egg and gave it to Piro –'

A sudden downdraught of air and a thump made them both turn. Fyn could hardly credit his eyes as an old, battle-scarred male wyvern, easily twice as tall as him, landed on the deck between them and the foenix. Judging by the scars, this beast had faced down many wyvern males in mating battles.

It must have been drawn by the foenix's scent. Affinity beasts would often fight, the winner devouring the victor to absorb its power. The wyvern exuded a rank predator scent that, combined with the untamed power which rolled off its skin, almost stunned Fyn. Fear held him immobile. He was armed only with a short all-purpose knife.

Above and behind them, the lookout give a belated cry of warning.

The wyvern pivoted, leathery wings lifting in an aggressive display. Fyn's heart quailed. The beast was so big it might just be able to carry one of them off. The wyvern fixed on the foenix, which had frozen instinctively. One day it would stand taller than a man, with a chestplate of hardened scales and spurs that could tear through armour, but now it was vulnerable.

'No!' Piro sprang forwards, trying to distract the wyvern from her pet.

The wyvern's great head, with its massive jaws, swung to face her. She was defenceless.

Through the rushing in his ears, Fyn heard the sea-hounds shouting as they called for weapons, but they were too far away.

'You idiot, Piro!' Fyn shouldered her aside and tore off his cloak. He swung it around so that he seemed twice his height, mimicking the wing display male wyverns used to intimidate their opponents.

The wyvern backed off a step. Isolt darted in to drag Piro behind Fyn. The wyvern's gaze followed them. It opened its jaws and roared a challenge.

Fyn swung the cloak again, yelling a challenge of his own.

How long would his trick confuse the beast?

Wyverns weren't stupid. If raised by people the fresh-water kind were more intelligent and loyal than dogs. All too soon the beast would realise Fyn was a single puny creature, not a rival wyvern.

Jakulos roared as he raced up beside Fyn with a long spear, its tip ended in a vicious barbed spike. The big man sprang in, jabbing the beast's belly where it met the chestplate.

The wyvern took a swipe at Jakulos with its short front paw, claws splayed. Bantam sprang forwards on Fyn's other side. With a crack, the quarter-master flicked a whip at the wyvern, stinging its skin and drawing blood.

It roared its dismay and fury. Fyn flung his cloak into the beast's face.

In a frenzy it tore at the cloak, teeth sinking through the fabric, claws shredding it. Then it leapt into the air, dropping the mangled material like a dead body. The downdraught of its massive wings nearly knocked Fyn off his feet. Jakulos went for it again as it hovered a body-length above them, the spear's tip just missing its target. Bantam's whip cracked a warning.

With a bellow of anger, the old male worked to gain height, circling above them, before heading off.

Fyn dragged in a chest full of air and bent double. Jakulos clapped him on the back so hard he fell to his knees on the deck.

Bantam dragged him to his feet. 'Thought you'd tackle a lone male wyvern without us?'

Fyn shook his head, unable to speak.

Captain Nefysto joined them and studied the sky through his farseer, then lowered the tube and clicked it shut. 'Looks like he was a loner. But still... Bantam, set a watch. Select three of our best archers and have them on deck.'

Bantam hurried off to obey and the captain looked at Fyn. 'You never cease to amaze me, Agent Monk. Well done.'

'I was only protecting... Isolt's maid.' Fyn managed not to reveal Piro's identity. Had he shouted her name? He didn't remember.

Nefysto glanced at Piro.

'The wyvern came after my mistress's foenix,' she explained.

'So you thought you'd take on an adult wyvern to protect it?' The captain grinned. 'Wyverns consider foenix flesh a delicacy. I suggest you take that bird into my cabin until we are sure it's safe.'

Bantam arrived back on deck with the bowmen.

'Fun's over, back to work!' Nefysto called.

Jakulos took his spear below decks. Piro collected her foenix and climbed down the ladder to the cabin. Now that it was all over, Fyn felt shaky and slightly nauseous.

Someone tapped him on the shoulder. He turned to see Isolt standing there with his torn cloak.

'I'll mend this for you.' She smoothed the material over her arm.

He gaped.

So stunned was he by the thought of Isolt Merofyn Kingsdaughter mending his clothes that she was gone before he had time to speak. Now she would think him a lout.

ONCE IN THE cabin, Piro sat her foenix on the floor. The bird went straight to the screen, which the pica pair were caged behind. Luckily, he was too small to be a threat to them, but had he been larger he might have found a way past the screen to devour them.

Isolt entered with Fyn's cloak.

'Seela.' Isolt used her assumed name even when they were alone. 'See if you can find me a sewing kit.'

'You don't have to mend Fyn's cloak. I'll do it,' Piro said. 'As your maid I should do it.'

Isolt hugged the cloak to her chest. 'Bring me the sewing kit.'

When Piro returned with a pouch of needles, thread and a pair of sharp scissors, Isolt had spread the cloak out to survey the damage. There were several long rents caused by the wyvern's razor-sharp claws and a whole section had been chewed to ribbons.

'It's going to take more than invisible darning to mend that,' Piro said.

'I wanted to mend it as a way of saying thank you.'

'Well, there's enough good material left in it to make a jerkin.' She smiled at Isolt's expression. 'I often helped my mother make-down my father's clothes for my brothers. At least until they grew bigger than him.'

'Queen Myrella had to make-down clothes for her sons?' Isolt looked aghast. 'Why didn't she pass them on to servants and get new ones?'

Piro stiffened. 'Father wasted nothing. The Merofynian war, combined with the revolt by the Servants of Palos, nearly ruined the kingdom. So times were tough. It was only after I was born that peace bought prosperity. And, by then, Father was set in his ways.' She felt a half-smile tug at her lips. 'Besides, my mother didn't mind. Why, sometimes she would roll up her sleeves and prepare a meal for him with her own hands, just for the fun of it. He loved it when she did that.'

Isolt shook her head slowly. 'I'd trade every gown and jewel I have for what you have.'

'*Had*.' Anger, sharp and hard as winter wind sliced through Piro's memories. 'My parents are dead, Lence is dead, and all because your father wanted Rolencia for his own.'

The kingsdaughter went very still. Then she looked up at Piro. 'Why would my father attack, if he'd betrothed me to your brother?'

'That was a diversion, to lull us into a false sense of security. He meant to invade all along. Deeds speak louder than words.'

The silence stretched. After a moment, Isolt spread her hand across the remains of Fyn's cloak. 'Can you show me how to make this down into a jerkin?'

Piro had to draw a long, slow breath to change tack. Then she nodded. 'First I'll need one of Fyn's for size.'

When she came back, Isolt was fingering the torn material thoughtfully. 'I've never seen anyone take on a full-grown wyvern armed with nothing but a cloak before. Fyn must know no fear.'

Piro laughed, remembering Fyn's reason for not joining the warrior monks.

'What?'

'A secret I can't share.' Piro saw Isolt's expression. 'I would not betray my brother's confidence, even for you.'

Isolt was silent for a moment.

'How strange,' she said. 'A warrior who hates to kill. A brave man who is afraid.'

Piro's Affinity tingled, making the foenix nudge her hand with his head.

'You'll make a good queen one day,' Piro said, with a strange air.

Isolt shivered. 'You just gave me goose bumps. Why?'

Piro shook her head and placed Fyn's jerkin on the desk. 'Let's see if we have enough material.'

BYREN HID HIS annoyance. The warlord of Leogryf Spar had sent his nephew, a man who insisted on being called Lord Leon and had an exaggerated sense of his own importance. At least Lord Leon came promising his uncle's support.

Last night they had feasted. Today they talked tactics. Lord Leon was not like most spar warriors. Byren did not blame a man for being wary, but Leon's smile did not reach his eyes. Still, he had come with the promise of seven hundred warriors, so he had a right to his place at the council of war.

They stood around Feid's war table, Master Catillum, Orrade and Feid himself. Unistag's representative had sailed home to await Byren's call for the promised warriors.

This war table was not as finely detailed as the one Byren had grown up with. Instead of three-dimensional models the map was drawn on a square of fine vellum, stretched on a frame. Instead of delicately moulded metal inset with jewels, the pieces were carved from wood.

Lord Leon indicated Feid's spar. 'So you plan to go over the pass, take the fort and attack Rolenhold from behind?'

Byren nodded. Anyone could guess his plans. There were only so many ways he could attack. Feid went to speak but, just in case he had been about to reveal the secret pass, Byren spoke over him. 'We have four hundred men from Unistag Spar, Foenix's six hundred, my own men and the seven hundred your uncle promises. Plus, as soon as I march over the Divide the people of Rolencia will rise up.'

Lord Leon nodded, his eyes on the map. He tapped the last spar, the one that ran north from the far tip of Rolencia's crescent. 'Nothing from Manticore?'

'Nothing from Manticore, yet.' Byren felt his supporters watching him, felt the weight of their expectation. 'And nothing from Cockatrice. After Rejulas's death the warriors of Cockatrice Spar had to appoint a new leader. We've heard they have chosen one now and I expect he'll be eager to swear his allegiance.'

'And when will you attack?'

'When the moment is right.'

Lord Leon lifted his hands palm up. 'It will take days to return to Leogryf Spar, call in our warriors and return.'

'I know,' Byren said. 'I'll figure this into my calculations.' The alternative was to send for the warriors now and let them eat Feid's food set aside for summer, while waiting to attack. 'I'll let you know when I need Leogryf's men.'

'Why not call them in now?' Orrade suggested.

Byren tensed. It wasn't like Orrade to speak at cross purposes to him, especially in front of the others.

Lord Leon turned to Byren. 'Is that what you want?'

'No. I'll let you know.'

'Very well. I set sail tomorrow, to report to my uncle.'

As Feid and Catillum escorted the Leogryf warrior from the room, Byren fell behind, catching Orrade's arm. 'What were you thinking? We can't ask our host to feed seven hundred men.'

'I don't like this Lord Leon. I wanted to call his bluff. Did you see how he reacted?'

'He offered to bring the warriors.'

'Yes, but...'

'But?'

Orrade shrugged as if he couldn't explain.

'Have you had an Affinity vision?'

'No...'

Byren waited. Orrade didn't elaborate, so he strode off to catch up with the nephew of one of the stronger warlords.

Later that evening, while their men played games of dice in the castle's great hall and sang drinking songs, Feid turned to Byren. 'You didn't tell him our plan to go over the old pass and attack the fort from Rolencia's undefended side?'

Byren had just taken a mouthful of mutton and Orrade answered for him.

'Because the fewer who know, the fewer who can betray us.'

No one spoke as they watched the men eat their way through the castle's stores. It would be a lean, late summer before the crops came in. Byren was surprised Feid wasn't encouraging him to attack already.

'And besides,' Orrade muttered, 'Lord Leon has probably already guessed how we came across the Divide. I wouldn't be surprised if each spar had a secret pass.'

Byren blinked. Of course, that made sense.

Here he was, obsessed with his own problems and Orrade saw further. What would he do without him? He put his ale down and turned to Feid. 'Are there more secret passes?'

The warlord lifted his hands in a shrug. 'If there are, the warlords haven't shared their whereabouts with me.'

Byren was not surprised. Alliances between the spar warlords were short-lived and prone to betrayals. He drained his ale. Across the hall, near the stairs to the bedchambers, he noticed Florin. She beckoned and his body tightened in anticipation.

But this was not an assignation. Florin did not play those kinds of games. Whatever she wanted to see him about it would not result in him tupping her up against the wall. More's the pity. And, after the trouble he'd gone to, to ensure Winterfall and others like him didn't get the wrong idea about her, he should be ashamed to even think it.

The problem was he couldn't help his body's reaction.

Byren stood and stretched casually, glad his jerkin came down to mid-thigh. 'Think I'll turn in.'

Orrade met his eyes, not fooled for a moment. But he said nothing.

They hadn't seen much of Florin. She'd spent her days with Feid's wife, who avoided the great hall and its noisy drinking.

Byren caught Orrade's eye and nodded to Feid.

When his friend diverted the warlord with an arm wrestle, Byren slipped away, his heart pounding despite himself.

He passed the monks' table, where Catillum spoke earnestly while his men listened. It was unlike the table where Old Man Narrows sat. There, the maimed player entertained them with ribald stories, amidst shouts and laughter.

When Byren approached Florin, she backed out of the hall into the dark corner at the base of the stairs. Despite everything he'd told himself, Byren's body quickened in anticipation. He saw her only as a dark shape, her pale face surrounded by midnight hair.

She reached for him, pulling him closer. Not into an embrace, but so that her words would not be overheard. 'You can't trust the warlord!'

'I don't trust him. He says one thing, but his eyes

say another. Still, he has given his word to bring seven hundred fighting men and I can't afford to –'

'Not Lord Leon. Feid!'

Byren blinked. 'Mountain-girl, you –'

She thumped his chest. 'I might be nothing but a mountain girl, but I have eyes and the wits I was born with. You asked me to watch Feid's lady.'

To keep her out of harm's way.

Florin did not wait for his reply. 'Lady Cinna has pet birds. She spends hours talking to them in her own language.'

'No harm in that. She's lonely.'

'They talk back to her.'

'Eh.' Byren grinned. 'My mother had a pet parrot. It could say a dozen things. She wept when it died. I remember, I was seven and –'

'These aren't parrots.' Florin's glare seared him.

Ah, but she was fetching when she was angry. He hid a smile.

Florin glanced over her shoulder and stepped closer still. 'Today, after we heard about Lord Leon's offer, Cinna disappeared into the chamber where she keeps her birds. Later, I checked. One of them was missing. She said it must have escaped and pretended to look for it, but I think she sent it off with a message.'

Byren felt the laughter leave his body. 'Are these bird black and white?'

'Yes.'

He took a step back, and felt the solid wall behind him. *Ostronite messenger birds? Only the elector and his spies had access to pica pairs.*

'Byren?'

What would a humble kitchen maid be doing with Ostronite messenger birds? What if she wasn't a humble kitchen maid, but one of the elector's spies? Ostron Isle was a powerful ally, if a fickle one. Byren's head spun. Why plant a spy on Foenix Spar, of all places?

'You believe me now,' Florin said.

'Aye.' He believed the warlord's lady had black and white birds for pets that could be possibly be a pica pair. But he also believed Feid's marriage was a love match. Perhaps it was, and the elector's spymaster had enlisted her? Yet, Lady Cinna seemed to adore her warlord husband and Byren's gut instinct told him to trust Feid.

'What will you do?' Florin pressed.

'Nothing... for now.' Byren smiled at her impatience. 'As my old nurse used to say, *actions speak louder than words*. Feid has taken us in and fed us.'

'But –'

'Watch the Lady Cinna. If Feid betrays us, we will not be taken by surprise. Thank you, Florin.'

She shrugged his thanks off as if annoyed and went up the stairs. Byren watched her go, mesmerised by the unconscious sway of her hips.

If Feid was betraying him to Ostron Isle, then the warlord was a better actor than Byren had given him credit for. If the warlord's lady was the betrayer, then she was a consummate actress.

Chapter Sixteen

PIRO LACED UP Isolt's bodice, her fingers flying. Being a lady's maid was not so hard. She stepped back and Isolt let her hair fall down. Long and sleek, it fell to her waist, a sheet of black silk. They were about to meet the mage or, at the very least, his agent.

'You look every bit a kingsdaughter,' Piro told her.

Clothes had been provided in both their sizes. They wore rich satins, laces and velvets with tight bodices and full skirts that finished just above the ankle to show off their exquisite slippers, Ostronite-style.

'Either they have some marvellous seamstresses, or the mage knew my size and the colours I like,' Isolt said. She turned Piro around to do her laces, though her fingers were not as skilled. 'But how did he know your size?'

Piro shrugged and held her hair out of the way. When Isolt finished she gave a wriggle to settle the bodice in place then let her hair drop. 'Who knows? Perhaps they have a range of clothes ready-made. Perhaps the mage is a good guesser.'

Isolt met her eyes, suddenly serious. 'We must be wary of this mage, *Seela*.'

Piro understood the warning and heard the added emphasis on her assumed name. But the singing of the porters unloading cargo came through the open cabin windows on warm air, bringing the scent of salt-water and fish, mixed with spices and seaweed left in the sun too long.

Piro shrugged off Isolt's fears with a laugh. 'Spring is here.' There was a knock at the door. 'That'll be Fyn. Shall we go?'

Isolt rolled her eyes. 'This time, don't let Captain Nefysto get me alone. If I have to listen to another of his songs composed in my honour, I'll fake a fainting fit.'

Piro grinned and opened the door. She hardly recognised Fyn. He looked very fine in Ostronite fashion, a well-cut velvet vest, full silk sleeves, leggings and boots. But he was not so fine as the captain, who wore a hand's span of lace at each cuff. She hid a smile, thinking what her father and Lence would have made of a sea-hound who wore lace and wrote love songs.

'Ready?' Fyn asked. He looked Piro up and down. 'Don't you have a dress more fitting for a maid?'

'I can't help it. All the dresses in my size are like this.'

'They fight like brother and sister.' Nefysto shook his head and offered his arm to Isolt. 'May I escort you to the carriage?'

Piro saw Isolt put on her Merofynian face, the mask that hid her emotions.

'You are too kind,' she said, but Isolt's voice held a hint of warmth that hadn't been there in Merofynia, for the kingsdaughter genuinely liked Nefysto.

Piro hid a smile, then noticed how Fyn's mouth tightened.

Piro's foenix gave a soft call of dismay as she walked out. She glanced back to where he sat in the cage. 'They'll send him with our things?'

'It is all organised,' Fyn said.

They went out on deck and across the gangplank to the waiting carriage, which rattled over the cobbles. It was hard to see much of Ostron Isle through the small window. Piro caught flashes of lattice-covered balconies, and heard laughing people chatter in a language spoken too quickly for her to follow. She was better at reading Ostronite than speaking it. As of today, she would get the practice needed to improve her mastery of the spoken language.

'Will you be coming to see the mage with us?' Piro asked Captain Nefysto before he could take out his citole, run his fingers across the strings and serenade Isolt with another ode to her beauty.

'Only as far as the courtyard. I report to one of his agents.'

'We're nearly there,' Fyn announced. 'Look out the window, Isolt, and you will see the tallest tower in the world.'

As they rolled across a stone bridge, Piro peered out of Isolt's window. They had to crane their necks to see the top of the slender tower. It glistened white and fresh against the intense blue of the sky.

They entered the shadow of the bridge's gate-towers and rolled into a courtyard. Eager to help Isolt from the carriage, Captain Nefysto stepped down and slung the citole over his back. Fyn stood on her other side, offering his arm. Isolt laughed and ignored them both, jumping lightly to the ground. Both men began pointing out things of interest, ignoring Piro, who shook her head in wonder as she climbed down. What was it about Isolt that made men act so stupidly? Isolt certainly didn't welcome their attention.

Nefysto pulled off his feathered hat and swept a courtly bow, taking his leave of them. A boy of about twelve, wearing a less ornate, miniature version of Nefysto's clothes right down to the feathered cap, came over to them. He swept an identical bow and asked them to follow him.

'How's your brother's foot?' Fyn asked.

The lad frowned at Fyn and turned his back with great dignity. 'Follow me.'

Fyn dropped back, whispering to Piro and Isolt. 'Beware what you say in front of him. In fact, beware what you see. Things are not as they seem here.'

Piro nodded, although she didn't know what he expected them to do. Did they have to prod everything to make sure it was real?

She took another look at Fyn. He seemed outwardly composed, but his shoulders held tension, there was a grimness around his mouth, and his eyes were too sharp. Her stomach clenched in response to his unspoken trepidation. If he feared this meeting, then so should she.

They were led inside, up three flights of stairs and down several corridors until they came to a circular chamber. A balcony at the far end overlooked the Ring Sea.

Sunlight reflected from the water below, creating rippling patterns across the white ceiling. From the circular shape of the chamber, she guessed they were in the tower. The floor was covered with blue tiles so shiny they glistened like water. A large war table dominated the room, with a perfect replica of the known world.

A single figure stood on the balcony, the slight breeze stirring his long black hair.

'I hoped we'd see the mage himself,' Fyn muttered. 'This is only his agent, Tyro. But he has renegade Affinity too, so watch out for him.'

Piro nodded, relaxing a little. Then she stiffened as the agent strode into the room. She had the strangest feeling she knew him. But she would have remembered this intense, thin, young man. From his narrow chin to his high forehead and black eyes, he was... Those eyes...

Fyn gave an abbreviated bow. 'Meet Isolt Merofyn Kingsdaughter and her maid, Seela. Turns out, Isolt knew nothing of the betrothal and did not want to marry Palatyne.'

Piro was aware of something unspoken passing between Agent Tyro and Fyn.

'So she is happy to take sanctuary on Ostron Isle,' Fyn finished. 'Where is Mage Tsulamyth?'

'Dealing with other, more important matters,' the agent said. 'I have been his voice for many years.'

Piro thought this must be an exaggeration for he looked no older than Lence. But then Lord Dunstany had been much older than he looked. Ah, that was it. The agent bore a strong family resemblance to the noble scholar and Dunstany did say his long life was a by-product of his Affinity.

Every now and than, as if his shielding was imperfect, she could feel a wash of Affinity roll off the agent. It reminded her of the way the air around Lord Dunstany used to hum with power. It made her dizzy.

She took a step back and Isolt steadied her, sending a look of query.

Too much Affinity, Piro mouthed.

When Tyro turned towards Isolt, Piro blended into the background as a maid should.

The agent gave Isolt a Merofynian bow as he spoke in her own language. His deep voice also struck Piro as familiar. 'You have come a long way, kingsdaughter. Welcome to Mage Isle.'

Piro watched as the kingsdaughter assumed what she thought of as Isolt's Merofynian court face.

'I thank Mage Tsulamyth for offering me sanctuary. In truth, I had little choice. Duke Palatyne will be furious when he learns where I am. I don't wish to be a burden to Ostron Isle.' Isolt looked down, then up, her mask slipping to reveal a flash of defiance. 'But I refused to stay and play Palatyne's game of Duelling Kingdoms.'

'In my capacity as his agent, I offer the mage's protection. You don't need to worry about Palatyne. He leads by fear, not example, and such men do not live long,' Agent Tyro said. Piro thought him slightly pompous. 'Palatyne will be furious but, while you are on Mage Isle, you are safe. However, you cannot hide forever. Have you thought what you will do?'

Fyn spoke quickly. 'Since Lence Kingsheir is dead, by the laws of Rolencia and Merofynia, Isolt is betrothed to Rolencia's uncrowned king, Byren.'

Agent Tyro fixed Fyn with gleaming dark eyes. Piro thought she saw a hint of laughter in their depths. 'At this moment Byren Kingsheir, or should I say the deposed king, is trying to unite your father's warlords, Fyn Rolen Kingson. So far, only two have offered their support. He needs the support of all five to stand a chance of retaking Rolencia.'

Piro hid her joy. This was the first real news she'd had of Byren.

Fyn's eyes narrowed. 'How –'

'Mage Tsulamyth has a very good spy network, Fyn. Now perhaps you would like to share another of your secrets?' When Tyro turned to Piro, she had the feeling he had been avoiding looking her way. 'Introduce me to your sister.'

Piro's heart skipped a beat and heat raced up her cheeks. She hated being caught in a lie. How had he guessed?

Fyn cleared his throat. Piro could tell he was quietly furious but he spoke courteously. 'Lord Tyro, this –'

'I am no lord,' the agent said, voice cold and cutting. 'My father did not acknowledge me. My mother sold me to the mage when I was five.'

Isolt took a step back as did Piro, scalded by his fury. Born the wrong side of the blanket – now she understood why the agent was so pompous. She'd seen the same response in those who felt disadvantaged in her father's court.

'I've met lords with less scholarship than you, Agent Tyro,' Fyn said.

Tyro's eyes widened, then he almost smiled. 'Your tongue is as fast as your sword. A valuable trait. Now, introduce your sister.'

Fyn cleared his throat. 'Agent Tyro, meet the sister I thought dead, Piro Rolen Kingsdaughter.'

The agent bowed then took a step back, looking at Piro. Waiting. Waiting... His obsidian eyes held hers, intense and quizzical. When she merely stared right back at him, a wry smile tugged at his lips. 'Don't you know your old master, Seelon?'

'Lord Dunstany!' Piro gasped. 'But... but you're young. The noble Power-worker was ninety even though he looked fifty.' She frowned. 'You must have used your Affinity to augment a player's disguise and –'

'No,' Isolt spoke up. 'Lord Dunstany has served the Merofynian royal family since my great-grandfather's time, so this agent can't be him.'

Tyro turned to her. 'You are right. Lord Dunstany died of natural causes, without any heirs. He was my master's trusted friend and agent. Dunstany arranged with the mage to keep his death a secret. Since I bore a strong resemblance, being born on the wrong side of the blanket on Dunstany's estate, I took his place so that Lord Dunstany could continue to serve the mage.'

'But I slept on the floor next to your bunk,' Piro

objected. 'I rubbed lineament on your... on Lord Dunstany's swollen fingers.'

'You offered and I could not resist. So kind.' For a heartbeat his eyes twinkled as Lord Dunstany's used to and Piro felt a tug of recognition. Then he was the cold, pompous young man again. Maybe not as young as he appeared. 'A disguise is only as good as its detail, kingsdaughter. A maid servant would not have clean toes and fingers.'

'You knew it was me from the start!'

'Why do you think I was so quick to get you away from Palatyne? His Utland Power-worker is a dangerous man.'

'But you... when you were Lord Dunstany, you mocked the Utlander, made him out to be weaker than you,' Piro countered.

'I did,' Tyro conceded. He glanced to Fyn. 'What happens if two equally skilled swordsmen meet?'

'They don't battle unless they are forced to, because they know one or both will die.'

'What if one swordsman knows the other is more powerful?'

'He bluffs,' Fyn said, and his eyes widened. 'Sounds as if you were playing a dangerous game, Agent Tyro.'

'We play the game we must. Each of you knows that.'

They were all silent for a moment.

Then Piro had to ask, 'But why? Why play at all? Why did you accompany Palatyne when he invaded Rolencia? Why didn't the mage go? Is he too frail and old? Is he truly over two hundred years old?'

'The mage is a very great man and he does not discuss his plans with a slip of a girl,' Agent Tyro told her, turning to speak to Fyn.

Furious, Piro walked away, pretending to study the war table. She hated Agent Tyro, felt he'd made a fool of her. Her face burned, as she tried to recall everything that had passed between Tyro and herself, when he had been disguised as Lord Dunstany.

Believing him an old man she had treated him like a grandfather, but Dunstany had not treated her like a slave. He had been kind to her.

Only Tyro wasn't Dunstany. He was a cold, arrogant young man. Her mind raced.

At least she knew why Dunstany had pulled the bed curtain every night. The agent could not maintain his disguise while he slept. His Affinity must be powerful to maintain a disguise all day, even aided with the player's arts.

Fyn's voice reached her. '... met Dunstany in Marchand. So that's why he... you sent me to the *Wyvern's Whelp*.'

Piro turned. Fyn had told them how he'd failed to assassinate Palatyne, finding the noble Power-worker in the bed instead. That was the night Dunstany had locked her in the cupboard, to protect her, he'd said. To keep her away from Fyn more like. And to think they had been so close.

'I had to get you safely out of Rolencia.' A wry grin tugged at Tyro's lips, reminding her of Dunstany and how much she missed him. Only he had never existed. At least, the Lord Dunstany she knew hadn't existed. There was an odd pain in her chest.

'I could not believe my luck when you tried to kill me,' Tyro confessed.

Piro laughed outright.

Isolt and Fyn both stared at her. When Tyro met her eyes, his held a smile. He understood.

She found this unnerving so she confronted him. 'Lord Dun... Agent Tyro. I can understand why you let Palatyne give me to Isolt. You had no choice. But why did you leave Merofynia just when Isolt needed you?'

'The mage called me back. He has many irons in the fire.'

'Another thing,' Fyn said. 'If you knew Seelon was Piro all along, why didn't you tell me? Why did you send me off to... rescue Isolt?'

Piro caught the slight hesitation and guessed Fyn had not been sent to rescue Isolt, but to abduct her.

Lord Dunstany... *Tyro* knew Isolt. He had to realise she wouldn't want to marry Palatyne. Ahh, he had been testing Fyn. She let the revelation slide, eager to hear what Tyro had to say.

'Serving Isolt was the safest place for King Rolen's daughter. But I was not sure if Piro would be with her when you found her.' The agent drew something from his pocket, fingering it absently. Piro recognised a Kingdoms piece, a monk. 'The mage was testing you, Fyn. You had to pass or your piece would have been flawed.'

'You speak in riddles.' Fyn bristled.

'Forgive me,' Tyro said, but Piro could tell he didn't mean it. He meant, *you have to forgive me, because you have no choice*. She really didn't like him. 'Being obscure is a failing of those with Affinity and I was raised by the master of all mages.' He changed topic abruptly. 'Do you want to see your brother restored to the throne of Rolencia, Fyn?'

'Of course I do. But what is it to you, or the mage for that matter?'

'For you to understand, I must tell you a little about my master. Mage Tsulamyth has been playing the game of Duelling Kingdoms for nearly two hundred years, gradually building power and influence. A hundred and fifty years ago, he convinced the five powerful noble families of Ostron Isle to elect a ruler, instead of assassinating each other in a bid for power.

'Under this system Ostron Isle has prospered. Not that there haven't been attempts by ambitious nobles to set themselves up as kings instead of electors,' Agent Tyro admitted with a half-smile. He spread his hands. 'Then the mage spent many years trying to bring about a peace between Rolencia and Merofynia, only succeeding when Myrella Merofyn Kingsdaughter married King Rolen.'

Piro looked away, recalling the price her mother had paid for that peace. Rather than reveal her Affinity, Myrella had let her own father sail off to his death.

'So Rolencia is part of Mage Tsulamyth's Duelling Kingdoms game?' Fyn asked.

'It is hardly a game, Fyn Rolen Kingson. When Palatyne unleashed the hounds of war his warriors ravaged your kingdom.' Tyro lifted his hands in a helpless gesture. 'Palatyne is ruled by ambition. While playing Lord Dunstany, I did what I could to lessen Palatyne's evil influence, and I did save the kingsdaughter.' He nodded to Piro. 'Not that she wasn't doing a good job of saving herself.'

Piro flushed. Was Agent Tyro trying to charm her? She had instinctively wanted to trust Lord Dunstany, but he had never existed. Instead, this agent had played on her affection for an old man. At least that explained why Dunstany had entrapped her soul in the amber pendant. It was something Agent Tyro would do, because he did not truly trust anyone. How could he, when he was so good at deceiving people?

No one spoke. A ship passed by on the Ring Sea, the tips of its masts level with the balcony. They heard someone on board singing a song about parted lovers.

'So, do you want Byren to become king of Rolencia, Fyn?' the agent said.

'Of course.'

'What of yourself?'

'I was never raised to be a kingson. I was meant to renounce the world this midsummer when I became a monk.'

Fyn cast Agent Tyro a wary glance. 'Since the mage's spies know so much, they probably know that some of Halcyon's monks survived. My friends are waiting for me to return. When Byren is king we will rebuild Halcyon Abbey.'

'Very well. Captain Nefysto will take you to Rolencia.' Agent Tyro retrieved something from inside his deep sleeve. 'Take this to Byren Kingsheir. It will convince the remaining warlords to support him.'

Fyn eyed the brass message cylinder. From here Piro could see it was embossed with an image of the abeille, the butterfly-winged bee of Ostron Isle.

'What is it?' Fyn asked.

'An offer of alliance from the Elector of Ostron Isle.' Relief flooded Piro.

But Fyn did not accept the cylinder. 'The elector is failing. He'll be replaced and this will be worthless.'

'A fair point, Fyn, but the warlords don't know that,' Tyro countered. 'While they're fighting for your brother in the belief that Ostron Isle supports him, the mage will be negotiating the support of the new elector.' He offered the message cylinder again.

Fyn accepted it, speaking stiffly. 'I thank you, Agent Tyro. It seems I have misjudged you and your master. I'm sorry. I was not trained for the game of Kingdoms.'

'Sometimes our path chooses us. Perhaps it is not your fate to renounce the world, Fyn Kingson. Here.' Agent Tyro passed Fyn the Kingdoms piece he had been toying with. 'Your piece.'

'But I wasn't playing,' Fyn said, taking it. 'It's warm to touch.' He glanced down at the piece and his eyes widened. 'Why, it looks just like me!'

Piro and Isolt hurried closer to study the Kingdoms piece. It was unmistakably Fyn. Did that mean...

Piro ran to the far end of the war table, locating Ostron Isle. The elector's piece wore his turbaned crown and there was a hooded piece, the mage. Amongst the many others were also two female pieces. 'Come look, Isolt. It's you. Why, it has your high forehead and small nose.'

'Don't touch,' Tyro warned, as he joined them.

Isolt leaned close. 'Why am I holding a sword?'

Agent Tyro gave her a rueful smile. 'The war table is Mage Tsulamyth's invention. According to this you are on the way to becoming a warrior queen.'

'Me? But I hate war!'

Fyn laughed. 'What about you, Piro? What does your piece reveal?'

She blinked, skin suddenly cold. 'Why do I have no face?'

As Tyro glanced to the piece, she read surprise and alarm, quickly hidden.

Isolt slid an arm around her shoulder. 'Don't worry, Piro. It is only a game.'

But they all knew it was much more. Fyn turned to the agent. 'What will happen to my sister and Isolt while I'm gone?'

'They will be safe here on Mage Isle. Even the elector has no power over this island. Wait.' Tyro held up his hand. 'Before you go. You wear a pendant around your neck?'

'Yes.' Fyn tugged on the chain, bringing Halcyon's Fate into view. 'Do you want it? You let me keep it in Port Marchand.'

'I've been hiding King Rolen's kin from the Utlander since Rolenhold fell. That Fate was nearly your undoing, Fyn. It was lucky I was the one who sensed it the first time you used it. I've felt it each time since, and others will feel it too. Don't use it again until I can train you in the art of defence.'

'That's it!' Isolt announced suddenly. They all turned to her. '*Tyro* is an old Merofynian word for apprentice. You are Mage Tsulamyth's apprentice. That is why you have such strong Affinity.'

Agent Tyro gave her a mocking bow. 'You have exposed all my secrets, kingsdaughter.'

And still Piro didn't like him.

BYREN WATCHED WARLORD Corvel as the gangplank was lowered. The sight of Corvel's fabulous manticore chitin armour reminded Byren how he had killed a manticore pride and given the chitin to his father, to be fashioned into armour. There had only been time to make a chestplate before the castle was besieged, and it hadn't helped King Rolen when Palatyne killed him under a flag of truce and confiscated the chestplate for himself.

Byren returned his attention to the warlord of Manticore Spar.

The spar's emblem, the red manticore, glistened on a field of black. Corvel was half a head shorter than Byren but thicker around the chest. The long temple plaits that hung from his helmet were iron-grey and bound with many gold circles, celebrating the enemies he had killed.

Last midwinter, when Corvel should have been swearing allegiance to King Rolen, he had been accused of slipping over the Divide to raid Rolencian villages. The warlord had denied it, claiming anyone could have planted the Manticore standard to implicate his warriors, and had eventually given his allegiance. But it had left Byren wondering about his loyalty.

Now they stood on the wharf in Feid Bay, Byren Kingsheir, his loyal Warlord Feid and Orrade, captain of his honour guard, along with their most trusted men-at-arms. Byren had thought they looked impressive in their armour, cloaks lifting in the breeze, until he got a good look a Corvel's ships.

Each must have held at least a hundred warriors. The sides bristled with oars and the deck could not be seen for shields and helmeted heads. The message was clear. Warlord Corvel would make a good ally or a very bad enemy.

What could Byren say to win this canny old warrior's support?

'Corvel must have sailed as soon as he got my message,' Feid whispered to Byren. 'That's a good sign. But he doesn't look too friendly.'

'He never does,' Orrade muttered. 'It's the eyebrow. Most people have two.'

Byren snorted and swallowed his laughter.

'Corvel gathered his warriors right away and sailed. Either he comes to aid me,' Byren whispered grimly, 'or he comes to wipe me out.'

He felt Feid shift uncomfortably. They were exposed on the wharf with a ceremonial guard. The Foenix warlord had not called his men in from their outlying farms. In the township women and children far outnumbered those who could defend themselves from seasoned warriors.

Corvel's boots thudded on the wharf as he strode towards Byren and his supporters. He came to a stop just beyond arm's length, with four of his seven sons at his back.

'This time we meet in very different circumstances, Byren Kingsheir,' Corvel said. 'This time I am not defending my name against baseless accusations.'

'It's the king's duty to protect his people.' Byren held the warlord's eyes, making no apology. 'Someone ordered the raid on that village.'

'Not me. Yet, I rebuilt it as a sign of good faith. Now, King Rolen's dead and you come crawling to me, needing my support.'

Corvel indicated the leogryf-tooth necklace which rested on Byren's chest. 'They call you Byren Leogryfslayer, say you killed the beast with your bare hands.'

'I had a knife,' Byren admitted. 'And the beastie was old.'

'But not toothless?'

'He was when I finished with him.' Byren grinned, determined not to beg Corvel to join him. This old warrior respected strength.

Corvel studied him. 'Now your cousin Cobalt sits on your father's throne, with the backing of Merofynia. Cobalt is not old and toothless.'

'Cobalt is a snake,' Byren said. 'Toothless but dangerous.'

Corvel's eyes narrowed thoughtfully. 'You talk well, second son, but can you lead an army?'

Since Byren had asked himself the same question he had no easy answer. 'Only Halcyon's Fate knows. And, since the mystics master does not have the Fate, he can't glimpse the future. As I see it, you have two choices, Corvel. Break your oath to my father, give Cobalt your loyalty and let him tax your spar to line his pockets, or join me and throw him out of Rolencia.'

'Perhaps I have a third choice. Break no oath and resist Cobalt myself.'

'You cannot stand alone. If Cobalt chose, he could chase your people down the length of Manticore Spar, raiding and looting until he drove the last warrior into the sea and took your women and children for slaves. United, we can defeat him. He can't fight on five fronts. If the warlords don't unite behind me, he can pick you off one by one.'

Corvel considered this, then he held out his right hand. 'They say you can be trusted, Leogryf Slayer.'

Relieved, Byren took his hand off his sword hilt and stepped forwards to grasp the warlord's. Without warning Corvel pulled him off balance, sweeping his legs from under him. It was a wrestling move Lence had used on him many times.

Byren reacted without thinking. Even as he went down he scissored his legs, trying to catch Corvel, but the older man's sons saved him, hauling him back and steadying him.

Orrade drew Byren upright. 'Say the word.'

At his signal there would be bloodshed, a pitched battle on the wharf. Byren waited, watching the warlord's face. If Corvel had meant to kill him he could have.

The warlord eased his shoulders, threw back his head and laughed. His laughter echoed up the steep-sided bay, echoed by the cries of the gulls circling overhead.

Corvel opened his arms and Byren stepped in,

ready for anything, but this time Corvel clapped him on the shoulders, leaning close.

'Your father belittled me. My men would not have respected me if I hadn't done the same to you.' And he went off into another deep belly-laugh.

Blood roaring in his ears, Byren joined him. It seemed he had passed the old warrior's test.

But now he had to strike soon. No doubt Corvel would have brought food. Even so, Feid would be making up the shortfall, supplying wine and ale. The warlord could not afford to keep this up for long.

Chapter Seventeen

As FYN STEPPED off the gangplank onto the deck of the *Wyvern's Whelp*, Bantam nudged Jakulos, who straightened up. Both men grinned at him.

'Did you have your way with the pretty little maid?' Jakulos asked.

Fyn shrugged. 'She's not my type.'

'What, you fancy the kingsdaughter?' Bantam asked. 'Think she'll lift her skirts for a common sailor, even if he was a monk?'

Fyn's hand shot out, fixing on Bantam's throat, lifting him off his feet. Jakulos grabbed Fyn, his sheer strength breaking his hold.

'A jest, little monk. 'Twas only a jest,' Bantam rasped, massaging his throat and watching him warily.

'Come here, Agent Monk,' Captain Nefysto called, frowning from the cabin door. Fyn hurried over to him.

Nefysto closed the door after them. 'Don't threaten my crew, kingson. As far as they are concerned, you're the mage's agent, a monk out for revenge.'

'He insulted the kingsdaughter,' Fyn said.

'He's an ignorant man but he's a good sailor, and loyal. Something a deposed kingson should appreciate.'

Nefysto was right. 'I'm sorry.'

'So you should be. We're risking our lives so you can play Kingdoms and we are not even your men-at-arms.'

Nefysto gestured for Fyn to enter his cabin. As the captain placed a rolled-up map on his desk, Fyn wondered how much Tyro had revealed. Obviously not Piro's true identity.

Nefysto spread out the map, holding it in place with an inkwell and several books. 'The *Wyvern's Whelp* will avoid the shipping lanes. When we approach land again we will be deep inside Rolencian waters. We'll make our way around the spars to Foenix Spar. Byren Kingsheir has taken refuge with Warlord Feid.'

'Good.' The sooner he reached Byren, with the offer of support from the Elector of Ostron Isle, the better were his brother's chances of winning over the other four warlords. 'How long?'

'Nine, ten days.'

'So long?' The warlords might turn on Byren and hand him over to Cobalt.

Nefysto placed a hand on Fyn's shoulder. 'The *Wyvern's Whelp* is the fastest ship of her size on the seas. No one could get you there sooner!'

* * *

PIRO CREPT INTO the war table chamber to look at her piece. They had been on Mage Isle five days and the little carving still had no face. Did that mean she was going to die?

She wished she'd never seen the war table. Going to the balcony, she stepped out and looked across at the steep slope of the encircling island, Ostron Ring. It was covered in terraced gardens and villas. A strange bird cried above her and she turned to look up at the tower. From the top floor she saw someone release an Ostronite messenger bird. The Pica's black wings and white vest flashed as it arrowed out in search of its mate. The female could find her way anywhere in the world to her mate. And, if either died, the other sang a song of love and lay down beside them, refusing to eat. Since only Agent Tyro went to the top of the tower, he had to have released the bird.

Piro took to her heels, waiting in the shadows for Tyro to come down the stairs. They'd hardly seen him since the initial meeting. She suspected he was avoiding them.

Hearing his footsteps, she moved to confront the agent. 'Was there news from Fyn?'

He shook his head.

'News for Fyn?'

'Not this time. The mage has his fingers in many pies, Piro.'

She bristled. Every time he said her name, he made it sound like he was laughing at her.

Tyro kept walking, so she followed. They came out

into a courtyard where Isolt sat feeding the foenix.

Tyro bowed. 'Mage Tsulamyth invites Isolt Merofyn Kingsdaughter to attend the elector's feast with him.'

Piro and Isolt exchanged looks.

'But you said Isolt was safe as long as she stayed on Mage Isle,' Piro countered. 'Why should we risk this?'

'The elector is dying. The other four powerful families are preparing to choose a new elector. The mage will need the new elector's support. Tonight my master needs to show the powerful nobles that he holds the winning piece.' Tyro nodded to Isolt. 'The mage will be by your side and you will be under the protection of the elector himself.'

Isolt released the foenix, which flew over to Piro. She caught him but had to put him down, as he was getting too big to hold. She knelt to stroke his long neck, noting how the brilliant red comb was already coming through on the crown of his head.

'Is Mage Tsulamyth's position so precarious?' Isolt asked.

'We are approaching nexus points in every kingdom.' Tyro turned to Piro. 'The mage asks that you tell him if you have any Affinity visions.'

She nodded.

'Then he knows who Piro is?' Isolt asked.

Tyro barely hesitated. 'Of course.'

He lied. *Why?* Piro wondered.

'I don't like appearing before Ostronite nobles like a Kingdoms piece,' Isolt said. 'But then I've had to do a lot of things I haven't liked.'

Piro straightened and came over to her. 'Don't

worry. I'll be with you.'

'Speak only Merofynian,' Tyro warned. 'Piro, let the nobles think you don't understand Ostronite. Report everything you hear.'

She both nodded. Since the mage had taken them in and promised to protect them, spying for him was the least she could do.

FYN LIFTED HIS face to the morning sun and inhaled the sea breeze. A messenger bird gave its cry, alerting him, and he lifted his arm, adjusting for the bird's weight. It was marvellous how the picas could find this ship on the faceless ocean. They chose to come to him, because of his natural Affinity.

According to the mage's spies three of the spar warlords had sworn to fight alongside his brother. Fyn had suggested they send a message directly to the spy in Feid's stronghold but Nefysto explained the *Wyvern's Whelp* pica would fly only to Mage Isle.

'Then the mage must send a message to the kingsheir,' Fyn had said.

'That is up to the mage. He may not want to reveal his spy.' Nefysto had shaken his head. 'Let the mage play the game his way, Agent Monk.'

Now Fyn headed towards Nefysto, who was taking a reading of the height of the sun above the horizon to work out their position. 'A message, captain.'

Nefysto put his sextant aside and offered his hand to the bird, taking her into his cabin, where the male sang sweetly in greeting.

The bird knew it would not be placed with its mate

until it delivered its message and began to warble in fast, garbled tones that Fyn found almost impossible to understand.

Fyn watched Nefysto, trying to read his face. 'Bad news?'

The captain walked the bird over to the cage, where its mate hopped around in excitement, singing loudly. He slipped the cage door open and the female fluttered over to the stand. The two birds wrapped their heads around each other and set up a soft cooing. And Nefysto slid the screen across.

'Not bad news of Isolt and her maid?' Fyn pressed.

'The warlord of Leogryf Spar promised to support Byren Kingsheir, but he has been seen moving his men over the Divide into Rolencia. And there is still no word from Cockatrice Spar.'

'Leogryf has betrayed him?' Fyn cursed. 'When the Leogryf warlord hears of the elector's alliance he will regret his choice.'

'You'll have to wait three days.' Nefysto laughed. 'The *Wyvern's Whelp* can't get you there any faster.'

'A lot can happen in three days,' Fyn muttered, but he had to be content with that.

PIRO DECIDED THAT she did not like the mage. He had a terrible temper. When Agent Tyro was late he told the coachman to set off without him. Isolt and Piro exchanged glances and huddled in their seats. The mage was the oldest man Piro had ever met – so frail and bent he was barely taller than her. His face was webbed with wrinkles, and bristly white brows hid his eyes.

He grumbled when they had to walk from the coach to the chambers, where the elector's feast was being held. He grumbled while they waited in line to be received by the elector. But Piro was not fooled. His grumbling hid a mind as sharp as the winter wind.

At last they stepped onto the dais to greet the elector, who lay on a daybed. The couch was cast from bronze, decorated with wyverns. Even the couch's legs ended in wyvern claws. Piro was aware of the nobles watching, listening avidly. At Isolt's name there was a ripple of reaction and excited speculation.

Piro stood behind Isolt, as a maidservant should. The elector's couch was only a body length from her. When Isolt and the mage stepped aside, she caught sight of the elector for the first time. Her vision shimmered and shifted to Unseen sight. The bones of the elector's skull showed through his skin. She gasped and glanced around. Had no one else noticed?

'And who is that behind Isolt Merofyn Kingsdaughter?' the elector asked in Ostronite.

'Her maid, Seela.' The mage gave Piro a nudge forwards, speaking Merofynian.

Struggling to hide the fact that she viewed the Unseen world, Piro somehow remembered her role, gave a servant's bow and said the first thing that came into her head. 'Your wyvern couch is a wondrous thing.'

'Do you like wyverns?' The elector spoke Merofynian out of courtesy. Since his face was little more than a talking skull, Piro found it hard to meet his eyes.

'A big male nearly killed us.' Piro winced. He was going to die and all she could talk about was death.

'They're not all like that. You must see my pet wyvern. She's a beauty.'

'You are very kind,' Piro said, and he was, to notice a mere servant. She bowed, and they stepped down from the dais as other nobles claimed the elector's attention. Piro tore her gaze away from him.

'What is it, girl?' the mage asked. But before she could answer a beautiful middle-aged woman approached them.

'This is Comtissa Cera. Her husband, the Comtes, died last year and she fancies herself the next elector,' Mage Tsulamyth whispered to Isolt and Piro. 'Beware this cat. She has claws.'

'Mage Tsulamyth?' The comtissa bestowed a bow on him.

'Comtissa,' the mage greeted her with no more than a nod.

Comtissa Cera ignored Piro, who dragged in a ragged breath and tried to control her Affinity-induced sight. The world no longer shimmered.

'I hear your father grows weaker every day, my dear,' the comtissa said to Isolt. 'What will you do when he dies? You cannot let a barbarian duke claim the throne of Merofynia.'

Piro stiffened. But Isolt was used to dealing with this kind of courtier.

'Oh, Father is much better than he appears,' Isolt replied. 'It is the elector's health I fear for. What will Ostron Isle do when they lose him? With the Twin Isles in upheaval, Ostron Isle needs a strong leader.'

The comtissa's eyes narrowed.

Just then another group came over to meet Isolt and the mage introduced them. Comtes Abeillus began to pay Isolt extravagant compliments, which Piro knew would bore her silly.

Piro glanced out through the arches to the courtyard where a fountain played over a pool. Servants had poured oil on the pool's surface and lit it. Statues of wyverns frolicked in the flames as if frozen in stone. Such extravagance.

Behind her two old noblemen, who thought Piro could not understand their language, spoke frankly of Duke Palatyne. For all they cared he might conquer Rolencia and the Snow Bridge. They did not fear him, because of the logistics of attacking Ostron Isle. The Merofynian army would have to sail across the Stormy Sea and enter the Ring Sea. But they would never get that far because Ostron Isle had the greatest navy the world had ever seen and, as a last resort, they could tighten the chain across the entrance to the Ring Sea.

All around her the nobles jostled and jockeyed for position, shoring up alliances. They were like carrion birds waiting for the elector to die so they could pick over the bones.

Piro felt a touch on her back.

'We have been seen and discussed, we can go now. My bones are too old for these late nights.' The mage leant heavily on Isolt's arm. 'But first we must take formal leave of the elector.'

Due to the crowd, they had not moved more than a few steps from the edge of the dais. Piro looked over at the elector.

In a blink, her sight shifted to the Unseen world again. The elector was just a skull, bare bones, no skin, no life. With a start she realised this was one of the nexus points Tyro had spoken of and she had failed to heed her Affinity.

The elector was going to die tonight.

Piro slipped through the nobles, running lightly to the dais, where she dropped to her knees. The elector clutched his chest, straining to breathe. His eyes were frightened. His hand seized hers, squeezing so hard her bones hurt.

'Mage,' Piro cried, her high voice cutting through all conversation. 'The elector needs you!'

The musicians stopped mid-note. The elector's breath rattled in his throat. Once, twice, he gasped. Then no more. As his spirit left, Piro's sight returned to normal.

There was absolute silence and, though she hadn't known him, tears stung Piro's eyes.

Mage Tsulamyth knelt at her side to gently close the elector's eyes, smoothing the lines of pain from his face and placing his hands neatly on his chest.

A sob escaped Piro. She had not wept for her father and mother, or Lence. There had been no time. Now she wept for a man who had been kind to a maidservant, someone who could do him no favours.

'Murderer!' roared a voice.

Piro wiped tears from her eyes and spun to see Comtes Abeillus pointing an accusing finger at Tsulamyth.

'I saw the mage slip something into the elector's drink earlier,' Comtes Abeillus claimed. 'He killed the elector. Arrest him!'

'Rubbish.' Piro leapt to her feet, forgetting she was not supposed to understand Ostronite. 'The mage gave him nothing.'

Tsulamyth placed a restraining hand on Piro's arm, struggling to his feet with great dignity.

Comtes Abeillus ignored her, calling for his private swordsmen. A dozen armed men in emerald-green cloaks barged into the room with their weapons drawn.

'They came too quickly,' Isolt whispered as she joined Piro and the mage. 'This was planned.'

'I fear you are right,' Tsulamyth muttered. He raised his voice, suddenly finding strength. 'Comtissa Cinnamome. I am accused of murdering your kinsman. What do you say?'

'The accusations are false. My uncle died of natural causes.' The comtissa spun to face the other nobles. 'Abeillus only accuses Mage Tsulamyth because he seeks to discredit the mage. He knows Tsulamyth doesn't favour him and won't vote in his favour. The elector's death was a natural death and by law, I propose Comtissa Cera of Cerastus House as the new elector.'

'I accept.' The comtissa stepped forwards.

'I propose my uncle, Comtes Abeillus,' a youth announced. 'House Abeillus is due to hold the electorship.'

'It is not a child's game, to be taking turns. The position requires competence and reliability,'

Comtissa Cinnamome snapped.

'What of Merulus House?' a youth with prematurely silver hair spoke up. 'I propose myself for the position. Cerastus House held the electorship before Cinnamome's.'

'Transport my uncle's body back to his chamber,' Comtissa Cinnamome ordered.

'No,' the youth from Abeillus House objected.

'Will you fight over my uncle's dead body?' The comtissa signalled the elector's swordsmen. 'Show some respect. Throw these buffoons out.'

The chamber erupted. Hired swordsmen clashed, tables overturned. People screamed and fled, others drew their own weapons and sought to settle old scores. The mage grabbed Piro and Isolt, displaying unexpected strength as he ran from the room. A single swordsman blocked the doorway, weapon drawn. Piro came to an abrupt stop, heart thundering.

'Do you want to live out the rest of your life unable to make love to your wife?' the mage asked, soft voice filled with menace.

The man stepped aside.

They ran down a corridor. Servants fled alongside them. Caped swordsmen ran in the opposite direction, as they went to aid their masters.

The mage hesitated at the courtyard to the city. The main gate was closed and around fifteen swordsmen waited, obviously ordered to stop anyone from leaving.

'Back this way.' Tsulamyth led them up a flight and down another corridor. At the end of this, they had to wait for a dozen caped swordsmen to settle what appeared to be a private dispute over a woman, before they went up another stair. An eerie howl rang through the palace, making Piro's skin prickle. Thrusting open carved double doors, the mage led them into a chamber. It was simply decorated by palace standards.

The Comtissas Cinnamome and Cera, and two others, had gathered around a bed. All of them turned at the intrusion. The howl came again, haunting and bereft.

'Comtissa Cinnamome,' Tsulamyth greeted her, hardly out of breath.

'We brought his body back here, to have a healer proclaim it is a natural death –' Another howl cut her short. Stepping away from the bed, she revealed the dead elector and a young wyvern no bigger than a large wolf hound. The Affinity beast lifted its head and howled again, forelimbs on the elector's bed.

'Will someone get rid of this creature!' the comtissa demanded.

'Abeillus will claim you bribed the healer. The matter will have to go before the Council of Five,' Mage Tsulamyth told her. 'Ask each of the major houses to send their own healer to verify your man's verdict.'

'I'll send for mine,' Comtissa Cera said, and spoke with a servant, while Cinnamome beckoned one of her servants.

The wyvern sank its head onto the elector's chest and whimpered.

'Why, the poor thing's sad,' Piro exclaimed. 'I didn't know wyverns could be so devoted.'

'Their nature grows to resemble their owner's,'

Isolt said. 'At least, that is what I've read.'

'Get her out of here,' the comtissa ordered, shocking Piro until she realised Cinnamome meant the wyvern, not Isolt.

A youth, who looked enough like the comtissa to be her son, tried to drag the wyvern off the bed, but the Affinity beast planted her claws in the covers and the elector's body nearly fell to the floor.

'Fool!' Comtissa Cinnamome shrieked.

'I was only trying to help, Mother,' the youth protested.

The healer arrived. The wyvern howled. Screams and smashing glass echoed up from the courtyard below. Piro fought a rising panic. They had to get out of here. At any moment Comtes Abeillus's swordsmen might overcome the elector's and they could be arrested.

'Poor pet,' Isolt whispered, as she stroked the wyvern's neck.

'Behind the ears,' Mage Tsulamyth told her. From the table by the bed he took a glass jar filled with odd-shaped fruit and gave it to Piro. 'Open this jar, my old hands are too weak. Give Isolt a wyvern-nip for the beastie.' Then he went to speak with the healer.

When Piro opened the jar a vile fish smell almost made her gag, but it caused the wyvern to leave the bed and sniff hopefully.

Isolt put her hand into the jar, wrinkling her nose in distaste. 'They're all soft and squishy. Ugh. Some sort of sea food?'

'Sea fruit,' the mage corrected, returning to them.

'Give the wyvern one and come with me.'

Isolt fed the wyvern who took the wyvern-nip delicately in her claws. She sat on her haunches, which made her as tall as Isolt, to nibble the treat. Piro sealed the jar and went to return it to the table.

'No, bring it *and* the wyvern,' Tsulamyth said.

Half a dozen swordsmen barged into the room, wearing yet another noble family's colours.

'Ahh, the House Picollus,' the mage muttered. 'I think it is time we slipped away.'

Isolt waved her fishy fingers under the wyvern's snout. 'Come, my pretty.'

The comtissa began a shouting battle with the old woman leading the Picollus swordsmen.

Tsulamyth led them further into the elector's chambers, to a wood panel on one side of the fireplace. He unhooked a lantern and pivoted the silver hook. The mahogany panel rolled aside to reveal a secret passage. Seeing Piro's surprised expressions, one corner of his mouth lifted in crooked smile. 'A secret passage. No respectable Ostronite noble would be without one. Come.'

The mage went first, then Isolt with the wyvern at her heels, and lastly Piro. Before the panel slid shut after her, Piro heard something smash and a shrill cry from the comtissa. Ostron Isle's run of peace and prosperity had come to an abrupt end.

She followed the others down the secret passage, which eventually led out to a deserted alley. In the next square they hired carry-chairs to take them back to Mage Isle. Tsulamyth declared he could not walk another step. Piro was amazed he had been able to lead them so far.

There was a short argument with the carry-chair men, who had to be paid double to carry the wyvern in Isolt's chair. Piro had no idea why the mage was taking it with them. What would they do with the Affinity beast?

Chapter Eighteen

PIRO STOOD ON the gate tower, hands gripping the stone. Smoke rose from the palaces atop Ostron Isle. All night the fighting had raged.

She'd thought it through. The upheavals did not matter to Fyn for, as long as the warlords did not know the elector was dead, the document he carried would still be useful to Byren. And since the heads of Ostron Isle's five great houses would hardly be sending messenger birds to the spars, no profit there, news of the elector's death would have to travel by ship.

The big question was, would the mage be able to convince the next elector to honour the alliance? How long before the fighting settled down and they knew who the new elector was?

No time soon, judging by the way people were still fleeing.

From up here she could see boats laden with

families and their possessions fleeing across the Ring
Sea to the safety of the outer island.

A child's cries carried to her and she looked back
to the inner island. On the low wharf not far from
the bridge to Mage Isle a woman was pleading with
a captain to let her onto their boat. She carried an
infant and its cries were what had attracted Piro.
Several more children hung onto her skirts, all
looked tired, hungry and dishevelled.

Piro couldn't actually hear the words, but she
could read their actions. The captain refused her.
No room. The woman climbed wearily back up
to the road. Where it met the bridge she hesitated
undecided. Obviously she could not go back. One
of the small boys climbed onto the bridge's rail
and stood there, yelling abuse at the boat that had
refused them passage.

Just then a dozen riders, magenta cloaks flapping,
rode past at a gallop, heading for Mage Isle. Tyro
had been turning them away all night. The mage
would not interfere with the five families. They had
to choose the next elector. Piro anticipated these
men would also be turned away. People scattered to
let them pass.

Startled by the horses' clattering hooves, the boy
toppled off the bridge, falling into the sea. Only Piro
noticed. His mother was too busy with the other
children. He bobbed up again but he struggled to
keep himself afloat and the current started to take
him away from the shore.

Piro looked about. No one had seen. No one else
could save him. She darted down the stairs from the

tower, onto the wall-walk. As she ran she tore off her over-dress and sprang onto the stone rim. She was a good swimmer. Judging the distance and direction of his drift she dived out and down, dropping two storeys into the sea.

The water was shockingly cold, and deep. She fought her way up, towards the light that danced on the wavelets above. Tossing hair from her face she turned, looking for the boy. From the bridge she saw the mother waving frantically. Alerted by her screams, people on the boats were starting to turn, but they were at the wharf.

Now that the boy realised he was being swept away, he panicked and floundered. Piro struck out for him. Six strong strokes and she was there. Surprisingly strong arms wound around her neck. He clung to her like a limpet, dragging her down. Shivering and sobbing, he coughed up sea water.

She soothed him, treading water until he had calmed enough to follow her instructions, then she turned him about, hooked an arm across his chest and set off for the shore.

The mother had clambered down onto some seaweed-strewn steps by the time Piro reached the stones, and several people helped them out. The woman alternately hugged and scolded the boy, who stood there, miserable and shaking.

Piro brushed the mother's thanks aside.

'I don't know what I'll do. My house has burned down. I've nowhere to go. Two of these children aren't even mine. I found them wandering in the street, after their family was killed.'

'Do you have people on the outer isle?' Piro asked.

'No. I hoped someone would take us in.'

Piro pushed wet hair from her face. 'Come with me.' She scooped up one of the smaller children and marched up to the steps to the road and across the bridge to Mage Isle.

Five warriors in magenta cloaks waited at the gates, their mounts stamping impatiently. Agent Tyro stood on the gate tower, in discussion with their leader.

Piro strode through the men, dripping wet, followed by the children and their mother and more homeless townspeople, who had come to watch.

'Open the gates!' Piro had lost her shoes, or she would have kicked the wood.

The warriors muttered at her effrontery.

Tyro stared down at Piro, looking stunned. 'I can let you in, but not the townspeople, by the mage's orders.'

'By the mage's orders?' Piro was furious. 'My father never turned people away. It is the mage's duty to take these people in and protect them. Let me in and I'll tell him so, if you're afraid to.'

Tyro looked grim. After a moment he said something to the men behind him and turned back to the bridge. 'Stand aside, captain. Mage Tsulamyth offers asylum to the people of Ostron Isle.'

Even as he spoke the gates swung inwards and the soldiers backed their horses with bad grace. The captain shook his fist at Tyro.

'I'll report this to the comtissa!' he roared and rode off.

Piro ignored him and marched onto Mage Isle

with a dozen people at her back. By the time Tyro came down the stairs she'd sent the children and their mother to the kitchen and ordered a hot bath run for the half-drowned boy. Word was already spreading back to the crowded wharf.

'The men can bed down in the stables,' Piro told the gate-keeper. 'Women and children can go through to the hall.' She turned and found Tyro beside her. 'If that's all right with you.'

'It's the mage's decision,' he said, then his eyes widened as he saw the number of people flocking towards the bridge.

'They're desperate. You did the right thing,' Piro told him. 'Sometimes you have to do what you believe to be right, even if other people don't understand.' She bit her bottom lip. She had no reason to like Tyro, not after the way he had tricked her. But... 'Will you get in trouble with the mage?'

One corner of his mouth lifted. 'No more than usual.'

'BYREN,' ORRADE WHISPERED, face so close to his in the dim predawn that the warmth of his breath brushed Byren's skin.

He woke instantly, pulling back, only too aware of his honour guard asleep on the floor.

Orrade placed one knee on the bed. 'Byren, listen –'

He lifted a hand to silence Orrade but his friend kept speaking.

'...saw them, coming over the Divide. The sooner we strike the better.'

'Come all the way in.' Byren pressed his back to the carved head-board, as Orrade climbed onto the bed and let the canopy fall, so that they were private from the others. 'Now start again and keep your voice down.'

'I saw Leogryf's warlord march his warriors over the Divide. They wore cobalt-blue ribbons on their helmets.' Orrade rubbed his temples, frowning in concentration.

'An Affinity vision?'

Orrade nodded. 'Complete with thumping headache, and now I have grey moths clouding my sight.'

Fearful of someone overhearing and Orrade's Affinity being exposed, they both glanced to the canopy at the end of the bed, beyond which the honour guard slept. They could see nothing, of course, and the soft snoring continued as normal.

'I knew we could not trust Lord Leon,' Byren whispered.

'It wouldn't surprise me if he'd already made a pact with Cobalt before he came here to judge our strength and discover our plans.' Bitterness stretched Orrade's voice thin. 'I had a bad feeling about him. But I...' He shrugged. 'Will you commit your army on the strength of my vision?'

'I'm alive because of one of your visions.'

They were silent for a moment. Byren could not help but recall the kiss when Orrade found him in the seep and they both thought he was dying. To be on the receiving end of such love...

The bed curtain on the other side flicked open as someone slipped in, letting it fall behind them. Blinded by the darkness, they felt for Byren.

He lunged forwards, caught their arm and pulled them flat across the bed, pinning them with his body, feeling the firm curves of a woman's body, smelling the scent of... 'Florin?'

'Get off me.' She thrust at his chest with all her strength. It was not enough. And Byren realised she might be trained, she might be fast but, if a warrior got past her weapons, she had the strength of a lad. He wouldn't send a boy into battle, not if he could help it.

Florin thumped him, annoyed by her inability to make him budge. 'Off me, you great lump.'

Orrade chuckled.

Florin went still.

'Orrie had a vision,' Byren explained. 'Why are you here?'

She shoved and Byren pulled back. There was rustling as she sat up. 'The Lady Cinna's bird returned with a message. It must have been important because she ran right back to Feid's bed and they were whispering madly under the canopy. I heard something about betrayal.'

'So the warlord's pretty new wife is an Ostronite spy after all,' Orrade whispered.

'And Feid,' Florin added.

'But that does not mean Feid intends to betray me,' Byren said.

There was a knock at the chamber door. All three of them froze. Winterfall answered. Someone asked for Byren.

Before Winterfall could discover Orrade and Florin in his bed, Byren thrust open the canopy and stepped out. 'What is it?'

'The warlord's sent for you.' Winterfall kept his voice low. 'Do you want me to come too?'

'No.' He wanted Orrade with him. Anything was better than leaving him in a warm bed with Florin. But he could hardly ask Orrade to step out from his bed canopy now. 'I'll be right there. Wait here.'

He threw on breeches, a shirt and boots. The stone floor was cold as he followed the servant down the passage. The pool of golden lamplight illuminated just enough to see where to place his feet.

At the warlord's chamber Feid sent the servant off and invited Byren in. A lamp burned, illuminating a chamber much like his own. The fire had been lit and Lady Cinna waited, wrapped in a blanket on the floor by the fire. She scrambled to her feet as Byren entered.

'What is this?' Byren asked, wondering if half a dozen of Feid's honour guard waited in the next chamber with their swords drawn, but he did not think Feid would risk his pregnant wife in a brawl.

'We've had news,' Feid said. Like Byren, his breeches and shirt looked as if they'd been thrown on in haste. 'Leogryf's warlord has taken his men over the Divide. We need to strike now, before he can unite with Cobalt.'

'How do you know this?'

Feid deliberately did not glance to Cinna. 'A spy told me.'

'Do you trust this spy?'

'With my life.'

Byren let his breath out slowly as Cinna came to stand behind Feid, slipping her hand into his. Clearly,

Cinna was more than a kitchen maid become lady. Yet, just as clearly, she adored Feid.

'Byren?' Feid pressed.

'You're right. Send word to Unistag Spar.'

Back in his chamber he found his honour guard awake and Orrade with them. He didn't dare ask how his friend had slipped out of the bed without being seen.

Enough pale dawn light filtered in for him to see his honour guard's faces. They all turned expectantly, as he entered.

'I've sent a message to Unistag Spar. We leave today.' His last words were drowned by their cheers.

Orrade sent him a wry look.

At Byren's signal the others fell silent. 'It's lucky Corvel is here with his warriors. Without the women and children we'll move fast. I'll lead Corvel's men and the majority of my men over the secret pass and across the foothills. The Rolencian side of the fort won't be as heavily defended. Orrie?'

His friend nodded.

'You wait here for Unistag's warriors. Lead an attack on the fort, at dawn on the fifth day. Don't waste lives, but make it look like you mean it. I want the fort's defenders firmly focused on the threat from Foenix Spar when we attack the other gate.'

Orrade smiled. 'Understood.'

Byren looked into their expectant faces. 'Right. Let's get ready.'

Byren's honour guard had already rolled up their sleeping mats, now they filed out, eager for breakfast and a chance to reclaim Rolencia. Last out was

Orrade, who glanced once to the bed before shutting the door behind him.

Heart thudding, Byren pulled the bed curtain back to find Florin kneeling, head cocked to one side, listening intently. There was nothing wanton in her pose, but his body thought otherwise.

'They're gone?' she said.

He nodded.

'Good.' She thrust past him, tantalisingly close. 'I can be ready to leave in a few moments.'

Byren's heart sank. He already had Garzik and Elina's deaths on his conscience. He stared at her. How could he convince her to stay in the Foenix stronghold?

He couldn't. Short of locking her up, and that was just insulting. But he didn't have to put her in harm's way.

Thinking they were done, she turned to leave.

He caught her arm. 'You stay with Orrie.'

She brushed his hand off. 'I'd rather go with you. If Orrie's not with you, someone has to watch your back.'

'I watched my own back for years before you came along, Mountain-girl.'

She sniffed, then a thought occurred to her. 'Did Cinna admit to being the elector's spy?'

'No. Feid admitted only that someone spies for him, someone he trusts. That's why I need you here, for now. I need you to keep your eyes open.' *I need to keep you safe.*

'Of course.' She glanced up to him. 'What is it?'

The words were on the tip of his tongue but he

could not ask it of her. He would be denying who Florin was. Sylion take her, why did she have to be so stubborn?

'Be off. And keep out of trouble.' It was no more than he'd say to any of the lads.

She grinned. 'I'll serve under Orrie's command, but we'd better catch up with you in time to take Rolenhold!'

With that she was gone.

By mid-morning they were ready to leave. Men milled about in the stronghold courtyards, double-checking their travelling kits. Word of Leogryf's betrayal had spread, leaving a bad taste in everyone's mouths.

Byren caught Orrade's eye and led him into the shadows of the stable. It was quiet here. 'There's something I need you to do for me, Orrie.'

'Name it.'

But Byren hesitated. If he asked Orrade to watch over Florin, Orrade would know how he felt and Byren knew she loved one of his men. It might just be Orrade. In fact, it probably was, they'd spent enough time in each other's company. He didn't want his friend to hold back. Orrade enjoyed Florin's company and admired her. Let him marry Florin and settle the whispers once and for all.

It would be so much simpler if Orrade wed the mountain girl and made his wife available to his king. It wouldn't be the first time a king had come to such an arrangement with one of his loyal lords.

But Byren was not going to be that kind of king.

He cleared his throat, aware that he had taken too

long to answer. 'Make it look like a concerted effort to take the fort, but don't waste lives.'

Orrade nodded, a half-smile lightening his sharp eyes. 'And?'

And nothing. If Florin wanted to be a shield-maiden, she had to face death just as his warriors did. 'It's Winterfall. I overheard him giving Florin a hard time –'

'So that's why you arranged for her to sleep in Lady Cinna's chambers.' Orrade grinned. 'Don't worry. I'll keep her close by me.'

Byren swallowed. This was not the outcome he wanted, but it would be for the best. So he nodded.

'By the way, I told Catillum you wanted him and his monks to march with me,' Orrade said.

Byren cursed. He had forgotten the monks in his preoccupation with Florin. 'I thought you'd want the mystics master as far from you as possible, Orrie.'

'And I thought you'd want to keep him as far from the renegade Affinity at the old camp as possible.'

'Good point.' He didn't want Catillum anywhere near those caves with their old, untamed Affinity. Byren grinned and squeezed Orrade's shoulders. 'What would I do without you?'

Orrade shrugged. 'Flounder on, I suppose.'

Byren laughed and thumped him. As they marched out of the stable a horn sounded.

Everyone froze.

Byren met Orrade's eyes. Were they under attack?

He bounded up the tower stairs with Orrade at his heels. Here they found Feid already holding the Ostronite farseer to his eye.

'What is it?' Byren asked.

Wordlessly, Feid passed him the tube and Byren looked through it. He spotted three ships bristling with warriors, their helmets and shields gleaming in the sun. The wind lifted the banners to reveal the rearing cockatrice. Relief flooded him.

Byren closed the farseer with a snap and shouted the news. People cheered.

They headed down to the wharf, where the first ship retracted its oars as ropes were thrown across and secured. A young man marched down the gangplank, hand on sword hilt.

'That cub's too young to be the new warlord,' Orrade muttered.

'Well, he brings three hundred warriors, whatever he is,' Byren said and went down the wharf to greet the boy-warrior who stood almost as tall as Byren, but looked no more than fifteen.

'Byren Kingsheir?' he demanded.

Byren nodded.

He dropped to one knee. 'I'm Aseel, younger brother of Warlord Hrost, of Cockatrice Spar. I've come with three hundred men to help you retake Rolencia.' He got up, dusting off his knees and added apologetically, 'Hrost has kept back the rest. He doesn't trust Leogryf Spar.'

Byren snorted. 'For good reason. Lord Leon promised to support us then rode over the Divide!'

'He betrayed you?' Aseel demanded. 'He joined Cobalt?'

'Don't worry.' Seeing himself only a few years ago, Byren slung an arm around Aseel's shoulders and turned him towards the others. 'A warrior from the spar is worth two from the valley. Come meet Orrade and Warlord Feid.'

Chapter Nineteen

FYN STUDIED THE map. At last, they had entered the deep narrow bay that would bring them to Feid's stronghold. By midday he would see Byren and bring him the good news. He couldn't hold back a smile.

'Bad news.' Captain Nefysto walked into the cabin, with a messenger bird on his wrist, his expression grim. He crossed the cabin and placed the bird in its cage, behind the screen. 'The old elector is dead and there's been fighting in the streets of Ostron Isle. As yet there is no elector and we don't know if the new one will honour the alliance.'

Fyn came to his feet, mind racing. 'Only we know about this and, when the new elector is named, the mage will endeavour to win their support. Tell no one, Nefysto. Understood?'

'I was serving the mage when you were an abbey brat, little monk.' But there was a smile in his eyes.

Fyn had the grace to grin then remembered a comment Tyro had made. 'I gather the mage has a spy on this spar. Will Feid know about the elector's death?'

Nefysto shrugged. 'I'm not privy to the mage's machinations and I certainly don't know the identity of his spies.'

Midday saw Fyn on the deck of the sea-hound, studying the warlord's stronghold as they approached. Below it, a collection of cottages clung to the steep slope that led down to Foenix Spar's only harbour. Even from here, he could see pigs and chickens wandering the muddy streets, squabbling and squawking. After Ostron Isle the comparison was not favourable.

Their ship had been sighted, and as it drew near, mothers called for children to come running. The women retreated, clutching the little ones' hands, and closed up their houses, to watch no doubt through peek holes. The spars were wary of everyone and the sea-hounds owed them no allegiance.

Word must have been sent up the steep road to the stronghold. By the time the oarsmen had guided the *Wyvern's Whelp* into its berth and made the ship secure, a delegation strode down the slope. Fyn searched for Byren's broad shoulders but could not find them.

'My brother isn't there,' Fyn said to Nefysto. Had Byren fallen foul of his injuries after all? Then he spotted Orrade. He would know. Fyn waved. 'Orrie!'

As his brother's best friend sprinted along the wharf, Fyn charged down the gangplank. They collided, laughing and hugging.

'You've grown, Fyn,' Orrade said, stepping back to look at him.

'I'll never be as big as the twins...' Fyn broke off, remembering Lence's loss all over again. He looked around for Byren. 'Where's –'

'You missed him. He's gone ahead to attack the fort across Foenix Pass. And I'm leaving tomorrow to aid him.'

'Then I'm coming with you. I've news for him.' Fyn patted his vest where the message cylinder was hidden. He glanced over at the waiting men. 'I don't see Garzik?'

Orrade's thin features tightened with sorrow and his voice grew rough. 'He fell the night Palatyne took Dovecote. We lost Elina and Father that night, too.'

Unable to find the words, Fyn hugged him again.

As he pulled back, Orrade managed a smile. 'So where have you been? Playing sea-hound-and-Utland raider?' It was a game they'd indulged in as children.

Fyn laughed. 'I've much to tell you, Orrie.' He nodded past Orrade's shoulder to the spar warriors. 'Can we trust them?'

'As far as we can trust anyone from the spars.' Orrade slung an arm around Fyn's shoulders. 'Come on. I'll introduce you. Ah, but you're a sight for sore eyes. We heard Piro lived, but no one knew what'd happened to you.'

'About Piro...' Fyn fell into step with him, then remembered the sea-hound captain. 'First, you must meet Nefysto.'

They'd agreed to pretend the sea-hound had

delivered Fyn for a fee and the chance to trade. It felt wrong to lie to Orrade, but the mage's secrets were not his to share.

By now the rest of the delegation had reached them, and Orrade made the introductions. Most notable amongst them was the handsome youth, who turned out to be a mountain girl called Florin, and the warlord's new lady, Cinna. When Nefysto greeted Lady Cinna, he acted as though they'd never met, but there was a hint of laughter in his black eyes, which was echoed in hers.

While the sea-hounds were setting up their goods on the wharf and the inhabitants of Feidton gathered, eager to begin bargaining, Fyn slipped over to speak with Nefysto.

'So you do know the mage's spy,' he said.

A smile tugged at Nefysto's lips but he didn't answer.

'Orrade tells me she was a kitchen maid in some merchant's house when Feid met her, and it's a love match,' Fyn pressed for a reaction. 'Does the mage deal in love potions now or is she such a fine actress she'll bear his children?'

Nefysto caught Fyn by his vest, swung him behind some tall bales and thrust him up against them. 'That's my cousin you're talking about.'

Fyn gulped. 'My apologies, captain. I meant no insult.'

Nefysto let him slide to the ground.

Fyn adjusted his clothing. The women of the five families were renowned for handling finances, driving hard bargains and marrying to cement alliances. 'If Lady Cinna comes from one of the five families of Ostron Isle, what's she doing spying for the mage?'

Nefysto looked as if he wouldn't answer, then he let out his breath in a huff of annoyance. 'Cinna was born the wrong side of the blanket, so she can never be acknowledged, but she could have served the family safely. She would never have gone hungry. Cinna, however, always preferred excitement. If she's married this spar warlord it's because she loves him. And he's a lucky man.'

'Yet, she's still spying for the mage?'

'Be glad she is, for your brother's sake.' And Nefysto strode off, offering the Lady Cinna his arm to show her the sea-hounds' wares.

Fyn watched Nefysto and his by-blow cousin. If Feid married her after meeting her in a merchant's kitchen and was unaware of her connections to one of Ostron Isle's wealthiest families, then he'd married her for love. Fyn almost envied him. It was something a kingson would never be sure of.

A kingson had to be careful where he spread his seed. Not that Byren or Lence had been particularly careful, if the stories were true. You'd think they would have learnt from King Byren's mistake.

When he was only sixteen, their grandfather had dallied with a passing player and produced a son. Born the wrong side of the blanket, destined never to inherit, Spurnan's very existence had triggered a civil war. Then Cobalt, Spurnan's son, betrayed King Rolen for his chance at the crown. Seventy years on, they were still paying for his grandfather's indiscretion.

'There you are.' Orrade found him. 'Something wrong?'

'No.' Fyn mustered a smile.

'Then come up to the stronghold and tell me what's happened to you since Merofynia invaded.' Orrade had only taken three steps when he came to an abrupt stop. 'Fyn, the abbey mystics master is here with us.'

'Good, I –' Fyn registered Orrade's serious expression. 'What?'

'One of the monks told me he struggles with renegade Affinity. He could betray us.'

'Catillum? Never!' Fyn pulled away from Orrade. 'Are you sure?'

'It was your friend Feldspar who warned us.'

Fyn digested this. He'd misjudged Cobalt, but then he hadn't known his cousin well. He did know Feldspar and Catillum. Could his friend be mistaken? They hadn't begun their monks' training, how could Feldspar judge the mystic master's true state?

Besides, now that Fyn had met renegade Affinity in the form of the mage's agent, he knew Power-workers could live outside the abbey's teachings and not succumb to evil. Come to think of it, there had been some shining examples of evil within the abbey. If the monks were wrong about Power-workers, what else did they have wrong?

'Fyn?' Orrade prodded. 'Can I trust the mystic?'

Then it came to him. This was the meaning of the vision back on the *Wyvern's Whelp*, when he'd seen Catillum battling a wyvern. 'The mystic master won't betray us. He'd die before he bowed down to Merofynia.'

'You sound certain.'

'I had a vision.' Fyn's hand went to his chest, to where the Fate lay hidden under his vest. Even as Fyn did this, he realised that if Catillum discovered he was the mage's agent he would denounce him. Fyn's skin went cold as his mind raced. He'd been so focused on reaching Byren, he hadn't thought this through. He could never go back to the abbey. It would mean living a lie.

His head spun as he tried to make the mental adjustments. If anyone from the abbey asked how he came to be here on Foenix Spar with the sea-hounds he'd tell them he'd fallen in with one of the elector's agents and leave it at that.

'The vision told you Catillum is trustworthy?' Orrade pressed.

'Absolutely.'

'Good. Because I don't want to battle renegade Affinity without his support. The Merofynians are sure to have brought one of Mulcibar's mystics with them.'

Fyn nodded. Unlike Halcyon, the Merofynian god of summer was the patron god of war. A bull with a coat as hard as stone, its breath could incinerate. In the last great battle the Merofynians hurled burning balls, known as Mulcibar's dung. Anything they touched burst into flames.

'So, Fyn,' Orrade said, resuming their walk up to Feid's stronghold. 'Where have you been and how did you come to be sailing with sea-hounds?'

And Fyn began to lie.

That evening, after the meal, as he stood on the mezzanine overlooking Feid's great hall, Bantam and

Jakulos joined him. When Nefysto had assigned them to accompany him as his honour guard, neither had been particularly impressed to learn who he really was. Fyn was relieved they treated him no differently.

'Did you make a pretty profit?' Fyn asked.

Bantam grimaced. 'No profit to be made from spar trading. They're too poor. Cap'n's taking the *Wyvern's Whelp* around to Port Marchand.'

Fyn nodded. No doubt Nefysto would be reporting to the mage on the state of affairs in Rolencia. Fyn was glad to have the two sea-hounds watching his back and wanted to tell them, but before he could, Feldspar and Joff sought him out.

'There you are, Fyn,' Feldspar said, eyeing the two sea-hounds warily. Bantam gave Fyn a nod and he and Jakulos moved off as if they hadn't been told to shadow him. Joff and Feldspar joined Fyn at the rail, overlooking Feid's great hall.

'Catillum wants to see you,' Feldspar said. 'What happened after you left us? How did you end up with the sea-hounds?'

Fyn straightened up. This was what he'd dreaded, but for their own good, he must deny his old friends. 'That's between the king and I.' He'd never given Byren this title before. 'Did you say Master Catillum wants to see me?'

Feldspar stiffened and took a step back. 'Yes, kingsheir.'

Fyn wanted to tell him to drop the title. But it was better to let Feldspar think he was too ambitious to maintain friendship with a monk, who could do him no favours, rather than have Feldspar tainted by association if Fyn's relationship with the mage was ever revealed.

So Fyn nodded dismissively. 'I'll be along soon. Where is the mystics master?'

'In his chamber. It's –'

'I'll find it. Thank you.' Fyn turned away from them. It was hard, but it had to be done.

What could the mystics master want with him? He stayed and watched the hall, until enough time had passed for Joff and Feldspar to go back downstairs, then he went in search of Catillum.

'You sent for me, mystics master.'

'Ah, Fyn.' Catillum turned with a tired smile. His eyes were red-rimmed and the skin below them bruised but he was still the man Fyn remembered. As Catillum glanced to Fyn's head of dark hair, Fyn noted the mystics master had shaved his head. Now that he thought about it, so had Feldspar and Joff. 'It is good to see you. Feldspar and Joff expected you to bunk down with us, but I told them you might feel you had to serve your brother, before coming back to the abbey.'

Fyn nodded. He was grateful for Catillum's tact, but he couldn't dedicate himself to the abbey now. He couldn't live a lie.

'If you mean to serve your brother until he is restored to the throne, you should return Halcyon's Fate,' Catillum said. 'As mystis master, it is my responsibility.'

'Of course.' Fyn should have thought of this. Since he no longer meant to go back to the abbey, he had no right to the Fate. His hand went to his chest, where the Fate rested beneath his vest. It was with a surprising reluctance that Fyn undid the clasp and removed the Fate from around his neck.

'Thank you for keeping it safe.' The mystic's fingers closed around the Fate and he hung it around his own neck, tucking it away safely. 'Any visions I should know about, lad?'

Fyn looked up. He could hardly admit to seeing Catillum's possible death. He swallowed. 'No.'

SINCE THE MAGE had opened his gates, Piro had cared for the sick and wounded, while the battle for the electorship raged across Ostron Isle.

As she finished her day shift, Isolt arrived looking fresh and determined for the night shift. Following Merofynian royal custom, she was also trained as a healer.

'I saw Agent Tyro outside. Is there news of your brothers?' Isolt asked.

'Not that I heard. The agent didn't come in here.' Piro hadn't seen much of Tyro since she insisted he open the gates, and she was reasonably certain he was avoiding her. Perhaps Tyro had borne the brunt of the mage's anger.

She handed over care of the sick to Isolt and hurried out into the corridor looking for the agent, but he was nowhere in sight.

She should explain to the mage how she had put Tyro in a position where he could hardly say no but, since the night the elector died, they had seen nothing of Tsulamyth.

If only the Ostronites would decide on a new elector.

The solution came to Piro in a flash. Why hadn't she thought of it before? The war table piece would have the new elector's features. Driving her weary legs, she ran up the stairs and down the corridor to the war table room.

She'd avoided this chamber since she'd been in here to view her faceless piece. Now she darted over to Ostron Isle and peered across the table, careful not to touch anything.

'The elector's piece has no features yet,' Tyro said, coming out of the shadows. Piro gave a little start of fright, but she hadn't done anything wrong. She squared her shoulders.

Tyro stepped closer, the nuances of his expression hidden by the twilight. 'The piece's face went blank the night the elector died and has remained blank since. It was the first thing I checked.'

'Pity...' She tilted her head, trying to make out the agent's expression. 'Why doesn't the mage force the five great families to agree to a new elector?'

'If a decision was forced upon the five they would resent the mage. The four losing families would unite against Tsulamyth. No, Piro. It is better to let them sort it out.'

'By killing each other?'

'Ahh, but then they can resent each other and not the mage.' One corner of Tyro's mouth lifted in the wry smile she had come to know so well. Dunstany's smile.

She felt an odd tug in her belly. She'd hardly eaten today. 'Was the mage angry with you, Tyro?'

He looked blank.

'Because you opened the gate.'

He turned away. 'No. We came to an understanding.'

His reply did not ring true. She should find the mage and make it clear that she was to blame. Where to start looking?

First she had to slip away from Tyro.

Piro used Isolt's new pet wyvern as an excuse to slip away. 'I'd better feed Loyalty.'

'I'll come with you,' Tyro said.

They found the wyvern and foenix playing in a private garden courtyard, complete with its own fountain. Piro upended a bucket of fish scraps from the kitchen. The wyvern leapt on the fish, gulping them down, while the foenix nibbled one at a time.

'It's lucky for my foenix that Isolt's wyvern is too young to know they should be deadly enemies,' Piro told Tyro. With the fish fast disappearing down the wyvern's throat, the Affinity beast looked decidedly deadly. Piro eyed Loyalty uneasily. 'How long before she grows horns?'

'Another year or two,' Tyro answered. 'That's when she'll have to be let loose if she hasn't bonded properly with Isolt. She'll be too dangerous.'

'Agent Tyro?' Ovido came trotting into the garden. He ignored Piro as if she was an interloper. 'The mage has been called to meet the new elector, Comtissa Cera of House Cerastus.'

'At last!' Piro turned to Tyro. 'Now the mage can –'

'The new elector will want to clean up Ostron Isle before interfering in other kingdoms' squabbles,' Tyro warned.

He was right. Piro's heart sank. 'But my brothers –'

'The world does not revolve around the troubles of House Rolen,' Tyro snapped, then seemed to regret his temper. 'First thing tomorrow, Tsulamyth will try to convince Elector Cera of the importance of this particular squabble.'

BYREN HAD FORCE-MARCHED his men over the secret pass and across the foothills, through slopes of winter-bare grape vines, to what had been Cedar tradepost. Now it was a well-built fort. He'd kept his followers out of sight and he was glad he had. Originally, he'd intended to wait until he heard Orrade's attack on the far side, before launching his own, but he'd had an idea. Why use force when trickery would do? He took Corvel and Feid aside to explain his plan.

Both warlords heard him out, then tried to find flaws.

'So you'd approach the fort late in the day as a trader returning home to the spar with a wagon of goods to sell?' Feid rubbed his jaw. 'That'll get you inside overnight until they open the gate on Foenix Spar-side but, if your identity was discovered, you'd –'

'No one will recognise me.' Byren didn't mention that he knew the tradepost's keeper, and he expected the man not to reveal him. Besides, he trusted to his mother's training. Piro was not the only one who had enjoyed acting out the myths. All he needed was padding to make him look fat, ash to age his hair, and he could hunch over to make himself seem shorter. The Merofynians were looking for a young, tall kingson. 'I'll need three or four likely lads to come with me.'

'Take my sons,' Corvel offered. 'They're spar-born. They can pass for a trader's sell-swords.'

Byren had been meaning to take his honour guard, but Corvel was right. Winterfall and the others were not spar-born, and might unwittingly betray him.

So, just on dusk, Byren dressed in a trader's serviceable cloak and joined three of Corvel's four sons. The youngest drove a wagon borrowed from the sympathetic vintner. Its wheels moved slowly under the weight of a dozen barrels of fine Rolencian red as they headed for the main road over the pass.

With the player's assistance Byren had disguised himself, rubbing ash into his face and beard to turn them grey, and affected a limp. Old Man Narrows had loaned his own staff to complete the transformation. Seela was right, warriors in the prime of life tended to dismiss the old and the lame.

Cedar tradepost came into view, the top floor of the third storey visible over the palisade. Last time he was here, he'd been defending the scholar and his family. He wondered briefly what had happened to them and little Rodien. He could only hope they were safe somewhere.

Then the tradepost had nestled in the valley, near the narrow defile that led to the only path over the Divide. Now, hastily built but sturdy wooden fortifications had been extended so that a palisade surrounded the tradepost, blocking the defile's entrance. Everyone had to pass through the fort.

Defended by one gate tower, the gate facing Rolencia was sturdy, and already closed. Byren led the horses, leaning heavily on a staff. When he rapped on the wood, the gate-keeper opened the slit and accepted Byren's story without reservations.

'Your goods must be worth protecting to hire three sell-swords,' the gate-keeper said. 'What do you carry?'

'Rolencian red for the warlord's own cellar.'

The gate-keeper closed the slit, slid the bolts out and swung the gate to let Byren and the cart in. Corvel's youngest son flicked the reins to get the horses moving, and the other two walked alongside the wagon.

They'd entered the courtyard and the gate was closed behind them, when the gate-keeper announced, 'There's a new tax for crossing the Divide, one-fifth of your wares.'

'One-fifth!' Byren spluttered as he knew a trader would. 'That's daylight robbery.'

The gate-keeper smirked. 'If you want to sell your wine to the warlord, that's what you'll be paying.'

Grumbling energetically, Byren ordered Corvel's sons to unload the right number of barrels.

As they were being rolled away, the gate-keeper turned back. 'There's also the charge for housing and feeding your horses, and yourselves.' He named an exorbitant price.

Byren threw up his hands. 'You'll ruin me.' But he paid, after some haggling.

In the tradepost proper, he found several other travellers, none of whom were happy with the new charges. But they kept their voices low. From the gossip, he learnt how the keeper of the tradepost had objected when the Merofynians first arrived. Now he and his family worked as servants in the kitchen.

Byren bristled on the keeper's behalf. The sooner he reclaimed Rolencia, the sooner he could right the wrongs done in King Merofyn's name.

When the keeper's son served their meal, the lad's gaze fixed on Byren, then glided deliberately past him. In a few moments, the keeper himself came out to supervise. The fort's forty or so Merofynian solders crowded the tables, claiming the best of the food.

The keeper put a tray of pastries on Byren's table, pausing just behind him.

'Is there anything else I can do?' he asked softly.

Byren's reply was equally soft. 'Be free with your measures of ale and wine tonight.'

The keeper nodded and retreated to the kitchen.

Byren forced himself to eat. If this failed, not only would he pay with his life but the keeper and his family would also die. He hoped Orrade attacked at dawn, as planned.

FYN LAY ON a rock beside Orrade to study the fort in the fading light. Spar locals had known exactly where the fort's lookouts were posted and had eliminated them, preventing word of their approach from reaching the fort.

But all their precautions were pointless, for the fort was ideally situated. Built at the end of a narrow defile, just before the pass path opened out into the

Rolencian foothills, there was only one approach and it was heavily guarded.

'This will be a slaughter,' Fyn muttered.

'It only needs to be a diversion for Byren,' Orrade said. But Fyn could hear the anger and regret in his voice. They were going to lose good men in a hopeless assault.

They climbed down, returning to where Aseel, Catillum and Bearclaw from Unistag Spar waited. Bantam and Jakulos were within hearing distance. They were never far from him.

For some reason Florin was present. Fyn had noticed she slept next to Orrade, in his fire circle, and assumed she was his lover, for all that they were being circumspect.

When Orrade explained the situation, the older warriors exchanged looks.

'We knew it wasn't going to be easy,' Catillum said. Fyn noted that he did not offer to cast an illusion to get them inside the gate.

'Let me lead the assault, with my honour guard,' young Aseel offered, eager to wipe out the shame of his cousin Rejulas's betrayal.

Fyn noticed Orrade flinch. He didn't want to send the untried youth to almost certain death, but to refuse Aseel would dishonour him. Fyn stiffened. It wasn't right, asking men to die for his brother while he sat back and watched.

'I'll lead the attack,' he heard himself say.

'You can't,' Orrade objected. 'Byren would kill me if anything happened to you. You're his heir now. I'll lead. We attack just before dawn.'

*   *   *

TOWARDS DAWN, BYREN woke his three companions and they slipped out of the tap-room.

'Wait here.' He left them in the dark entrance, to stumble his way across the courtyard to the privies.

The fort was silent, no hint of trouble. And, lucky for Orrade, it was a cloudy night. Byren could barely see his hand in front of his face.

Across the courtyard, by the spar gate, the night watch congregated around a burning brazier. After relieving himself, Byren limped back to join the others.

'Six men guard the gate winch, none too alert. Take them down silently if you can. I'll distract them.'

They nodded their agreement and kept to the building's edge so they presented no silhouette.

Byren made the trek across the courtyard a second time.

'Here, you?' One of the night watch proved more alert than the others and strode over. 'Weren't you just out here?'

Byren shrugged, remaining bent over as he leant on the staff. 'I've the old man's curse, a leaky tap.'

The man chuckled and waved him on.

As he turned away, Byren whipped the end of the staff around and caught him in the back of his knees. Before the man hit the ground, Byren followed him, bringing the staff over in an arc to strike his head. All thanks to Florin and the days spent practising to best her. He mustn't think about her.

In that moment, he realised he was risking his life to make sure she didn't fall at the gate in some foolhardy attempt to prove she was better than his men.

If he was lucky, Orrade would never guess how Byren really felt.

A soft whistle drew his attention. He looked over to find the others had dealt with the remaining night watch.

Byren hurried to join them. 'Drag the bodies out of sight, winch the gate open.' As they did this, he lit a lantern and stepped into the open gateway.

THEIR LOOKOUT HAD reported activity. Fyn and Orrade tried to make sense of what they saw.

'The gate's opening,' Orrade muttered. 'I don't believe it.'

'Someone's signalling with a lantern,' Fyn said. 'We must have supporters inside the fort.'

Orrade scrambled to his feet. 'Quick, before they are discovered.'

With Aseel and the volunteers at their heels, they hurried down the narrow defile, trying to make as little noise as possible. Bantam and Jakulos followed Fyn.

As they came closer to the gate, the man with the lantern lifted it to reveal his face.

'I swear that's Byren!' Orrade said as he ran.

Fyn sprinted to keep up with him. What had happened to his brother? He looked terrible.

Orrade hugged Byren and pulled back, low voice rich with laughter. 'How did you do it?'

'A little play acting. Eh, Fyn, don't you recognise me?' Byren gave his familiar crooked grin and Fyn threw his arms around his brother. His brother squeezed him so hard Fyn thought he'd break a rib. Byren stepped back to study his face, voice thick with emotion. 'We thought you dead, little brother.'

Aseel and the volunteers poured into the courtyard. They were excited, nervous, ready for action. Any time now, their presence would be discovered.

Byren glanced past Fyn's shoulder and Fyn turned to see the two sea-hounds. 'Uh, this is Bantam and Jakulos. They're...'

'We're his honour guard,' Bantam said. And Jakulos dipped his head in agreement.

'Good.' Byren offered his arm, pulling them each in for a hug and clapping them on his back. As he pulled back from Jakulos he grinned. 'Don't often meet a man I can look in the eye. How did you come to serve m'brother?'

But before they could answer, there was some sort of altercation and Aseel came over, dragging a prisoner.

'This man claims he knows you,' Aseel said.

'Let him go, lad. It's the tradepost keeper.' Byren turned to Orrade. 'Go with him. He'll show you where the Merofynians sleep.'

As the others left them, Byren turned back to Fyn, who took a few steps away from the sea-hounds and reached for the message cylinder inside his vest. 'Byren, I –'

'A moment, lad.' His brother strode off, after one of the warriors, caught him by the shoulder and spun him around. In the lantern light, Fyn recognised the mountain girl.

Byren glared at her. 'What're you doing here?'

'Orrie called for volunteers.' She glared right back

at him.

'Did he know you were one of them?'

She lifted her chin.

For a moment, Byren seemed too angry to speak. Then he lowered the lantern. 'You can make yourself useful, Mountain-girl. Run back to the rest, tell them to come down here.'

'Yes, my king.' She darted off.

Fyn watched Byren watch her go. 'It's not Orrie's fault. He didn't know. He wouldn't have sent the girl he's bedding on a suicide attack.'

Byren stiffened, then let his breath out slowly and rubbed his jaw as if tired.

So much rested on Byren's shoulders. Fyn knew just the thing to cheer him up. He removed the message cylinder from inside his vest. 'Here. The elector offers you his support.' No need to mention that the old elector was dead.

'Better and better.' Byren took it then glanced to Fyn. 'So how is it that you bring an alliance with Ostron Isle?'

And Fyn lied to his brother.

Chapter Twenty

By dawn, Byren had called his captains together, and taken over the tap-room. He could smell spicy sausages, eggs and beans cooking, and his stomach grumbled. The traders had congratulated him, then backed out. They were happy, believing taxes would return to normal. They wouldn't be so happy when he had to confiscate their edible goods to feed his army.

Orrade was last to arrive and join them at the long table. 'The fort's secured. Your men took down the night watch. The rest surrendered without a fight.' He grinned. 'Hard to be brave when you're unarmed, barefoot and only half-awake.'

'Our losses?'

'None dead. One injured.' Laughter lit Orrade's thin face and Byren felt an answering grin tug at his lips. 'He dropped a barrel of looted wine on his foot and broke it.'

'The barrel?'

'No, his foot.'

'Just as well.'

The others chuckled, as Byren meant them to. They were all pleased with the easy victory, but jumpy because they knew the real battle still lay ahead.

'What will you do now, Byren?' Feid asked. 'They say Rolenhold can't be taken by force.'

'It never has. Deceit opened the gates for Palatyne. Cobalt won't fall for that.' Byren was reminded of tactics lessons with Captain Temor. The old warrior's death was another he had to avenge.

'Word of Byren's return will spread,' Orrade said. 'The people will rise up and join us.'

'The Merofynians could sit in the castle and ignore us,' Bearclaw countered. He was from Unistag Spar and eager to prove his loyalty to Warlord Unace, by supporting Byren who had helped her gain leadership.

'I hope they do stay safe in the castle,' Byren said quickly. The secret to leading men like this was never to appear at a loss. 'It'll give me time to gather warriors, retake the abbey and wipe out any Merofynians not within the castle walls. In fact, they don't know we're here, yet and I'd like to keep it that way for as long as possible. Before Cobalt knows it, he could have lost Rolencia.'

'But he'd still be safe in Rolenhold,' Corvel muttered.

'If I were Cobalt, I'd ride out to do battle before you're at full strength,' Feid said.

'But Cobalt doesn't know we're here yet.' Byren

knew Palatyne had left a third of the Merofynian army under Cobalt's command, plus Lord Leon's warriors had joined him. He was outnumbered three to one. 'And that's why I need a secure base to strike from.'

'Dovecote's overrun with Merofynians,' Orrade began, 'but –'

'The Narrows is empty,' Old Man Narrows suggested. 'And it's secure, surrounded by the lake and cliffs on three sides. The palisade on the fourth side would have to be rebuilt –'

'We've got the men to do that. Excellent.' Byren turned to Orrade. 'See how many horses we have. Take twenty or thirty good men and the Narrows family. Go prepare the tradepost for us.' That would get Florin out of his sight and, hopefully, out of his thoughts. 'We'll follow on foot.'

As the keeper and his family brought out breakfast, Byren noticed that Catillum had slipped out of the tap-room. He'd have to catch him later and ask his advice on retaking the abbey. Recapturing Halcyon Abbey would inspire the valley people, and it was an easier nut to crack than Rolenhold.

FYN STOOD ON the fort's gate-tower. Looking across the valley, he drank in his homeland. It was good to be back. To his right the sun had just risen. So far it only picked out the tip of Mount Halcyon and, much nearer, Rolenhold itself. The Rolencian valley lay shrouded in early morning mist, with only single spires and tall trees spearing the fog. It was all so peaceful.

But not for long.

'Your brother did well, but winning one battle doesn't win the war,' Bantam muttered. 'He has a long, hard haul ahead of him, before he can call himself King Byren the Fifth.'

Fyn shrugged. 'Byren's up to it. Before summer's over, you'll have good news to report to Nefysto.'

'How do you know we won't claim lordships, riding on your coat tails?'

Fyn laughed. 'You have salt-water in your veins, not blood. I can't see you settling down on dry land, Bantam. But as for Jaku here –'

'I plan to settle on Ostron Isle. I bear Merofynia no love after the way she treated me, and Rolencians bear me no love, after the way Merofynia began this war. No, it's Ostron Isle for me.'

Below him, barely visible through the mist, Byren's army was cooking breakfast. Soon they would pack their kits and march out. Fyn should find Byren and see what his plans were.

Footsteps on the wooden ladder told him someone was coming.

Feldspar climbed up. 'Master Catillum wants to see you, kingsheir.'

His former friend's gaze skimmed past Fyn, who wanted to explain, why he was keeping his distance, but then Feldspar would have to denounce him for associating with renegade Affinity. So he held his tongue and hardened his heart.

Fyn nodded. 'I'll be along soon. Where is he?'

'Behind the stables.'

Fyn turned away from Feldspar's disappointment and heard him go down the ladder.

'What does the mystics master want?' Bantam asked.

Fyn's hand went to his chest but the Fate was gone. Odd how he missed its warmth over his heart. 'I don't know. I've already returned the abbey's Fate.'

Had he somehow given away his association with the mage? He didn't think so. Bantam and Jakulos followed him down the ladder as he headed for the stables. They waited just out of sight around the building.

'You sent for me, mystics master.'

'Ah, Fyn.' When Catillum turned, Fyn was struck by how much worse he looked. He had always been thin and intense, now he looked positively gaunt. Was the master sickening from something? He hoped not. Catillum was the only master-level monk left alive. When they retook the abbey, he would be their abbot. 'There is something I must ask you, kingson.'

Fyn waited.

'You are torn by two loyalties now, the abbey and your brother. Byren Kingsheir intends to retake the abbey. Only you and I know about the secret passage. I don't want rough warriors traipsing through the goddess's Sacred Heart. I want you to leave this to me. Don't tell him what you know.'

'Of course.' It was none of his business, now that he had turned his feet away from the goddess's path.

'Very good. Thank you, kingson.'

The mystic master left and the sea-hounds joined Fyn.

At Bantam's raised brows, Fyn explained. 'Abbey business.'

Bantam did not look pleased.

Just then there was a commotion from the front of the stables, so Fyn headed around to see what was going on.

Through a gap in the crowd, Fyn saw Byren with the warlords. His brother laughed at something Corvel said, and the man's sons laughed along with him. These violent men respected his brother for the good-hearted warrior he was. But did Byren have the cunning to beat Cobalt, who according to Piro was both brilliant and devious?

There was always Orrade. As if his thoughts had conjured him up, his brother's best friend thrust through the horses and men to join Fyn.

'We looked for you at the war table,' Orrade said.

'I was speaking with Master Catillum.' Giving up the Fate had been hard, but being excluded from retaking the abbey brought home to him that he was no longer going to become a monk. Strange how much that hurt.

'I've set aside three horses for you.' Orrade's glance included Bantam and Jakulos. 'We're riding ahead.'

The mountain girl approached, with her travelling kit slung over one shoulder.

'Over here, Florin.' Orrade beckoned her, explaining to Fyn as she approached. 'We're making for Narrowneck. Byren is going to reinforce its defences and make that his base until he can take back Rolenhold.'

'Good idea.' Fyn nodded to Florin. He didn't know what Orrade saw in her. She was half a head taller than Fyn and could look Orrade in the eyes. Handsome rather than pretty, she moved and spoke with none of the unconscious grace that made Piro and Isolt so desirable.

Florin eyed the horse Orrade had selected for her. 'If I fall off this beastie and break my neck, I'm never speaking to you again.'

'You rode well enough the night we fled Merofynians in Waterford.'

'That wasn't riding. That was holding on for dear life!'

Orrade grinned, winked at Fyn and offered Florin a leg up.

She tossed her braid over her shoulder, slipped her boot into the stirrup and swung onto the saddle.

As Fyn mounted up, he heard her muttering under her breath.

'...can't be any harder than facing down a manticore pride.'

And he hid a smile.

PIRO LAY IN wait for the mage's return all morning, eager to hear if the new elector would honour the last elector's alliance.

All morning people left Mage Isle, returning to their homes. The Ring Sea was busy with small boats ferrying people back to Ostron Isle.

By midday Piro was starving, but she would not leave her post. Her patience was rewarded with the return of the mage in his closed carriage.

When the horses came to a stop, she was there opening the door. 'Mage Tsulamyth?'

'Who?' He glared at her. 'Oh, it's you. Can't an old man have a moment's peace?'

She offered her hand to help him out. 'Did you see the new elector? What did she say?'

'Manners, that's what young people lack today. Won't even let an old man rest his feet and take a sip of mulled wine to ease the bone-ache.'

His Affinity rolled over her, making her skin tingle and the hairs on her arms lift. He was powerful but frail, so she let him lean on her shoulder. As she guided him across the courtyard, a family hurried past, pausing to make a low bow of deference to the mage.

He waved them off. 'And good riddance. Eating me out of house and home –'

'You mustn't be angry with Tyro. It was my fault,' Piro told him. 'I opened the gate.'

'That boy...' The mage's mouth lifted in a wry smile. Tyro's smile. Dunstany's smile.

Piro saw through the disguise in that instant.

Just as he had pretended to be Lord Dunstany on the mage's orders, now Tyro was pretending to be the mage. But why?

Poor Tsulamyth must be so sick. Perhaps he could not leave his bed. Or perhaps the mage was somewhere else tending to one of his other 'irons.'

She hid a smile. This pretence would explain the mage's rumoured ability to be in two places at once. More likely, he was sick. The excitement the night the elector died must have been too much for him. So he'd sent Tyro to see the new elector today.

Hiding her discovery, she asked, 'Did the elector see you?'

'One-track mind, that's what you have, girlie. But to answer your question, yes, she did. When I pointed out that Palatyne's next invasion would be of Ostron Isle, with the might of both Rolencia and Merofynia at his back, the elector agreed to support your brother in –'

'Wonderful.' Piro hugged him.

Tyro disguised as the mage pushed her off, wincing as if his back hurt. She hid another smile. Tyro was such a good actor. In fact, he seemed more comfortable acting a part than being himself.

'You must let Byren and Fyn know,' Piro told him.

He glared at her. 'If I let a little slip of a girl tell me what I must and must not do, I would be a sorry excuse for a mage. Now, leave me in peace.'

Delighted with the news, Piro went to find Isolt. She found her on the tower stairs with the wyvern.

'Guess what?' Piro beamed.

'Let me see.' Isolt put her finger to her chin, pantomiming deep thought. 'The new elector has agreed to an alliance with your brother.'

Piro had been about to tell her that she'd caught Tyro playing the mage, but thought better of it now. Isolt might worry if she believed the mage was too frail to protect her. 'You heard?'

Isolt laughed. 'What else would it be? Truly, this is good news for your family and Rolencia.'

But there was no good news for Isolt, who was still estranged from her father and lived in fear of Palatyne discovering her whereabouts and claiming her. Surely the mage could do something for her too?

'Piro? Day dreamer?' Isolt smiled as Piro focused on her face. 'I feel bad about neglecting Loyalty these last few days, so I'm taking her for a swim. Do you want to come?'

Deep below the tower was a grotto, which opened onto the Ring Sea. Sunlight filtered through a hole in the roof, bathing the white stone in rippling light, and a hot spring of fresh water fed the pool, making it warm enough to swim in. Since water was her natural element the wyvern liked to go there once a day.

'Another time,' Piro said. 'I just thought of something I must do.'

Isolt nodded and led the wyvern off. Piro suspected King Merofyn's daughter was happier living as an outcast on Mage Isle than she had been in her own palace. But Isolt had to go home eventually.

Piro glanced up the stairs, thinking of the mage lying up there in his bed, too sick to go out. Poor thing. She should make sure he understood that she was to blame for opening the gates, not Tyro.

She went past the war table chamber on the tower's third floor. The curving stairs followed the wall. At the next floor the door opened into the chamber housing the library. She'd seen this room when Tyro showed them about. According to him, this was as far as they were allowed to venture. Which meant the mage had to be on one of the next four floors.

He would probably enjoy a visitor.

Piro crossed the library, entering the next stairwell. When she reached the top, she thought she heard a scurrying noise. Rats. They should get the terriers in.

The door opened at her touch. This chamber contained an odd mix of treasures, reminding her of her father's trophy room, except these treasures were all covered in dust.

There was, however, a clear path across the dusty

boards to the far door, so someone came up here regularly. No doubt to deliver the mage's food and bring him news.

Following the trodden path, she passed strange objects so powerful they made her teeth ache with Affinity build-up. These treasures were nothing like her father's trophies. Only the Mirror of Insight had set off her Affinity and it responded to power, rather than having any of its own.

Telling herself that if she wasn't meant to go further the door would be locked, Piro pressed on the handle. The door swung open and she went up the next set of stairs, heart pounding.

Mouth dry, she entered the sixth and second-to-last floor. This chamber contained ancient weapons, some beautiful in a terrible way. Again, a path had been trodden across the dusty boards. And, again, she felt the tug of power from some of the objects as she passed.

Again, the door was open, so she went up. But at the top of the last flight of stairs she found the door locked.

No one answered her tentative knock.

It had to be Tsulamyth's room. Perhaps the old man was lying sick in bed. She felt sorry for him, shut away all alone. He needn't worry, she wouldn't give his secret away. But she wanted to see the mage to explain. Suddenly, it was very important to make sure he wasn't angry with his agent.

How was she going to get to Tsulamyth?

Piro returned to the floor below. If she remembered correctly the balconies were directly under each other. She went through to the balcony doors, opening them wide and stepping out. Immediately the wind whipped at her, tugging at her hair and clothes.

The balconies were on the far side of the tower, facing away from Ostron Isle and the buildings on Mage Isle. From here she could see the terraced slopes of Ostron Ring. Below her the Ring Sea glistened a brilliant azure, with boats dotted on its surface.

Turning away from Ostron Ring, she faced the tower. As she had guessed, there was a balcony directly above this one. Could she... *dare* she climb onto the balcony rail, grasp the floor of the balcony above and swing her weight over? She'd always had a good head for heights.

Climbing onto the balustrade, she placed one hand on the tower wall and stood up, balancing. The bottom of the top-floor balcony was too high for her to reach.

Piro jumped down. She needed a rope and a grappling hook. The chambers were filled with weaponry. Surely, she would find something useful.

Avoiding the objects that gave off the tingle of Affinity, Piro searched the weapons, until she found a three-pronged hook. After making sure the rope was not frayed and the connection tight, she returned to the balcony.

Standing on the very edge, she put her back to the balustrade and swung the hook around and around, letting it build up momentum, before releasing it. The distance was so short the wind did not have a chance to spoil her aim. The hook clanged against the stone, loud enough to alert anyone in the room. She held her breath.

No one came out to investigate. Either Tsulamyth was so sick that he couldn't get out of the bed, or the mage was off in Merofynia spying on Palatyne and that was why Tyro was pretending to be him.

Emboldened by this thought, Piro slipped off her shoes, tied her skirts out of the way and climbed up onto the balustrade. She shimmied up the rope, grateful for three older brothers who'd teased her until she could do everything they could. The wind tore at her hair, pulling it free of its bindings and whipping it across her face. Tears stung her eyes.

The only tricky part was transferring her grip from the rope to the balustrade. She ignored the drop, swinging her leg over the balcony rail.

Leaving the rope dangling, Piro went to the balcony doors. Each of the glass panels reflected a different patch of clear blue sky or hillside, and she couldn't see in. Cupping her hands, she peered into the dim chamber. It did contain a bed, though from this angle she couldn't tell if anyone was in it.

Tentatively, she touched the balcony doors. If they were unlocked, she was meant to go in. They opened at her touch. Not surprising really – she was on the top floor of the tallest tower in the known world.

Feeling pleased with herself, Piro slipped into the room. She expected to be greeted by the stale smell of old age and illness. Instead, she smelled freshly laundered sheets and messenger birds. Fresh herbs lay on the polished wooden floor. They crushed under her bare feet, filling the air with their pungent scent. Hardly daring to breathe, she padded lightly across the floor to get a better view of the bed.

Empty... Piro's mental picture of a sad, lonely old man evaporated. The mage must be in Merofynia, or even Rolencia. Helping her brothers, she hoped.

Pica birds cooed. She turned to find a wall of cages. Gentle Affinity creatures generally liked her, so she went over. Most cages contained a pica pair. Only three of the birds were alone and she guessed their mates were off carrying messages. The remaining pairs perched on their rods, necks entwined, crooning to each other, a picture of devotion. She reached through the bars to stroke one bird's back, feeling her own Affinity build up and flow down her arm. Even though she kept her foenix nearby and petted him every day, her Affinity still built up. It had to be increasing. How would she ever control it? Would she have to join Sylion Abbey after all?

No point in worrying about that now. Byren still had to win back...

A presence grew behind her, making the space between her shoulder blades throb with a presentiment of danger. Piro swallowed. So the mage was here after all.

She turned slowly.

A dark figure stood in the shadows beside the fireplace. No, the figure exuded shadow. 'M-mage Tsulamyth?'

'Others have died for daring to do what you have done,' he told her, his old voice paper-thin but menacing.

'I had to see you, had to explain. It wasn't Tyro's

fault. I was the one who insisted we open the gates. You mustn't be angry with him.'

The mage said nothing.

Had she offended him? She was only trying to make things better.

'Mage Tsulamyth?'

He stepped out of the shadows, a fragile old man, stooped by age so that he stood barely taller than her. The light from the balcony flooded his face. She caught a flash of clever dark eyes, set deep behind those bushy white eyebrows in a nest of wrinkles.

'What are you doing here, kingsdaughter?'

She sensed power. Familiar power. Of course it would be familiar, she'd met him before. 'I thought you might be lonely. So I came up to keep you company.'

'Over the balcony?' A wry smile tugged at his lips.

Tyro's smile. Tyro's power!

Anger banished her fear. Why was the agent playing with her? Did he think she was stupid?

'I am sorry, mage.' Eyes down so he could not read her anger, she took his arm as if she believed he was old and weak and led him in front of the fireplace.

'I had to come over the balcony. Your chamber door was locked.' She gave him her best cheeky smile and patted his veined hand. It looked so real, felt real. Equal parts resentment and admiration for Tyro's skill churned within her.

'The door was locked for a reason. Can't an old man get any peace?'

'Peace is for the grave,' she repeated her old nurse's saying. 'Could the door be locked because you have something to hide?'

Without warning, she tucked her leg behind his, just as Fyn had taught her, and shoved.

Quick as a cat, the frail old mage regained his balance. His image shifted then settled back into that of Tsulamyth. If she'd blinked, she would have missed it.

But she hadn't. 'It is you!'

Hands grasped her upper arms, swung her around, and slammed her up against the wall. For a moment all she saw was stars. When her vision cleared, it was Tyro who pressed her to the wall, her feet off the ground, her eyes level with his. Tyro who had coarsened his features with player's putty and bushy eyebrows.

Tyro who looked very, very angry.

Her mouth went dry, even as her heart raced, but she would not be cowed. 'Did you think I was stupid?'

'No. Never that. Just young and foolish.' His gaze dropped to her mouth, and lingered.

Suddenly he let her go, stepping back stiffly. 'What are you doing here, Piro?'

'I told you. I thought the mage might be lonely and... and I thought he might be angry with you. I shouldn't have worried.' For some reason she was more angry than frightened now. Why did she feel as if he had betrayed her?

When he didn't speak she plunged on. It was all quite clear now. 'You played the mage the night of the elector's death That's how he ran so fast.'

'I did. But that didn't make you suspicious. What gave me away just now?'

'I've seen you play Lord Dunstany. With some player's putty to change your face and your Affinity to smooth the illusion, you are a consummate actor. But, when you smile at me, your smile is the same whether you are Dunstany, Tsulamyth or Tyro!'

He said nothing, seemed to loom over her. Why was he so serious? It was clever, this deception. It meant the mage could be in more than one place.

'Have you told anyone your suspicions, Piro?'

'Of course not. So where is the mage?'

'Tell anyone what I am about to tell you and I will have to kill you.'

She laughed, then realised he wasn't joking. It was no longer a game. She was out of her depth. She should never have come here. But she would never betray a trust and he should know that. 'As if I would!'

He let his breath out on a long exhalation. 'The mage is dead.'

Piro's knees went weak and she sank onto the chest in front of the fireplace, knocking a velvet-covered book to the carpet. Automatically she picked it up and smoothed the dust from the cover. 'Dead? But I thought he was all-powerful.'

'No one is all-powerful, Piro.' Tyro paced the chamber. 'Are you sure you haven't told anyone, not even Isolt?'

'She's placed her faith in the mage. I don't want to see her haunted expression return.' Piro frowned and put the book down. 'Maybe you should tell her. She has a right to know the truth.'

'Tell no one!' Tyro strode over to her and dropped to his haunches. His eyes held hers, intense and compelling. 'You want the truth? The truth is that I am the mage. No one lives for two hundred years. Upon his death I was supposed to inherit the role of Mage Tsulamyth from my master just as he inherited it from his. Only we did not anticipate him dying for at least another twenty years.'

Tyro sprang to his feet and threw himself into the chair by the fireplace. For once he didn't look pompous and composed, he looked like a troubled youth. And she felt for him.

'No one must know, Piro. I don't ask this for me. If it was known that Palatyne's twin Utland Power-workers had killed Mage Tsulamyth, Ostron Isle would no longer be safe. Palatyne would sail his army across the sea and strike. You must not reveal the truth.'

'The Utlanders killed Mage Tsulamyth?'

'They meant to kill Dunstany.' Words poured from him as if a dam had broken. 'I'm sorry I lied to you, Piro. I had assumed Dunstany's identity. This much you guessed. Lord Dunstany was a good friend of my master's. He believed in my master's dream. He died at a nexus point, when King Sefon was murdered. Rather than lose Dunstany's influence in the Merofynian court, my master assumed his identity. And he trained me to do likewise. Sometimes, I played Lord Dunstany, sometimes the master did.

'Two summers ago while both the master and I were in Merofynia, the Utlander and his twin brother laid a cunning trap for Lord Dunstany. They had been fierce rivals ever since Palatyne climbed over the Divide and marched his army into the king's very palace, claiming he was there to pay homage to his king.

'I had a head cold. Lord Dunstany didn't, so my master played him that day. The twin Utlanders ambushed Lord Dunstany and they battled, two against one. Somehow, my master escaped and made his way back to me. I was frantic, he had been missing for hours. I found him dying in the secret passage under the Dunstany town mansion. I couldn't save him.' He sat back, long legs stretched out, and stared past her into the fire. Brooding. 'But for a head cold, I would have been the one who died.'

'I don't understand. How could the Utlanders kill the mighty Tsulamyth, even two against one?'

'They didn't set out to kill Tsulamyth. They wouldn't have dared. They set out to kill Lord Dunstany. The Utlanders were prepared with stolen Affinity.' He saw she did not understand. 'They keep Affinity-slaves. The Utlander's twin had one when we arrived in Rolencia. She escaped when he was killed.' Tyro's top lip lifted in a grimace of distaste. 'They siphon Affinity off the living. It's the opposite of what you do with your foenix. Worse than this, they can steal a person's Affinity when they die. Your mother...' He glanced at her, as if not sure whether to go on.

'I saw the Utlander capture my mother's essence in the stone on the tip of his staff. Is she in there? Does she know –'

'I don't know. I hope not.' He shuddered. 'Upon her death, her Affinity would have returned to the world. The Utlander stole it. And it was just this kind of stolen Affinity that he and his twin had gathered in preparation for the day they ambushed Lord Dunstany. They never realised they had Tsulamyth cornered. I believe he would've fought them off, if not for his heart. It gave out. He was lucky to escape alive. They thought he'd crept off to die. But they never had the chance to gloat.' Tyro's lips parted in a fierce grimace that was not a smile. 'For I assumed Lord Dunstany's disguise and met the Utlanders at court the very next day, hale and hearty, but for a slight head cold. They nearly passed out. After that they were most careful of Lord Dunstany. And now that one of them is dead, the remaining Utlander is doubly careful, for all that he hates me.'

'Fyn was right. You must have nerves of steel.'

Tyro's dark eyes fixed on her. He looked tired and worn, but determined. 'I have been bluffing since my master died two summers ago. Without him I must train myself from the books the previous Mage Tsulamyths collected during their lifetimes. I miss my master's advice, but most of all I miss him.' He glanced across to Piro, defiantly apologetic. 'I was his natural grandson.'

'Oh, Tyro. I'm so sorry,' Piro whispered. She caught herself reaching out to him, hesitated, then tucked her hands in her lap. 'But I thought you said you were born on Dunstany's estate, that your mother sold you to the mage when you were five.'

'She did. Dunstany was my other grandfather, her natural father. She was a serving girl, born the wrong side of the blanket. She fell in love with my father, who should have been the next Tsulamyth, but he was too keen on wenching and acquiring wealth. It's a tawdry tale. He seduced her, left her pregnant and got himself killed before I was born. So I'm a bastard twice over, with too much Affinity to live a normal life.'

No wonder he was angry at the world.

Piro licked her lips. She wanted to reassure him, but was pretty certain he would bridle at the sympathy. So she changed the topic. 'If this charade is so dangerous, why continue?'

'This is not a game, Piro. I continue the original Mage Tsulamyth's great dream. Peace through a balance of power. Why... the first Tsulamyth invented the game of Duelling Kingdoms to teach the warring nobles the value of diplomacy.'

She didn't tell him that the way her father played it involved resolving disputes with strategic battles.

Tyro continued. 'Each mage since has continued his work. My master is the reason you exist. Without his interference, Myrella Kingsdaughter would never have married your father.'

Piro found it hard to imagine. 'So I owe my existence to a meddling mage?'

'To Tsulamyth's dream of peace,' Tyro corrected, and this time he didn't sound pompous.

Piro picked at the hem on her sleeve which had begun to unravel. 'There is one thing... I don't see how the different Tsulamyths could carry out this deception. How did they hide the fact that it was a different man each time the mage died? I mean –'

'Two things worked in our favour, Affinity is hereditary and our line is long-lived. The mage always selected one of his descendants to train as his apprentice, so there was a family likeness. And his descendants never knew about him, unless he came for them. He would test the males of each generation and –'

'So he tested you when you were five and chose you for his apprentice?'

'Just as he had chosen my father. But strength of Affinity does not correlate to strength of character.' Tyro shook his head. 'If I had failed the mage's tests, I would have worked on Dunstany's estate, unaware of my relationship to him.' He sounded as though this might not have been such a bad thing. Piro knew how he felt.

'Even so, how did the different mages hide the switch-over?'

'The mage did not select an apprentice until he was over fifty. He had few close friends. Dunstany was one. The people he dealt with grew old, they saw him perhaps once a year, then not for several years. Basically, they forgot.' He shrugged. 'Besides, people see what they expect to see.'

Piro nodded. She accepted it could be done. 'And I suppose you all trained in the art of illusion.'

'The skill runs strong in my family. My master should have lived another twenty years. When he died in my arms, I vowed to carry on. But things have gone from bad to worse. It all started with Palatyne conquering the other spar warlords. His next step was to ingratiate himself with King Merofyn, by invading Rolencia. I tried to stop him. I told him invading Rolencia would be his death.' Tyro looked bleak. 'But instead of preventing Rolencia's invasion, he set off to kill King Rolen's kin.'

Piro blinked. Tyro was responsible for Palatyne's vendetta against her family? 'But –'

'He would have executed your brothers anyway. He only let Cobalt live because he's a bastard and useful to him. It's all gone from bad to worse.' Tyro sank his head into his hands.

Piro felt sorry for him. He'd tried to curtail Palatyne's ambition and failed. But at least he tried. She was about to slip off the chest and go to him, when he lifted his head.

'Palatyne's next goal is to conquer Ostron Isle. With Rolencia and Merofynia behind him, he has the resources. I can't let this happen. Palatyne hesitates only because the mighty Tsulamyth lives here. That's why you must not tell anyone about me, not even Fyn and Isolt.'

'But we can help you. We can –' She broke off as Tyro reached under his vest to pull out the amber pendant.

'I don't need your word, Piro, not when I have this. If I break the stone, your essence escapes and, unless you are within touching distance, you'll die.'

Anger rushed through Piro, driving her to her feet. To think, she'd wanted to console him. 'You don't trust me!'

'Should I, kingsdaughter?' His eyes glittered strangely. 'Isn't your loyalty to your brothers, your kingdom and even your friend Isolt, before me?'

She didn't know what to say. He was right. Wasn't he?

'Besides, the things I've seen in the courts of Ostron Isle and Merofynia have not given me reason to trust anyone.'

'Then I pity you, for loyalty coerced is not loyalty at all!' Piro blinked away tears of fury. If she stayed here another moment she would disgrace herself. 'I'm going down to the grotto... that is, if I have your permission?'

Tyro said nothing.

She marched out, leaving him alone in the tower room.

Piro had found Mage Tsulamyth and she wished she hadn't.

Chapter Twenty-One

BYREN ARRIVED AT Narrowneck to find Orrade had already reinforced the palisade, which was built across the narrowest part of the isthmus that stretched out into the lake. The men, who were building a new gate, paused to give a cheer as he rode past, then went back to work.

In the last few days the ice had melted and the lake was no longer frozen. There was only one place where anyone could approach Narrowneck over water, and this small beach was defensible with steep cliffs. Byren grinned, remembering Florin's challenge to him. She claimed she'd tried to climb those cliffs and failed and if she couldn't, no man could. He had vowed to come back next summer and prove her wrong.

Then the smile disappeared, leaving a bitter taste in his mouth. He should be happy now that Orrade had claimed Florin. It made sense, since his friend was Lord Dovecote, he had to marry and produce an heir. Maybe a mountain girl was not the kind of wife his father would have chosen but in these troubled times, she was just the kind of wife a man needed. Someone who would stand beside him, shoulder to shoulder.

Riding up the winding path, Byren noted where trees had been felled. Soon, every clearing on Narrowneck would be crowded with camp circles. Give him a day or two to send out scouts and find out where the Merofynians were nesting, then he'd lead his men out to clean up the valley. He intended to make Cobalt so furious, his cousin would leave the safety of Rolenhold to engage him on open ground.

'Byren!' Orrade appeared around the bend, heading down the path from Narrowneck tradepost, with Florin at his side.

Byren swung his leg over the mount, jumping to the ground. He should be happy for them. He couldn't speak, his throat was so tight, but he hugged Orrade, slapping him on the back, then tugged on Florin's braid. She brushed his hand away, grumbling without heat.

By Sylion, he should have been a player.

They fell into step with him, one to each side as he led his horse around the back to the stable.

'I've prepared the chambers for your warlords. And I've checked the larder,' Florin said. 'We had to slaughter the hens and drive the cows to a nearby farm when we fled. They've returned the cows and sent more laying hens. I can feed two dozen men for ten days on what's left in the larder. After that...' She shrugged.

'I've rebuilt the palisade and the new gate will be finished soon,' Orrade said. 'Now that everyone's here, I'll finish the ditch across the narrows and plant it with stakes.'

'You've both done a fine job,' Byren said, handing his mount over to Leif. The boy grinned and led the horse off.

Old Man Narrows welcomed Byren at the tap-room door. A fire burned in the grate, fresh bread and cheese were laid on the long table and he could smell a roast cooking in the kitchen. So different from last time he had been here. Then, they'd huddled in the kitchen and planned how to survive the manticore pride. 'Whatever happened to Leif's dogs?'

Even as he said this, the two wolfhounds bounded out of the kitchen to greet him. Byren laughed as they reared up, putting their paws on his chest. Now this was the kind of greeting a man should come home to. How he envied Orrade.

Behind him, the warlords and their captains poured into the tap-room. As Catillum arrived with several of his monks, Byren lost track of Florin. Men took their seats at the long table and Florin reappeared with Leif and her father. They moved about, serving tankards of ale.

When Fyn passed by Byren grabbed his arm.

'Join me.' He indicated the bench beside him. Orrade made room. 'In a day or two, when my scouts come back, I'll be leading raids. I intend to wipe out all Merofynians not living in the castle and the abbey. While I'm away, I'm putting you in charge of Narrowneck.'

'Me?' Fyn almost squeaked. 'What about Orrie –'

'He'll be with me.'

'Or Feid, or Corvel or –'

'They'll be leading attacks. We'll strike in several places at once, strike fast, before the Merofynians realise what's happening and can gather their forces.' Byren grinned at Fyn's expression, then he sobered. 'You're seventeen now. You're my brother and kingsheir. By appointing you captain of Narrowneck, I make it clear to my followers that I trust you. If anything happens to me, you'll be –'

'No.' Fyn would have pulled back, but Orrade didn't let him. 'I don't want –'

'D'you think I want this? How do you think I feel, turning the valley into a battlefield?'

Fyn blinked. 'The valley first, then the abbey, then Rolenhold?'

Byren nodded and laughed as he ruffled Fyn's newly grown hair. 'You'll do, lad.'

FYN WOKE, HIS heart racing. Even as he sat up his dream faded, leaving him with a sense of being lost in the caverns below the abbey, trying to keep the young boys safe from wyverns.

It was almost dawn.

Byren had made him responsible for Narrowneck. Equal parts pride and trepidation filled him. But Byren was right, he was a man now. He'd turned seventeen without noticing, because the sea-hounds hadn't celebrated spring cusp. Time to take on a man's responsibilities.

He stretched out on his bedroll, listening to the snores of Byren's honour guard. Tonight he'd have the chamber to himself, as Byren headed out today. Each of the warlords had an objective. Strike fast, strike before Cobalt could prepare and anticipate.

His stomach churned. He couldn't sleep.

From today, he would be responsible for protecting Byren's bolt hole and the lives of everyone in it. Might as well start now.

He rolled to his feet, grabbed his boots and crept between the sleeping bodies.

Bantam lifted his head.

Fyn signalled for him not to get up. No point in the sea-hounds also going without sleep.

He padded lightly down the stairs and through the tap-room, where more men slept. On the porch he found the man on duty sleeping, huddled in the doorway. Fyn slipped on his boots, and still the man did not wake.

So he kicked him, just hard enough to hurt.

The warrior woke with a start and sprang to his feet, reaching for his knife.

'You're lucky I'm not a Merofynian, planning to slit your throat and assassinate King Byren,' Fyn told him.

He left the chagrined man trying to gather his wits and wandered down to the lookout over the lake where the winch was built to haul loads up from the small beach. Here the three sentries were awake, at least. They were talking softly, their bodies clearly silhouetted against the stars.

Fyn paused, selected a rock and threw it straight into someone's back. The man gave a grunt of surprise and spun around.

Fyn stepped out from the shadows. 'If I had a bow and arrows, all three of you would be dead before you could raise the alarm. Tomorrow night, I want stuffed decoys on guard where you are and the real guards back in the trees, or stretched out on the cliff edge, where they present no silhouette.'

'But the ladder is up and no one could climb the cliff from the beach. That only leaves the winch and we're protecting it,' one of them said.

'You wouldn't be, if you were dead.'

Fyn moved off, thinking some people must walk around half-asleep. Skirting the tradepost, he headed down the winding path towards the Narrows and the palisade.

The scent of incense told him he was downwind of the monks' fire circle. Catillum must have been performing a protective ritual, before venturing out tomorrow. Fyn had no intention of waking Joff and Feldspar, but his old friends weren't there. The monks were missing. Where...

Fyn's steps slowed and then he realised the mystics master must have volunteered his monks to take the dawn watch.

He headed for the palisade. The monks wouldn't be as careless as the other sentries. At least he hoped not.

Four monks manned the single gate, which could be lowered to form a bridge over the ditch. Fyn could see their silhouettes by the starlight but not their features.

'All well?' Fyn asked.

'Yes, kingsheir.'

Fyn moved on. There were two platforms, one each side of the gate. They were built in the tree tops, halfway along the palisade. From these vantage points, lookouts could watch the approach to the Narrows and Fyn headed towards one of these now, curious to discover how far they could see from up there.

'Who is it?' a voice called down.

'Fyn Kingsheir.' He was glad the monks were alert. It would have felt odd, reprimanding men who had ranked above him in the abbey.

Fyn climbed the ladder and joined the three men, who knelt on the dappled, starlit platform. Only when he identified Joff and Feldspar, and felt a spurt of relief, did he realise his true motivation. He wanted to be reconciled with his friends.

Selfish fool. He must not lay his burdens on them. They'd be horrified to learn he'd allied himself with Mage Tsulamyth. This hurt. To distract himself, he crept to the edge of the platform. 'How far can you see? How much warning would we have?'

Only one monk joined Fyn at the edge of the platform. Whetstone had given his vow three years earlier, when he had joined Master Sunseed's gardeners, but they had all been trained as abbey warriors and he'd marched out with the abbey into the Merofynian ambush so few survived.

'In daylight we can see Rolenhold, off to the south-west. At night...' Whetstone hesitated.

Fyn frowned. A shadow moved under the trees on the shore.

'That's no shadow. That's an attacking force!' Fyn gasped.

'Hundreds of them,' Whetstone said.

'Where?' Joff and Feldspar joined them.

Fyn pointed.

Feldspar sat back on his heels abruptly. 'I don't believe it. Cobalt is making a sneak attack on our watch.'

'What luck!' Joff crowed.

'Luck? Stupid boy. You've no idea...' Whetstone shuddered and went still.

Fyn gulped. Whetstone's fear seemed to leap into Fyn's body like flames leaping onto dry leaves. Was this going to be another massacre?

'Fyn, what do we do?' Feldspar asked.

That snapped him out of it. 'Joff, run up to the tradepost, give the alarm. I'll run to the gate. Warn them.'

Fyn scrambled for the ladder.

'What about me?' Feldspar asked.

Fyn glanced, over his shoulder. 'You've bows and arrows.'

'Yes. A dozen arrows.'

'Make every one count.'

Feldspar's terrified expression remained impressed on Fyn's mind as he scurried down the ladder. Joff jumped the last three rungs. They separated without a word.

Fan ran towards the gate. Was that the creak of the winch? Surely not.

He sprinted, hoping he wouldn't break his ankle on the uneven ground, only slowing when he neared the gate.

Two of the monks bent to wind the winch that lowered the drawbridge, the other two stood back, while a fifth person, the mystics master, watched.

This wasn't right. In his vision Catillum didn't aid the Merofynians, he fought them to the death.

'M-master?' Fyn struggled to catch his breath.

When Catillum turned, his features were the same but his expression was alien. Fyn knew instinctively, this wasn't Catillum. And he understood his Affinity vision, the mystics master had fought... and lost.

Fyn's mouth went dry with fear, as a great backwash of Affinity rolled off the being who had inhabited the mystics master's body.

'What are you doing?' Fyn demanded.

'Lowering the gate,' one of the monks explained, as if this was completely reasonable. 'Master Catillum wants to check the outer palisade.'

In the dark? Didn't they realise this wasn't Catillum? The renegade Power-worker had to be using the monks' own Affinity against them, making them blind to the subtle differences in Master Catillum's behaviour.

'Raise the drawbridge.' Fyn's voice scraped his throat raw and his heart raced. The monks ignored him. 'Raise the drawbridge. Byren has appointed me captain of Narrowneck. I outrank Catillum. Raise it. We're under at...'

His voice went completely, in fact his throat began to close, narrowing with each breath. Desperate, he ran past the renegade Power-worker, heading for the winch. But every step he took became more of an effort, until he could hardly move his limbs, could hardly drag a breath into his chest.

Time stretched. His breath came in horrible rasping gasps. He fell to his knees.

One of the four monks blinked and looked troubled. 'Kingsheir, are you...' His voice cracked and he fell to his knees, clawing at his throat.

The pressure on Fyn's chest lessened, as though the Power-worker was over-extending himself. Fyn lurched forwards, trying to reach the winch. Grey moths fluttered in his vision.

One of the monks at the winch straightened up. 'What's wrong with...' His voice cut out as he clutched his chest.

Fyn dragged in another breath.

There was a roaring in his ears. No, it was men shouting. The attackers charged the gate. He spared them one glance. Not Merofynians, spar warriors. Enemies all the same. He was too late. He'd failed Byren. Despair flooded him.

Hands grabbed him. The last two monks lifted him, swung him around and thrust him against the palisade beside the gate.

The renegade Power-worker reached out to Fyn. Reached into him.

Fyn watched in horror as fingers sank into his chest, through his flesh, through bone, to seize his essence. He found himself staring up into black, bottomless eyes. As the light faded, he thought he saw Bantam and Jakulos running through the trees towards the gate. But what could they do? They weren't Power-workers.

Even as he thought this, the world shifted and he was falling through the back of his skull, spiralling away.

Nothing could save him...

BYREN CAME AWAKE to find one of Catillum's monks trying to force his way through the door, shouting at Winterfall.

'Let me in. I must see Fyn's brother. The Merofynians are attacking.'

'Let him in.' Byren sprang out of bed, mind racing. Even as he reached for his breeches, his honour guard dressed and armed themselves. A pale grey light came through the casement windows. Dimly, he heard shouts from outside, from below.

The youth hurried over. Byren recognised Joff, who gave his report, but he knew no more than he'd already said.

Byren grabbed Joff's arm, suddenly afraid that the mystic master had betrayed them and lured Fyn to his death. 'You said Fyn sent you?'

Joff nodded. 'He went to make sure the gate was secure.'

'Don't worry, his sea-hounds are with him,' Orrade said, pointing.

Byren glanced to where the odd pair had been sleeping. Their bedrolls were empty.

'Good.' Byren rubbed his face. At least Fyn was at the gate and the camp was on alert. The palisade would hold, but for how long? He shoved on his boots. 'Come.'

Collecting the spar warlords and their honour Guards, he charged down the steps into the tap-room.

Florin tumbled out of the kitchen, her face creased by sleep. 'What's going on?'

'We're under attack. Stay here.' He ran past her, out of the tap-room.

Byren headed for the path to the gate.

Screams and the clash of metal on metal told him his men were already battling the enemy, and the depth of the sound told him it was in great numbers.

Worse, as he rounded the bend he saw the enemy pouring up the slope. They'd breached the gate. Impossible – the palisade should have held. Ravening spar warriors swept his half-armed, partly dressed defenders before them.

'They're not Mero –' Orrade began.

'No. They're Leogryf's men, sent in first to break us, so the Merofynians can clean up after!' Byren despised such tactics.

With a roar, he raced into the fray.

Byren shouldered a man aside, hacked at another, ran on. There was no time to judge the strength of the forces against him. He could only slash and block, with Corvel and Feid at his side. Aseel and Bearclaw yelled to their men, spreading out to form a line.

Where was Fyn?

Dead, if he'd tried to hold the gate.

Byren had to find him. He kicked men aside, ploughed through bodies, plucked an axe from a dead man's hand and swung it left-handed, using it to block. Orrade fought at his side, protecting his back as he'd always done. All about them in the growing light of a fresh day men fought for their lives.

Where was Warlord Leogryf and his smooth-tongued kinsman, Lord Leon? They had to be here somewhere. Byren wanted to get his hands on them, either of them. Preferable both!

But he was pinned on the spot, fighting for his life. For every spar warrior Byren knocked aside, three took his place.

He'd never make the gate, never find Fyn.

Step by bloody step, they were forced back, through the overturned camp sites, the trodden camp fires, over men's scattered belongings, over bodies still groaning in pools of blood.

Until they came to the bend in the path, and there they made a stand. The sheer mass of men behind them, hemmed in by the cliffs, forced them to hold.

Byren felt the weight of the battle, felt it turning in their favour. He laughed and his laughter inspired those nearest him, spreading along the line.

Orrade tugged at his arm and he allowed himself to be drawn back from the fray. Even as he did this, someone shoved in front of him to take his place. All along their line, fresh men replaced those who were spent or dead.

'We're going to hold,' Byren shouted.

'Aye. Catch your breath.'

He bent double to drag in great lungfuls of air.

A strange whistling roar made him lift his head. What was that coming towards them?

'Mulcibar's balls!' The words had barely left his mouth when a spinning ball of fire, big as a melon, smacked into a tree a bow-shot down the slope below. Instantly, the tree went up with a great whoosh of flames. The fire drove Leogryf's warriors into a frenzy of fear, striking out at Byren's men to escape the flames.

'They have a renegade Power-worker with them,' Orrade cried. 'Where's Catillum when we need him?'

Where indeed? How had the Merofynians breached the gate so quickly, if they hadn't been betrayed? Byren rubbed sweat from his eyes. 'You were right. I should have let you kill Catillum.'

Orrade shook his head. 'Fyn swore Catillum was loyal. He had a vision of the mystic.'

Had Fyn tried to stop Catillum? Byren's heart clenched with fear for his brother.

The horrible whistling came again as more fireballs flashed over. This time they flew above the tree canopy and came crashing into a stand of oaks. Flames engulfed the trees.

Men screamed and scrambled away from the blaze.

'It's an indiscriminate weapon,' Orrade yelled. 'As likely to kill their men as ours.'

Above the roar of the battle, Byren heard another roar, louder and fiercer. He knew that sound. Forest fire.

No ordinary fire, this one raced through the tree canopy, leaping from tree crown to crown.

'Mulcibar's breath,' Orrade gasped. 'I've read of it. I never thought to see it.'

Even as he spoke, the fighting slowed on both sides, as men saw flames racing towards them. A great gout of hot wind drove the fire front towards the top of the rise. Burning leaves, twigs and the fronds of pine needles showered them. The embers fell on the leaf litter, on the heads of unprotected men, singeing their faces, igniting their hair.

They broke off what they were doing to stamp out the flames. Suddenly, the air was almost too hot to breathe.

Throat parched, Byren glanced over his shoulder to discover that the tradepost was well alight. Old Man Narrows' pride and joy. All that old wood lovingly carved, pegged joists and wooden roof shingles, ablaze.

His men were trapped between the cliffs and the advancing fire. And Leogryf's men were trapped with them. Cobalt must have decided to sacrifice them.

'Byren.' Orrade grabbed his arm. 'You need to get away.'

He was right. Byren forged through the men, shouting. 'To the cliffs, jump for it. Swim to shore. Meet at Feid's stronghold.'

They passed along the message.

Word spread as men ran, dodging flames. In the mad scramble for the cliffs, he realised he'd lost sight of both Corvel and Feid. As for Aseel and Bearclaw, he'd lost track of them as soon as the fighting started.

A man could not fight god-driven fire. They had to go over the cliffs and swim for it. Byren could see no other way out. Many would escape on foot, or on borrowed horses riding across Rolencia for the Divide. Cobalt's Merofynians would pick off the slowest.

Florin could pass unnoticed, if she'd just slip on a woman's skirts. He hoped she was already well clear and had the sense to keep her head down.

A flash of dawnlight reflecting on the lake through the tree trunks told Byren he was nearly at the cliffs. Just as well. The air was so hot his throat rasped. A tree in front of him burst into flames. He dodged it.

And collided with Feid. They grabbed each other to steady themselves.

Byren blinked. His eyes burned, dried out by the furnace-hot air. 'We'll meet back at your stronghold.'

Feid nodded. 'But I don't understand. How could it go so wrong? How did the gate fall?'

'Catillum betrayed us,' Byren guessed. 'Left us at the mercy of Mulcibar's breath!'

And they ran on. He reached the cliff edge, not far from the platform where the winch stood. One glance below told him the water was full of men, floundering, swimming, struggling.

'Come on,' Feid said, tossing aside his weapons.

'Can't.' Byren turned back, looking for Orrade.

There he was, struggling with a leg wound. Luckily someone supported him... Florin? What was she still doing here?

Byren tossed his sword and borrowed axe aside. Running over to them, he slid his arm under Orrade's shoulder and took his weight. Ignoring his friend's attempts to drive him off, he swung Orrade right off his feet and ran for the cliff edge. Reached it and realised Florin was not with him. Turned, saw her hanging back.

'Come on. We've got to jump.'

She shook her head. Was she afraid of heights?

He let Orrade's legs slide to the ground and lunged back to grab her arm, hauling her to the edge. 'It's not far –'

'It's not that.' Her arm trembled in his hand. 'I can't swim.'

She couldn't swim? Orrade wouldn't make it to the shore with that leg wound. And if he did, he couldn't run far.

Byren couldn't... *wouldn't* leave either of them behind.

Without warning, Orrade shoved him in the small of the back.

He fell, dragging Florin with him. Free arm swinging, Byren caught Orrade's hand. Then all three of them were falling, plummeting towards the lake.

The lake hit Byren square in the back, driving the air from his chest. Cold black water closed over his head. Down, down he went into the shockingly cold depths.

He kicked up, hauling Florin with him. He'd lost Orrade in the fall. Above them, the surface glowed red with the fire raging over Narrowneck.

He broke through, sucked in a breath. Florin's head surfaced next to him. She clung to him, terrified. If he hadn't been so much stronger, she would have dragged him down. Somehow he managed to turn her around so her back was to his chest, and he trod water.

Where was Orrade? 'Orrie!'

While supporting Florin, he turned an awkward circle, searching for Orrade.

'Where is he?' Florin cried.

Red fire light danced on choppy waves. All he could see were wet frantic faces, plastered with strands of black hair. More people hit the lake, their impacts sending out more waves. Dark heads went under. Some bobbed up again, some did not.

'Why did you let him do that?' Florin demanded, struggling against Byren's arms.

'Stop it. Or I'll lose you.'

'You've lost him. Now you'll hate me.'

'Orrie?' His voice was raw from all the shouting and the heat of the flames.

Was that Feid over there? 'Feid?'

The head turned at his name. Byren struck out for Feid, pulling Florin along behind him. At least she wasn't fighting him.

Treading water, he pushed her into Feid's arms. 'Get her safe to the shore. I have to find Orrie.'

As Feid grabbed Florin, she turned a bedraggled face and haunted eyes on Byren. 'Find him.'

So it was true, she loved Orrade. 'I won't stop looking.'

Byren swam around, searching for the familiar thin face. So many wet, dark heads of hair. Had Orrade even surfaced?

How could Byren have let him go? His hold should have been stronger. 'Orrie. Orrie, where are you?'

He swam a little further. Called again and again. So many men, calling out. Their voices almost drowned by the roar of the fire above. The water's surface had turned to bronze.

'Orrie, where are you?' His teeth chattered so badly, he bit his tongue. 'Orrie...'

Refusing to give up, Byren swam in larger and larger circles. At last, he neared the shore. Dawn sunlight lit the trees. Orrade must have made it this far. Maybe he was already ashore, trying to escape the Merofynian search parties.

That had to be it, because Byren could not have stayed in the water any longer and lived. He was half-numb already.

As he waded out onto the shore he felt the mud under his feet. Like an old man, Byren struggled upright and stumbled through the reeds into the trees. Long shafts of dawn sun speared through the trunks, offering no warmth as yet. He wanted to yell Orrade's name, but dared not. He could still hear the roar of the fire.

He leant on a trunk and tried to think. So cold. Had to keep moving. His heart thundered with exhaustion.

No, it was a horse galloping. Several horses came through the trees towards him, flashing in and out of shafts of sunlight. Shouts. 'We have him.'

Who? Orrade?

No. Him. They circled around behind.

Byren spun, staggered.

'Lord Leon. We have him. Over here!'

It couldn't be. It was.

Byren weaved, trying to escape. Big, sweating horse flanks cut him off. He lurched and turned.

Something hit his head. He went down to his knees.

Someone jumped off their mount to stand in front of him. Caught his hair, jerked his head. Lord Leon's sneering face. Byren knew he was a dead man. It didn't matter. He'd failed Orrie.

'Not so proud now, eh, king?' Lord Leon said, breath heavy with ale.

'Cobalt's... sacrificed your warriors, b–burned them up,' Byren told him, the words chopped to pieces by his chattering teeth. 'What of your uncle?'

'Dead. He led the attack.'

Byren saw satisfaction in Lord Leon's black eyes. His uncle's death meant Leon was warlord of Leogryf Spar. What manner of man sent his own kin to their death?

'Do your men know you sacrificed –'

A fist slammed into Byren's face and the world went away.

Chapter Twenty-Two

PIRO SAT UP in bed, a cry on her lips. Her heart raced. In her mind's eye she still saw the wyvern with its gleaming green eyes laughing at her as its companions dragged Fyn and Byren away.

'What is it?' Isolt asked.

Pale dawn light fell across the foot of Isolt's bed where her pet wyvern slept. Loyalty lifted her head like a curious puppy and made a soft, interrogative sound. Isolt crawled up her bed to rub the beast's head reassuringly.

'A bad dream,' Piro confessed. 'I was with Byren and Fyn. We were running away from something. It caught them and now it's coming for me.'

'It could be a nexus point,' Isolt said. 'Piro, you must tell the mage.'

Piro hugged her knees. Tell the mage? What good would that do? There was no mage, only a half-trained apprentice, not much older than Byren.

And that half trained apprentice had entrapped her essence. In all this, who could she really trust but herself? She'd have to...

'Piro?' Isolt prodded. 'What are you up to?'

'Nothing.' She had promised not to reveal Tyro's secret, and the goddess knew he did not deserve her loyalty, but... she could not bring herself to destroy Isolt's faith. For once, her friend did not look haunted.

'I hate being trapped here. I've finished Fyn's jerkin and now I can't give it to him until he comes back.' Isolt gave an odd little laugh and sprang off the bed, pacing the room. Loyalty followed her, making soft worried noises.

Piro's foenix woke up then flew across the room to land on the head of her bed. She sat with her back to the headboard and he climbed into her lap for a cuddle. 'There, there, boy. There's nothing to worry about...' But she feared there was.

Isolt spun to face Piro. 'You've got Affinity. Could this be a warning for your brothers?'

Piro hugged the foenix. He made a purring sound as though sympathising with her.

'It's possible,' Piro admitted. 'But I don't know. I had dreams of wyverns prowling Rolenhold for ages before Palatyne captured the castle and finally made it come true.'

'We must warn them.' Isolt lit a candle, shielding its flame. 'The mage can use the Fate Fyn wears to contact him. It will be faster than a messenger bird. Come on.'

'Yes... but we'll go to Tyro.' Piro pushed the foenix aside and swung her legs off the bed. The cold floor made her toes curl. 'The mage is old and grumpy and we don't want to wake him.'

Isolt accepted this without question.

They hurried down the dark hall with the wyvern and foenix following. Piro rapped on Tyro's bed chamber door. 'It's us. Wake up. It's important!'

After a moment, Tyro opened the door, blinking in the light of Isolt's candle. His chest was bare and his hair hung down his back, tousled from sleep. It was the first time she had seen him looking vulnerable and Piro forgot what she was going to say.

'Piro's had a dream and we think it's a nexus point,' Isolt announced. 'Tell him, Piro. He can decide if we should wake the mage.'

Tyro caught Piro's eye. 'By all means, tell me, Piro.'

She did so, finishing with, 'If you use the Fate, you can contact Fyn, see if he is all right –'

'And warn him!' Isolt insisted.

Tyro hesitated.

'Use the Fate,' Piro urged.

'Now,' Isolt added.

Tyro smiled. 'Very well.'

He pulled on a pair of slippers and tugged a shirt over his shoulders, reminding Piro that she and Isolt wore nothing but their silk nightgowns. It didn't matter. Tyro saw them only as annoying game pieces, which he had to shelter until they could play their parts in the Duelling Kingdoms.

Tyro borrowed Isolt's candle to light a lamp and adjusted the wick. 'Come with me.'

He led them through the quiet corridor. Far away, Piro heard the servants stirring in the kitchen. The smell of baking wafted up the stairwell as they entered the war table room. Her stomach grumbled.

'Stir up the fire, Piro,' Tyro ordered.

She crossed the floor and knelt on the hearth tiles, adding fresh kindling and stirring up the coals.

If Tyro contacted Fyn and there was nothing wrong, she would feel silly, but at least her brothers would be warned.

She turned and joined Isolt, who was sitting cross-legged on the brilliant Ostronite rug in front of the fireplace with her wyvern's head in her lap. Piro sat stroking her foenix for reassurance. Isolt met her eyes, impatient with the delay.

Piro glanced past her. Tyro was over near the war table. 'What are you –'

He joined them, holding up a piece. 'It's Fyn.' He sat down. 'I'll use it to help me focus.'

'I can help you find him,' Piro offered, recalling how Tyro, while playing Lord Dunstany, had inadvertently drawn on her Affinity back in Rolenton.

'No need. Fyn wears the Fate. Its power will draw me to him.' Tyro closed his eyes.

Piro watched him, his face lit by the glow of the fire. The lamp had been left near the war table and the room was dimly lit behind him. Dawn light filtered through the tall balcony doors.

'The Fate is a great source of power, a channel for Affinity. It calls to me. Ah, there...' Tyro whispered. 'Now, I'll wake its sleeping owner. I...' he stiffened. His face twisted in a grimace of shock, then pain.

Without another word, he toppled sideways across Piro's knees. Her foenix gave an indignant cry and darted aside.

At the touch of Tyro's flesh on hers, a powerful force swamped Piro and she felt herself being sucked under.

'Piro?' Isolt lunged across the carpet.

Dimly, Piro felt Isolt catch her shoulders, shake her, call her... to no avail.

Smack. A palm collided with her cheek, then another and another. Shock and pain made her eyes fill with tears.

As suddenly as it had begun, it was over. Tyro rolled off her lap onto the floor. Face down, he struggled to push himself up, arms trembling. The wyvern watched them all, tail lashing from side to side like a vexed cat.

'Are you two all right?' Isolt whispered. 'What happened, Piro?'

Piro looked to Tyro, who pushed his hair from his face with a shaking hand.

'It was an enemy Power-worker. He nearly had me.' Tyro raised shocked black eyes to them. 'You two saved me, distracted him long enough for me to gather my defences.'

'But you were looking for Fyn,' Isolt protested.

'Does that mean he's been captured by a renegade Power-worker?' Piro demanded.

'I found the Fate. I didn't find your brother.'

'Fyn's dead?' Isolt went pale.

'No. At least, I don't know.' Tyro confessed. 'The Fate has fallen under the power of an enemy.'

'Fyn wouldn't give it up without a fight. It belonged to the abbey,' Piro insisted. 'Something has happened to him, maybe to both my brothers.'

'I fear so,' Tyro agreed.

'We must wake the mage and tell him,' Isolt decided, coming to her feet.

Piro and Tyro exchanged looks.

'I'll tell him,' Tyro offered. 'He hates being woken. No need for you two to catch the sharp edge of his tongue.'

'It wouldn't worry me,' Isolt said.

Piro stood and slid her arm through Isolt's. 'I think we should let Tyro tell him. Let the mage deal with the enemy Power-worker.'

Isolt saw the sense of this. 'Come, Loyalty. Breakfast.' She turned to Tyro. 'But if there is any news you must send for us.'

He nodded and gave Piro a grateful look.

FYN WOKE TO the soft padding of heavy feet. A terrible sense of dread swamped him. He smelled wyverns and heard their harsh breath as they exhaled. They stalked him.

He could see nothing, but he felt the stone under his hands and knees. Crawling along, he came to a wall and stood up. By the feel of it, he was in the caverns under the abbey. His hand grazed the embossed wyvern symbol and he fingered its shape. Follow the wyvern to get out, the abbot had said. He had to escape the wyverns. Terror rose up in him, threatening to choke him.

Think!

How had he become lost down here? Where were the others?

Every time he tried to focus and find the answers, he came up against a kind of mental bruise that made him wince and gasp.

What was going on?

The soft padding of wyvern feet on the stone and their acrid smell came to him. No time to think. He must run.

Follow the wyvern to escape the wyvern. If he kept that fixed in his mind he would be safe. Fyn ran.

And kept running.

BYREN WOKE TO find himself tied across a horse's saddle. His head ached. With each lurch of the horse's back his gorge threatened to rise. He couldn't breathe through his nose and suspected it was broken.

Men on horseback rode around him, visible in the light of the setting sun. He recalled waking more than once, tied across this horse's back. Each time he'd woken they'd knocked him senseless.

Now, judging by his upside-down glimpse of the world, they were nearing the top of the steep switch-back road that led to Rolenhold.

He bit back a groan as it all came back to him.

He'd been captured. He'd failed Fyn and Orrade. Soon he would face his traitorous cousin, Cobalt, and execution.

At least Florin was safe. He hoped she was safe.

Merofynians cheered as the returning warriors entered the castle courtyard. Someone jumped down and reached under the horse, cutting the rope that held him in place. They shoved him and he slid backwards off the horse, staggering, arms still tied at the wrist. His knees almost gave way. But he found his feet and looked up, blinking blood from his eyes.

Behind the cheering Merofynians, he saw the silent, sad faces of his father's people, watching from vantage points around the courtyard. They'd put their hopes in him. He'd failed them and now they were a subjugated people, slaves in their own land.

Lord Leon shoved Byren between his shoulder blades, driving him ahead of them into the stronghold, through King Rolen's great hall and up the stairs to the trophy chamber.

Here, his cousin waited across the other side of the war table, which had been shifted from its original room. He wore royal Rolencian red in the Ostronite style – nipped waist, lace at the collar and wrists. One sleeve hung loose and his long hair was threaded with red garnets, so that it gleamed in a shaft of setting sun that streamed through the oriel window.

Behind him, to one side, stood a Mulcibar monk, perhaps the very one who had sent the fire to consume Narrowneck and the warlord of Leogryf Spar.

Once, Byren had been blind to Affinity, but now he could sense power exuding from the monk's skin, so he had to be a mystic. Avoiding the monk's unnerving black gaze, Byren vowed to give Cobalt no satisfaction. He wouldn't plead for his life.

'A present for you, King Cobalt,' Lord Leon said. 'The pretender, Byren Kingson.'

So he was a pretender now? Talk about the pot calling the kettle black.

Cobalt looked him up and down. 'Not so fine now, are you, cousin Byren?' A cruel smile lit his handsome face. 'Looks like I've won this game of Duelling Kingdoms!'

As Byren stood, hands bound in front of him, he did not regret trying to avenge his parents and brother's murders. But he did regret failing the men who had followed him. At least Piro still lived and she knew Cobalt for the treacherous liar he was. Which reminded him...

'The game's not over until the king takes a queen,' Byren said. 'Piro will never marry you. My mother cut off your arm. Piro will cut off your –'

'I'll cut out your tongue!' Cobalt lunged across the war table, grabbing Byren's vest, pulling him off balance and jerking him forwards so that their faces were only a hand's breadth apart. 'I'll cut off your balls and see how cocky you are then! Won't that make your lover weep?'

Byren's stomach lurched. Death he could face, disfigurement and torture he dreaded.

Mulcibar's mystic touched Cobalt's shoulder. It was enough to make Cobalt release Byren with a shove, so that he fell backwards, into Lord Leon's arms.

'How is Orrade, by the way?' Cobalt asked. 'Did you know he spied for me, reporting on your every move?'

'I know that's a lie.' Just as Byren knew denying Orrade was his lover would achieve nothing. 'And I know the people of Rolencia will never accept you as their rightful king, not as long as Piro could be their queen.'

'Speaking of queens...' Cobalt sneered. 'You'll never get the chance to claim Isolt. Palatyne has plans for her. And,' he glanced to the mystic, 'as much as I'd like to spike your head over the main gate of Rolenhold, Palatyne has plans for you. You're going to Merofynia, where you'll be tried for treason.'

'Against Rolencia? A child could see through that ploy!' Byren threw back his head and laughed. The sound echoed off the trophy chamber's high ceiling.

His laugh startled his enemies, who stared at him.

'You won't be laughing when Palatyne's finished with you!' Cobalt bristled.

'Now that I've delivered the pretender, I want my reward,' Leon announced. Clearly, he'd grown tired of waiting. 'You promised to appoint me overlord of the spars.'

'Overlord of the spars?' Cobalt echoed. 'You seek to emulate Palatyne. Very well, come here.'

Lord Leon thrust past Byren as he went around the table to stand before Cobalt.

'A man who will send his own uncle to his death cannot be trusted,' Cobalt said, and nodded to the mystic.

'What?' Leon protested. 'You said –'

'Look out!' Byren yelled. Too late, the mystic caught Leon around the neck and drove a knife through his ribs.

Behind Byren the chamber erupted as Leon's five honour guards leapt to defend him and were cut down by Cobalt's swordsmen.

Byren ran around the far end of the table, meaning to fling his bound hands over Cobalt's neck from behind and use him as a hostage to escape. But Cobalt was already turning.

Cobalt brought his one good arm up in a blow aimed for Byren's temple. Byren tried to duck but Cobalt's fist caught him on the ear and he went down, clipping his head on the edge of the table so that he knew no more.

PIRO HAD BEEN waiting on news for three days now. She sprang to her feet as Tyro walked into the grotto. 'What of Byren and Fyn?'

Isolt went very still. Attuned to her, the wyvern slowed in its play and swam to the side, slithering out, skin gleaming. Reflected sunlight filled the grotto, playing on the oyster-shell ceiling and walls.

'Captain Nefysto sent word.' Tyro looked grim.

Despite the warmth rising off the water Piro went cold.

'Fyn was wounded,' Tyro said. 'Nefysto is on his way back with him.'

'Then he is safe.' Isolt brightened. 'Piro and I are both versed in the healing arts. We...' She ran down, seeing Tyro's expression.

'It's not that kind of wound.' The look Tyro sent them made Piro's heart falter. 'From what I've pieced together, it seems the abbey mystics master was consumed by the Mulcibar mystic. Fyn tried to stop him betraying them. From Nefysto's description of Fyn's state I think I know how to reverse it. The Power-worker used Fyn's own Affinity against him. We have to hope he has the strength to last until he gets here. Bantam is caring for him, dribbling water into his mouth, massaging his throat to make him swallow.'

'Poor Fyn. If only –'

'What of Byren?' Piro asked.

It was clear Tyro did not want to answer.

'Dead?' she whispered, stricken.

'We don't know. It was a slaughter. Some of Byren's men escaped. They were supposed to meet back at Warlord Feid's stronghold. He was meant to join them there but...'

'He's survived before,' Piro said. 'I won't give up hope.'

'You're right.' Isolt squeezed her hand. 'And the mage can cure Fyn.'

What mage? Piro felt like shouting. Tyro should have let her tell Isolt. He should have trusted her.

She turned away to stare through the grotto entrance. Outside, brilliant sunshine made the Ring Sea sparkle. Anger and confusion churned in Piro's stomach.

'I'm so sorry.' Isolt hugged Piro. 'I never had a brother, but I would have loved to have someone to look after me.'

Piro snorted. 'Tease you, you mean.' Tears spilled down her cheeks. She held Isolt's eyes. 'You would have loved Byren. He had a good heart. He brought

me the foenix egg and helped me hatch him. He...'
A sob shook Piro and she fought to speak. 'At least
Fyn still lives.'

'And he will be back soon. The mage will fix the
mystic's Affinity curse and we'll nurse him back
to health,' Isolt said with conviction. She smiled
through her own tears. 'You will see.'

Tyro put a hand on Piro's shoulder. 'She's right.
We'll do everything we can for Fyn.'

Piro stared up at him. This renegade Power-
worker had her soul trapped in an amber pendant.
If it hadn't been for that she would have trusted him.
But now...

Chapter Twenty-Three

BYREN HAD A miserable sea voyage to Merofynia, chained at the ankle and wrists, but otherwise free to wander about his cabin. They did not fear him, for what could he do? One man couldn't take over a ship and sail it. And if he jumped overboard he would drown or be eaten by wyverns.

Now, he knelt on the window seat watching Mulcibar's Gate grow distant behind him. It was dusk and the fiery finger of falling lava was reflected in the sea.

Soon they would be in Port Mero and Palatyne would have his circus of a trial. He was a duke now, this Palatyne. In reality he was no more than a warlord whose ambition was to crown himself king.

Byren snorted. How Duke Palatyne could justify charging him with treason was beyond him, but he knew the men of law that Palatyne hired would make it appear legal. Then they could execute Byren with a clear conscience, not that men like that had a conscience.

Byren stared at the black water, Mulcibar's flames dancing on the waves. Maybe he should have jumped overboard to prevent their triumph.

But he had never been one to give up. He would fight with the last breath in his body. He would never give Duke Palatyne the satisfaction of breaking him.

To think Affinity had been his downfall, just as it had been his grandfather, King Byren's. He should have surrounded himself with abbey-trained mystics. Then Fyn and Orrade wouldn't be... no, he had to hope they lived, just as he hoped Feid had managed to slip back over the Divide with Florin.

WHEN THEY CARRIED her brother in, Piro had to hide her dismay. Fyn had never been big like Byren and Lence but, without his personality animating his body, he seemed dangerously fragile. Isolt said nothing, her fingers biting into Piro's arm.

'Tell the mage I've done everything I could for him,' Nefysto said. 'Sometimes he moans and his eyes dart about under his lids. I don't know –'

'This way,' Tyro ordered. He led them upstairs to the chamber next to his. The bed had been made with fresh sheets and a fire laid in the grate, though it was warm enough without one. Tyro dismissed them all except for Piro. 'You go too, Isolt.'

'I can help. I'm a trained healer.'

'Later, if all goes well, then we will need you. What I must do now calls for a different sort of skill.'

'Why isn't the mage here?'

'He told me what to do.'

Piro took Isolt's hand to lead her to the door, where Isolt glanced back to the bed. 'He'll be all right won't he, Piro? I mean if it were really serious the mage himself would be here.'

Piro couldn't bring herself to answer. She shut the door and turned to Tyro.

'I should tell her the truth.'

'She has enough to worry about. Now come here.' He beckoned Piro to the bed, where he sat holding Fyn's hand. 'Take his other hand. He has done well to hold on this long. It is not the lack of food and water that is most dangerous, but what he faces.'

Piro's mouth felt too dry to speak. She went around the far side of the bed and took Fyn's hand.

'Using Fyn's Affinity the Power-worker trapped him in his own mind, trapped him with what he fears most.' Tyro met her eyes. 'Do you know what that is?'

'Fear. He fears that he is a coward.'

'Amazing!' Tyro's eyes widened. 'Nefysto said he never faltered, not once. He saved them from the Utland raiders when they ventured into the Skirling Stones.'

All this was news to Piro, so she just nodded. The last time she had faced the Power-worker with Tyro it had almost crushed her. She dreaded what they must do now but... 'Tell me what to do to save Fyn.'

'He knows you, he trusts you. I will lead you into his mind. You must convince him to face his fear. Only then can he escape.'

Piro gave a relieved laugh. 'To escape he must face his fear? Is that all?'

Tyro nodded. 'Face it and die, or face it and live. Only by facing it will we know.'

'Oh Fyn...' Piro smoothed her brother's hair from his forehead. At seventeen, his cheeks were still as smooth as a boy's. It hurt her to think he wouldn't live long enough to need to shave. As she watched, his eyes moved under his lids as if he dreamed.

'Piro?'

She looked across Fyn's vulnerable form to Tyro.

'I must be honest,' the half-trained mage whispered. 'If he confronts his fear and fails, I may not be able to bring you out. You don't have to do this. I can go in on my own and –'

'No. You're right. Fyn trusts me. I must do it.'

'You are very brave, Piro. I knew it from the first moment I saw you.'

She shook her head. 'Once I thought I was brave. But not now. Now that I've known true fear, I...' She shivered and summoned a smile. 'Let's do this.'

Tyro nodded and reached across Fyn's chest to her free hand. Their fingers entwined. 'Close your eyes and imagine you are walking down a path with me.'

Piro dropped her guard and found herself on a forest path. It was very grey and overcast and the big pine trees loomed above them. Tyro held her hand, leading her to a granite outcropping. He pointed into a narrow cave mouth.

Piro did not want to go in there. 'I don't have a lamp.'

He cupped his hands and a small ball of light appeared. 'In this place you make your own light, Piro.'

She held up one hand and the ball of light came to her, settling on her wrist like her foenix used to do, before he grew too big.

Tyro cupped her cheek with his hand. 'Be brave, little Piro.'

She brushed his hand away. Why did he have to be kind all of a sudden? It was easier if he was abrupt with her.

Ducking her head, she entered the cave.

FYN FELT TIRED, so tired. His body ached with every step and his night-blind eyes burned, the gritty lids scraping his eyes each time he blinked. He couldn't remember the last time he'd slept. All he wanted to do was rest, but if he sat down, he would fall asleep and to sleep was fatal. The wyverns would get him. He could still hear them snuffling behind him, tracking him through the dark.

He must keep going.

Something sparkled.

Stars?

No, it was a golden light.

He squinted, his tired eyes producing tears so that the light fractured into prisms.

'Fyn?' Piro called.

He blinked the tears away to see Piro walking down the tunnel towards him, with a light in one hand. No, the light hovered over one hand. How strange.

'Oh, Fyn!' She ran the last few steps, throwing her arms around him. It felt so good to hug her.

She pulled away to look at him. 'You poor thing.'

'Shhhhh!' He pressed his fingers to her mouth, glancing behind him. 'They'll hear you.'

'What?'

'The wyverns. They're after me. I don't know how many.'

'Wyverns? Oh, Fyn, you're not being chased by wyverns. You're running away from your fears!'

He stared at her. 'Can't you smell them, hear their footsteps, the scrape of their claws on the stone?' Grabbing her arm, he pulled her with him, heading up the tunnel. 'We've got to keep moving.'

She planted her feet. 'No. You can't run for ever. You have to face them. That's the only way to overcome –'

'I can't fight a full-grown wyvern and there's more than one.' He wanted to shake her. 'Piro, you must keep moving. You'll get us killed!'

'Where are we?'

He dragged her another step. 'In the caverns under the abbey. Come.'

'No, we are trapped in your mind.'

Fyn stopped pulling at her and stared into her sweet but determined face.

'The Power-worker trapped you. Don't you remember?'

He probed his memory and felt pain as if from a deep bruise. But, as much as it hurt, Piro made sense. Hadn't he wondered how he got here?

'He used your own Affinity to trap you. The wyverns are your fears given form. The only way to defeat them is to face them.'

Snuffling came from behind them. The wyverns were nearly on them. 'But it seems so real.'

'Look.' Piro held up her lamp. Only it wasn't a lamp. It was a ball of golden light, hovering over her skin. 'We are both in your mind. That's why I can make light.'

Fyn stared at the glowing ball.

'Face your fears, Fyn. Defeat them and we can escape.'

She turned him to face the wyvern. The golden glow picked up every chip in the stone floor, every vein of coloured rock in the walls. Beyond there was only darkness, and in that darkness the wyverns waited to tear him apart.

Fyn could imagine wyverns crouching just out of the light, eyes glinting, muzzles pulling back from their teeth.

'Face your fears.' Piro took a step forwards, her circle of light moving with her.

No wyverns were revealed. Fyn peered into the shadows. He imagined the beasts leaping to attack, pouncing on them...

Piro took his hand, lifting it. The ball of light jumped from her hand to his. 'Face them and free yourself.'

'What happens if I fail to face them down?'

'You die and I die with you.'

Heart hammering, Fyn lifted his arm higher. The light revealed only bare walls and floor. He took a step. Still no wyverns.

'What wyverns live underground?' Piro said.

She was right. They loved the fresh air, nesting on

cliffs over the water. Why hadn't he remembered that? Because he'd been too frightened to think.

Sucking in a breath, Fyn forced himself to stride forwards. No wyverns.

At his heels, Piro laughed.

He felt lighter.

Piro tugged on his hand. 'Come on.'

And he was running with Piro next to him, running with his light. Running into the light.

PIRO WOKE WITH a gasp. She'd fallen asleep with her head on Fyn's shoulder, his hand in hers. Tyro leant over her.

'Are you all right?'

Piro sat up. 'Fyn?'

Her brother's eyelids flickered open.

'Piro?' His voice creaked from lack of use.

'Here.' Tyro offered him a sip of something.

Fyn took a mouthful then coughed. When he caught his breath he looked up at Piro wonderingly. 'We were in the caverns under the abbey. You came to me with a light.'

'And you escaped. You beat the trap the Power-worker placed on your Affinity.'

Fyn shook his head, tears filling his eyes. 'Byren. Have you heard –'

'Fyn?' Isolt opened the door. 'You're awake?'

'You were listening at the door,' Piro accused.

'Of course.' Isolt hurried across the chamber. She studied Fyn critically. 'You're too pale and thin. You need building up. I've mixed a tonic for you. Ovido is bringing it.'

Piro fought down a wave of resentment. Fyn was her brother and she was just as good a healer as Isolt.

'Tyro?' Fyn pulled himself onto one elbow, fixing on the mage's supposed agent. 'Has there been word of my brother?'

'Nothing. The mage has no spies among Cobalt's men and the spy from Feidton knows nothing. Byren was meant to meet up with the others there.'

Fyn sank back to the pillow. 'I failed him.'

'Nonsense,' Isolt said briskly. 'From what I heard you tried to save the whole camp.' She broke off as Ovido backed into the chamber with a tray of medicines and jars. 'Good boy. Put it here next to the bed.' Isolt turned back to Fyn. 'Now listen to me. You must get better. Piro and I need you.'

An odd smile tugged at Fyn's lips.

'Lift his head,' Isolt ordered and, while Tyro held him, she tipped a spoonful of broth into his mouth. Fyn swallowed. 'As soon as you finish this, I have something to make you sleep. You are safe with us now.'

When he had finished it was clear just drinking the soup and the tisane had exhausted Fyn. He sank back onto the cushions and fell asleep even as they watched.

'I'll stay with him,' Piro said.

'I'll stay too.' Isolt pulled the chair nearer to the bed and sat down, her face close to Fyn's. She watched him sleep with total concentration.

Tyro caught Piro's eye and nodded towards the door. They left quietly.

'Get some sleep while you can. It will be a long night,' he told Piro, once they were out in the hall.

'With Elector Cera soon to be crowned there is peace in Ostron Isle, but the news of Byren's defeat may make her wonder about the alliance. I have much to do.'

Piro nodded. But when Tyro left her, she opened the door and leant against the door jamb, watching Isolt with Fyn. The Merofynian kingsdaughter held Fyn's hand in both of hers.

Noticing Piro, Isolt sent her a fierce smile. 'Don't worry. We'll soon have him strong again!'

She loves him, Piro thought. *I wonder if Fyn knows? How could he, when Isolt does not even realise it?*

And, understanding this, Piro was able to leave her brother in Isolt's care.

DESPITE HIS CHAINS, they escorted Byren out of his cabin at sword point, then walked him down the gangplank onto the wharf at Port Mero. The chain between his ankles was so short he could only shuffle. By the light of many torches he saw Duke Palatyne on his horse, looking grand in full battle armour, wearing the manticore chitin chestplate that Byren had given his father. A skinny, silver-haired Utland Power-worker hovered at Palatyne's side.

'Kneel before the duke!' A soldier kicked Byren in the back of the knees so that he fell to the wharf.

Palatyne walked his horse closer. Sliding a leg over the saddle, he jumped to the ground and grabbed a handful of Byren's hair, hauling his head up. 'Let's see what King Rolen's traitor looks like. This is the son who ran off, leaving his brother and father to fight his battles, leaving his mother and sister to die. Then he tried to claim the kingdom for himself. Is this the sort of man we want as the king of Rolencia?'

People jeered.

'Who killed King Rolen under a flag of truce?' Byren yelled. 'Who killed Queen Myrella in her own hall? Not I. It –'

Palatyne backhanded him with such force he saw stars. Men hauled him away, unlocked the chains at his wrists and ankles, picked him up and threw him into a cage on a cart. Head ringing, Byren stared out through the bars at angry faces.

FYN WOKE TO find himself in a strange bed. Sunlight streamed through the window panes, making rainbow patterns. For one perfect moment he was glad just to be alive and free of fear, before it all came back to him.

Master Catillum was dead, his body possessed and his Affinity used to betray Byren. If his brother still lived, he would have made it back to Feidton by now, so he must be dead. How could everything go so wrong?

Fyn turned his head away from the window. On the other side of his bed Isolt curled up, asleep in a chair. The shawl had slipped from her shoulders, silk tassels hanging on the floor.

With Byren and Lence dead, Isolt was officially betrothed to Fyn. His mouth went dry with longing and his heart hammered against his ribs.

Terribly thirsty, he tried to lift the mug by his bed, but it slipped through his clumsy fingers and fell to the floor, rolling on the carpet.

Isolt woke with a start, springing from the chair. 'Oh, you're awake!' She picked up the mug. 'Now you'll need some more broth and –'

'Broth? I'm not a toothless old man.'

She laughed. 'Certainly not. You just bit my head off!'

He wanted her for his own. Heat flooded Fyn as realisation swept him. He had wanted her all along but refused to admit it, because she'd belonged to Byren.

Byren... How could he feel glad his brother was dead? His eyes burned with unshed tears and he turned his face away from Isolt.

'What's wrong, Fyn?'

Now was not the time to tell her that he loved her, not when she had been feeding him like a baby. Besides, what if she laughed at him? He could not bear it.

The door swung open. Piro raced into the chamber, face glowing with happiness. 'Good news, Byren lives! He was sent to Palatyne to be executed. Lord Dunstany's spies saw him arrive.'

Fyn closed his eyes, overwhelmed.

For a moment he could not bear to think.

Isolt belonged to Byren. She would never be his.

Thank the goddess he had not revealed his true feelings. A morass of emotion swelled in his chest.

His duty was clear. He must rescue his brother.

When he tried to sit up, his elbows trembled with the effort. Frustration raged through Fyn. How could he save Byren when he was so weak? 'When is Byren to be executed?'

'Palatyne has him in a cage. He accused Byren of treason against his own family. It's very clever the way he worded it. I think Cobalt had a hand in that,' Piro admitted. 'The traditional means of execution is death by starvation, but Lord Dunstany's servants will slip him food and water if they can.'

'I must get up.' Fyn tried to swing his legs to the floor, groaning as his head swam.

Isolt held him down without trouble. 'You've been all but dead for days. You need time to recover.'

He brushed her hands off him. 'I don't have time. Why doesn't the mage send Lord Dunstany's people to free Byren, Piro?'

She looked away. 'I don't know the mage's plans. Maybe he will.'

'I must get up,' Fyn muttered.

'And I say you must stay in bed.' Isolt glared at him.

She looked so adorable when she made that fierce expression, Fyn had to turn away.

He came face to face with a wyvern. It stood on its hind legs, with a paw on the high bed. Fyn's heart missed a beat. 'Freezing Sylion. Where did that Affinity beast come from?'

'Hush, you'll hurt Loyalty's feelings,' Isolt said. 'She was the last elector's pet and now she's mine. Speaking of which, they will crown the new elector tonight. Will you be well enough to come? You look flushed. Are you running a fever?'

She felt his forehead. Fyn knew it was the touch of a healer for her patient, but he ached for more. He sank into the pillow, heart-sore and weary beyond belief.

He would have to leave Mage Isle as soon as he could, for he couldn't bear to be near Isolt, knowing she belonged to his brother.

* * *

PIRO WATCHED FYN close his eyes, a bitter twist to his mouth. He was in pain. Suddenly, he lifted onto one elbow and fixed on her.

'Go to the agent, Piro, find out when he's sending someone to save Byren. I'll go with them.'

Isolt cast Piro a swift worried look.

'Of course,' Piro said. 'I'll ask him now.'

Out in the corridor, she headed straight for the war table room, where she found Tyro studying the pieces.

'Is Fyn well enough to come to the elector's inauguration tonight?' he asked her. 'He can rest all day. We can take the carriage and he can sit down while we're there.'

'Fyn wants to save Byren. He wants to know if the mage is sending a rescue party. Is he? Are you?'

'Your brother is being held in the heart of the enemy's stronghold. How many men would you send to their deaths to rescue Byren, Piro?'

She opened her mouth, then closed it. 'There must be some stealthy way, some way that uses subterfuge.'

'I'm working on it,' Tyro muttered, as if he'd never cupped her cheek and tried to reassure her. 'I'll have formal clothes sent to Fyn's chamber. He must dress appropriately for the celebrations tonight. As must you and Isolt.'

'Strangely enough, I don't feel like partying when my brother is being starved to death,' Piro snapped. 'How can these Ostronites feast with war hanging over their heads?'

'Would you deny the Ostronites their butterfly existence? Their symbol is the abeille, after all. The beautiful but industrious butterfly-bee.'

She stiffened. 'The people of Ostron Isle play games while people are dying.'

'Could a butterfly stop the serpent from devouring its prey?'

'No.'

Tyro smiled and his dark eyes glittered. 'Then why not enjoy the butterfly? Don't deny its right to exist, leave the serpent-slaying to the mongoose.'

A shiver moved over Piro's skin. 'You mean to see Palatyne dead!'

Tyro nodded. 'He is a dangerous man. If he becomes king, he will not accept Lord Dunstany's guidance.'

'Why not free Byren and let him kill Palatyne for you? At least tell Fyn your plans.'

'What happens if a cook takes the cake from the oven before it is ready?'

'It sinks,' she answered automatically.

He nodded and would not elaborate.

She fumed. Tyro thought he was so clever, but he could not think of everything. Besides, she didn't like her fate to be in anyone's hands but her own.

Chapter Twenty-Four

BYREN HAD SLEPT well, considering he was lying on the bars of a cage, hanging in the square in front of the palace. After forced marches to deal with spar upstarts he'd learned to sleep anywhere. He'd tried licking the condensation from the bars to slake his thirst. Now he was hungry.

Merofynian ceremonial guards stood at intervals along the courtyard walls. They wore brilliant azure cloaks and blue and black feather crests on their helmets, but the swords they carried were not just for show.

Byren's stomach rumbled. He could smell baked potatoes and cinnamon cakes in the market beyond the courtyard. Already the market was busy. Voices carried, as did the pipes of a performer.

Byren heard a shout, several curses. Something was knocked over and crockery smashed. A child screeched. No, it was a dancing monkey, which had broken free of its chain and run into the courtyard. The guards along the wall above him laughed as a pretty young woman ran around the courtyard after the monkey, trying to catch it. It managed to stay just out of her reach, scampering back to the market.

The guards began laying bets on whether the monkey would escape her altogether. While their attention was distracted a beggar boy scurried into the courtyard, coming over to Byren's cage. The floor was level with his chest.

He tossed something at Byren who ducked, used to rubbish and abuse being hurled at him after last night. At the last moment he caught the object, which was clean cloth and tied with string.

Byren hid it under his cloak, picking at the ties. By the smell, it contained hot cinnamon buns. His mouth watered.

With his back to the guards he snuck mouthfuls of bun and silently thanked his unknown benefactor. It seemed some of his men had managed to infiltrate Port Mero. Things were not hopeless!

FYN STRODE BACK and forth across the orchard courtyard, driving himself. His arms and legs were weak and strangely numb, but the more he used them, the better he felt. He had slept for most of the day and now it was late afternoon. Depending on the winds, it would take four to five days to sail to Port Merofyn. He feared Palatyne would change his mind and order Byren's execution by a more immediate method such as beheading.

He ducked under a mandarin tree, its branches bending under the weight of early-ripening fruit. All around him other trees were blossoming and the whole courtyard was awash with their fragrance, but he could not enjoy it. Not when Byren's life hung in the balance.

'Fyn, that is enough pacing. You'll bring on a fever,' Isolt warned.

'Twice more,' he said, not looking her way.

He knew Piro and Isolt were exchanging looks. They sat under a cherry tree, their hair and clothes speckled with pale pink blossoms. He had been sitting there with Piro until Isolt joined them, bringing hot pastries fresh from the kitchen. He'd eaten three, then had to get up to pace. He knew his withdrawal had hurt Isolt.

'Fyn,' Piro called. 'You are taller than me. Pick one of those passion fruit for Isolt. They are her favourite.'

He stopped his pacing and went to the trellis. Plucking several, he offered Isolt one with a quick smile. 'Sweets for the sweet.'

'Don't start sprouting poetry, Fyn.' Isolt laughed. 'Next you'll be singing like Captain Nefysto.'

'So, you are well enough to pick fruit,' Tyro said, coming up behind him. 'Good, Mage Tsulamyth wants you to attend the elector's ceremony tonight as Fyn Kingson.'

Fyn frowned. 'If the mage would only give me Captain Nefysto and the *Wyvern's Whelp*, I'd lead a raid deep into Merofynia to rescue Byren.'

'The mage doesn't want you both dead. He has his own plans. Byren is safe for now.'

'Safe? In a cage at Palatyne's mercy?' Fyn exploded. His head swam and he staggered. Isolt rose to help him. He brushed her aside. 'Freezing Sylion, Tyro. You can tell your mage, Byren is not a piece in his Kingdoms game. If Fyn Kingson appears in Ostron Isle tonight, Palatyne will find out. He knows about the alliance, he might kill Byren!'

'Or he might offer to ransom him to you.'

'He might,' Fyn conceded slowly. 'But I don't want to gamble with my brother's life.'

'Fyn's right,' Piro spoke up. 'Who would pay this ransom? We are destitute. The food we eat and the clothes we wear come from the mage.'

'He would gladly pay,' Tyro revealed. 'He wants to restore the balance of power in the three kingdoms.'

Piro seemed convinced, but Fyn was not.

'You can tell the mage I am too weak to attend the ceremony tonight,' he told Tyro. 'I'm going back to bed.'

'I'll help you,' Isolt said.

'I can manage.'

'I am a healer, Fyn.'

'Rest is all I need.' He marched off. It was only when he got out of sight that he leant against the wall to catch his breath and wait for the grey specks to vanish from his vision. He cursed himself for being rude to Isolt.

She would hate him. Good.

That was better than her ever guessing how he really felt. And he needed privacy for he was going to rescue Byren. As soon as the others left for the elector's coronation he would slip off Mage Isle.

* * *

PIRO WATCHED ISOLT climb into the mage's carriage, lifting her ankle-length silk skirt and revealing the jewelled clasp on her slippers.

'What took you so long?' The mage thumped the roof of the carriage with his cane and it lurched, sending Isolt onto her seat with a thud.

Piro hid a smile. Tyro was good at this.

'I had to check on Fyn,' Isolt said primly, slipping back into her Merofynian court persona. 'He was sleeping. I think he overdid it in the garden today.'

'The arrogance of youth,' Mage Tsulamyth muttered. 'Now you two keep your ears open. Any interesting gossip, report back to me.' His deep-set eyes gleamed. 'Many men make the mistake of thinking power comes from the sword, but real power comes from information. Remember that. One day you will both be queens.'

Piro snorted. 'I don't want to be queen.'

'But think of the good you could do,' Isolt countered.

'How will you do good, while married to Palatyne?'

'I will never marry Palatyne. In fact...' Isolt's small mouth settled in a grim line, 'I will never marry!'

FYN'S SKIN FELT clammy with sweat as he jumped down from the borrowed horse. Luckily the wharfs were almost deserted. Everyone who could wrangle an invitation was up at the gardens for the inauguration ceremony. Fyn headed for the *Wyvern's Whelp*. Everything rested on his ability to bluff Nefysto, and the captain was no fool.

A single sailor stood on watch, having his own feast of wine and a leg of ham. He waved to Fyn. 'Good to see you back on your feet, little monk!'

'Captain in his cabin?' Fyn asked.

'You missed him. He's with his family, up at the ceremony.'

Fyn cursed silently. He should have anticipated this. He slid out a message cylinder, pinched from the war table room. 'We're supposed to sail at first light. Give this to the captain when he comes in.'

The sailor shook his head. 'Can't be done. Half the crew won't be back till midday and the ship has to be provisioned.'

'Very well. But my mission is of the greatest urgency. I will return at lunchtime tomorrow.' Fyn strode off. As soon as he was out of sight he bent double to catch his breath.

A snatch of music and laughter wafted down from the elector's gardens.

Isolt was up there. He'd pretended to be asleep when she came to check on him. It had been on the tip of his tongue to apologise. Since he was going to rescue Byren, so his brother could marry her and unite their kingdoms, he deserved one more chance to see her.

Fyn headed up the slope. He would blend into the crowd, watch her from afar. He entered through one of the many garden archways and made for the lantern-dotted terraces. Now that he was here and saw the crowds he realised how hopeless it was. Still he wandered, listening for Isolt's voice in the laughter and music. There were rock pools amid artfully constructed gardens, and heavenly scented flowers glowed in the velvety night.

He thought Isolt would be up on the main terrace where the elector was, with the aristocracy of Ostron Isle, but he found her alone by a pool. Pale flowers floated on its surface, barely disturbing the stars' reflection.

She wore something white and filmy, and her head-dress was threaded with zircons that glinted like stars in the black sable of her hair. She was so beautiful, she took his breath away. He should leave.

He meant to take one look and go but she gulped back a sob and wiped her fingers across her cheeks.

'What's wrong?'

'Oh, Fyn. What are you doing here?' She turned away from him and hastily wiped her face, turning back with a smile. 'I thought you were sleeping...' She frowned, putting it all together. 'You're leaving, aren't you? You're going to rescue your brother.'

He nodded. 'I'm sailing on the *Wyvern's Whelp* tomorrow. Don't tell the mage.'

'Of course not. Take me with you!'

There was nothing Fyn would have liked more.

PIRO PACED THE terrace searching for Isolt. That stupid woman, the new Elector Cera, had told Isolt her father was very sick. Her friend had gone very pale and slipped away as soon as she could.

Now Piro couldn't see the kingsdaughter anywhere. Her heart missed a beat. What if Isolt had been kidnapped? Should she find Tyro in his mage's disguise, or keep looking for Isolt?

Piro leant her elbows on the balustrade and stared down into the lantern-lit gardens below. Was that Isolt's white gown by a rock pool? Was someone with her?

Trying to keep the location fixed in her head, Piro threaded her way down shallow steps, through arches, around fountains and winding streams. A night-bird sang its sweet mournful song. Piro rounded a bend in the path and saw Isolt and her companion through the fronds of palm trees. Even by starlight Piro recognised Fyn.

She was about to call out when she overheard Fyn speak.

'I can't, it's too dangerous.'

'I can help rescue Byren. After all, I am still Isolt Merofyn Kingsdaughter.'

'The guards would tell Palatyne and you'd end up his captive.'

'Not all the guards are loyal to him. Some are still loyal to my father. Besides, we'd be away before Palatyne discovers we've been into Port Mero.'

Fyn considered this. 'We'd have to tell Piro. She –'

'We can't tell her. She'd give us away.'

'Nonsense!'

'Oh, Fyn. You haven't been here. I've seen the way she and Tyro send each other secret looks.'

Fyn looked stunned. 'Piro's in love with the mage's agent? Are you sure? She doesn't seem to be in love to me.'

Isolt gave an odd little laugh. 'Men, what would they know about love? So, I'll pack a few things and meet you tomorrow. But how will I get away? I know. I'll wait in the grotto under the tower. Sail a boat around to me.'

'You would risk your life for Byren?'

Piro suspected Isolt was risking her life for Fyn.

But Isolt only nodded. 'It's decided then. I'll meet you in the grotto.'

Piro's first impulse was to tell them they were wrong. She was loyal. But it would mean disclosing why she and Tyro had been exchanging meaningful looks, and his secret was not hers to reveal. Sad at heart, she retreated.

On the terraces the celebrations continued, and Piro found Mage Tsulamyth hobbling around looking annoyed.

Seeing Piro, he beckoned. 'You don't join in the games and entertainment? A pretty young thing like you should have some fun.'

'One party is much like another. I'm no butterfly –'

'What are you then, Piro?' he asked, slipping into Tyro's voice.

She looked away. She had been Piro Rolen Kingsdaughter, expected to marry well for the sake of her family, but she had hated it. Ironically, in some ways she had been happiest as Lord Dunstany's slave. Then she recalled how Palatyne had claimed her for Isolt's slave and how Isolt was considered a prize for the victor... 'I wish I were a man!'

He laughed and her cheeks burned at his tone.

'Consider this, Piro,' Tyro said. 'Who taught you to speak three languages, heal and stitch a wound?'

'My mother. But it was a man who killed her.'

'True,' he acknowledged. 'In the Duelling Kingdoms game which piece is the most powerful?'

'The king.'

'No. The game is lost if the queen falls before her king does. But if the king falls, the queen fights on.' He smiled and slipped back into the mage's voice. 'Find Isolt. We have done our duty. We can leave now.'

Piro nodded. Should she tell Tyro about Fyn and Isolt's plans? She was sure he had plans of his own. But he still wore the amber soul-pendant around his neck.

If he did not trust her, she could not trust him.

THE NEXT MORNING, Piro looked up as Isolt bustled into the room to collect her basket of herbal remedies.

'Fyn's awake at last. I'm going to check on him.'

'I'll come with you.' Piro slipped off the bed. The foenix and wyvern padded after them.

Fyn looked up as they entered his chamber, his expression guarded.

Piro forced a smile. 'Feeling better?'

'A bit. I think I overdid it yesterday. My head's aching.'

'Hmm. Could be fever. You should stay in bed and rest today,' Isolt advised, just as Piro knew she would. Didn't they realise they couldn't fool a player like herself?

While Isolt mixed a tonic and something for Fyn's head, Piro sat on the windowseat with the foenix on her lap, stroking his soft feathers. She felt the moment he fell asleep, his body relaxing completely. If only Isolt and Fyn would trust her. If only she could tell them the truth about Tyro and the mage.

'There.' Isolt packed her things away. 'I'll tell the servants not to disturb you. Come on, Piro.'

She slid out from under the foenix, leaving him asleep in Fyn's room. Back in their chamber, Isolt went to the mirror to comb her long hair. She met Piro's eyes in the looking-glass. 'I've been neglecting Loyalty. I think I'll take her down to the grotto for a swim.'

'I know where you are going.'

Isolt's hand stilled for a second, then kept moving. 'You're welcome to come for a swim.'

'You're going with Fyn. He sails for Merofynia today.'

Isolt lowered the comb. 'Your Affinity told you?'

Piro let her think that. 'Tyro has plans –'

Isolt spun around. 'I know you like Tyro, but we can't trust the mage. Tsulamyth doesn't have to save Byren while he has Fyn in reserve.'

Piro's mouth went dry. They were right. One kingson was as good as another, as long as there was a legitimate heir for the people to rally behind.

'Don't give us away, Piro,' Isolt pleaded.

'Of course not.' But they didn't trust her and this hurt. They should have asked her to come with them.

'I must go.' Isolt slipped a jar of wyvern-nip in her basket then clicked her tongue to call Loyalty. The wyvern scrambled over, reared up on her hind legs and put her front paws on Isolt's shoulders, nuzzling her neck.

Isolt laughed. 'She knows it's time for a swim.'

The wyvern sank to her feet and padded to the door. Isolt looked over at Piro, troubled. 'I don't want you to get in trouble with the mage because of us. Pretend you didn't know our plans.'

Piro could not think of a thing to say as Isolt slipped away. Right up until the door closed, she had been expecting Isolt to ask her to come along.

Tears stung Piro's eyes.

Byren and Fyn needed her. They all needed her. Surely this was a nexus point? She was not going to be left behind.

Piro blinked her tears away and darted out into the corridor. Down the spiral stairs she went until she reached the landing where the stairs split. One branch went to the kitchen, the other went far below to the grotto.

There was a sound behind her. Piro spun in time to see Ovido run away. She cursed. He would report to Tyro. Even if Tyro did not suspect, he might come down to the grotto to picnic with them, and that would spoil everything.

Piro ran after Ovido, but the boy knew shortcuts and by the time she reached the war table chamber, he was already at the door. With a grin of victory he slipped inside.

Piro heard Tyro's amused voice. 'Yes, Ovido?'

'Isolt goes to the grotto.'

Piro entered in time to see Tyro leaning over his war table. He held a piece as if he had been about to move it. Piro would not let herself look at her piece.

'Go play, Ovido.' Tyro dismissed him.

Now that Tyro knew they were going down to the grotto he would suspect something if she didn't invite him. But he looked too preoccupied to join them, so she took a gamble. 'Isolt and I are going to spend the morning in the grotto. Would you like to have lunch with us?'

Tyro glanced at Piro, taking in her open sandals, light muslin tunic, her hair loose to her waist. 'Tempting as that offer is, I must refuse. I have work to do. Come closer.'

Piro stepped forwards, determined not to let him see through her.

'Can I trust you, Piro?'

She went cold. 'I haven't told Fyn and Isolt about you.'

'No. Perhaps I should ask if you trust me?'

'Should I?'

He laughed softly. 'Good answer.' Then he grew serious as he removed the chain from around his neck, bringing the amber pendant into the light. Her mouth went dry with fear and she tried to draw back. He caught her hand, his eyes holding a plea.

'When I created this, I did not know the Piro I now know.' He turned her hand over, putting the amber in her palm. 'Accept it with my apologies.'

She lifted the chain so that the stone swung. Holding it to the light she expected to see herself trapped inside. Instead she saw an innocent air bubble. She gasped.

'It was illusion, Piro. I used the starkiss-scented candles to lower your resistance. I needed a way to keep you by my side, so I could ensure your safety. It was for your own protection but, by doing this, I forfeited your trust.'

She stared at the amber. She had never been trapped. A rush of anger filled her. She hated being manipulated.

'Stay with me today, Piro.'

Startled by the change of subject, she met his eyes. They were too searching. For her own protection, she pulled back. 'I can't stay. And I don't want this either.' She dropped the stone and its chain onto the war table. 'I don't like being tricked.'

'Then I have played the game badly.'

Piro turned on her heel and left him.

FYN LEANT HIS head against the cold wall of the landing. The smell of savoury pastries wafted up one stairwell. Isolt had gone down the other stair. Despite promising otherwise, he was going to leave without her.

Last night he had tossed and turned, too troubled to sleep. It was wrong of him to take Isolt along just because he wanted her by his side. She was safer on Mage Isle. He would never forgive himself if anything happened to her.

Even if she was furious with him, he had to tell her before he left. He could not leave her waiting in the grotto for him, that would be too cruel.

Feet heavy with reluctance, Fyn padded down to the steps to the grotto, where he found Isolt paddling her feet while the wyvern frolicked in the water.

A pearly light made the limestone walls of the grotto glow, made Isolt's skin translucent and her eyes luminous. And he was going to refuse her. Fyn hardened his heart.

She sprang to her feet. 'I thought you were bringing a boat. I'm ready. I've brought the wyvern-nip but no clothes. I can wear yours and roll up the legs... What's wrong?'

'I'm not here to take you with me. I'm here to say goodbye.'

'No, Fyn!' She ran up the grotto's shallow steps to the entrance where he stood. 'Don't go without me. You could be killed.'

'I can't leave Byren to die, and I can't take you into danger.'

'You can't take me into...' Her eyes widened. 'How dare you decide my fate, marrying me off to your brother to save his kingdom? Maybe I want to make my own future!'

Fyn shook his head. 'I won't take you.'

Isolt's eyes blazed.

He was sure she hated him. It was for the best. Without a word he turned and left, striding up the stairs.

So deep in thought was he, he almost did not hear someone running down the steps. There was just time to duck into a storeroom doorway before Piro flew past him, hair streaming behind her.

What was she up to now? Silly little Piro.

PIRO JUMPED DOWN the last two steps into the grotto, expecting to find it empty, but Isolt was there by the pool with the wyvern's head in her lap, weeping silently.

Isolt turned at the sound of Piro's feet, her face awash with tears. When she saw who it was, she looked away, clearly disappointed.

'He didn't come?' Piro asked.

'He came to tell me he would not take me.' Isolt's voice grew thin with anger. '*Too dangerous*, he said. But the real reason is that he sees me only as a prize. Fyn meant to use me in his game of Kingdoms, just like all the others. And I thought he was different!'

'Fyn is different.' Piro knelt beside her. 'I'm sure he was thinking only of your safety.'

Isolt wiped the tears from her cheeks with tight, angry gestures and stared across the pool, refusing to meet Piro's eyes.

'Look!' Her lips parted hopefully.

Piro followed her gaze. A shadow appeared in the low arched entrance to the Ring Sea. A small boat was riding the gentle swell into the grotto.

'Fyn?' Isolt stood and ran around the pool's edge.

Piro followed. Loyalty whined uneasily.

On the next up-swell, the boat slid into the grotto and four men lifted their heads. They were not Captain Nefysto's sea-hounds. Piro had a bad feeling as two of them swung coils of rope. With a powerful stroke of the oars, the oarsman drove the boat across the pool, reaching the far side. The men climbed out, blocking off their escape.

Piro glanced to the arch – could they swim for it?

Isolt made a dash, clicking her tongue for the wyvern. A man confronted her. The wyvern reared on her back legs, roaring. The skin on Piro's arm's lifted in primal response.

The first man grabbed Isolt as she tried to duck under his arm. Loyalty leapt for him. A second man stepped in front and slashed at the wyvern, who squealed in pain and writhed in mid-air, falling with a splash into the pool.

Isolt screamed. Her captor covered her mouth. She bit his hand, and he cuffed her over the head, stunning her. His companion hefted her over his shoulder.

Piro jumped on his back, knocking him sideways. He almost fell in the pool. Someone grabbed her from behind, pulling her off him. She tossed her head back into his face, heard a satisfying crunch of bone. Her feet were off the ground and she swung them hard, connecting with her captor's shins. He grunted in pain. They already had Isolt in the boat.

Piro strained to break free. 'Isolt!'

Then she was flying through the air, thrown like baggage. She hit the ground and rolled to her feet. Turning, she found the men were all in the boat. They rowed past her, aiming for the low arch. They were leaving her behind.

Piro took a running leap and jumped, landing in the boat. It tipped alarmingly. Someone slammed their hand on her back, driving her down into the belly of the boat. She lay amidst the men's boots next to Isolt, who was pale and silent, blood seeping from her nose.

Down here Piro felt a hum of power. It set her teeth on edge with its wrongness. As they passed under the grotto's arched entrance, the power rose until her temples throbbed with each heart beat.

And just as suddenly it passed. They were out in the

Ring Sea, stolen from under the mage's protection.

Chapter Twenty-Five

FYN CONTINUED UP the steps after giving Piro a few moments to reach the grotto. He'd only climbed five treads when he met Tyro coming down. Fyn was dressed to travel, and the agent was no fool. He would try to stop him. Fyn's hand reached for his sword hilt.

Tyro's gaze went to the weapon, then to Fyn's face. 'Is this how you repay the mage?'

'Let me pass,' Fyn warned, fingers closing on the hilt.

Tyro lifted his hands and Fyn felt the agent's Affinity rise. He knew himself outmatched. Still, one quick strike before the Power-worker could infiltrate his abbey-trained Affinity wardings, and it would be over. Luckily the weapons master had taught him how to draw and strike in one motion.

'I won't let you take her into danger,' Tyro said.

Fyn's fingers relaxed. 'You seem to know what's going on, but your spies don't know everything. I just told Isolt I would not take her with me. She hates me now.' He felt weary. 'Let me pass.'

Tyro lowered his hands. 'Then pass. I told Captain Nefysto to take you to Merofynia, when you were ready. Everything you've done has been according to my plan.'

Fyn frowned and his cheeks flamed as he realised his subterfuge had been for nothing. He drew breath to reply but, before he could, a terrible roar echoed up the stairwell.

'Freezing Cyena, what was that?' Tyro said.

'An attacking wyvern.' Fyn shuddered, the memory fresh in his mind.

The wyvern squealed in pain. Isolt screamed.

Fyn turned and ran down the steps with Tyro at his heels. If that wyvern had attacked Isolt, he'd kill it himself.

As Piro screamed Isolt's name, his stomach twisted in knots. Fyn leapt the last five steps, did not feel the impact as his shoulder crashed into the far wall. Rounding the bend, he came to an abrupt halt in the empty grotto.

No, not empty.

The wyvern floated face down in the pool, its blood staining the water. Fyn looked for Piro and Isolt's bodies but did not find them.

'Where are they?' Tyro said. Fyn felt the agent's Affinity build. 'My wards have been breached. I fear –'

At the sound of his voice the wyvern lifted its head and whimpered.

'Help me.' Fyn unbuckled his sword and plunged into the pool, reaching for the wyvern.

Tyro dropped into the water next to Fyn.

'I feared the wyvern had turned on Isolt,' Fyn confessed. 'But I was wrong. It was trying to protect her.'

Tyro nodded, and grunted with effort as they dragged the Affinity beast onto the broad stone lip of the grotto pool. The agent tugged his shirt off, packing it in the wyvern's wound, murmuring gently to the beast as she whimpered again.

Feeling useless, Fyn sensed waves of power roll off Tyro. The agent knelt, his head bent, lids lowered. As Fyn watched, Tyro's eyes moved rapidly under his lids and he grimaced as if in pain. When he straightened and looked at Fyn, his expression was hard.

'Palatyne's a cunning brute. He sent the Utlander to retrieve Isolt. The Utlander knew his power would trigger my wards, so he sent ordinary men in a boat with just enough power to reveal the grotto's disguised entrance.'

'You know this how?'

Tyro glanced to the Affinity beast. 'I skimmed the wyvern's memory.'

'What of Piro?'

Tyro looked down, then winced. 'She jumped into the boat to be with Isolt.' His voice caught. 'Brave, foolish girl.'

'That sounds like Piro. The little...' He could not go on, his throat felt too tight to speak. Water sloshed in his boots as he stood. 'I'll take the *Wyvern's Whelp*, intercept them −'

'Wait,' Tyro ordered. 'We cannot leave this beast to bleed to death. I must help her. Wyverns heal remarkably fast.'

'You heal her. I'm going.'

'This time I'm going with you, Fyn. Isolt and Piro are safe enough for now. They won't be in danger until they reach Merofynia, and then Palatyne's plans are to wed Isolt, not execute her. He still thinks Piro is Isolt's maid so, as long as she keeps her head down, she will be overlooked. We have time to prepare. This is too important for the mage to send anyone but me.'

Fyn nodded reluctantly.

Tyro gave him a wry smile. 'I need your help. I exhausted myself dipping into the wyvern's mind to learn what happened here. I need to draw on your Affinity to help her. I'm not a true healer, the best I can do is hasten the healing. Are you willing to lower your walls, or are you still blinded by your abbey training? Am I just another renegade Power-worker to you?'

Fyn grimaced. 'Having seen how Master Catillum died, I know evil is in the man, not in the power.'

'I'm sorry, Fyn.'

He shrugged this aside. Now that he was reminded of Feldspar and Joff, he sent a silent prayer to the goddess to watch over them. He hoped they'd survived the attack on Narrowneck. 'Let's get started.'

Together they sealed the wyvern's wound and made her comfortable. Then they packed, taking both the wyvern and the foenix with them to board the *Wyvern's Whelp*. Captain Nefysto was not keen on carrying a wyvern, even a half-grown, wounded one. But Tyro invoked the mage's name and he acquiesced with wry grace.

PIRO CROSSED THE Merofynian captain's cabin. It was beautifully appointed, with brass fittings, stained-glass windows and polished wooden cabinets, but it was still a prison.

All the while, she felt the Utland Power-worker watching her. So far she had played the maid, shielding her Affinity from him as she had done back in Rolenton, when she'd been Lord Dunstany's slave.

The roll of the ship's deck changed, telling her they were on the open sea. Piro adjusted her step, returning to the bunk with a bowl of cool water to sponge Isolt's face. Her friend had just woken, pale and nauseous.

Isolt tried to lift her head, winced, dropped back and rolled her face towards the Power-worker. 'How is my father, Utlander?'

He sighed and shook his head sadly, but Piro could sense his malicious triumph. 'The old king has lost touch with reality. He is haunted by night terrors, claims wyverns stalk him through the palace corridors. He leaves the running of the kingdom to Duke Palatyne.'

'And what is to be my fate?' Isolt asked, her voice low and determined.

'I'm taking you back to your loving betrothed,' the Utlander said. His eyes held mockery.

Isolt turned away from him. 'I look forward to seeing my father.'

'Show Duke Palatyne proper gratitude, girlie, he holds both your life and your father's in his hands,' the Utlander told her sharply, then he left them alone, locking the door after him.

Piro sat on the bunk next to Isolt, and squeezed her hand.

'Is it safe to talk?' she mouthed.

Isolt made a rude noise. 'What could we say that would interest men of action? We are mere females, prizes to be married off!' Tears filled her eyes. 'They killed my sweet wyvern!' A sob escaped her, and another.

'I know. I know.' Piro hugged her, rubbing Isolt's back until the crying eased. Then Piro lowered her head so that her lips were near Isolt's ear. 'It looks like we are going to Merofynia without Fyn's help.'

Isolt nodded, and whispered, 'I thought we were safe on Mage Isle.'

'That's what Tyro thought, too,' Piro said, glancing resentfully to the locked door. She caught Isolt's eye. 'Someone's listening.'

Now her Affinity helped her. Why hadn't it warned her of the kidnapping? Of course, the Utlander had cloaked his intentions. Besides, she had been focused on Isolt and Fyn's plans.

'I'm glad they came for us after Fyn had left,' Isolt whispered. 'He would have died trying to protect us.'

'He will come for us. *Nothing* will stop him.'

Isolt nodded, her cheeks flushed with colour. Satiny black eyes met Piro's, as Isolt deliberately raised her voice. 'I'm glad you are with me, Seela.'

Piro squeezed her hand. It was lucky Fyn had insisted his rescue of Isolt back in Merofynia should look like a kidnapping. Now, even if they suspected, no one was sure if Isolt had changed allegiances. 'You must be happy to be going home, kingsdaughter.'

'Oh, I am,' Isolt agreed. 'If the Utlander's men had only told us they were coming to take me home, I would have jumped into their boat!'

Piro smiled.

FYN WALKED THE wyvern around the deck. She seemed to enjoy the sun and sea air, and was picking up after only three days despite the severity of her wound.

'Never thought I'd see the day we carry a wyvern as a passenger!' Bantam muttered.

Fyn smiled at his grumbling. 'Careful. You'll hurt her feelings.'

'Is it true this Affinity beast tried to save the kingsdaughter's life?' Jakulos asked, scratching the wyvern behind her horn nubs. She tilted her head, eyes closing as she enjoyed the sensation.

'Loyal as they come.' Fyn scratched her throat.

'I always suspected Nefysto was serving the mage,' Bantam admitted. As they crossed the midship, Bantam paused and nodded to the captain's open cabin door, where they could see Nefysto and Tyro consulting the maps. 'Should have jumped ship and signed on to an honest sea-hound who was out for nothing but profit. This playing of Kingdoms will be the death of us.'

'At least we have the mage backing us up,' Jakulos said.

'So speaks a man who knows nothing of Power-workers!' Bantam said and spat over the side.

Fyn winced, the memory of his confrontation with the Mulcibar mystic still fresh in his mind. 'Jaku is right. If we have to work with renegades, the mage is the most powerful and, more importantly, the most honourable.'

BYREN HUNG FROM the bars of his cage, doing chin-ups, legs bent so he could rest his full weight on his arms. It was the darkest part of the night and he was too cold to sleep. It had rained earlier, and consequently he was soaked through, despite his cage being hung from the lowest branch of a giant linden tree. Half a body length below the cage, starlight glinted in puddles of rain water.

Different street urchins, or the same one in different costumes, had slipped him food each day, and Duke Palatyne had been too busy to taunt him. As long as Byren did not take a chill, he would be ready when the moment came to break out.

A scurry of movement at the courtyard entrance caught his attention. As he watched, the figure crept from the wall shadow to the linden tree's shadow, then to his cage.

'Byren?'

He knew that voice. 'Orrie?' Too overcome to speak, he reached through the cage, clutched his friend and pulled him into a hug. 'I thought you'd drowned.'

'Can't drown me. I was born with a caul...' Orrade broke off and pulled back a little, though he didn't release Byren. 'Father didn't want it known, didn't want to give me up to the abbey.'

'Wasn't Nun Willowtea the midwife?'

Orrade nodded. 'When I was born Father had already lost three sons.'

Byren laughed softly. He never would have guessed the Old Dove capable of convincing an abbey healer to break the law. 'So you would have developed Affinity eventually?'

'Something would have triggered it. Listen, Byren. Cobalt has attacked the spar. So far Feid's held him off at the pass fort but what's left of your army are captives on Foenix Spar. I'm here to get you out.'

'What of Florin? Is she safe?'

'I don't know. She –'

'Who goes there?' a guard demanded. Torches flared as a dozen guardsmen hurried from their posts.

Orrade spun around, knocked the man to the ground, darted between two others, then ran straight up the right-angle bend in the courtyard wall like a monkey. He'd always been nimble, but that was remarkable.

'What was that?' someone asked, after making the sign to ward off evil.

'An acrobat, nothing more,' the leader of the guards snapped. 'Don't just stand there. Go after him.'

Several guards ran out the courtyard, while the leader raised his torch so that he could see Byren's face.

'So your men came for you? Don't get your hopes up, pretender. Duke Palatyne has the palace and its courtyard tied up tighter than an Ostronite merchant's purse. Nothing gets in and out without his say so.'

'Then who was that?'

'A performing monkey, something to keep my men on their toes.' He spat. 'They'll be even more vigilant after this. Go back to bed, your majesty!'

And he walked off laughing, calling to his men to sweep the courtyard and surrounding streets.

Byren huddled to keep warm. He was not disheartened. Orrade lived... more than that, he was here. Orrade would help him escape. All they needed was a diversion to set him free.

PIRO WAITED WITH Isolt in the ship's cabin as their vessel docked with the morning tide. Isolt had been supplied with clothes suitable for her station and Piro was dressed as befitted the future queen's maid.

If they could just escape, they'd run to Lord Dunstany's residence. His servants could hide them.

The Utlander and half a dozen warriors arrived to escort them off the ship. There was no chance to escape as they were led to a waiting carriage and the Utlander climbed in with them. Isolt's features settled into her Merofynian court face. With her high forehead, plucked brows and tilted back eyes, she was beautiful as a porcelain doll, and she gave nothing away.

The carriage swayed when it turned a corner. They could hear the noises of the city stirring. Piro felt Isolt stiffen.

'This is not the way to my father's palace.'

'No. It is the way to your betrothed's townhouse. You told me your dearest wish was to see him upon landing,' the Utlander informed her.

Isolt said nothing, her lips compressed. Piro wondered if there was some way she could get a message to Dunstany's servants.

The carriage rolled through arched gates into a private courtyard. As the carriage door opened, Piro climbed out and looked up to see a four-storey building, all faux columns and windows. Servants scurried to let Palatyne know they were there.

The Utlander marched straight'in, his half-dozen warriors escorting them. Glorious artifacts littered Palatyne's mansion. Paintings, carpets, statues and golden plates were stacked on tables and floors as if the owner had collected trophies and never had time to sort them.

Isolt and Piro exchanged uneasy looks. Ahead of them, the Utlander scurried down a corridor. A servant threw open a tall door to reveal a long room, patches of early morning sunlight glistening on the marble floor. Palatyne was seated at a table breaking his fast with honeyed mead and hot beef. Despite the silk dressing gown and aristocratic setting, there was no mistaking his spar origins, as he tore into the meat with strong white teeth, grease dripping onto the mahogany table. Without a word to the girls, the Utlander took a seat at the massive table. No one offered them a seat, or food.

Piro hovered a step behind Isolt, who squared her shoulders as though determined not to be browbeaten.

'I see you have returned with my little bird,' Palatyne greeted the Utlander, clearly pleased. 'We will have to make sure the cage doors are secured this time.'

'Rescuing the bird was easier than I thought. On his own isle the mage thought himself invincible,' the Power-worker boasted. 'A mistake I would never make.'

Palatyne downed his tankard and called one of the warriors over, paying him off with a bag of gold. As soon as the man and his companions left, the duke called an unsavoury-looking man from the room beyond and whispered something to him. He nodded, following the other warrior out.

Piro and Isolt exchanged another uneasy glance. They both suspected the warriors would not live to tell how they had kidnapped Palatyne's reluctant bride. The duke did not want to be the laughing stock of Merofynia.

'To my bride and her trophy maid.' Palatyne came to his feet, lifting a fresh tankard. 'Welcome home, my pretties.'

Isolt gave him a distant, queenly bow. 'I thank you, Duke Palatyne. Without your help I might never have escaped the mage. My father will be most grateful.'

'I heard Mage Tsulamyth presented you to the elector as his companion, not captive,' the duke countered. To Piro he appeared amused by Isolt's tone, but if he were truly secure in his power, he would not feel the need to assert his authority.

'The mage is a great Power-worker. I did not dare to make a move while I was in his clutches,' Isolt replied swiftly. 'I wish to see my father. I have been most concerned for his health.'

Piro bit her bottom lip to hide a smile, for it was the prim kingsdaughter talking now, not the Isolt she knew.

'Understandably, kingsdaughter.' Palatyne shared a look with the Utlander. 'But I must warn you, you will find your father changed. The healers fear his mind is going. He dreams of wyverns stalking him and screams so much in his sleep that he can hardly talk the next day. It has become so bad, he refuses to fall asleep. The healers have been giving him dreamless-sleep to ease his mind.'

'Then I must go the palace, immediately,' Isolt insisted, growing just a little agitated. Even though King Merofyn was a cunning, ruthless man, Isolt loved him. Piro supposed it was evidence of her good heart. She didn't think she could have been so forgiving.

'He will be better for seeing me,' Isolt said.

'Let us hope so.' Palatyne bowed, eyes gleaming maliciously. 'If you will excuse me, I will finish my meal. Do you care to join me?'

Isolt shook her head. Piro swallowed and ignored the rumbling of her stomach.

He sat down, sawing off a hunk of meat. Recalling his insistence on using a food taster in Rolencia, Piro realised Palatyne must trust his own cook. Could she use that against him in some way?

Then she noticed the unistag horn lying next to his plate as though it was nothing more than another knife, and not a rare and valuable Affinity tool. So that was where Byren's unistag horn had ended up. He'd given it to Lence, to present to King Merofyn, who went in dread of poison. Well, it explained Palatyne's lack of a food taster, for the pure white horn would discolour if the food it touched was corrupted.

'Take a seat.' The duke waved a hand to the other chairs. 'When I'm ready, I will escort you myself.'

Isolt gave a gracious bow. 'You are too kind, Duke Palatyne. But I will not break my fast until I have seen Father.'

She nodded to Piro and they retreated to the window seats, where Isolt gave her a tight smile. Piro squeezed her hand. She dared not speak in front of Palatyne and the Utlander, but the king's suffering sounded very much like what Fyn had suffered from. She suspected the dreamless-sleep was making King Merofyn susceptible to hallucinations planted by the Utlander, hallucinations designed to rob him of his reason and the support of the nobles.

It was cruel but clever. A kingdom needed a king who was in his right mind.

By the time Palatyne and the Utlander were finished destroying King Merofyn's credibility, the people would be eager for the duke to take over.

Chapter Twenty-Six

FYN STOOD ON the deck of the *Wyvern's Whelp* as the boat was made fast to Port Mero wharf. She flew a Merofynian merchant ship's flag.

Once ashore, Tyro headed for Lord Dunstany's grand town house, striding off up the street, followed by a servant carrying the foenix in a covered cage. The wyvern would follow in a closed crate, later. Lastly came Fyn. His head had been shaved to reveal the abbey tattoos.

Servants opened the gate to the courtyard, greeting Tyro by name, and explaining that Lord Dunstany was not presently at home. He arranged for 'Monk Sunseed,' as he introduced Fyn, to be housed in the mage's regular chambers, then left, with the news that Lord Dunstany would be arriving presently.

Not twenty minutes later, Lord Dunstany arrived with his travelling bags and, after going to his chambers, sent for Fyn to welcome him. Fyn was there in the background as one of Lord Dunstany's spies reported that Isolt and her maid had been seen disembarking that morning. They had been escorted to Duke Palatyne's mansion and, as yet, had not come out. Meanwhile, the captured Rolencian king had been hanging in the square outside the palace for several days now, and the spy had arranged for food to reach him once a day.

'But they doubled the guards, after someone was caught talking to him during the night.' The plump middle-aged man, who looked like a friendly baker, sniffed in disapproval. 'That person made it much harder for us to reach him.'

'Who was it?'

'Had to be one of King Byren's supporters. The local people hate him. Palatyne has them convinced he hid while his family were killed, then tried to take the crown for himself.'

Fyn stiffened, but said nothing.

Lord Dunstany thanked the spy, then dismissed him and stared out the window at the Landlocked Sea, which sparkled under the midday sun.

Even though Fyn knew Lord Dunstany was Tyro, a youth not much older than Byren, the greying hair and dignified bearing made Fyn instinctively treat Dunstany with the respect due a grandfather. And he caught himself waiting for Lord Dunstany to speak.

Reminding himself, yet again, that it was only Tyro, Fyn paced. Byren was safe for the moment. It was Isolt he worried about. 'If only I could get inside Palatyne's mansion.'

Dunstany pulled a bag out from under his desk and tossed it to Fyn. 'With the contents of this bag you can go anywhere.'

Fyn caught it eagerly, opened the drawstring and sniffed. 'Grease paint?'

'Player's make-up, but we can disguise the smell. From candle maker to tanner, every trade has a smell.'

'Then I can get into Palatyne's mansion, but how will I get Isolt and Piro out again?'

'He will bring them out and deliver them to us. I have spies in the palace. This morning I want you to reach your brother.'

'Right. I'll free him and –'

'No. Give him food and water. We'll free him when the moment is ripe.'

'Why not now?'

Tyro studied him. Fyn tried to see the mage's agent, behind Lord Dunstany's disguise, but failed. 'Do you trust me, Fyn?'

That was a difficult question. It was not in Fyn's nature to lie. 'To a certain extent.'

Tyro smiled grimly. 'Then trust me on this. It is not enough to free your brother. Palatyne has convinced the people that Byren is a coward. To defeat Palatyne, we must restore Byren's reputation and win over the people of Merofynia.'

BYREN'S STOMACH RUMBLED. Since Orrade came two nights ago, the guard had been doubled and only one food parcel had reached him. He longed for a wash, a shave and a change of clothes. Above him bees hummed, busy in the flowers of the linden tree. The blossoms' scent made the air fragrant and reminded him that summer's cusp was drawing close.

Over near the fountain, the guards chattered and laughed, their voices a fraction too loud. From the market beyond the wall, Byren registered a subtle change of tone, a suppressed excitement mingled with bravado. He pressed against the bars of his cage, trying to make out individual words from the marketplace. Could Orrade be making his move?

'Ready for your bath?' Three guards approached with buckets of ice-cold water. 'After all, we don't want you stinking up the palace courtyard.'

As they tossed the first bucket of water over him, Byren opened his mouth to get a gulp of fresh water. It was so cold he gasped.

'Not with the kingsdaughter due back today,' the next guard said, as a second bucket hit Byren full in the face. 'Can't have your stench offending her pretty nose.'

Byren flicked water from his hair and eyes.

'Rescued her, Palatyne did, all the way from Ostron Isle. Bet those merchants didn't know what hit them!' The third bucket sluiced over him and the guards marched off, their duty done.

Byren shivered, creeping to the far corner of the cage where a patch of sunlight filtered through the tree's canopy. The dappled spring sun hardly warmed him. But now he understood why the market bubbled with repressed excitement, and why the guards were so edgy.

Soon he would see the young woman Lence had been betrothed to, the young woman who, despite anything Palatyne might say, was legally betrothed to him. She would ride by in a gilt carriage, while he hung in a cage. If he was lucky, she probably wouldn't even look at him.

DRESSED AS A beggar, wearing a moth-eaten wig, Fyn limped through the crowd, leaning heavily on a staff. People jostled him, eager to see Isolt Merofyn Kingsdaughter pass by. They spoke of how she had been rescued by Duke Palatyne, who swore revenge on the wicked mage and arrogant elector for this insult to Merofynia.

If Palatyne was planning to invade Ostron Isle, as Tyro had suggested, he had primed the people well.

Mingling with the crowd, Fyn worked his way into the courtyard, where Byren's cage was suspended from the branches of a huge linden tree. A long avenue of these trees led across the courtyard to the palace steps.

Bored with waiting, people had gathered around the cage, throwing rubbish through the bars. Guards looked on, enjoying the sport. Byren huddled in the far corner, shielding his face. His clothes were tattered, his hair in tangles, his face half-hidden by a beard. He seemed utterly beaten and dejected.

But he was alive, and Fyn's heart leapt with fierce joy. While the Merofynians taunted Byren, he kept his eyes down, waiting for the right moment.

'She comes!' someone cried. 'The kingsdaughter comes!'

The crowd rushed to see, including Byren's tormentors. For a few moments the guards were also distracted. Fyn drew out food and a water-skin from under his rags. Before he could approach, another beggar pulled a knife from his rags and rushed towards the cage. Fyn intercepted him, grabbing the knife, twisting his wrist, and only just preventing himself from breaking the assassin's wrist as he recognised Orrade.

'Orrie?'

'Orrie?' Byren echoed, having come to the very edge of the cage. 'And Fyn?'

All the while, people cheered and called out to the Merofynian kingsdaughter. Fyn released Orrade and helped him to his feet. 'I thought –'

'I came to free Byren.'

'We can't –'

'Fyn, I thought you dead.' Byren's eyes gleamed with unshed tears and he reached through the cage to catch Fyn's arm, pulling him into a hug.

Fyn thrust the food in through the bars. 'Take this.'

Byren accepted the food. Meanwhile, Orrade put his knife to the cage lock, trying to pry it open.

Fyn glanced over his shoulder. Any moment now, the guard could look this way. 'Put the knife away, Orrie.'

'Not on your life. I'm setting Byren free. I may not have another chance.'

'We can't free him yet. It must be done right.' Fyn saw Orrade did not understand. 'If we free Byren now, the people of Merofynia will always believe him a coward.'

Orrade stiffened. 'I've heard what they're saying. It's not true.'

'I know. But it is what they believe. There's a better way,' Fyn said, hoping Tyro would prove him right. He was very aware of Byren's gaze on his face, weighing what he'd said. 'Trust me.'

'What better way?' Orrade asked.

Fyn hesitated.

'I'm ready,' Byren said. 'I'm stronger than I've made out. Someone's been slipping me food –'

'I know,' Fyn said. 'That's Lord Dunstany's doing. I'm working with him to free you. But not just yet. It must be done in such a way that it clears your name.'

'How?' Orrade persisted.

'Yes, how?' Byren muttered. 'I must admit it eats at me to be called a traitor.'

Fyn reached through the bars to squeeze Byren's hand. 'We'll get you out and save your name. Don't give up hope.'

Byren grinned. 'Not with you two come back from the dead.'

Fyn noticed the cheering had lessened. 'We must go.'

Orrade hesitated.

'Go with Fyn.' Byren jerked his head.

'Here, what's going on?' a guard demanded.

Fyn stepped back, rattling his staff on the cage, yelling abuse at the prisoner. Orrade followed his lead, while Byren hastily hid the food and water under his clothing.

Fyn blended into the crowd, Orrade one step behind him.

'I hope you know what you're doing, Fyn. Who is

this Lord Dunstany and why is he helping Byren?' Orrade asked.

'You'll see.' Fyn kept walking, weaving his way across the square towards the palace. He had to get a glimpse of Isolt. All about him, people spoke of her innocence and beauty.

'With the old king fading we'll need a new king,' a sensible matron told her companion.

'So true. We can't have war in Rolencia and the merchants of Ostron Isle encouraging sea-hounds to rob our ships. We need a strong king to look after our rights,' her companion agreed. 'Palatyne can marry Isolt and claim the throne with my blessing!'

The matron nodded.

'Stay near me, Orrie.' Fyn worked his way to the palace steps, to where he could see Isolt and the royal party. It was relatively easy. No one wanted to get too close to a couple of smelly beggars.

'Is that Piro?' Orrade whispered. 'What's she doing with the Merofynian kingsdaughter?'

'I'll explain later.' Fyn's heart turned over as Isolt walked up the broad steps to the entrance, where King Merofyn waited. Fyn could only think of him as the usurper, Uncle Sefon's murderer. He could still hear his mother's voice, *Poor little Sefon*. He'd been a boy of two when she was sent to Rolencia, and he had always remained that little boy in her mind.

King Merofyn sat on a litter, with a blanket over his knees. Isolt gave a cry and ran up the last few steps to him, throwing her arms around the king's shoulders.

The people cheered. Fyn's throat felt tight. He knew that Isolt had good reason not to love her father, yet she did. It did not mean she was weak, only good-hearted.

Palatyne drew Isolt's arm through his and turned her around to wave to the crowd. Then he led her inside. Piro followed behind the king.

At least Piro and Isolt were safe for now. Tyro, as Lord Dunstany, was waiting for them inside the palace.

Satisfied that there was nothing more he could do for them or Byren, Fyn turned to make his way back towards Dunstany's mansion. 'So how did you get here, Orrie?'

'A farmer took me in and sewed up my leg. I heard they had Byren and tried to reach Port Marchand in time to save him, but I was too late, so I took passage on a ship and followed. What of you? Last I heard, you tried to hold the gate. We thought you dead.'

'I looked dead. That's what saved me. My sea-hounds realised I was Affinity-wounded and stole my body. They took me back to their ship. Where are you staying? We'll get your things.'

'I don't have any things. I've been sleeping in the streets.' A grin creased Orrade's thin face. 'This isn't a costume.'

Fyn laughed. 'I bet you'd love a hot meal and a hot bath.'

An hour later, after being let inside Dunstany's mansion by his spy, Fyn watched while a much cleaner Orrade enjoyed a hot dinner.

'You look like you haven't eaten properly in days.'

'I haven't.' Orrade took a mouthful of ale and fixed sharp eyes on him. 'What's going on, Fyn?'

'You heard them out in the street. They hate Byren. They're ready to accept Palatyne if he marries Isolt. And it wouldn't take much to convince them to attack Ostron Isle.'

'I don't much care what happens to Merofynia or Ostron Isle. I just want to make sure Byren's safe,' Orrade said.

'No one, not Byren or Piro or Isolt, will be safe until Palatyne's dead, and if we assassinated him, we wouldn't get out of here alive.'

'You're right,' Orrade conceded. 'So, what are we going to do?'

Fyn sank into the window seat overlooking the Landlocked Sea. 'I've no idea. Yet.'

Chapter Twenty-Seven

PIRO WAITED UNNOTICED towards the back of the crowd that filled the king's bedchamber. The great bed stood in the centre of the room on its dais. Like a restless sea, ebbing and flowing, courtiers clustered around it.

There were representatives from every noble family of Merofynia as well as warlords from beyond the Dividing Mountains. Several healers hovered over the bed consulting.

Back home in Rolencia, there would have been Sylion nuns and Halcyon monks, here they were renegade Power-workers, eager to make a name for themselves, plus nuns and monks from Merofynia's abbeys. Her father had always considered them little better than Affinity renegades. Three Cyena nuns in purest white sang and did the warding symbols at the chamber's three entrances. Five Mulcibar monks with their abbot walked around the bed praying for the king's soul as they swung tiny brass braziers filled with burning herbs. Renegade Power-workers chanted and made gestures over the bed. The room smelled of too many bodies, pungent Mulcibar herbs and beneath that, barely disguised, old age and death. It made Piro feel ill. She wished she could open a window and take a breath of clean air.

Isolt was speaking intently with the healers and, from her tight expression, the news was not good. So far the king had met his daughter's eyes only once with a flicker of recognition, and then resumed his senseless muttering.

Silence fell as Palatyne marched into the chamber with the Utland Power-worker by his side.

'Kingsdaughter.' He bowed.

'Duke.' Isolt inclined her head only slightly.

'I fear there is no hope, Isolt,' Duke Palatyne said, his voice cutting through all the others. 'The king lives but his mind has gone. For the sake of the kingdom you must appoint a regent to rule until you are of age. Consider appointing me as your regent. Better still, before he lost his reason King Merofyn asked me to put his mind at rest and marry you, so that both you and the kingdom would be cared for.' His triumphant eyes never left Isolt. 'For peace and stability we must marry as soon as possible. The people of Rolencia are planning an uprising and the elector of Ostron Isle cannot be trusted.'

Isolt opened her mouth as if she would argue, but Palatyne rushed on.

'After all, you do not know how long your father

has to live, and you want him to see your wedding, don't you?'

Isolt winced visibly then recovered her composure, assuming her Merofynian court face, but Piro knew she was seething.

'And so, he springs the trap,' Lord Dunstany whispered.

Piro bit back a gasp and turned to meet Tyro's eyes. In some ways she was more comfortable with him when he was disguised as the noble Power-worker. Why couldn't Lord Dunstany be the real person, then he could be her friend, not her... what was Tyro to her, but an angry, pretentious youth, who had only recently begun to trust her? Too late for her to let her guard down.

'Fyn's safe?' she breathed.

'At Dunstany's mansion.'

'Byren?'

'Caged, but safe for now.'

'We must free him.'

'When we are ready.'

Piro felt the force of furious eyes and turned to see the Utlander glaring at them. At Lord Dunstany.

The Utland Power-worker left Palatyne's side and joined them. 'So you have come back to us, Lord Dunstany.'

'As soon as I could, I came to serve my king.' He gave a gracious bow.

'Not soon enough, I fear.' The Utlander pretended sympathy. 'Your patron has not long to live and soon my patron will be king.'

As if to confirm this they heard Isolt's clear voice.

'You are right, Duke Palatyne. We must marry soon. I see all of Merofynia's noble families are present. Since they are here, why not marry tomorrow?'

'Tomorrow?' Palatyne was surprised, but willing.

'It would take time to prepare such a grand occasion,' Lord Dunstany spoke up. 'There is the food for the feast, the decorations –'

'It can be done. *I* can do it!' the Utlander insisted. He turned to the duke. 'Give me a day to organise the joint wedding and coronation.'

Palatyne laughed. 'Very well. Make it the day after tomorrow. I want this to be a grand occasion for my bride.'

With a flourish, Palatyne kissed Isolt's hand. Her face betrayed nothing as the nobles, healers, nuns and monks all offered their congratulations.

Isolt excused herself as soon as she could, claiming she had preparations to complete. The kingsdaughter swept from the room, Piro at her heels.

When they were out in the almost deserted corridor Piro whispered, 'Why did you suggest marrying him so soon? You hate him.'

'I do. But I hate seeing my father suffer even more. As soon as I am queen I shall dismiss those healers and the Utlander –'

'You forget, you will be queen, subject to your king. Palatyne!'

'As queen, I will be subject to no one.' Isolt's eyes blazed. 'For Palatyne will not live long enough to be king. You must find out where he keeps the poison he meant to use on my father. Before the wedding you must slip it into his food while I distract him.'

'It's in the ring he wears on the little finger of his left hand. The stone lifts off.' Piro fought a surge of panic. It did not worry her that Isolt had ordered her to commit murder. Palatyne deserved to die. Like Cobalt, he was corrupt and nothing would make him whole. What worried her was carrying this off under the Utlander's nose. 'I don't see how I can get the ring off his finger.'

'Then we must ask Lord Dunstany for some poison of our own,' Isolt whispered. 'Slip it in Palatyne's food.'

That was when Piro remembered Palatyne owned a unistag horn. Poison would not get past it. They'd have to come up with another idea. Before she could mention this, they reached Isolt's chambers, where they were greeted by three of Duke Palatyne's own warriors, battle-scarred veterans from his time on the spar.

'You may go. I have my own guards,' Isolt told them.

'We cannot leave your door, kingsdaughter,' the oldest said. 'The Utlander uncovered a plot to kidnap you and if you are taken we lose our lives.'

'It is good of the duke to care for my safety.' Isolt caught Piro's eye. 'Seela, bring my dressmaker. I need a new gown for my wedding. The seamstress and her girls will have to sit up all night.'

If Isolt could not reach Dunstany, Piro could. But, when Piro turned to go, one of the men fell in step with her. Seeing her expression he explained. 'My instructions are not to let you out of my sight, Mistress Seela.'

Piro hid her dismay. And by the time she had run her errands she had decided not to tell Isolt about the unistag horn. As long as her friend had hope, she would not do something desperate.

'MY SPYMASTER TELLS me you've brought home a stray, Fyn?' Tyro challenged, as he entered the chamber. Fyn noted that he'd put aside his Lord Dunstany disguise before appearing.

'Tyro, this is Orrie, he...' Fyn hesitated. How was he to explain? 'He grew up with us.'

The mage's agent studied Orrade, who had stripped off his disguise and bathed, and was now dressed in borrowed clothes that were too short for him. His clothing might be slightly absurd but his expression was intense.

Tyro glanced to Fyn. 'But can he be trusted?'

'I would die for Byren.' Orrade took a step forwards, his voice rich with repressed emotion.

Tyro was not impressed. 'So you say, but Fyn is asking me to make you privy to secrets that could be the death of us all.'

Orrade made an impatient gesture. 'What can I say to convince you?'

'Nothing you say could convince me. Normally the mage would have me test his tools, but...' Tyro studied him. 'I sense you have Affinity, so I can use a shortcut. Lower your walls and let me taste your essence. If it is pure, I'll trust you.'

Orrade swallowed audibly.

Fyn shifted. Since when had Orrade had Affinity? But he kept his mouth shut.

'Very well.' Orrade dropped his arms. 'Do it.'

Tyro gestured to a chair. 'Sit, otherwise you may fall. Fyn, come hold him.'

'No one needs to hold me.' Orrade went to the chair and sat down. 'I won't resist.'

Tyro ignored this and caught Fyn's eye. Following his unspoken instructions, Fyn came around to stand behind the chair, hands resting on Orrade's shoulders.

He felt the tension in Orrade's muscles and the force of his repressed Affinity. As Tyro approached, Orrade's body tightened further.

'Who says I can trust you?' Orrade asked, his voice light. At odds, Fyn could tell, with how he really felt.

The agent hesitated.

'I jest. Just do it.'

Tyro placed his fingers on Orrade's temples, much as a monk might do when he searched for Affinity. Fyn felt a rush of awareness. His mouth watered, his eyes stung, his breath felt sharp as winter air in his nostrils. And he recognised Orrade's essence. Byren's friend would die for him because he loved him.

Naturally, they all loved Byren.

Tyro stepped back.

'Satisfied?' Orrade asked, voice bitter.

'You've chosen a hard path.'

'We don't choose our paths, they choose us.'

'Too true.'

Fyn didn't understand. 'What –'

The agent turned away. 'Isolt is to be married to Palatyne the day after tomorrow.'

Fyn cursed. 'Couldn't you... couldn't Lord Dunstany stop it?'

Tyro glanced to Orrade, then back to Fyn. 'With the king near death, Dunstany has lost power. He tried to delay the wedding but the Utlander stepped in and took over.' Tyro smiled grimly. 'He should have encouraged a quick marriage and then the Utlander would have delayed it just to spite him.'

Fyn stepped in front of him. 'We must contact the mage to ask his advice. Send one of your Pica birds.'

'By the time the bird reached him, Isolt would be married,' Tyro said. 'We are on our own.'

Fyn stared at him.

'I am the mage's agent and apprentice. He trusts me. You should too.'

Fyn nodded. But Tyro was not much older than Byren.

He went to run his hand through his hair and discovered he had none. That's right, he'd had to assume a monk's disguise, at Tyro's suggestion.

What could he do to save Isolt? Knees weak, Fyn sank into a carved cedar-wood chair beside Orrade. Everything was richly decorated, from the mosaic floor to the gilt and plaster ceiling. But what good was wealth if they did not have the mage to guide them? 'What about King Merofyn? Couldn't Lord Dunstany warn him about Palatyne's plans?'

'The king barely knew his own daughter. I fear the Utlander has weakened his mind to such an extent that Merofyn will never recover his wits.'

'Then we have no choice.' Fyn sprang up and prowled the length of the room. He came to the window, which looked up at the palace far above. The wyvern padded after him, her claws scraping on the mosaic floor. She rested her chin on the window sill and whimpered, almost as if she knew Isolt was at the palace. Fyn empathised with the Affinity beast and rubbed behind her horn knobs. The wyvern had nearly died to save Isolt. He would do no less.

A rush of conviction filled him. 'We can't let the marriage go through.'

'We can't let Palatyne execute Byren, and he will if we make a move against him,' Orrade said. 'That cage –'

'I already have a copy of the key. That's not the problem.' Tyro crossed to take a chair at the table, opposite Orrade.

Fyn joined them. 'Freeing Byren isn't enough, Orrie. Palatyne has been feeding the Merofynians a pack of lies. They believe he is their saviour and Byren is a threat.'

Orrade bristled. 'It's Palatyne who's the ambitious coward, not Byren.'

Tyro lifted his hands. 'The mage says what is written in history books is only the victor's version of the truth.'

Orrade laughed. 'I like this mage, already.'

Tyro looked away.

The foenix flew over to settle next to Tyro's chair.

'He misses Piro,' Fyn said.

The Affinity beast turned his head inquisitively to one side, much as Piro often did.

Tyro stroked the foenix's neck.

'Can't you foresee a way to reveal Palatyne's real nature?' Orrade asked Tyro.

'The past is like a road unfolding behind us, but the future is unwritten. The day of the wedding has solidified as a nexus point, the focus of many possible paths. Piro's Affinity gives her visions at nexus points.' Tyro's fists closed in frustration. 'Palatyne made sure Lord Dunstany can't get near her.'

Orrade cleared his throat. 'Ah... I get Affinity visions. Mostly they are just flashes of danger that seem to make no sense. They make my head ache so badly I can hardly think.'

'Any headaches now?' Tyro asked with a half-smile.

'None.'

'Then we are lost,' Fyn whispered.

'Not at all,' Tyro corrected. 'We must force Palatyne to reveal his true self. Fyn, I'll give you the key to Byren's cage. Dress as a player, so you can get close enough to free him. Tell him not to move, until he gets the sign. We'll have sea-hounds throughout the crowd, ready to act.

'Fyn, your part is crucial. After Palatyne marries Isolt, there will be speeches. Lord Dunstany will speak. When he rises, throw off your disguise to reveal yourself as one of Halcyon's monks, eager for revenge. Attack King Merofyn, but don't kill him. Palatyne will be right beside the king. We need to give people the time to see what Palatyne does. He'll make no attempt to defend Merofyn, because I know for a fact that Palatyne means to kill him. Isolt will spring to her father's defence. Take her captive, Fyn. Threaten, but don't hurt her. Byren can save her from you.

'This will give Byren a chance to win the people's love, while revealing Palatyne's true nature.'

Fyn nodded to himself. It seemed like a good plan.

Orrade cleared his throat. 'In my experience, plans never go the way you expect. There are too many factors beyond our control.'

'I know,' Tyro conceded. 'We'll have to adapt as things happen. But we must reveal Palatyne's true nature and give Byren a chance to clear his name.'

'Agreed.' Orrade glanced to Fyn, then back to Tyro. 'What of Fyn? You say his part is crucial. He could be killed.'

'Lord Dunstany will be there. He'll protect Fyn.'

'I don't mind taking a risk for Byren,' Fyn insisted. As long as Isolt was safe. He licked his lips. 'But what of the Utland Power-worker and the mystics from Cyena and Mulcibar Abbeys?'

'They are the factors we have no control over,' Tyro admitted. 'It could get interesting.'

Orrade laughed. 'That's one way of putting it.'

Fyn smiled. He'd missed Orrie.

'Right.' Orrade sat forwards. 'I'll watch Byren's back. Lord Dunstany will watch Fyn's. Who will make sure Piro is safe?'

'As far as Palatyne knows, Piro is a lowly slave girl,' Tyro said. 'If she keeps her head down, she's safe.'

Fyn said nothing. Since when could you rely on Piro's discretion?

IT WAS DUSK and Byren's stomach rumbled. It was always rumbling. He was grateful for the food Fyn had slipped him.

From the insults the townsfolk had hurled at him, he knew Isolt married Palatyne tomorrow, legitimising the ambitious murderer's claim to the Merofynian crown. Meanwhile, Byren hung here in a cage, impotent.

It was getting dark. Over the wall, he heard the market hawkers offering the last of their wares at bargain prices. The smell of roast chicken carried to Byren, making his stomach cramp painfully.

'Half a dozen roast potatoes going a begging,' a hawker called, wheeling his barrow into the courtyard.

'Be off with yer,' the guard nearest the entrance told him.

'Have one on me and tell me if they're not the tastiest tatties you ever had? Here, I'll top it off with onion and bacon.'

Several more guards came over, lured by the smell and the offer of free food.

Byren's stomach tied itself in knots.

As the potato hawker opened his barrow doors to prepare the guards' food, a figure slipped out from under the barrow.

Byren recognised Orrade, who darted over, taking advantage of the twilight to shove a couple of hot potatoes into his hands. 'We make our move at the wedding. Be ready.'

Then he was gone, before Byren could ask if there had been news of Florin. He hoped not, no news was good news. He hugged the potatoes, letting them warm him from the outside, before eating them to warm his innards.

His heart raced. Tomorrow, they freed him. He was more than ready.

Chapter Twenty-Eight

As Piro woke on the morning of the wedding, a brooding dreamscape faded, leaving her with a sense of menace. If it was a vision, it was hardly useful, since she had woken before she knew the details.

Untangling her legs from the bedclothes, she padded over to the door to Isolt's chamber. Her thigh muscles trembled as if she had been running all night. That triggered a memory of running in her dreams.

Opening the door to the next chamber, she checked on Isolt, who lay fast asleep on the silk sheets. Squares of early morning sunlight came through the balcony doors casting patterns across the floor and the bed. Everything looked safe and normal, but Piro knew otherwise.

She didn't need Tyro to tell her that today was a nexus point and her dream a warning. All day yesterday Isolt had been overrun with officious persons trying to arrange the marriage and coronation. There had been no sign of Lord Dunstany, although Palatyne's guards may have excluded him.

'What's the matter, Piro?' Isolt asked, sitting up, her cheek creased from the pillow.

'For someone who's about to marry a man she hates, you look to have slept well!'

'I'm not going to marry him. And if I do, I'll kill him on our wedding night, before he can touch me. So I'm not worried.'

Piro studied Isolt. Was she delusional or just desperate? Palatyne could easily overpower her.

'What's wrong?' Isolt asked.

'I had a dream,' Piro said.

'A vision?'

Piro nodded.

Isolt patted the bed. 'Come, tell me.'

Piro climbed onto the high bed. Leaning against the headboard, she set about diverting Isolt. 'Before Palatyne took my father's castle, I was troubled by dreams of wyverns prowling the corridors, terrorising servants and hunting me. This became reality when Palatyne's soldiers did just that. But this time...' And she had a dream flash so vivid, her whole body jerked with fright.

'What is it?' Isolt reached for her.

'I had to escape. A grown foenix stepped in front of me.' Piro shuddered. 'It had clever cruel eyes and it hated me. Terror filled me. I couldn't move.'

Isolt rubbed Piro's arms. 'Your skin's gone cold and clammy.'

Piro turned to her. 'Don't you see? If the wyverns represent Palatyne, then the foenix represents a threat from Rolencia. That means one of my brothers is a traitor!'

'No, Piro. I refuse to believe Fyn a traitor. As for –'

'Byren is the best of brothers. He'd never hurt me or Fyn,' Piro insisted. 'The dream makes no sense. If only I could ask Tyro.'

'Well, we'll see him soon enough. The wedding starts at noon.'

'But we'll be surrounded by courtiers, and the Utlander will be watching.' Just then there was a knock at the door.

'What is it?' Piro called.

'Breakfast. Fresh-baked apple tarts and cream, and hot chocolate.'

Piro slid off the bed, getting to her feet. She struggled to smile. 'Come, kingsdaughter, this is your wedding day, and my last day as your maid. I'll run your bath and scent it with starkiss perfume.'

Isolt wrinkled her nose. 'Wasted on Palatyne, I fear.' But she called for the servants to enter and set the table.

FYN PEERED INTO the mirror. After painting his face with the traditional jester's white, he exaggerated his eyes, drawing his eyebrows as big arcs of surprise. Everything was going according to plan, if you ignored the fact that they had only the barest of plans.

'All set?' Tyro asked, entering the chamber.

'Yes.' Fyn turned as Orrade came to his feet. He

wore unremarkable clothes, so he could blend in the crowd.

'Where will you be during all this?' Orrade asked Tyro.

'Hidden, watching.'

Orrade nodded. 'How will we see your signal?'

'Fyn will know.' Tyro dropped a large key in Fyn's hand. 'In that costume you'll be able to get close enough to Byren to unlock the cage and slide him this sword.' He drew the weapon from under his robe.

Orrade took the sword, testing its weight. 'You're a good judge. It feels just like Byren's old sword.' He laughed. 'Byren would say a man makes his own future.'

Tyro gave him a grim smile. 'And so he will, with a little help from us.'

BYREN TENSED AS the guards came towards him. They carried buckets of water. Ice-cold, he did not doubt.

'Come to clean you up for the wedding,' his chief tormentor said. 'Can't have you stinking up Duke Palatyne's coronation.'

'Be King Palatyne by sunset,' another said. 'And about time too.'

'Palatyne can't be king while the old king lives,' Byren pointed out, then dredged up his mother's lessons on royal protocol. 'Kingsdaughter Isolt will be regent, and her husband becomes her consort.'

'Oh, he'll be king soon enough,' one guard said, with an exaggerated wink.

Before Byren could comment, they tossed the cold

water over him. He shivered and shook himself like a dog as a horse dray was backed under the cage. The cage was lowered onto the dray and the horse walked the streets of Port Mero to the palace's terraced gardens overlooking the Landlocked Sea.

They left his cage on the dray, but released the horses, propping the dray in place. It was parked below the first terrace where the wedding would take place. He could just see through the balustrades of the terrace railings. At least he was in the sun and would soon dry off. Below him the terraces descended to the sea.

While Byren and his guards waited, most of the population of Port Mero and surrounding countryside filtered into the gardens, or sailed their boats across the Landlocked Sea to get a view of the proceedings.

Byren's stomach rumbled. One way or another he would not be hungry after today.

PIRO TUCKED HER hair behind her ears, to keep it out of the way while she did Isolt's. Though it was only late spring a summer storm brewed, nature reflecting the gathering of forces at this nexus point, and humid, oppressive heat hung over the city, as the sun neared the zenith.

For the wedding and coronation, Isolt wore an azure gown of Ostronite silk, gathered under the bust with a long train at the back. Her bodice was encrusted with zircons. Zircons also covered her crown, but for now, her hair needed to be done simply so that the crown could sit in place once she was made regent.

Piro gathered Isolt's long hair into a fine silver net and fastened it to a clip at the back of her neck. Sapphires hung from her ears. She looked perfect, but her face was a mask as she stared, hard-eyed, into the mirror.

Piro tried to reassure her. 'Fyn will –'

'I don't want Fyn to risk his life for me.' Isolt squeezed Piro's hand. 'No. I must save myself. I had hoped to kill Palatyne before the wedding but he has not come near me, not even to boast. So I must kill him after. He has to take that ring off sometime and when he does I will take the poison out and save it.'

Piro bit her bottom lip.

'You doubt me?'

Piro shook her head. 'What if Palatyne tries to poison your father on your wedding day? He's so weak it would carry him off quickly and no one would suspect a thing.'

A travesty of a smile illuminated Isolt's face. 'I shall be watching the duke. When he slips the poison into my father's drink, I will distract him while you switch drinks.'

Piro gulped. That just might work. If Palatyne had already tested his drink, he would not test it a second time. So much rested on her.

Isolt twisted from the waist, clutching Piro's arm. 'You must do this for me. Palatyne murdered your parents and brother – we can't let him get away with murdering my father too!'

Piro agreed, but she feared the Utlander's cunning

eyes. If he and his twin were powerful enough to kill Mage Tsulamyth, what chance did she have against him?

Isolt stood. 'I am ready.'

Piro squeezed her hand.

Palatyne's guards escorted them down to the terrace, where favoured nobles of Merofynia had already taken their places on the stage overlooking the gardens and the Landlocked Sea.

The Utlander had been busy indeed. Food had been delivered by the wagon load and prepared in the stifling heat of the kitchens, ready for the feast.

A dais had been hastily built for the royal entourage, right up against the balustrade in the centre of the top terrace, so that Isolt and Palatyne could be observed during the ceremony and feast.

The Utlander had made good use of his army of palace servants, Piro thought as they took their place on the dais. Urns as high as her waist were filled with dark red bougainvillea, topped with azure flags that hung limp in the still air. Sprays of flowers tumbled from hanging baskets, their scent almost overpowering.

Piro's diaphanous gown stuck to her shoulders and her hair hung limply, damp tendrils clinging to her neck and back. Nothing stirred in the oppressive heat, even the birds were still.

Clouds obscured the sun, sullen and threatening. But the impending storm hadn't deterred the people, who had turned out in their thousands. A huge crowd had gathered in the gardens along the Landlocked Sea shore. Many more had hired boats or paid for places on the decks of merchant ships.

The noble families of Merofynia, each with their own loyal guards in the coloured cloaks of the house, filled the next terrace, and more were scattered throughout the crowd. To Piro it was obvious no one trusted anyone in Merofynia. Isolt's father had acquired the kingdom through deceit, and this had tainted his rule.

A little shiver crept over Piro's skin and she turned to see the Utland Power-worker watching her. Did he have her ability to sense nexus points? Had he foreseen Isolt's plan?

She must stay calm and give nothing away.

Piro looked down into the gardens. It gave her a pang to see that Byren's cage had been brought around to rest just below the terrace so that he could stare up through the bars at the new regents of Merofynia, and starve as they feasted.

She willed him to look up and see her, but he didn't. His attention was on the crowd.

FYN EDGED THROUGH the nobles, gentry and wealthy merchants, until he was within a body length of Byren's cage. Dressed as a jester, in black leggings, boots, a multi-coloured tunic, and a tasselled cap on his shaved head, he passed unremarked, if not unnoticed.

Two guards stood in front of Byren's cage, which sat on a dray so that everyone could see the Rolencian pretender's degradation. Fyn caught his older brother's gaze.

Byren's eyes widened slightly as he recognised Fyn, with Orrade behind him. Byren nodded his understanding. They were ready to make their move.

A hushed murmur ran through the crowd as Isolt Merofyn Kingsdaughter arrived on the terrace and took her position on the dais. Fyn caught a glimpse of Piro, standing one step behind Isolt. The Merofynian kingsdaughter looked beautiful, but distant. He longed to reassure her.

Luckily they'd put Byren's cage right under the terrace. This meant, once Tyro-disguised-as-Dunstany gave his signal, all Fyn had to do was climb onto the cage roof, and onto the terrace.

As yet Fyn saw no sign of Lord Dunstany. He searched the crowd urgently for Bantam or Jakulos. It was noon, so the sea-hounds should be here now.

'I always knew you'd make a fine jester!' Bantam nudged Fyn's ribs. 'Let's see your tricks.'

Relief flooded Fyn. He gave a mock bow. 'At your service, sir.' Dropping his voice, he asked, 'Where's Jaku?'

'Not far,' Bantam whispered. 'Our ship's down there.'

Fyn followed Bantam's gesture and recognised the *Wyvern's Whelp's* masts. 'Good.'

BYREN'S HEART RACED as Fyn, dressed as a jester, capered towards him. He teased the guards with his bell and ribbon-tipped staff, then scuttled away when they threatened him.

The crowd cheered him on, always happy to see authority mocked.

Surreptitiously, Byren flexed his shoulders and stretched his legs. Just let him get out of this cage and he would make Palatyne regret the day he had invaded Rolencia.

Fyn darted in, poking Byren with his bell-tipped staff. On impulse Byren grabbed the bells. They came off in his hand. Fyn, the jester, stomped his foot and made a big show of demanding his bells back.

The crowd laughed.

The two guards looked at each other and shrugged. Too bad. They hadn't liked the jester anyway. Fyn scuttled away.

Byren looked down at the bells. Tied amid the little silver baubles was a key. The key to his cage. He hid a smile.

PIRO HAD SEEN Fyn pass something to Byren, right under the guards' noses. She smiled, admiring his skill. People laughed as the jester wandered off forlornly. He blended into the crowd, where many players kept people entertained until the real performance could begin.

Trumpeters sounded from the turrets at each end of the royal terrace and a hush fell over the crowd. All around her, the cream of Merofynia's nobility jostled for position, pushing Piro towards the back of the dais. Rich matrons and jewelled lords fanned themselves fiercely, their make-up and elaborate costumes wilting in the heat.

Piro climbed onto an urn base to get a view over the nobles' ornate head-dresses. Isolt stood silent and stiff in her zircon-embroidered silk. Palatyne joined her, a hungry, possessive gleam in his eyes. The old king sat in a litter drooling, unaware that the prize he had murdered to gain was about to be taken from him, as an upstart barbarian spar warlord married his only daughter.

The Utlander stood behind and to the right of Palatyne. He looked very pleased with himself. Piro felt a surge of intense dislike. It was clear he intended to be Palatyne's right-hand man when the duke became king.

Where was Tyro? Surely Lord Dunstany was invited to the wedding? If only she could get near enough to ask him about her dream. She had thought her dream's events took place at dusk but, with the heavy grey clouds, it felt like twilight now.

Her spirits lifted as she caught sight of Dunstany's iron-grey hair. Tyro, in Lord Dunstany's guise, met her eyes over the heads of the nobles. His expression was tense and preoccupied.

Piro stepped off the urn base and began to wriggle through the press towards him. No one wanted to relinquish their position, especially to an unimportant servant. Try as she might, Piro could not get near Lord Dunstany. She climbed onto another urn base and tried to catch his eye, but the abbot of Mulcibar and the abbess of Cyena had arrived. The wedding was about to start.

Piro despaired. Isolt was right. What could Fyn do to save them, or Byren? Palatyne had won the people with his half-truths and lies. They would have to win the hearts of everyone in Merofynia to defeat Palatyne.

The trumpets sounded again and the crowd fell silent.

The abbess of Cyena and the abbot of Mulcibar called on their goddess and god, praying for wisdom for the queen, who would be regent in her ailing father's place, with support from her husband, the royal consort.

Piro held her breath, willing something to happen but, apart from foreboding dark clouds coming so low that they seemed to touch the topmost spire of the palace, and the sultry heat growing ever more intense, nothing intervened to stop the ceremony.

The abbess took Isolt's hand. The abbot took Palatyne's and placed it over Isolt's. They gave their vows.

With a flourish Palatyne removed the pendants from around his neck. He draped them over Isolt's head so that they rested on her chest, glinting gold and silver. 'As a bridal gift, I present my queen with these tokens, the royal emblems of Rolencia!'

Resentment flooded Piro. To Palatyne those emblems were symbols of triumph, to her family they had contained the dignity of office.

In unison, the abbot and abbess each blessed the crown, then lifted it, taking one side each to place it on Isolt's head. Together they proclaimed her regent. Piro hid a smile. Clearly, the rivalry between the two great abbeys was as strong here as it was back in Rolencia.

Then the abbot and abbess repeated the process with Palatyne's crown, but it was Isolt who lifted it from the cushion.

The ambitious duke knelt at Isolt's feet. She picked up the crown, held it high for all to see, then placed it on Palatyne's head. Piro thought Isolt very restrained, considering she wished him dead.

And, suddenly, the combined wedding-coronation ceremony was over. The crowd cheered.

Piro sagged, exhausted by the heat and the tension.

The nobles parted so that the servants could carry the long tables forwards to the edge of the terrace. Other servants waited with food-laden trays. As soon as the tables and chairs were in position the nobles scurried to claim their places. Below them on the next terrace, less lucky nobles, gentry and wealthy merchants waited while their servants spread food on tables they had brought with them. Down on the lower terraces, people spread blankets on the grass and opened their picnic baskets. Musicians began to play from each turret, the music oddly thin and dull in the thick air.

All around Piro, the nobles talked and congratulated themselves, while the sky grew darker and the clouds took on an odd greenish tinge, giving the day an unreal quality. Piro's head throbbed. The very air felt strange to her, it seemed alive with more than the threat of the thunderstorm.

Her Affinity screamed a warning. She sensed Tyro drawing his power to himself, but with the Utlander ready to counter anything he attempted, Piro did not see what he could do.

Servants brought out roasted fowl, peacock, whole pigs, fresh fruit and glazed sweetbreads. And for the royal couple, whole white swans, Cyena's Affinity beasts, blessed by the abbess herself. Because Piro was Isolt's maid, she stood behind the regent's chair. Many servants, advisors and food tasters stood behind their lords and ladies. The Utlander sat next to the old king, whose chair had been placed next to Palatyne's. Isolt was on his right. Piro could not bring herself to think of him as the royal consort.

Palatyne came to his feet, lifting his goblet, signalling for silence to make a toast. A gem flashed on his little finger. Piro froze, recognising the poison ring.

This was the perfect opportunity for Palatyne to use it. Even if he ate or drank nothing else, the old king would automatically take a sip of the toast when his food taster held it to his lips. The king would appear to have died of natural means. After all, he was old and frail. Piro frowned. But if the food taster also died people would become suspicious.

'To Merofynia, greatest and fairest of all kingdoms!' Palatyne was used to roaring commands on the battlefield and his voice carried down to the shore, where town criers echoed him so that those on the boats and ships could hear. 'I promise I will seek out all those who threaten our peace and slay them!'

The people cheered.

Anger twisted inside Piro. Why didn't they see through Palatyne? He promised to make war, not peace.

Palatyne drank from his goblet, and everyone followed suit including the king's taster who took a mouthful and swallowed then held the goblet to Merofyn's lips. The old man managed a sip. Piro had been watching. Palatyne had not used the poison. Neither had he used his unistag horn.

Of course, he could not use it in front of Merofyn. By rights, such a valuable Affinity tool belonged to the king. Consumed by fear and greed, Palatyne had kept the horn for himself, but this meant he could not use it today at the feast.

The abbot of Mulcibar stood and made a speech, praising Palatyne, his allegiance clear. While everyone was watching him, Piro saw Palatyne lean close to Isolt. To everyone else he appeared to be making a lover's remark, pointing to her new emblems. Even the food taster was listening to the speech. Only Piro saw Palatyne flick the top off the ring and empty the powder into the king's goblet, the goblet which the food taster had already tested.

The abbot of Mulcibar finished his speech and lifted his goblet. Piro watched in fascinated horror as the king's food taster held the poisoned goblet to Merofyn's lips.

Palatyne smiled down the table at the abbot and drank from his own goblet. He wasn't even looking at the king as the old man bent his head to take a sip.

Piro had wanted to see King Merofyn dead, but she could not stand by and let Palatyne murder him. 'No!'

Palatyne looked up over his shoulder at her in irritated astonishment.

Even Piro was surprised. The plan had been to switch the goblets, but without Isolt's help to distract Palatyne she could not do it. 'Don't let King Merofyn drink. The wine is poisoned.'

'Nonsense!' Palatyne's voice boomed in the horrified silence. 'The food taster tested it.'

'You dropped the poison in while the abbot was speaking. I saw you do it.' Piro pointed to Palatyne's hand. 'Look at his ring. It has a false stone.'

'Let the ring be examined,' Isolt ordered.

Palatyne surged to his feet, knocking his chair over. A murmur of disquiet ran through the crowd. He flung a hand at Piro. 'She lies. Who would believe a slave, over me?'

Piro straightened. 'I am Piro Rolen Kingsdaughter. And I swear on my murdered mother's soul that I do not lie.'

'And I am the regent of Merofynia.' Isolt stood, small but commanding. 'If Piro Kingsdaughter lies, prove it, Palatyne. Drink freely from my father's goblet!'

The nobles muttered amongst themselves and Palatyne eyed the goblet. It contained certain death yet, if he refused, he confirmed his guilt.

Fierce justice poured through Piro. Thanks to Isolt, her family's murderer would be punished.

FYN GROUND HIS teeth in frustration. He'd been watching Dunstany, ready to make his move on his signal, only to have Piro thwart their plans.

Now what should he do?

Movement in Byren's cage caught Fyn's eye. Even as he watched, his brother undid the lock on the cage door but held it closed. Unaware that their plan was in chaos, Byren waited for Fyn's signal.

Oblivious to the fact that their captive was free, the guards watched events unfold on the terrace. All around Fyn, Merofynia's finest citizens focused on Palatyne and Isolt.

Lord Dunstany came to his feet. 'I have been advisor to the kings of Merofynia for seventy years. Heed my advice, Royal Consort Palatyne. The nobles and commoners will not trust you to rule Merofynia unless you prove your innocence.'

'Prove it!' Fyn shouted, quick to play along. 'Drink up.'

'Drink up. Drink up!' Bantam yelled, two body lengths from Fyn. Others took up the cry, telling Fyn that not everyone had been convinced by Palatyne's lies.

Palatyne hesitated. He glanced to the Utlander, but Fyn knew the old Power-worker could do nothing for him. Palatyne had been caught in his own trap.

Isolt raised a hand for silence. 'If what Piro Rolen Kingsdaughter says is true, then let poison be the traitor's fate!'

'Drink up. Drink up. Drink up!' the townspeople urged without prompting from Fyn.

Palatyne glared at Piro and drew his ceremonial sword. 'You won't be the death of me, King Rolen's brat!'

Fyn cried out, far too late to save his sister. Isolt threw herself in front of Piro. For a heartbeat it seemed Palatyne would gut them both.

The crowd gasped.

'I challenge you, Palatyne, to prove yourself worthy of ruling Merofynia!' Lord Dunstany cried and he slammed his staff on the stones. The tip flared to life. At the same moment, Dunstany sought

Fyn's face in the crowd.

Fyn leapt forwards, using the end of his jester's staff to knock out the nearest guard. Orrade dealt with the other one.

Byren flung his cage door open. Orrade tossed the sword to Byren. He caught it and laughed to feel its weight in his hands.

'Save Isolt!' Fyn pointed.

'Kill Palatyne!' Orrade urged.

Byren swung onto the cage roof, leaping from there onto the table top.

Fyn undid the tie and stripped the bells and ribbons from his staff, revealing a sword. 'For King Byren! For Rolencia!'

'King Byren!' Orrade echoed.

Chapter Twenty-Nine

BYREN'S HEART LEAPT for joy as he vaulted onto the dais, landing on the feast table. He planted his feet amidst the food and faced his tormentor at last.

The upstart spar warlord gaped.

'Fight me, Palatyne Or would you rather kill defence-less women and children? Show your true colours. Show the people of Merofynia how you attacked Rolencia while my father was negotiating peace.'

But Palatyne grabbed Piro, holding her in front of him as a shield. He backed away from Byren, pressing his sword tip to her throat. A horrified hush fell over the crowd.

Byren stalked Palatyne, stepping lightly amid the food platters down the length of the table top. He couldn't risk Piro but all he needed was one opening and he would have Palatyne.

Lightning flickered through the heavy, low clouds.

An ominous rumble of thunder growled above them. From the corner of his eye, Byren saw the abbot of Mulcibar make a grab for Isolt. She ducked under his arm, lunging towards the table. Byren caught her hand, pulling her up beside him. 'Release Piro, Palatyne, and I will return Isolt.'

'Kill her for all I care!' Palatyne laughed.

His bluff called, Byren cursed. He slipped his bare toes under a goblet, driving its contents into Palatyne's face. Piro dropped her weight and, quick as a cat, ducked away from her captor.

As Palatyne backed off, blinking wine from his eyes, Byren jumped for him. Metal on metal rang, shrill in the horrified silence, when their swords met.

Too close to strike, they sprang apart, swords lifted, taking each other's measure.

Out of the corner of his eye, Byren saw Mulcibar's abbot climb onto the table and lunge for Isolt. She lifted her skirts and ran down the long table, her gown tearing with a sound that was almost a cry of pain as the train came away. Her hair spilled from its silver net as she leapt over the bowls of fruit and whole roasted pigs.

'Stop her,' Palatyne bellowed. A dozen of his supporters blocked the end of the table. Two climbed onto it.

Isolt hesitated, trapped.

EVEN AS ISOLT ran, Fyn followed on the terrace below. She stopped running, trapped and desperate above him.

'Come to me!' he cried.

She looked down. It was a drop of more than two body lengths. Fyn tore off his jester's cape. Orrade took one corner without needing to be told, and Bantam and Jakulos took the other corners.

'Jump!' he cried. If she hesitated she was lost.

But no. She trusted him. Isolt leapt, her azure silk flying up around her slender legs. As she hit the cape, one of the corners pulled free, but the others held. Fyn caught her, setting her on her feet.

Stunned, Isolt stared at him.

He never wanted to look away.

'Heads up, Fyn,' Bantam called. 'Here comes Palatyne's private bullies.'

Fyn cursed. 'Orrie. Take the sea-hounds and help Byren. I have to get Isolt to safety.'

Fyn grabbed her hand and headed for the *Wyvern's Whelp*, taking the stairs to the lower terraces at a run. People parted, cheering them on and impeding their pursuers.

Vessels were packed so tightly near the shore that, after Fyn climbed onto the first, he was able to leap from deck to deck, steadying Isolt as she landed next to him.

Fyn looked up, fixing on the *Wyvern's Whelp's* mast. They crossed another two ships, ending up on a small vessel next to the larger sea-hound ship. Catching Isolt around the waist, he lifted her above his head. Nefysto grabbed her arms and hauled up onto the ship's deck. Fyn scrambled up beside her, then bent double to catch his breath.

Isolt's wyvern gave a piercing cry and ran to her.

Rearing on its back legs, it nuzzled her face. Isolt laughed so much she cried. The foenix gave its happy cry and butted her, trying to get her attention.

Nefysto laughed and helped her disentangle herself.

'What now, Fyn?' Nefysto asked.

He looked around at the sea-hounds, masquerading as honest merchant sailors. They'd all come to know Piro and had grown fond of her.

'We must go back, help Byren save Piro. Save Seela!' he corrected. Fyn tore off his jester's tunic, dunked his head in the water barrel and scrubbed off the paint.

Captain Nefysto handed him the farseer. 'Take a look.'

Fyn leapt to the rail, holding the farseer to one eye. The Utlander had Piro. He only prayed he could get there in time.

Fyn jumped to the deck, amidst the remaining sea-hounds. 'This way!'

PIRO RAN THE instant she was free of Palatyne. But she only managed three steps before the Utlander stopped her, not with his hands, but by using her own Affinity to rob her limbs of movement. She toppled forwards, unable to save herself.

He caught her, his cruel eyes gleaming with satisfaction. In that instant she recognised the moment in her dream – oppressive dark skies, churning people and the sense of being trapped.

Pinning her shoulders against his chest, the Utlander held his staff in front of her face. The carved wyvern's head on the tip seemed to stare into her eyes. He pressed his thumb on a hidden catch on the stone and a needle sharp spike emerged from the wyvern's forehead.

'This spike contains foenix-spur poison. One scratch and you'll die in agony,' the Utlander told her. He raised his voice. 'I've caught the kingsdaughter, Lord Dunstany. Tell your men to stand back. I don't know how you survived the last time my brother and I killed you, but you won't be able to save your pretty little spy!'

Fearing a duel between the two Power-workers, the nobles fled the dais. King Merofyn lifted his head, blinking as if he had just woken from a drugged sleep.

BYREN DODGED AS the abbess and three white-gowned nuns dragged Mulcibar's abbot off the dais and down the terrace. No love lost there.

He lunged for Palatyne, intent on provoking him to attack. There was no sign of Isolt. Byren had lost track of her while concentrating on Palatyne. The spar upstart edged backwards, circling until the table hit his thighs.

Palatyne scrambled onto it, never taking his eyes off Byren. He began backing away down its length, kicking plates and bowls into Byren's face as he followed.

On the edge of his vision, Byren was aware of movement on the terrace.

'To me, men,' Palatyne yelled. 'Kill the traitor!'

Byren cast one swift glance behind him. At least twenty of Palatyne's loyal spar warriors charged across the terrace towards the royal table. Byren backed off, trying to keep both Palatyne and his guards in his line of sight.

Down the far end of the terrace Byren saw men running up the stairs from the gardens below. Orrade and Fyn and a dozen sea-hounds.

'To me!' Byren cried, just as the first of Palatyne's guards attacked him, hacking at his legs.

PIRO FLINCHED AS the Utlander spoke from just behind her ear.

'Come, Lord Dunstany.' His voice was strained and thin with hatred. 'Let's finish what we began. If you believed you could best me, you would have confronted me before this. I think you are all bluff. And today I call your bluff!' He waved the poisoned spike close to Piro's throat. 'Or must I kill her, first?'

Lord Dunstany... *Tyro*, met Piro's eyes. What she read there told her that he believed he was no match for the Utlander. 'Let her go and I will duel you.'

'No. I set the terms of our duel,' the Utlander crowed. 'Throw all your power at me. See if you can stop my hand from moving!'

Piro strained away from the spike as the Utlander brought it closer to her throat. She could feel the pulsing of the Utlander's power and another force battering against it like waves beating on a rocky shore. But Tyro's force was breaking on the Utlander's defences.

With all of Tyro's reserves channelled into breaching the Utlander's defences, Tyro's disguise wavered and dissolved. Dunstany's aged features faded to reveal the tall, thin youth she knew.

Piro felt the Utlander's surprise and anger. He attacked with renewed force. His fingers wound so tightly through Piro's hair that she had to blink back tears of pain.

Tyro fell to his knees.

Piro gasped. He was not strong enough.

He must not fail!

Once before, he had called on her strength to bolster his own. Gathering her concentration, she focused on Tyro and opened her Affinity to him. Because the channel was already there, she only had to focus for the process to begin. And, at the same time, she found herself drawing off the Utlander's Affinity, much as the renegade Power-worker had drained Nun Springdawn back in Rolenhold.

The Utlander went rigid with concentration, trying to block her. His breath rasped in his chest.

Power poured through Piro, heady and addictive.

FYN JUMPED FROM deck to deck with the sea-hounds at his heels. Once on land, no one obstructed their mad dash as they pounded up the terraces.

'Up the stairs!' Fyn sent them to each side of him, up the terrace steps, while he leapt onto Byren's cage. Swinging his weight onto the roof, he peered over the balustrade across the table top.

Piro was pinned by the Utlander, his staff to her

throat, but Tyro was coming to his feet, taking each step forwards as though he ploughed through a thigh-high snowdrift. The Utlander backed away. Fyn could feel the waves of Affinity coming off them with such force that it made the hairs on his body rise and his teeth ache. This was a battle Fyn was not trained to fight.

He looked for Byren. Palatyne's spar warriors filled the terrace. Orrade, Bantam and Jakulos fought to reach Byren.

Just to Fyn's right with his back to him, Palatyne stood, legs planted on the table, laughing as his warriors closed in on Byren.

Fyn was halfway onto the table when Palatyne noticed him and went for his head. He only just managed to scramble across and hit the terrace tiles in a crouch.

He gulped in a breath.

'Fyn! You took your time.' Byren grinned, chest heaving.

He glanced over his shoulder, fearing Palatyne would attack them from behind, but he was content to let his spar warriors do his killing.

Fyn cursed. The sea-hounds were still making their way up the stairs. Twenty spar warriors filled the terrace, avoiding the Affinity battle at the far end.

'I should have executed you when I had the chance, Byren Kingsheir!' Palatyne roared. 'Now the little brother turns up. Good riddance, I say. All King Rolen's kin will be dead by sunset. Kill them both!'

Two of his spar warriors charged Fyn. He dodged and cut past them, opening a path for Orrade and the two sea-hounds to join them. They broke through the warriors' defences, coming to Byren's side.

Fyn poised on the balls of his feet, ready to attack, but Palatyne's warriors pulled back, glancing to their leader.

A shout from the far end of the terrace heralded the arrival of the rest of the sea-hounds.

Palatyne's warriors turned, swords lifting as they prepared to fight on two fronts.

'We'll mop up these warriors, Fyn,' Byren yelled. 'Then I'll go after Palatyne!'

Grimly, Fyn put his shoulder to his brother's. 'Watch our backs, Bantam.'

With Orrade on one side of Byren, and Fyn on the other, they confronted the enemy. The spar warriors charged. In the mad mêlée Fyn saw Jakulos grab two men by the shoulders and crack their heads together. Orrade took a man down. Fyn saved his neck, cutting down another who was about to run him through from behind. The odds were getting better.

'Fyn!' Isolt screamed. 'Watch out.'

Isolt? He'd left her on the ship. He glanced over his shoulder to find she'd scrambled up onto the table from Byren's cage.

'Freezing Sylion, Isolt!' Fyn began.

Something whistled towards his head. He ducked instinctively, avoiding a sword to his head. The warrior recovered and swung for Fyn's throat. He threw himself sideways, tripped over an injured man and fell heavily on one knee. The impact sent his sword flying. The spar warrior closed in for the kill.

Behind the warrior's head and shoulders, Fyn saw Isolt pick up a jug of wine and throw it. The pottery smashed on Fyn's attacker.

The unconscious man fell across Fyn, knocking the air from his chest. The fight seemed to have moved on, leaving him like a beached whale. As he lay there gasping, he looked up at Isolt, two body lengths away on the royal table. Why had she followed him? She'd been safe on the ship.

She stood on the table with her wyvern at her heels, closing on Palatyne.

'So you came back to your husband?' Palatyne leered.

'Husband? Never. You are a barbarian warlord who dreams too high!'

'Where I come from a wife who runs away can expect a beating!' Palatyne lunged.

'Loyalty!' Isolt cried and dropped to her knees. The wyvern leapt over her, going straight for Palatyne's throat. The force of the wyvern's attack drove him off the end of the table onto the terrace. Fyn heard the thump as Palatyne hit the ground, then a terrible scream and the crunch of his bones. A hush fell and Fyn imagined the crowd drawing back, horrified.

After everything he'd gone through to see justice done, Palatyne's death struck Fyn as ironic. To think the man, who had caused so much destruction, should be killed, not by one of King Rolen's kin, but by one of the goddess's Affinity beasts, as if she was setting the world to rights.

'Freezing Sylion, what a way to die!' Byren muttered as he cleaned his sword and sheathed it.

He pulled the unconscious man off Fyn and hauled his brother upright.

Beyond him, Orrade and the sea-hounds chased down the last of the spar warriors, but Fyn had eyes only for Isolt. As soon as he was on his feet, he brushed past Byren, running to Isolt. He pulled her off the table, swinging her to the ground. 'What possessed you? You were safe on the ship. You could have been killed!'

She ignored him, trembling but triumphant. 'I did it, Fyn. I set him up. I knew my wyvern would go for Palatyne!'

She laughed unsteadily, tears glittering in her eyes.

Fyn wanted to shake her. No, he wanted to kiss her.

'Well done.' Byren clapped Isolt on the back. 'You have a cool head. Present me, little brother.'

It took all Fyn's resolve to release Isolt and turn her towards his brother. 'This is Byren, your betrothed.'

Isolt blinked, her lashes matted and damp with tears. 'King Byren?'

Fyn actually looked at his brother. He hadn't shaved for days, his hair was matted, he was covered in blood and he smelled. He looked like the worst Utland barbarian.

It was probably not the best time to introduce them.

Fyn turned at Piro's whimper of pain.

Chapter Thirty

PIRO'S HEAD POUNDED as if two giants were trying to battle their way out of her skull. She was dimly aware that the Affinity battle had centred on her.

When she opened her eyes, flashes of light obscured her vision, flickering like the after-images of lightning. Bile rose in her throat.

She tried to focus on Tyro, willing him strength with every beat of her heart. The Utlander had found a way to stop her drawing on his Affinity, and now he sought to steal hers, while assaulting Tyro. She felt the Utlander's body tremble with the effort, but he did not falter.

She was fully extended, had no more to give Tyro.

And it was not enough.

Beyond Tyro, she could just make out her brothers and Isolt staring in horror, not daring to intervene. From the corner of her eye, she saw King Merofyn come to his feet, clutching the arms of his litter to steady himself.

And Piro realised, with so much of the Utlander's concentration focused on the battle with Tyro, he could not maintain his hold over the old king. But what could one sick old man achieve against Affinity of this magnitude?

Face contorted by manic fury, King Merofyn launched himself at the Utlander. 'Curse you!'

He barrelled into the Utlander, knocking him sideways. That was all it took for Piro to drop and twist out of the Utlander's grasp. She threw herself forwards, avoiding the poison tip. Tyro caught her and she turned to face their attacker.

Before the Utlander could straighten up, King Merofyn grabbed the staff, driving its poisoned tip into the old Power-worker's throat. The Utlander collapsed backwards, mouth open in a silent scream.

As King Merofyn staggered, falling to the tiles, Fyn and Isolt ran to him, helping him to his feet.

Meanwhile, Piro ran to the Utlander. Before she could reach him, the carved stone on the tip of his staff flared bright enough to blind her momentarily. She tripped, landing on her knees. As a rush of stolen Affinity poured past her, she felt her mother's essence. For one fleeting heartbeat, Queen Myrella seemed to touch her cheek in blessing, then she was gone.

Tears rained down Piro's cheeks. Her mother was free of the Utlander's trap.

When her vision finally cleared, she found Tyro, now in his Lord Dunstany guise, kneeling beside the Utlander to check his throat for a pulse.

'Dead.'

'Killed by his own trick,' Piro whispered, meeting Tyro's eyes. 'Why pretend to be Lord Dunstany? Everyone knows who you really are.'

'Not so. People see what they expect. Only you and the Utlander pierced my disguise.'

'Father!' Isolt's despairing cry made them turn. King Merofyn clutched his chest and gasped, his skin going grey as he staggered back to collapse in the chair.

'Dunstany?' The old king beckoned Tyro, clutching his vest, tendons straining. 'Watch over my daughter.'

Piro came to her feet, but looked away to give them privacy.

'Is there anything you can do for him, Lord Dunstany?' Isolt pleaded.

'There is nothing anyone can do for King Merofyn,' Tyro told Isolt. 'His heart has given out.'

Isolt choked back a sob.

Still looking away from them, Piro blinked fresh tears from her eyes. This time, when her vision cleared, she saw the nobles were gathered about three body lengths away on the terrace watching. Their many men-at-arms stood waiting for orders.

Fyn's sea-hounds drew closer to him and her brother Byren, fingering their sword hilts. Orrade joined them and it looked as if the fighting was going to erupt again.

'Tyro?' Piro breathed a warning.

He took in the situation.

'Time for something showy!' He grabbed Isolt's

arm, pulling her away from Fyn, and onto the table top. From there, the anxious crowds below could also see them. Lord Dunstany held up his staff, an imposing figure in indigo robes.

FYN BLINKED AS the lightning, which had been flickering deep in the glowering clouds, suddenly lashed out, striking the orb on the tip of Lord Dunstany's staff. The flash bleached everything white and the crack of thunder was so loud many people screamed, falling to their knees, deafened.

The staff's orb glowed, illuminating Lord Dunstany and Isolt with otherworldly brilliance.

The wyvern howled in fear and left Palatyne's body. With a short burst of its powerful wings, it climbed into the air, landing on the table. Isolt lifted her arm and it went to her, nuzzling Isolt's hand for reassurance. The crowd marvelled.

Lord Dunstany pounded his staff on the tabletop, causing the globe to flare. 'Behold the true ruler of Merofynia, Isolt Wyvern Queen!'

The people applauded.

Fyn's heart soared. Isolt had been returned to her rightful place. She would make a fine, strong queen for Merofynia.

Lord Dunstany looked over his shoulder. 'Byren, quick, up here.'

Fyn's heart sank.

Byren leaped onto the table top. Only a few overturned goblets remained on the snowy white cloth and he kicked them aside. Lord Dunstany's glowing orb illuminated Byren's wild hair and his bloodstained, tattered clothes flashing on his sword's blade. He looked the warrior he was. What woman could not fail to love him?

BYREN SWEPT ISOLT a courtly bow that would have done his mother proud. How he wished she could be here today to see her brother Sefon avenged.

Dunstany took Isolt's hand and Byren's, joining them. 'Palatyne's treachery has been revealed. King Rolen and his kin were not planning war on Merofynia. In truth, the king was planning to wed his heir to King Merofyn's daughter. Behold the heirs of Merofynia and Rolencia. From this day forwards may these two kingdoms live in peace!'

People cheered, throwing their hats in the air. Byren's spirits sang. He had come far to see his parents' plans for peace realised. His eyes stung and his throat grew tight. If only they could be here to see this. He ached for them, for the twin brother he'd lost and the people of Rolencia, who had suffered because of Palatyne's ambition.

In fact, his people still suffered because Cobalt still lived.

Byren would not know peace until he set his kingdom to rights.

PIRO GASPED AS Byren dropped Isolt's hand and knelt on one knee before her. He lifted his head, dark eyes blazing from behind his matted hair. 'Isolt Wyvern

Queen. I cannot marry you in good faith.'

Piro glanced to Fyn, where she saw hope dawn on his face only to be dashed as Byren continued.

'For my treacherous cousin sits on my father's throne, eating from his table, sleeping in his bed, oppressing the people of Rolencia. Only when I have restored my family's honour can I come to claim you.'

Isolt stiffened. 'But –'

'I know. We will need to rid Merofynia of Palatyne's treasonous supporters.' Byren jumped to his feet and beckoned Fyn. 'In my place I offer my brother to lead your army.'

Fyn's mouth dropped open.

Piro nudged him. 'Go on, everyone's watching.'

Fyn took three steps, accepted Byren's hand and was pulled up onto the table beside Isolt. Byren placed Fyn's hand on Isolt's.

'Place your trust in my brother, Isolt. Fyn is the most loyal of kingsons.'

'Oh, I do trust Fyn,' Isolt began. 'It's just that –'

'Good!' Byren turned to face the crowd, an arm sliding around each of their shoulders as he stood slightly behind them. Byren raised his voice. 'I name Fyn Rolen Kingson, Queen Isolt's general of Merofynia!'

Piro's heart went out to Fyn and to Byren, who had no idea what he had just done. Isolt's wyvern recognised Fyn and nudged his chest until he rubbed behind her horn nubs. The crowd took this as a good sign.

Byren looked over his shoulder. 'Climb up, Piro. I haven't forgotten you.'

Tyro steadied her as she climbed up between him and Isolt.

A mournful cry sounded from above. Piro's foenix circled, its heavy wings beating the air as it swooped low. The nobles and common folk whispered and pointed in awe. The bird spotted Piro and cried out again.

She went to lift her arm but Tyro whispered, 'No. If the foenix lands on your arm, you will be forever remembered as the rightful heir of Rolencia.'

Unaware of this, Byren gave a happy chuckle. 'Why, look, Piro. It's your foenix.'

Piro deliberately kept her arms by her side.

Byren whistled and the foenix landed on his forearm, settling in his arms. A hushed murmur rippled through the crowd.

'This is a sign!' Lord Dunstany cried. A flash of lightning punctuated his words. Both the foenix and the wyvern cried out in alarm, settling at a touch from Byren and Isolt. 'Beware, Cobalt, Byren Kingsheir will soon sit on the throne of Rolencia!'

The crowd applauded as the first heavy spots of rain fell, hitting the hot stones of the terrace with a hiss.

The heavens opened with a roll of cavernous thunder, and rain plummeted onto the crowd. Byren laughed. He leaped to the terrace, turning to catch Isolt and swing her down. The wyvern leapt after her. Fyn joined them.

The nobles scattered. The Merofynian people picked up their baskets, held their blankets over their heads and ran for home. The sea-hounds headed back to the ship.

Byren called to Orrade. 'Come, drink a toast in the great hall.'

In bare moments, the terrace was empty of everyone except for Piro and Tyro. She had to shout over the drumming of the downpour. 'We should go inside.'

'Lord Dunstany isn't needed for now. I'm going back to Ostron Isle,' Tyro said. 'I'm sorry I deceived you with the amber, Piro. You are free to rejoin your family as Piro Kingsdaughter.'

She glanced back to the palace. If she returned, her brothers and Isolt would welcome her, but soon they would be planning her marriage to forge an alliance. If she went with them she would be a piece in the game of Duelling Kingdoms. Or worse.

'They know about my Affinity now and that it is much stronger than Fyn's. They'd want to send me to the abbess of Sylion.' Piro could not bear the thought of living closed in by the walls and rules of the abbey. She blinked rain from her eyes and looked up at Tyro. 'If I come back to Ostron Isle, will you teach me what you know?'

'If you come back with me you will be a player, not a piece.' His brilliant eyes examined her. 'Is that what you want, Piro?'

Suddenly she knew why her piece had no face. 'I will never be a piece on the mage's war table. I was meant to be a player.'

He nodded. 'Then let's go, before they come to take Palatyne's body away.'

It was over at last. She had a future, but she had lost her family to Palatyne's pointless war. Piro froze as a memory came to her. She pulled her hands from Tyro's.

'Why do you look at me like that? What is it?'

'You started this war. You told Palatyne that one of King Rolen's kin would kill him.'

He shook his head. 'I never meant to start a war. I could see Palatyne was set on conquest.' Tyro shrugged. 'I tried to divert him but I made a mistake. I told him that one day someone he had wronged would kill him, hoping that he would mend his ways. Instead he went to the Utlander and demanded to know who would kill him. It was the Utlander who said King Rolen's kin would be his downfall. So Palatyne set out to destroy your family, and in doing so, destroyed himself!'

Piro's head swam. Her parents and Lence dead, because of Tyro's meddling.

'Don't turn away from me, Piro,' Tyro pleaded. 'I'm not ready to fill Mage Tsulamyth's shoes but I must. It's hard to be alone. Come back with me.'

She found his dark eyes too intense. 'For now. Come on. We'd better get back to the ship.'

Tyro jumped down to the roof of the cage and turned to help her, but Piro leaped down beside him. They climbed off the cart and ran across the grass.

BYREN HAD SHAVED and bathed. His long black hair was still wet, and hung down his back. He could feel the damp through his borrowed shirt as he stood to make a toast. When no one was looking, he grinned at Orrade, best of friends, then turned to face the feasting hall.

It was filled with the old king's loyal aristocrats,

who jostled for seats at the tables. Servants had hurriedly transferred what was left of the feast into the palace.

'A toast. Peace and prosperity for Rolencia and Merofynia!'

'Peace and prosperity,' the people echoed.

Orrade met Byren's eyes and they both downed their drinks in one gulp, while the Merofynians sipped delicately.

Byren sat, thinking how different the people of Merofynia and Rolencia were. That reminded him that his people were suffering. He leant close to Orrade.

'Arrange our passage on a ship back to Rolencia, Orrie.'

His friend nodded and left the table.

Byren glanced to Isolt. She was such a pretty little thing, so reserved and thoughtful. He didn't know what to make of her. She made him feel large and clumsy. But it wasn't just her size, for Piro was not much bigger and he'd always felt comfortable around her. Which reminded him.

'Where is Piro?' Byren asked.

Isolt and Fyn glanced at each other.

'I suspect she has sailed for Mage Isle,' Isolt replied, with a secret half-smile.

Byren sensed that the kingsdaughter was leaving a lot unsaid.

'That reminds me, I meant to return your family's emblems.' Isolt lifted the chains over her head. 'I don't want to keep what isn't mine. This large gold one, was it King Rolen's?'

'Yes. It's Byren's now,' Fyn said.

As Byren accepted his father's emblem from Isolt, his vision clouded with tears. He had seen it resting on his father's broad chest so many times, never had he thought to wear it himself one day. The old seer's prophecy had come true, in part.

'And this silver one, Byren, was it your mother's?'

'Yes.' He blinked away the tears and his voice caught as he replied. 'I... I would like you to have it.'

Isolt blushed as he took it from her fingers and replaced it around her neck.

Fyn pointed. 'The electrum emblem was Lence's as kingsheir.'

None of them spoke.

Byren cleared his throat. 'I will save it for my first born. And I guess we will have to keep Piro's safe for her.'

'I have a feeling we'll be seeing Piro when we least expect it,' Fyn said softly.

'Where is your emblem, Fyn?' Isolt asked.

'Safely hidden and that is where it can stay. I make no claim to Rolencia.' His eyes held Isolt's. 'Or Merofynia.'

Byren wondered if he was missing something, but before he could ask, Orrade came back.

'We sail at dawn, my king.'

My king... that was what Florin called him. Byren felt a rush of excitement. He must find her, make sure she was safe.

'I can see you two want to make your war plans,' Isolt said, nodding from Byren to Orrade. She stood and bowed to Byren. 'I'm tired. Good night.'

Byren felt guilty, caught ignoring his betrothed. 'Fyn, can you escort Isolt up to her room? I don't want Palatyne's sympathisers trying to kidnap her. Set a guard on her door. Better still, stay and guard her yourself.'

Fyn opened his mouth, then closed it. 'Yes, my king.'

'Oh, I'm not king yet. I still have to reclaim Rolencia.'

FYN STRODE FROM the feasting hall with Isolt at his side, then realised he was making her run to keep up and slowed his pace.

'My pardon, Queen Isolt.'

'Fyn?' She stopped at the base of the long curved stair. Servants had lit scented candles and the flickering flames sculpted her face.

He feared to meet her eyes in case she saw what he could not hide.

'Don't call me queen. We've been through too much together to –'

'You are my brother's betrothed and rightful queen of Merofynia, what else could I call you?'

'Friend?'

Fyn swallowed and managed to smile. 'You are right. My pardon –'

'So formal.' She rolled her eyes.

Fyn laughed but his heart was heavy. 'Come, you must be tired.'

They walked in silence up the curving stair. Isolt led the way into her chambers, pausing at a window that overlooked the Landlocked Sea. It was dusk now and still raining. Fyn could just see that Palatyne and the king's bodies had been removed from the terrace.

'So the board is cleared, ready for another game of Duelling Kingdoms,' Isolt said.

Fyn's Affinity tingled as if something was on the edge of his perception. He frowned, trying to make it clear.

'What was that?' Isolt asked.

'Nothing.'

She sighed. 'Well, I am glad it is all over.'

'Yes, my queen,' Fyn said. But his Affinity told him otherwise.

ROWENA CORY DANIELLS

The King's Bastard

BOOK ONE OF THE CHRONICLES
OF KING ROLEN'S KIN

*"Royal intrigue, court politics
and outlawed magic make for
an exciting adventure."*
- Gail Z. Martin, author of
The Chronicles of The Necromancer

UK ISBN: 978 1 97519 00 0 • US ISBN: 978 1 97519 01 7 • £7.99/$7.99

*Seven minutes younger than the heir, Byren has never hungered for the throne, and
laughs when a seer predicts he will kill his twin. But his brother Lence resents Byren's
growing popularity, and King Rolen's enemies plot to take his throne. In a world where
the untamed magic of the gods wells up from the earth's heart, sending exotic beasts
to stalk the wintry nights and twisting men's minds, King Rolen's kin will need courage
and wits to survive...*

 WWW.SOLARISBOOKS.COM

Follow us on Twitter! www.twitter.com/solarisbooks

ROWENA CORY DANIELLS

The Uncrowned King

BOOK TWO OF THE CHRONICLES
OF KING ROLEN'S

"Pacy and full of
action and intrigue."
Trudi Canavan, author of
The Black Magician trilogy.

UK ISBN: 978 1 97519 04 8 • US ISBN: 978 1 97519 05 5 • £7.99/$7.99

Thirteen year old Piro watches powerless as her father's enemies march on the castle,
while a traitor whispers poison in the King's ear, undermining his trust in her brother,
Byren. Determined to prove his loyalty, Byren races to the Abbey; somehow, he must
convince the Abbot to send his warriors to defend the castle. And Fyn, the youngest of
King Rolen's sons, has barely begun his training as a mystic, but wakes in a cold sweat,
haunted by dreams of betrayal...

 WWW.SOLARISBOOKS.COM

Follow us on Twitter! www.twitter.com/solarisbooks

UK ISBN: 978 1 844165 31 5
US ISBN: 978 1 844165 31 5
£7.99/$7.99

Having escaped being murdered by his evil brother, Prince Martris Drayke must take control of his ability to summon the dead and gather an army big enough to claim back his dead father's throne. But it isn't merely Jared that Tris must combat. The dark mage, Foor Arontola, plans to cause an imbalance in the currents of magic and raise the Obsidian King...

UK ISBN: 978 1 844167 08 1
US ISBN: 978 1 844165 98 8
£7.99/$7.99

The kingdom of Margolan lies in ruin. Martris Drayke, the new king, must rebuild his country in the aftermath of battle, while a new war looms on the horizon. Meanwhile Jonmarc Vahanian is now the Lord of Dark Haven, and there is defiance from the vampires of the Vayash Moru at the prospect of a mortal leader. But can he earn their trust, and at what cost?

 WWW.SOLARISBOOKS.COM

Follow us on Twitter! www.twitter.com/solarisbooks

PAUL KEARNEY'S THE MONARCHIES OF GOD

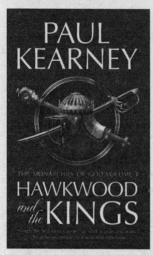